disappearing
in plain sight

By Francis Guenette

Produced by:

FriesenPress

Suite 300 – 852 Fort Street
Victoria, BC, Canada V8W 1H8

www.friesenpress.com

Distributed to the trade by The Ingram Book Company

For my mother: June Yvonne Guenette, 1936 – 1997. Your love of writing and your desire to be a published author inspired me and kept me going.

CHAPTER ONE

i.

Lisa-Marie woke to the sound of voices and the reflection of the lake rippling and running like melted butter along the sloped, cedar-planked ceiling above her bed. With all the agility of her sixteen years she sprang from the built-in futon. She barely avoided a knock on the head as she ducked along the edge of the window frame to peek out.

"Hi, Miss Shannon . . . how's everything going?"

"Oh good, Justin, good . . . just waiting to get the second batch of bread in the pans." Her Aunt Bethany was standing in the doorway to the bakery shed, drinking a cup of coffee. "It's going to be hot again today, hey? Don't let Izzy work you too hard."

"Oh ya, no way, I'll tell her you said that." Justin waved as he moved past the A-Frame to the trail that disappeared into the trees.

Lisa-Marie drank in the sight of Justin as if she were dying of thirst. He had glanced casually up at the window, tossing his long, honey-coloured hair out of his eyes. His white T-shirt clung to his lanky, muscular body and his slouchy work jeans hung on barely-there hips.

She flopped back onto the bed with her breath whooshing out in a sigh of intense longing.

She had been here two days and the high point so far was meeting Justin. She flew from Ontario to BC and boarded a further short-hop flight to the southern end of Vancouver Island. The flights were followed by an endless bus trip in which it seemed the aging coach stopped at every small town, gas station and even roadside mailbox. She was finally jolted awake by the grinding of the bus gears as the driver turned off the highway and bumped to a stop. Lisa-Marie stumbled off the Greyhound in the parking lot of the Dearborn hotel – a two-story, run-down building with a faded sign that advertised all-you-can-eat hot wings every Wednesday night in the pub.

With a shrug, she grabbed her heavy duffel bag and scanned the few vehicles lined up on the side of the parking lot. She spotted the red pickup her aunt had told her to look for.

Lisa-Marie saw a tall, thin woman leaning casually against the passenger door of the truck. She was dressed in jeans, the old-fashioned kind that came right up to the waist. A tucked in shirt glanced over a mostly non-existent bust. Steel wool-coloured hair stuck up in short spikes on her head.

Lisa-Marie hadn't been expecting a marching band or anything, but still . . . she paused to steal another quick look at the woman who was pushing herself to attention beside the truck. Would a smile crack that sour-puss face? Didn't the occasion warrant at least a small wave of recognition? It wasn't like there could be any doubt about who Lisa-Marie was. The only other person to get off the bus was an old man – probably pushing a hundred – who made a bee-line for the double-wooden doors under the pub sign the minute his shuffling feet hit the pavement.

Lisa-Marie decided that pleasantries on her part would be a waste of time. She walked straight up to the woman and said, "First things first. How am I supposed to say, B-E-U-L-A-H?" She had seen this name in letters from her Auntie Beth but she was never able to figure out how to pronounce it. Now that she was meeting the person attached to this odd combination of letters, Lisa-Marie's inability to pronounce the woman's name really pissed her off.

The woman was silent for a moment, seeming to take Lisa-Marie's measure. Then she relaxed the grim lines of her mouth to allow a slight twitch to play around the corners of her lips. Lisa-Marie was unable to tell whether her look was the beginning of a smile or a sneer. The woman repeated her own name out loud, twice for good measure, in a tone and volume well-suited to an army drill sergeant.

During the silence that followed, Lisa-Marie flung her long, brown hair out of her face and stood with her hands on her hips. "Let me get this straight; Beu sort of rhyming with phew, like phew-wee something smells bad around here and then la, like la, la, la? Beulah?"

Beulah nodded her head while gesturing toward the back seat of the truck. Lisa-Marie understood she was to stow her duffle bag. She had just struggled to pull it across the parking lot and it was clear that she could expect no assistance from Beulah.

The quick drive through the town revealed little of interest – a harbour jammed with fishing boats, a few restaurants, a post office, a grocery store and a large Petro-Canada station near the turn onto the highway. Dearborn was a small-town, crap place at the end of what had seemed, if she was to go by the view from the bus window, miles of nothing but trees.

Slouched down in the front seat of the truck she felt stowed into the old Ford in much the same way as her bag. Beulah paid no more attention to her sitting in the passenger seat than she would have given a duffel bag. A sharp turn off the highway and they were on a gravel road. The drive seemed to go on forever and at just about the moment when Lisa-Marie thought she couldn't handle the silence or the bumping along a second longer, the truck stopped at a pull-out across from a large building. The whirling and screaming sound of a saw broke into the quiet of the warm afternoon.

Lisa-Marie then suffered the indignity of climbing onto a green ATV behind her aunt's partner. She clutched her arms around Beulah's bony waist as they careened down the steep, narrow drive. Beulah took the bumps and corners like she thought she was competing for a million-dollar prize in some type of downhill race. Lisa-Marie arrived in the small, turn-around drive at the back of the A-Frame cabin with her heart thumping and her backside aching. But on the up side, she arrived just in time to be introduced to Justin Roberts. If timing is everything in life then maybe her luck was turning around because one look at Justin convinced her that there could be no better place on the planet to end up than here at Crater Lake.

Bethany had hurried out of the A-Frame, the screen door slamming as she rushed down the stairs and across the distance that separated her from Lisa-Marie. Two large dogs bounded out behind her. Wrapping her arms around Lisa-Marie, she hugged her close for a moment before standing back at arm's length, "Let me get a look at you." She twirled Lisa-Marie around. "You're so grown-up. I can't believe you're really here." She pulled Lisa-Marie into another hug while the dogs ran circles around them both, barking, wagging their tails and licking at the hand Lisa-Marie stretched out to them.

"Gertrude, Alice . . . give it a break . . . OK . . . for God's sake . . . get in the cabin." Beulah pushed the two German Shepherds ahead of her toward the cabin door before tossing Lisa-Marie's duffel bag up onto the porch with a loud grunt, "Jesus H. Christ, what did you pack in here . . . bricks?"

"Justin, this is my niece – Lisa-Marie. She's visiting from Ontario for the whole summer." Bethany squeezed Lisa-Marie closer, "It's going to be so good to have her here." As Justin stepped forward, Bethany added, "Justin lives at Micah Camp and he works next door at Izzy's."

Justin shaded his eyes from the slanting sun and looked at Lisa-Marie with a relaxed and easy comfort. When he reached out his hand to shake hers she felt a tingle run up her arm and plant itself right in her chest where the thudding of fear from the ATV ride was replaced with a different type of thud. There was something about Justin that was hard to describe. From the moment she laid eyes on him all Lisa-Marie wanted to do was step forward into whatever it was he had and wrap it tightly around herself – like the fuzzy blanket she'd curl up in when she used to lie on her grannie's old sofa.

i i .

Bethany leaned against the wall of the bakery shed and waited for the bread machine buzzer to go off. It would signal the next stage in a production line process that saw the Crater Lake Organic Bakery make a hundred loaves of bread and twenty-five dozen buns every day. Her mind was caught up in the memory of how her mother's voice had sounded on the phone – almost two weeks ago now.

She had walked over to Izzy's after getting the message that her mother wanted her to call. Then she had walked back to the A-Frame in a daze, thankful no one had been at Izzy's to hear her end of the conversation or see her reaction to her mother's news.

"I had to say yes, Beulah. What else could I say?"

Beulah stared open-mouthed at Bethany for a moment, "Jesus jumped up Christ, you could have said no is what you could have said. You could have told your mother that there's no bloody way we're looking after that kid for the whole summer."

"She's not just any kid, Beulah. She's my niece. She doesn't have anyone but me and Mom."

"Did your mother say why? Why now?" Beulah had been getting ready to do the nightly check on the fire in the bread oven and her hand was still on the door knob.

"No . . . no . . . not really," Bethany's eyes shifted away from Beulah's angry face, "She's old you know Beulah . . . maybe she needs a break."

"Oh, she needs a break, does she? So she's going to offload her responsibility for that kid on us?"

"Well, if you're going to get all worked-up about it maybe we should talk later." Bethany got up from the sofa and retreated to the bedroom to sit on the edge of the bed. She could hear Beulah stomping and ranting around the A-Frame.

"Don't suppose for a minute, Bethany, I don't know exactly who's going to be footing the bill for all of this. We both know your mom doesn't have two loonies to rub together by the end of every month. Who's going to pay to fly this kid out here? Don't you think I know it's going to be me?"

The rant ended with Beulah slamming out of the A-Frame toward the bakery shed where Bethany imagined she had vented her frustration by breaking down, cleaning and polishing every bit of the bread-making equipment – an exercise that took well into the wee hours of the morning.

iii.

On her first evening at the A-Frame, Lisa-Marie grabbed a novel from the coffee table and flopped onto the sofa. She didn't mind spending her time with a good book but she usually got to pick reading over other options. Here there were no other options – no TV, no internet and no phone. It was like being captive on an episode of *Survivor*. The dogs were lounging comfortably beside the sofa and Lisa-Marie stretched out a foot every now and then to rub each of their bellies in turn. The inside of the cabin was eerily quiet – in fact the whole area around the cabin was dead quiet and dark. Never in her life had Lisa-Marie seen it so dark outside.

Beulah strolled casually by the sofa flipping a brochure onto Lisa-Marie's lap. "Micah Camp . . . why not check it out? Maybe they need a cook's helper or something. Maybe you could get a job . . . better than lying around on your ass for the next two months."

Lisa-Marie had to give Beulah credit. That remark slid in like a well-aimed shiv in the prison exercise yard. And the timing was superb; her Auntie Beth had walked out of the room just moments before.

She held the brochure at arm's length for a moment then dropped it carelessly on the floor. She already knew all she needed to know about Micah Camp – Justin lived there. She headed for the stairs to her loft, "I haven't even been here for one fucking night. Maybe the employment police could let me get settled into this end-of-nowhere place before I need to find a job."

Though once she was up the stairs she couldn't believe her luck. She stretched out on the bed and flipped open the novel. The fact that Beulah's first request was for her to look for a job at the very place Justin lived seemed too good to be true.

i v .

Lisa-Marie was jolted back to the already-warm, July morning by Beulah's voice booming through the loft window just over her head. "Come on, Beth, let's get the lead out. That dough isn't going to hop into those pans by itself."

She rolled over onto her stomach and considered the fact that Beulah was irritated a lot. She reminded Lisa-Marie of some kind of tall and skinny porcupine – quills all aquiver and ready to defend her turf. Everything about Beulah and her Auntie Beth seemed to prove the saying about opposites attracting. Bethany was short and round to Beulah's tall sharpness. Lisa-Marie was surprised to find she was admiring her aunt's curvy figure and the long sweep of her blonde hair that was just beginning to show wisps of silver. Coming to this point in her thoughts she chose to veer off in a different direction; it was way too gross to entertain any images of her Auntie Beth's curves against Beulah's angles or anything else that Lisa-Marie hoped would happen only in their small bedroom at the back of the A-Frame's lower floor. Her mind skipped back to Justin.

V.

Beulah looked up at the window in time to catch the swing of Lisa-Marie's long hair moving out of sight. Having just watched Justin disappear down the trail, she vented a litany of cursing complaints to herself that included the useless little teenager now housed in their upper loft who was probably boy-crazy, lazy and sloppy to boot.

Arching her lean frame to ease the pressure on her lower back, Beulah glanced around. The lovingly-constructed bakery and the sound of the stream cascading down right behind their little bit of cleared wilderness was everything that Beulah had dreamed of – doing what she had always wanted to do and living with someone to whom she had become very attached. She would be damned if this little bit of nothing teenager, who waltzed about the A-Frame like she already owned the place, was going to throw a wrench into Beulah's well-planned and laid-out existence.

But the kid had spunk – that was for sure. The way she had looked spelling out Beulah's name in the parking lot the other day – it was all she could do to stifle a roar of laughter. Beulah had chuckled right out loud when she left the A-Frame the previous evening to take the dogs out and check on the fire smouldering in the stone oven across from the bakery shed. She would take spunky bursts of swearing over teenage pouting any day.

Her eyes went to the loft window again but this time there was nothing to see but the tall evergreens stretched up the slope behind the A-Frame reflecting back at her in clear, sharp detail. Would having Lisa-Marie here bring up a lot of stuff that would be better left buried? Beulah was a great fan of burying the unpleasant. Bury it deep and bury the shovel was her motto. Her gaze shifted to the bakery shed and she saw Bethany looking toward the upper window as well; her stunningly blue eyes appeared overly large in a face that was paler than usual.

vi.

In a small cabin just past Izzy's place, Liam woke up with a sore shoulder and back. Cleaning out the chicken coops was not as easy as it used to be and splitting firewood for the rest of yesterday afternoon hadn't helped. As if his aches and pains weren't enough, one of the chickens was out of the coop and making a God-awful racket right outside the cabin door.

He moaned and rolled over. Pulling the blankets up to cover his ears he let his thoughts drift to Izzy and how she had looked the other day, humming a tune under her breath, as they worked together in the greenhouse. Though her hair was pulled casually up on her head, the long mass of silky-black curls touched with the odd hint of grey, still managed to tumble like a cascade of dishevelled elegance over her eyes. She was wearing a pair of old, green coveralls. The sleeves were rolled up her arms and the long pant legs scrunched up to her knees. Beat-up white sneakers graced her bare feet. Liam recalled her sudden frown as she glanced at her watch and then turned to drop her hand-clippers into the tool box near the door. She walked into the nearby cabin and emerged, in less than twenty minutes, dressed in a skirt and crisp-white shirt. A necklace of silver medallions clinked softly against her exposed throat. He watched her stroll off along the trail toward Micah Camp where she worked.

Liam's last thought at night and his first thought each morning was of Izzy and this preoccupation was disturbing. He and Caleb had been like brothers and Liam was sure he had started thinking way too much about Izzy way too soon after Caleb died. His thoughts all too often strayed to a fantasyland where Izzy wore an inviting smile – the kind of smile she certainly never directed Liam's way in real life.

Liam wasn't entirely certain any of this was about Izzy at all. Maybe it was just a way to hold onto Caleb by wanting what he had. At any rate, in the two years that Izzy had been alone she had given no indication that she pined for Liam in the same way; so he kept his distance. Not a hard act to pull off since Liam was an expert at keeping his distance from Izzy.

Throwing back the blankets, he admitted that moving was the only way to ease the pain in his shoulder and back. As he struggled to a standing position and reached for his jeans, another memory popped unbidden into his head. He had been coming out of the sawmill yard a few days ago when Beulah pulled up from her daily trip to Dearborn with Bethany's niece. Liam watched the young girl get out of the passenger side of Beulah's old Ford. Her head was bent and her sweeping flow of brown hair hid her face. He saw how she stood on the gravel pull-out looking around and shaking her head like she couldn't believe where she was. He noticed that her tight jeans barely covered her behind. Her low-cut top didn't leave much to the imagination either. His stiffness migrated south and he shook his head in disgust. Too much flying solo wasn't healthy for a guy. He struggled into his pants and headed out to see what on earth the problem could be with that damn chicken.

Chapter 2

i.

Izzy had been awake for almost three hours. Since Caleb's death she never seemed to sleep much past five a.m. She filled the time marking papers, responding to emails and going over counselling case files. It was never hard to fill time. She grew to enjoy being present when the dark sky gradually turned to a grey light over the tops of the mountains. She anticipated the moment when the dawn quiet would be shattered by the incessant squawking of stellar jays as they perched in the tall trees, vying with the distant crowing of Liam's rooster to announce a new day.

After a well-deserved stretch she returned to her chair at the writing table. She saw Justin disappear along the trail toward the greenhouse garden on the other side of the cabin. Justin was a very attractive young man. It was more than the dark-golden glow of his hair or the brown eyes flecked with warm hazel tones; more than the generous mouth and slow smile that lit his whole face; more than the clean muscular lines of his broad shoulders and lean hips. Beyond all of this he possessed a quality that seemed untouched. Izzy's grandmother had once described the sensation of looking into some people's eyes as being in the presence of old souls. It was this quality – like something shiny and new but older than time – that caught Izzy's attention.

Justin had certainly turned out to be a golden triumph for Micah Camp. Not all the kids who came to the Camp were raving success stories but a large number were. They screened for success – that was part of the Board's mandate. Their client base was young people who were coming out of the foster-care system. They were looking for kids between the ages of eighteen to twenty who had a certain edge. Sometimes it was an artistic interest, drawing or music maybe; other times it was a high math or science score or advanced computer skills; or maybe that edge was the passion of a kid who had read every book that ever came her way. A year at Micah Camp would help fill in educational gaps, smooth the way to post-secondary opportunities and kick-start what would be a lifelong process of dealing with emotional baggage.

That was where Izzy came into the picture. Though she was not the type to brag, it was due in large part to her skills that so many of the young people who came to Micah Camp emerged a year later ready to capitalize on their talents. She was a gifted trauma counsellor and her skill was born of her ability to enter totally into the stories her clients told her. In the end it was all about hearing the story. Izzy believed that people had their own answers to what they needed in order to heal and that these answers were embedded in the stories they told. She knew she was good at what she did but was at a loss to explain how or why simply listening and bearing witness to someone's story was so powerfully healing. She often felt tongue-tied when asked by colleagues to explain her therapeutic skills and counselling methods.

Izzy glanced down to consult her daily list, a proverbial burden she couldn't do without. She carefully crossed off tasks already completed and then took a moment to write in a task done that hadn't made the list. She diligently crossed it off as well. She contemplated the day ahead. Beulah would be picking up the new tenant in Dearborn in the late afternoon and Izzy needed to be on hand to welcome him and get him settled in at the guest cabin.

Two months ago she had made the decision to put an ad on the internet offering the guest cabin for rent. There weren't many guests in the offing and having a cabin that sat empty day after day was a waste. She was surprised to get a response so quickly and even more surprised at who had responded. When she shared the news that the person who was going to take the cabin for a year was a Catholic priest, Liam had raised an eyebrow ever so slightly. Izzy could only describe his face as mostly inscrutable, all angular planes and dominated by those blacker-than-black eyes. That was it though – just a raised eyebrow.

Consulting her leather-bound daybook, Izzy noted back-to-back counsel-ling sessions scheduled for that morning. After she got the Reverend Patterson settled in she needed to prepare for the monthly book-club potluck. It would be a larger gathering than usual. Justin was invited. At Izzy's suggestion he had read Alistair MacLeod's novel, *No Great Mischief*. Bethany's niece, who had picked Beulah's copy off the table and apparently wolfed it down in a day, would also attend. The Reverend Patterson would be invited as well. It would be a good time for him to meet everyone and a convenient opportunity for Izzy to appear hospitable.

She leaned her elbows on the desk and cupped her face in her hands, glancing down the lake that was starting to ripple lightly in the breeze. The morning sun glinted off the top of each tight roll of water like row after row of sharpened steel blades. The book-club nights always took a toll. She missed Caleb when she had to plan or be part of a social gathering and book-club potluck night had really been Caleb's thing. He entered into each monthly gathering with a gusto that totally belied the fact that he would be the only one attending who had barely skimmed the novel in question. He would search out theme potluck dishes and would often come up with a prop or two to emphasize the book's theme. No doubt for tonight he would have had a Rankin family CD playing during dinner or maybe a Rita McNeil song or two. He might have served up a traditional Cape Breton meal and convinced Liam to join him in some spoon playing around the table. That level of planning was far beyond Izzy's capacity.

Book-club night stopped abruptly when Caleb died. For almost a year and a half, as if by some type of tacit agreement, they all knew they couldn't be in the same room at the same time. It was as if their collective grief would multiply, rebounding endlessly within any closed space like an image in a house of mirrors, until the pain would overcome them all. Then, as if emerging from some type of fog, Liam casually suggested the title of a book to Izzy and the monthly gatherings resumed. The first time, without Caleb, was as painful as they all knew it would be. But now that the ball was rolling, Izzy would make sure it kept on rolling. She would take her turn at picking a book; she would act as hostess; and she would make one of her trademark, potato dishes. The evenings obviously suffered in comparison to what they had been when Caleb was around, but at least it was a suffering for which they were now developing some tolerance.

A frown tightened Izzy's features. Every encounter, even the most innocent, was affected by Caleb's absence. This was as clear to her as if the others were shouting it to the mountaintops. A sharp line had been drawn across all of their lives that clearly defined every moment now as being less than it could have been if only Caleb hadn't died. Nothing she could do would change that. She knew that after the book club she would end up sitting alone on the cliff deck drinking too much wine and regretting it all when she woke with a splitting headache at five the next morning.

i i .

Bethany stood by the kitchen counter slowly drying the lunch dishes. She felt comfortable and totally at ease in her kitchen. She gazed with pleasure at the neatly arranged row of potted herbs on the ledge of the dormer window set in over the sink. The ceramic pots were painted with delicate sprays of flower blossoms. She brushed her fingers across the small leaves of one of the plants and the scent of chocolate mint filled the air. The window afforded a rare side-view of the mountains that formed the backdrop to the cove. Bethany loved the view of the trees marching up the slope in alternating bands of colour, from light to medium to dark-green and finally giving way to bright-white patches of snow on the mountaintops.

The screen door slammed and Beulah came across the length of the A-Frame's main floor. She stopped just slightly behind Bethany. Brushing the long blond hair from the side of her neck, Beulah kissed her softly. Bethany turned to rest her head on Beulah's chest. Tipping Bethany's chin up with her hand, Beulah said, "You OK, Bethy?"

Bethany smiled faintly and nodded, "Ya, I think so. I want to get out in the boat today. I probably won't be back when you come home from town."

Beulah was resting her hand lightly on Bethany's cheek and thinking about how blue Bethany's eyes were – the softest blue of a robin's egg, flecked with motes of darker-blue that seemed reflected over and over into their depths.

At that moment, Lisa-Marie came through the door and took in the scene across the bar in the kitchen. "Gross, go to your room or something . . . OK . . . have some consideration for your house guest. I am an easily influenced teenager, after all."

Bethany broke away from Beulah's embrace with an uncomfortable laugh, "Where have you been Lisa?"

"Been to London to see the Queen, Auntie Beth," Lisa-Marie sailed by them and out to the veranda to plop onto a deck chair.

Rounding up the Ford keys from the hook on the wall near the door, Beulah shook her head at the sight of Lisa-Marie sprawled out on the deck and then called back to Bethany, "Tonight's the potluck. What are we bringing?"

"I've got some chicken out. I'll fry it, I guess. People usually like that." Bethany's mind was already wandering to thoughts of her fishing tackle box. She wondered if she had the right lures for what was promising to be a warm afternoon.

"Sounds good . . . chicken and whatever potato concoction Izzy comes up with. We won't starve. I suppose that free-loader Liam will bring pickles or something. Maybe he'll outdo himself and bring a loaf of our own bread." Beulah ignored the way Bethany shook her head sadly at the reference to Liam. "I'd better get moving. That bread won't deliver itself." Beulah called out towards the deck, "Hey, impressionable teenager, help your aunt with that chicken for tonight. Make yourself useful."

Lisa-Marie wandered into the kitchen from the veranda when she was sure she could hear the ATV near the top of the trail. She sat down at the table and looked across the kitchen bar to catch her aunt's eye. "I went over to the Camp to check it out. I met this woman – Josie. She said she could use me for a few hours every morning to knock soap out of the forms and to do other jobs like that. They pay minimum wage but that's not bad."

Lisa-Marie was absentmindedly tracing the design that ran along the border of the tablecloth when Bethany looked up from whipping eggs and milk in a pie plate, "You didn't have to do that just because Beulah ribbed you, sweetie; you don't need a job. Maybe it would be better to hang around and help with the bakery."

Lisa-Marie caught the concern in her aunt's voice and she suspected that what she really meant was that it would be better if she stayed close where they could keep an eye on her. She wasn't sure how to handle the feelings that suddenly turned her face a hot-red colour and made her breath hitch in that awful way that could only mean one thing – tears. Lisa-Marie hated crying almost more than all the other things she hated combined.

"There's nothing wrong with me, Auntie Beth. You don't need to keep an eye on me like I'm a mental case or something."

Bethany began to dip the flour-drenched chicken pieces into the pie plate of frothing egg and milk and then into the dried bread crumbs. Each piece was on the way to the heavy, cast-iron frying pan that was already on the stove. Lisa-Marie rose from the table and walked around the bar to stand in front of the stove. She silently took the large metal fork her aunt handed her and began pushing the browning pieces of chicken around the pan. The kitchen was quiet except for the sound of the sizzling chicken.

Lisa-Marie spoke without raising her eyes from the frying pan, "I wish you wouldn't worry about me Auntie Beth. That's all. You know it will only make Beulah more pissed off, right?"

Bethany reached over to turn off the burner under the chicken, "It's good enough for now." She took the fork from Lisa-Marie's hand and laying it down on the counter she put her arms around her niece. "I'll try not to worry, sweetie."

She stroked Lisa-Marie's soft brown hair and they stood together like that for a few moments. Bethany was thinking of the effort she had put in over the years to be a long-distance aunt to Lisa-Marie. She wrote tons of letters. When Lisa-Marie was small the letters were on big pieces of paper in all sorts of bright, felt-pen colours with funny little pictures drawn in the margins. Lisa-Marie responded with pages of childish printing. These pages slowed to almost nothing when Lisa-Marie entered her teens and went to high school. Bethany wasn't daunted by the silence. She was rewarded for her patience with a birthday card each year – Lisa-Marie's large and looping handwriting declaring her love.

Bethany was not one to pray but if she were, she told herself, she would pray now. She would pray with all her heart that the closeness she had worked so hard to achieve with Lisa-Marie, over the miles and the years, was going to be enough to carry them into a new, more complicated relationship.

She wondered how to put together the thing she wanted to say to Lisa-Marie. It was a bit like a complicated fishing lure. It would have to be arranged just so if it was to go down with any sort of smoothness. She began to clean up the dishes while Lisa-Marie was putting the chicken into the baking dish. Slowly Bethany began to speak. "When I first came here to Crater Lake to live with Beulah I was pretty screwed up but I didn't really know it."

Bethany continued to talk as she ran water into the sink, "I knew that some bad things had happened to me in the past and I had seen a lot of counsellors and social workers and people like that and I felt like I had told a lot of people about stuff, but . . . I don't know how to say this, Lisa. It was like someone else was saying the words and sometimes it was like I wasn't really here at all." Bethany paused to see if Lisa-Marie was listening. Though her niece's back was turned, Bethany could sense the quietness in her and she saw Lisa-Marie nodding her head slightly.

"Beulah was pretty good friends with Izzy's husband, Caleb. He said maybe it would help if I talked to Izzy sometime. Beulah wanted me to and I didn't really care. Like I told you, I had talked to lots of people before; it wasn't a big deal to me. But when I talked to Izzy it wasn't like any of the talking I had ever done before. Izzy's different. I can't really describe it." Drying her hands on the towel hanging on a hook at the end of the counter, Bethany turned to pat Lisa-Marie on the shoulder, "I was thinking that maybe you might like to talk to Izzy sometime. It's up to you of course. It wouldn't work if you didn't want to do it."

CHAPTER THREE

i.

Beulah moved the flats containing the day's bread deliveries from the ATV trailer into the back of the pickup. Six days a week she drove the sixty-minute round trip to Dearborn to deliver the bread. She did the trip on her own because that's the way she liked it. Twice this week she was required to bring someone back to the lake with her. Picking up Lisa-Marie had been an irritating experience, but Beulah was looking forward to collecting Izzy's new tenant. Lately there had been little or nothing to interrupt the monotony of day to day life. When Caleb was alive there had been different house guests and gatherings nonstop at Crater Lake. Caleb had loved to be surrounded by people and he somehow managed to keep everyone on an even keel through the most diverse mixtures of personalities and temperaments.

Beulah was hoping the new guy would mix things up. At the very least he might become an object for her sardonic wit. Having only Liam to pick on was getting old. Lisa-Marie, though a convenient target, hardly counted in Beulah's books. It was certainly not worth Bethany's narrow-eyed glare and subsequent holding out on the sexual front.

Beulah parked the pickup at the top of Izzy's driveway and sidestepped down the first few feet of the slope to a large mailbox secluded in the bushes. The way down to Izzy's place was a steep and twisting, four-by-four drive. A trip down this road in a moving vehicle was best suited to those with a certain sense of adventure. Beulah and Bethany made do with their ATV trail and Liam had a foot path with several staircases.

Beulah bristled with irritation as she noticed the start of Liam's path that branched off to the right of where she was standing. It was obvious the salmonberry bushes and the salal needed trimming. If he didn't get to it soon the whole trail would be overgrown. That's how it was out in the bush – without constant vigilance any puny efforts people made to carve out their own space would quickly slip away. She wasn't surprised that Liam didn't think his messy trail was a problem. He acted like Izzy's driveway was his and he also drove Caleb's Dodge around any time he wanted. "Free loader," Beulah snorted as she stepped up to the box.

Beulah was the only one who had ever gone to town on a daily basis. Caleb had devised a system to deal with the way everyone was always asking her to pick things up for them. Requests were to be written clearly on a piece of paper, placed in an envelope with whatever form of payment was required and deposited in the mailbox at the top of the trail.

Beulah enjoyed the various errands she was sent on, though she would never let people know that. She took the written requests seriously and almost without fault returned with exactly what was ordered. The delivery was Beulah's favourite part of the whole process – it allowed her to make what she considered to be witty remarks about people's purchases. Izzy invariably wanted parcels picked up from the post office – books, CDs, the occasional boxed set of DVDs and clothes. Izzy was the only person Beulah ever knew who could shop almost exclusively for clothes via the internet.

Today, as always, Liam's request was a pain in the ass. His note was faultlessly polite and written in a neat hand. He asked that Beulah please pick him up a large bottle of Pepto-Bismol and he had included the exact change. What's up with him now, she thought – probably guilty about something.

Holding Liam's note and frowning, Beulah recalled how Caleb's requests had always given her the best laugh of the day. *God just get me anything sweet – jelly beans would be good, maybe some of those sour coke bottles they sell at the Petro-Can.* Caleb would scrawl these words on any old piece of paper he could get his hands on, including the back of other people's envelopes. Invariably his notes ended with the words – *I'll pay you later – OK?* And you could be sure of one thing – Caleb was always good for whatever he owed you.

Beulah strode up the rise from the mailbox and jumped into the truck. Tossing the envelopes on the seat, she noticed out of the corner of her eye a piece of stationery from the camp. Now and then kids from Micah Camp dropped off requests but Beulah didn't encourage this. She was sure it would involve the purchase of contraband of one form or another. She had enough to do in town without hassles like that to contend with.

She unfolded the sheet of paper to read – *Dear Beulah – could you be a pal and pick me up some BC Bud while you're in town. Thanks so much for your time – I'll pay you later. Lisa-Marie.*

Beulah laughed right out loud as she started the truck. Gravel whipped out from under the tires as she reversed to turn tightly and head out. She did like a good joke. There might be hope for that kid yet.

i i .

Shrugging into her hoodie, Lisa-Marie reluctantly followed her aunt out to the A-Frame's heavily-shaded deck. "Liam, hi," Bethany took the shopping bag full of egg cartons from Liam's outstretched hand and turned to put an arm around Lisa-Marie. "This is my niece, Lisa-Marie."

Liam reached out his hand and Lisa-Marie responded as she took in the man Beulah described as the freeloader who lived in Izzy's cabin. She saw a guy in his forties with dark eyes and a nose, sharp in profile. His cheekbones were high and his teeth very white against the dark of his skin.

Back home in Ontario they said Indian – right out loud. Her aunt had told her Liam was First Nations. Lisa-Marie had never heard the term before. She guessed that's what they called a guy like Liam in BC. She shook his out-stretched hand and looked into his eyes to see a warmth and acceptance that sent her a clear message – any niece of Bethany's was pretty OK by him.

Bethany brought out mugs of coffee for herself and Liam. They sat at the deck table overlooking the lake together. Lisa-Marie let her mind wander as Bethany and Liam's voices droned on about which of Liam's chickens were laying the best these days, how the new feed had made a difference and how a racoon had been digging in the garbage the last couple of nights at the A-Frame. With her head lying on the table atop her folded arms, Lisa-Marie could easily slant her eyes towards her aunt or Liam and manage the occasional smile or nod expected of her. There was no need to invest too much of herself in what she considered to be an amazingly boring conversation.

Her thoughts carried her back to the morning her grannie had taken her to the plane to fly to BC. As they sat in the airport lounge waiting for her flight, Lisa-Marie had looked closely at Grannie and she remembered thinking that she hadn't really done this in years. She was surprised to see that the woman beside her was old and tired. As they walked to the gate, Lisa-Marie noticed that her grandmother still limped from breaking her ankle the summer before. When they said goodbye, Grannie had held onto Lisa-Marie for a long time. She had pressed her tightly against her full soft body and then let her go with such a look of sadness on her lined and weary face. Lisa-Marie winced with guilt as she thought back to that look. Why did she have to be the one who had put such a look on her grannie's face?

Liam got up to leave, draining the last of his coffee as he rose. "Thanks Beth, I look forward to this one cup a day."

"Is your stomach getting any better, Liam?" Without waiting for his response, Bethany added, "It isn't getting worse, is it?"

Liam paused for a moment before smiling at Bethany. Lisa-Marie thought he was nice looking for a really-old guy when he smiled like that at her aunt. "It's fine. I better get the rest of these eggs over to the Camp." As he turned to go, he reached into his pack and pulled out a book-sized parcel wrapped in white tissue paper. He handed it to Lisa-Marie, saying, "I brought this for you – a welcome gift."

Lisa-Marie looked up at him in surprise. She felt rude all of a sudden. She hadn't been making any effort to be friendly and here he was giving her a gift. She reached out and took the parcel and laid it on the table in front of her. She slowly lifted the tissue paper to reveal the leather binding of a journal – the pages inside were made from the paper she had already seen and admired at Micah Camp. Josie had even given her a sample package of the stationery to take home with her. The journal paper was an oatmeal colour with small motes of embedded flowers and herbs dancing across the pages. She opened the book to the spot where a slim satin ribbon traced a line down the page – it was smooth and soft and rich to the touch. She slowly closed the book and ran her fingers over the cream-coloured, brushed leather and the intricately worked design of interlocking circles around the outside edge. It was one of the most beautiful things she had ever seen.

"You never know when you might have something really important to write down," Liam told Lisa-Marie as he waved to her aunt and turned in the direction of the path to Micah Camp. Lisa-Marie covered the entire first page that very night with an elaborate design of delicate leaves, vines and flowers that encircled a finely wrought name – Justin.

i i i .

Izzy glanced up and stifled a groan of impatience as Micah Camp's new, live-in director came through the door of her office, "This paper and soap making business is going to give me a nervous breakdown."

Her desk was overflowing with client files. She didn't have time for this. She had discovered over the last two months that there was a multitude of things that could possibly give Roland a nervous breakdown and each and every one of them could result in a lengthy discussion followed by inter-office correspondence. Izzy had been enjoying a cinnamon bun and sipping a coffee while trying to get caught up on some case notes. She saw now that crumbs had spilled over the top of her shirt and down inside her bra. She hastily tried to shake herself off, "I have an appointment in just a few minutes, Roland."

It was clear from the way Roland settled in the straight-backed chair opposite her desk that he had no intention of budging before her client came through the door.

"What did you think of the Board meeting, Izzy? I know it was my first but I did come away concerned about a number of issues." Roland opened a thick notebook and ran his finger down what looked to be a very long list. "I realize you have an appointment so I'll try to be succinct – I thought there was far too much emphasis on the importance of the paper and soap sales."

Izzy pushed the files on her desk to one side and accepted the fact that she had to allot the next ten or so minutes to Roland. "Well – the Board was impressed with Josie's five-year market plan. Everyone has nurtured the business along from the start and we're all proud of how well it has done. The paper and soap sales bring in a lot of money for Micah Camp – and almost all of that revenue goes to scholarships. Besides that, the workshop is a really convenient placement site and work experience is part of the resident's educational goals."

"What about quantifiable mental health goals, Izzy? I had hoped a larger part of the agenda for the meeting would have been allocated to my presentation on tracking outcomes based on the best practice guidelines I've drawn up." Roland stopped talking to scan Izzy's desk before asking, "You have studied the binder I gave you?"

"I'm going to get to it, Roland . . . this is a busy time with new residents coming in and others leaving." The place that Roland's binder occupied on Izzy's priority list was so far back that she would have needed high-powered binoculars to see it.

Roland abruptly changed the subject. "Izzy are you aware of what goes on here, after hours? People were running around until two in the morning with this latest soap order. I felt like I was living in the middle of a maquiladora border town. I just can't see how that type of behaviour can contribute to anyone's positive mental health. You have no idea what it is like to spend your nights here or eat every meal with the residents."

Izzy shrugged. It was hard to have any sympathy for Roland. It was part of the director's job to live on site.

Roland leaned forward in his chair to brush an imperceptible speck of dust from the sharp crease in his grey trousers, "I believe this type of work experience and emphasis on the trivial detracts from my clinical counselling." Izzy caught a look of what she perceived to be superiority flit across his face. "After all, the Board did hire me for my PhD in clinical counselling."

She watched Roland studying his well-manicured nails and thought that he looked exactly like a blown-up toad, with his I've-got-a-PhD crap. For two cents, minus his high and mighty PhD – probably bought and paid for from some mail-order place in the States – she'd tell him exactly what she thought of him and his clinical counselling skills.

When Roland looked up it was as if he had read a small portion of her thoughts, "Of course I mean our work, Izzy . . . our valuable work with the young people who need us so desperately."

With those words Roland rose just as Izzy's appointment breezed through the door. She watched the young man plop into the chair Roland had just vacated. His hand immediately snaked out to grab her half-finished coffee and he gulped it down while stuffing what was left of her cinnamon bun into his mouth. When he raised his eyes to meet Izzy's he said, "You were done with these, right?"

Izzy nodded, watching Roland stroll out of her office calling back over his shoulder as he went, "I'm really looking forward to book club tonight, Izzy."

Why she had ever allowed Cook to invite him along to book club was certainly beyond Izzy's ability to discern. Roland would probably go into his empty office and put his feet up on his empty desk, stare at his ceiling and come up with yet other ways to irritate her. It wasn't that Izzy couldn't recognize Roland's ability. In the months since his arrival he'd straightened out more than a few of the Board's headaches. He was an excellent manager with a real talent for establishing protocols, solving staffing issues, meeting financial goals and untangling complicated legal issues.

In Izzy's opinion, the Board didn't care if Roland ever used his so-called clinical skills on a single kid, no matter what they had led him to believe when they hired him. They liked the letters behind his name but what they really valued was his ability to push the paper necessary to keep a facility like Micah Camp financially afloat.

Izzy had been working at Micah Camp for almost seventeen years. George Lafferty, Micah Camp's first Director, had hired her. The Camp had been established just a year before and Izzy was their first counsellor. George had been just the type of Director the fledgling Camp needed. He was everywhere all the time, doing whatever needed doing. If a toilet was plugged after hours, George unplugged it. If a kid needed to go for a canoe ride to unwind, George was there to paddle right along. If Cook needed a hand hauling in a fifty pound bag of potatoes, George was at her side. If Josie needed someone to oversee a vat of soap, George threw on a black, plastic apron and grabbed a mixing paddle. And if Izzy needed to talk, he listened. George saw his primary role at Micah Camp as an educator and he tutored several of the courses in which the residents were enrolled. He and Izzy complemented one another rather than getting in each other's space.

George was gone now – retired for at least a year and backpacking around Ireland. The Board had decided to go in a different direction with George's replacement – by hiring a person with a more hands on approach to management, a person who was a clinically trained counsellor more than an educator, a person who was bound to encroach on Izzy's territory. It hadn't taken Izzy long to realize that Roland's approach to counselling was diametrically opposed to her own. In her opinion, Roland's style wasn't what Micah Camp needed and with each passing day she missed George more and more.

Izzy refocused her attention on the young man flopped on the chair across from her crunching down the last mouthful of her cinnamon bun, Micah

Camp's newest arrival. She glanced down at the single sheet in the open file in front of her: Jesse McAlister – age nineteen – high scores in computer science – working since high-school graduation waiting tables at a Boston Pizza.

"Hello, Jesse." Izzy rose and came around her desk. She reached out to shake Jesse's hand, "My name is Isabella Montgomery, but everyone just calls me Izzy."

"Ya, sure . . . nice to meet you. I want to say for the record that this place is totally budget in the accommodation department. The cabins are way too small for three guys to share and that prissy fart is fucking irritating." Jesse pointed in the direction Roland had headed.

"OK . . . watch the language, Jesse."

Jesse looked down for a moment and then back at Izzy with a wide grin, "I'm just saying is all."

Izzy grabbed her sweater from the hook behind the door and smiled back at him, "Let's get some fresh air while we talk, shall we?" Jesse followed her out of the office and down the hall to the wide double doors that led out toward the lake.

i v .

Liam walked along the path from the A-Frame to Micah Camp. The trail under his feet was closely bordered by banks of salal, ferns, huckleberries and a mixture of second-growth cedar, hemlock, spruce and fir trees. He thought about Lisa-Marie's face as her fingers moved gently over the pattern worked into the leather cover of the journal. He had seen a look of real pleasure and appreciation when she raised her eyes to thank him. He had learned to work with leather back in his treatment center days, though most of his time had been spent tutoring the other guys in English or getting them ready to take the grade twelve equivalency test. He kept up the leatherwork now as a hobby. It was a way to fill the winter evenings while the sound of country music came from old cassettes played on his stereo, the fire in the woodstove crackling and throwing a warm glow into the room. He had quite a stack of journals, hair pieces, wallets, small purses and belts stored away waiting for the right recipients to come along.

Liam enjoyed his early afternoon chats with Bethany. She mothered him a bit and he didn't mind her concern. He was used to his stomach complaint. He had suffered with it a long time. The doctors said maybe it was this or that but they never decided on anything for sure. Liam made every effort to eliminate or cut down on the things that really seemed to disagree with him. He treated himself with various herbal tea concoctions and Pepto-Bismol, which seemed to be as good as anything that Dr. Maxwell had prescribed – and cheaper too.

The trail opened onto a circle-drive in front of Micah Camp's main building, a large structure built in a chalet style. It was flanked on one side by the paper and soap workshops and a large maintenance shed, on the other by a row of resident cabins. The whole effect was somewhat like a squat figure in a pointy hat with two arms outstretched toward the lake. Liam followed the path around the back of the main building to the service entrance and through to the large, bright kitchen.

Cook was busy behind the long counter with a batch of her famous cinnamon buns when she caught sight of Liam and called out her regular greeting, "You are way too thin, Mr."

Shaking his head, Liam refused a large piece of cherry pie that Cook pointed to as she relieved him of the eggs. He knew that eating pie would play havoc with his stomach. He headed out of the kitchen and down the hall.

Roland came out of his office when he saw Liam pass his door. "Liam, it's good to see you; I'm looking forward to book club tonight." Liam nodded, taking in the wide expanse of Roland's perfectly clean desk. "Would you have some time next week to work with our maintenance guys on the annual power system check-up?"

Liam attempted to hide a haggard look. The Camp's hydro-electric system was modeled on the one Caleb had, so Liam was familiar with the ins and outs. In the past he hadn't minded moonlighting at the Camp for some extra cash, but in Liam's memory of the good old days he had always had plenty of time. He and Caleb and George would hike up the pipeline trail and spend hours hanging out together on the mountain checking the water flow and clearing debris from the intake area. But things were different now. Since Caleb's death, Liam was hard-pressed to keep up with everything that had fallen on him – managing the woodlot and the sawmill, working around his own place, looking after the chickens and doling out the eggs, as well as keeping up with what needed doing at Izzy's. Having Justin around to do the gardening helped but Liam was still working as many hours as he could manage and even so, things were slipping. He had only to glance at the bottom line of the latest bank statement for Crater Lake Timber, to see that.

"Let me think about it . . . OK, Roland? I'll let you know tonight." Liam carried on down the hall that led past Izzy's office just in time to see her come around the corner, walking beside a young man who was smiling and chatting amiably to her. Izzy stopped in front of Liam.

"Hey Liam, this is Jesse McAlister. Liam lives down the way and I'm sure you'll see him around now and then."

Jesse squinted at Liam, "You from the reserve at the end of the lake? Saw some kids from the reserve when I was in Dearborn. Some old guys hanging out near the hotel too. Well, more like passed out."

Liam studied the look on Jesse's face – a smart-ass kind of smirk. He's just a kid, he thought, but all the same, Liam still felt a sudden urge to reach out and shove Jesse in the shoulder.

"I'm Cree from Northern Manitoba."

Jesse continued to stare at Liam, "Ya . . . sure . . . Plains Indians, buffalo and horses. We studied them in school . . . think we even had a video."

"Well, I haven't been home in a while. Didn't see any buffalo around last time I was there." No horses either for that matter, he thought. More like snowmobiles zigzagging across the reserve most of the year. "And like I said, Northern Manitoba."

Liam glanced at Izzy but she had already turned to her office door and was juggling a file and her cup of coffee, while trying to get her key in the lock. She dropped the file. Liam heard her utter a half-whispered but clearly audible – shit – before she handed Jesse her coffee to hold and scrunched down to retrieve the file and the papers now scattered at her feet.

From the vantage point of their height above her, Liam and Jesse were both afforded a clear view down the front of her shirt to the top of her bra edged in lace. A faint tan line separated her exposed skin from a lighter colour below. Liam averted his eyes from Izzy's bent figure. Jesse made no such effort. Liam could see him ogling Izzy quite openly. Jesse finally pulled his eyes away to glance at Liam as Izzy rose with the file in her hand. Liam was sure now that Jesse was smirking as he headed off down the hall.

"See you soon, Izzy. Same time, same place, right?" Jesse slurped Izzy's coffee loudly. Liam's gaze followed after Jesse for a moment before he turned to Izzy. He stood just inside the doorway of her office admiring the atmosphere in which Izzy worked.

In front of the large window with its view of the lake, two comfortable chairs rested on a thick carpet. A low table sat in front of the chairs. The soothing sound of falling water came from a corner where a wooden ladle tipped a steady stream into a fountain's stone bowl. Fresh flowers adorned Izzy's desk. An entire wall of bookshelves contained a variety of interesting objects interspersed carefully among the many books.

"Shit . . . unbelievable . . . that guy took two coffees and a cinnamon bun from me in the first session." Izzy flipped open the client file in her hand and began quickly to jot down notes.

"Roland wants me to help out on the Camp's power system maintenance," Liam said as he moved further into the office, letting his eyes rest on Izzy's head of black curls bent over the file in her hand.

She raised her eyes from the file to stare at Liam for a moment. "Just tell him you can't, Liam. You already have too much to do. You know that – right?" Izzy was shaking her head now and tapping the pen in a staccato beat against the side of the file. "We have to try harder to find someone to help with that damn woodlot and sawmill." Liam nodded silently. They had been advertising for over a year now, looking for someone to take over the management of the business. So far there had been no takers.

"Maybe another person part-time would help. It could free up one of the other guys to take on some of the management." The tap, tap, tap of the pen increased and Liam saw Izzy get a sort of "aha" look on her face. "Maybe Jesse . . . his main interest is computer programming and stuff like that but some part-time work on the woodlot might be a nice change of pace."

Liam just nodded. He said goodbye and walked away down the hall. Great – that's just what I need, Izzy – to be out on the woodlot and have that smirk walking behind me with a chainsaw.

Chapter 4

i.

"Call me Dan or Father Dan if you must." The Reverend Patterson talked over his shoulder to Beulah as he juggled his large duffle bag and two other odd-shaped bags from the curb near the bus.

He certainly wasn't anything like the priests Beulah had ever known. Call-me-Dan was cut from a different type of cloth altogether. In the first place there was no clerical collar anywhere in evidence. He was dressed in jeans and a tourist T-shirt that sported an orca whale breaking out of the Pacific's coastal waves. A New York Yankees ball cap perched on his head.

Dan was around forty-five – Beulah's own age. He had what she had always heard described as a Roman nose below a high forehead that gave way to premature balding. This last trait was made evident when he doffed the Yankees cap to shake her hand. He seemed unusually cheerful for someone at the end of a three-day journey, the last leg of which had been an eight-hour ride on a Greyhound bus.

"I work in a large diocese in Ontario." Dan spoke while he crunched through the bag of chips he had bought at the gas station. "That's what we call a group of individual churches with a bishop in charge . . . a diocese."

The sound of spewing gravel came from under the Ford's tires as Beulah made the turn onto the road to Crater Lake. The local radio station pumped out classic rock tunes. The sound of Beulah cracking sunflower seeds and throwing the husks out the open window filled the cab. It was a warm afternoon and Dan inhaled deeply the smell of trees and water and something ineffably wild drifting in on the breeze.

"I like to move around a lot . . . from parish to parish . . . you know?" Dan paused for a moment, "That's what we call the churches . . . parishes."

Beulah gave him a slanting sideways glance, "I know what a parish is, Dan."

"Oh great – anyway, the bishop likes us to stay put for at least four years . . . stability and all that. I usually don't hang around any one place that long." He smiled over at Beulah and added, "I get itchy feet." Dan wiggled his new joggers for emphasis and laughed loudly.

As Beulah continued to crack her sunflower seeds, she chuckled more than once. Dan's habit of laughing at his own jokes, with a braying type of noise that put her in mind of Mozart's insane laughter in the movie, *Amadeus,* made it hard to resist. At first she was laughing at him but after a bit she caught onto the fact that some of what he said was really humorous. The humour was not always in the parts he thought were funny but that was half the fun of it.

"After seven years we're encouraged to take a year-long sabbatical. It's a bit of a break, a holiday but we're also supposed to be doing something intellectual."

"Geez, Dan . . . I wish I could have put a mirror up to your face when you said the word, intellectual. Are you in pain or something?" Beulah started to laugh and Dan joined right in. Beulah was now convinced this guy was going to be entertaining. She could hardly wait to see the look on Izzy's face when he laughed like that.

"I do hospital chaplaincy work and I'm planning to write a manual for other priests who do the same type of thing." Dan paused to look out the window as a breathtaking expanse of Crater Lake came into view around the bend in the road. "But to be honest I'm more of a hands-on kind of guy –," again the laugh, "– good thing right? You know . . . idle hands are the devil's playthings and all that." Beulah shook her head and rolled her eyes as Dan continued, "Writing will be something new to sink my teeth into. I'm mostly looking forward to kicking back and putting my feet up."

Dan took a moment to enjoy the view and then with the basics of his own story out, he asked Beulah, "How long have you lived at Crater Lake?"

"Fifteen years."

Dan plunged on, "On your own?"

"Nope." A sunflower seed husk zoomed right past Dan's face to fly out of the passenger window.

"What do you do?" Dan kept right on smiling over at Beulah. He had jumped back slightly when the husk flew past his nose but he didn't seem fazed by it.

"I bake bread."

Dan waited a moment, as if he thought Beulah might elaborate and then changed the subject, "How do you know Isabella Montgomery?"

"Neighbours,"

"Is she married?"

"Not anymore." Dan was silent for all of two minutes. His next question got Beulah's attention. "Are there any decent baseball leagues in the area? Can you see a good game around here now and then?"

The abrupt turn of Beulah's body to stare at Dan had the Ford careening toward the cliff. Beulah sharply corrected her placement on the road. She laughed when she noticed Dan clutching the dash and pushing his foot down hard on an invisible brake pedal.

"There was a mixed slow-pitch league in this area that was something to talk about, Dan. We had a team that was damn near impossible to beat."

i i .

Dearborn's mixed slow-pitch league had been Beulah and Caleb's passion. Actually they were passionate about everything to do with baseball but the Crater Lake Timber Wolves team was their baby. Caleb played catcher and Beulah pitched. Liam did a pretty fair job on third base and though Izzy was nothing much in the field, she could hit a decent grounder. George played center field but he seemed to cover the whole outfield most of the time. Cook held down first base. Players fooled by her five-foot-nothing stance, found they were tagged out before they knew what hit them. Josie played shortstop where she had an almost eerie ability to get under the ball at whatever trajectory it entered the field. Bethany was their scorekeeper. For all her shrinking-violet ways, she would stand toe to toe in a screaming match with any other scorekeeper who didn't come up with the same figures she had entered neatly in the little squares of the score sheet.

Caleb and Beulah ran the whole league. Everything to do with it engrossed them from the start of the season to the end – signing up the teams, putting together the schedule, booking the fields, arranging the out-of-town tournaments, coaching and playing in the actual games and drinking beer in the dugouts when the game was over. The fun times carried right on to the Legion where reliving each and every play seemed to be as enjoyable as the games themselves.

The end-of-season league barbecue at Izzy and Caleb's had been an event to rival any in the Dearborn area – buckets of beer on ice, a huge grill smoking with the smell of barbecued salmon heavy in the air, kids running around everywhere, players from all the teams swimming, laughing, eating and finally dancing under the stars long into the warm summer night to the music of whatever local band Caleb had badgered into making an appearance. Caleb's death had taken the heart right out of the whole league to say nothing of what it did to the Crater Lake Timber Wolves.

iii.

The rest of the drive went by quickly with talk of baseball filling the cab. As they approached their destination, Beulah anticipated with great pleasure the look that would appear on Dan's face when she hurtled the pickup down Izzy's driveway. The road plunged down what seemed like a ninety degree slope to end in a tight hairpin curve before flattening out and carrying on to the main cabin. A ride down the roadway with Beulah was something most people endured only once, preferring to walk up and down carrying heavy bags from then on if Beulah was the only other choice.

Pulling into the open space of Izzy's driveway, Dan rewarded Beulah with the appropriate my-life-has-just-passed-before-my-eyes look. He had actually reached for a rosary from his pocket when they neared the curve. That had been a bonus even Beulah could not have anticipated. She noticed Izzy coming out of the garden with Justin trailing behind her and Liam standing near the open door of the workshop. Quite the welcoming committee – all hands on deck. She began whistling as she jumped from the driver's side of the truck and turned to scoop her various deliveries from the backseat.

Beulah strolled across the drive and veered toward Liam. She pushed a package against his chest with more force than was required, "One bottle of

Pepto-Bismol as ordered. Got something eating away at you, Liam?" Without waiting for an answer she turned her back on him to pass Izzy a large stack of mail.

"Welcome to Crater Lake, Reverend Patterson." Izzy beckoned Justin forward to grab the bags. "I'm going to get you settled into your cabin first thing and we can worry about introductions, tours and other things as we go."

"Please just call me Dan – or Father Dan if you must." Dan reached out to shake Izzy's hand, "I always shudder a bit when I hear the word Reverend. It makes me think of a pot-bellied old man wearing a black hat and coat . . . delivering a eulogy." Dan added this last comment accompanied by the loudest laugh yet – a laugh that dissolved into a distinctive snort.

Izzy's double take and the fleeting expression on her face was everything Beulah was hoping for. She jumped into the Ford, did a quick turnaround in the drive and headed back up the twisting road.

i v .

Liam was hanging up the phone when Izzy breezed in from the garden. "The new blade for the saw should be on the bus tomorrow," Liam told her.

She glanced toward him with a roll of her eyes, "Please, for the love of God, do not tell me even one pain-in-the-ass thing about that sawmill."

Changing the subject, Liam asked, "Can I give you a hand with anything?"

Izzy was banging around the kitchen pulling things out of the fridge and cupboards. "If you would peel those potatoes you would make my day," she told Liam as she brushed past him to grab a large glass baking dish.

As he peeled potatoes neatly onto a piece of newspaper, Liam glanced over at Izzy grating cheddar cheese; her movements were quick though somewhat wild as bits of cheese fell to the floor at her feet. Dante, Izzy's russet-coloured setter, watched her every move and dutifully took care of each fallen piece – some before they hit the ground.

Liam rinsed the potatoes and asked, "The cleric all settled in?"

"Hmmm . . . that laugh is something else, isn't it?" Izzy gave a small snort of her own for emphasis. "He sure doesn't look like any priest I've ever seen," she added, scooping the cheese into a bowl before scooting around Liam to grab a knife. She began to chop onions in a flurry that made Liam a bit queasy. He backed away from the counter as Justin came through from the pantry carrying a large basket filled with fresh herbs and lettuce greens.

"Hey, kid," Liam greeted Justin and peered into the basket, "Looks like this hot weather is sure paying off."

"I'll say . . . there's enough lettuce out there to feed an army." Justin placed the basket on the counter and turned to Izzy, "I took the rest of Dan's bags over. He looked pretty comfortable, kicking back with a beer and the newspaper."

Izzy was already filling the sink and tossing the lettuce into the cold water. She nodded absently to Liam as he headed out saying, "I've got at least another hour or so on that tax stuff, Izzy. I'd better get back to it."

"If this heat keeps up, Justin, we'll have to be careful the rest of the lettuce doesn't bolt. I think I'll get you to pull out the shading covers for the cold frames."

Justin nodded, leaning in against the counter. His eyes tracked Izzy's movements. "Can I give you a hand with anything?"

Izzy laughed as she looked back over her shoulder at Justin in his garden-stained work clothes with his face flushed from the afternoon heat. "No, I don't need any help. Why not go catch a swim before everyone gets here? You look like you could use it."

"Ya, I guess –," Justin hesitated for a moment then raked his hand through his sweat drenched hair, "– OK, sounds great. See you later, Izzy." He pushed himself away from the counter and headed for the door.

Izzy watched Justin disappear toward the stairway to the beach before she turned to reach for a large wine glass from the cupboard. She filled the glass to the brim with Chardonnay and stood silent for a moment to contemplate the way the wine sparkled through the pattern of the glass in the afternoon light that streamed into the kitchen. She took a sip, then walked over to the stereo in the corner and shoved a Joan Jett CD into the machine. The combination of music, wine and cooking was enough to clear her mind of Jesse's unproductive first session, Roland's constant carping, Beulah's sneering expression directed at Liam and Dan's surprisingly non-priest-like demeanour.

Chapter Five

i.

Dear Emma:

My name is Lisa-Marie and I'm sixteen-years old. I'm going to call you Emma because when I read that Jane Austen book last year, I loved Emma – she was always messing everything up but in the end things worked out great for her. I would like that to be me.

You are a beautiful leather-covered journal that my aunt's friend, Liam gave to me – for no reason at all, Emma – he doesn't even know me but he gave me a gift. My aunt just loves him but Beulah (my aunt's super bitchy partner) can't stand him. Maybe she's jealous – haha – as if.

Do you wonder how I ended up with such a lame name? My grannie named me Lisa-Marie because she was such a total Elvis nut. If you aren't an Elvis nut then I'll tell you that Lisa-Marie was the name of Elvis and Pricilla Presley's daughter. I never saw my own mother – not even once. She died right after I was born. Grannie tried to say it in a nice way but bottom line – my mom was a junkie who cleaned up to have me. Then she went out on the street and scored some heroin that was way too pure for someone who had been on the wagon for nine months. She died of an overdose in a flop hotel in downtown Kingston.

Anyway – Emma – in this journal I promise to tell the truth, the whole truth and nothing but the truth. How does that sound? The first truth I will tell you is that I am spending the whole summer with my aunt and crabby-pants Beulah in their A-Frame cabin on a lake and next door is a place called Micah Camp and

I have met a guy who lives there and he is the cutest, hottest, nicest guy ever! His name is Justin Roberts and I promised the truth – right? I am totally in love! When I look at him I think I will just melt into a big puddle on the ground. He is nothing like any of the other guys I've been with. I'll tell you the truth about all of that on another day.

Tonight we are going to a potluck thing next door at a lady named Izzy's house and Justin will be there. I'm going crazy trying to figure out what to wear. Shit – Emma – I've got to stop writing – Beulah is screaming at me from downstairs to hurry up and get ready. She is such a bully-cow. (And if you snoop in my things and read that, Beulah – you deserve what you get.)

i i .

Lisa-Marie, her aunt and Beulah walked along the tree-lined path from the A-Frame and then through an orchard of mature apple trees. The glossy-green leaves of the large rhododendrons, interspersed among the fruit trees, shone in the late-afternoon sunlight. They came out of the orchard and along a wood-chip path to a large deck backed by an arbour covered in honeysuckle and sweet peas.

A friendly Irish setter scampered around the three of them licking any out-stretched hand he could get to. Lisa-Marie hunkered down to the ground and dug her hands into the thick fur around the dog's neck. She began to knead and pet him while the dog looked at her with already adoring eyes.

Izzy came out of a door from the kitchen when she saw them on the deck. In her hurry to pull an apron dotted with bright-red poppies over her head she got tangled up in its folds. Laughing, Beulah reached over to help her. Izzy stood in front of them. Her raven black curls were tousled around her face, a slightly abashed smile playing around the corners of her glossy lips, while her brown eyes sparkled and lit on each of them in turn.

"That's Dante –," she smiled at Lisa-Marie who was getting up from petting the dog, "I see you two have already met." Izzy reached out for Lisa-Marie's hand.

Roland and Cook came down the same path through the apple trees to join them on the deck and everyone was introduced to Dan. He had already been there when the group from the A-Frame arrived. He looked comfortable, ensconced in a deck chair drinking a beer. Dan greeted Beulah like a long-lost friend and got up right away to shake hands with Lisa-Marie and Bethany. "I feel lucky to be alive after the ride this woman took me on down that roadway earlier," he pointed to Beulah with his can of beer.

"Any more where that came from, old pal?" Beulah gestured towards the beer in Dan's hand and playfully punched at his arm.

After the introductions, Bethany stood off to the side of the deck. She reached down to deadhead some of the old petunia and marigold blossoms on the plants that spilled in reckless disarray from the brightly-coloured, ceramic planters that decorated the deck. Dan's eyes strayed more than once to the blonde hair that swung down over her face as she bent to her task. Bethany wore a periwinkle-blue dress that picked up the colour of her eyes and accentuated her curves. Dan's glance lingered on the endless row of tiny pearl buttons that ran from the sweetheart neckline to the hem of the dress.

Izzy moved effortlessly around the deck chatting to everyone as she filled wine glasses and passed around a tray of appetizers. She was clad in a red dress made of a beautifully draping fabric. The deep V in the front was matched by one in the back and the cap sleeves accentuated the shape of her arms. Her only other adornments were a necklace of overlapping silver medallions that caught the light whenever she moved and a thick, gold wedding band on her left hand.

iii.

Lisa-Marie leaned back against the deck railing and munched on the small pastry in her hand. The scent of the honeysuckle, draped in a wild tangle over the arbour, was heavy on the late afternoon breeze. She inhaled deeply and watched Izzy. She didn't want to stare but she couldn't help herself. Izzy was like someone from the pages of a magazine or a movie screen. Her aunt had told Lisa-Marie that Izzy was forty-five and that had seemed really old to her before she actually saw Izzy. Now age didn't seem to mean anything at all – Izzy was perfect. And it wasn't just because she was so beautiful. From the moment she had shaken Lisa-Marie's hand her warmth and acceptance had been like something solid between them.

Lisa-Marie was slammed with a crushing wave of self-consciousness. She felt gawky and embarrassed and she wanted to find someplace to hide. Her stomach rolled over with nausea and she wished she hadn't eaten the pastry.

She looked down at her tight, sleeveless top layered over her best push-up bra and at her black, hip-hugging jeans. The latter afforded a nice view of her belly-button ring in the front and her thong underwear in the back. She didn't understand what was wrong with her outfit but she was sure everything she was wearing was wrong and her makeup was probably wrong too. Everything about her was wrong.

With a shrug of misery she turned to stare out over the dazzling water, bright with the rays of the setting sun. That same sun shone on her face and despite the warmth, she felt cold. A litany now ran through her mind non-stop; *you are one fucking, pathetic loser.* She could feel herself descending to the bottom of a very familiar well of self-loathing.

As she teetered on the edge of total despair, Lisa-Marie spotted Justin coming from around the side of the main cabin. Her heart actually felt as though it missed a beat. Her downward spiral was arrested as if both her feet shot out to grip the walls of the well and her arms worked frantically to pull herself back up the slippery sides. Justin must have just showered because his hair was wet and he was buttoning up a shirt over a pair of faded, black jeans. She caught a brief glimpse of his chest – a view that was hot enough to make her blush. She felt her palms start to sweat and her mouth go dry. She had always wondered if the heart-missing-a-beat phenomenon she read about in novels could be true. She now had the answer to that question.

iv.

Liam came through into the kitchen of the cabin with a jar of pickles in hand. He put the jar on the counter only to realize that he had gotten it from Izzy in the first place. There was an identical jar already on the counter. He had hoped that the pickles he brought might have come from Josie. Oh well, you can never have too many pickles, he thought as he placed a box of Timbits beside the jars on the kitchen counter. He was hoping the doughnuts were still OK. They had been kicking around his place for a few days.

He looked out to see everyone gathered on the kitchen deck and his gaze quickly went to Izzy at the center. The red dress was one of Liam's favourites and he stood watching her for a few moments. Finally he walked out and greeted Lisa-Marie, "Hi, kiddo." Liam had always had a problem remembering names. He adopted a simple system to deal with the young people from Micah

Camp. He called all the boys kid and all the girls kiddo. It worked for him. He felt a pang of anxiety as he watched Lisa-Marie cross the deck towards Izzy who was standing next to Dan and calling Lisa-Marie over. There was way too much of that girl's body on display.

He turned back to the rest of the group in time to hear Izzy say, "One thing we have to establish before I show you two around –," she was glancing at Lisa-Marie and Dan in turn, "– is the common lexicon of directions." Liam and Beulah burst out laughing. Beulah unsuccessfully hid a scowl as she turned away. Liam knew it was because she didn't even want to share the same set of memories with him anymore.

Soon after Liam had arrived at Crater Lake, Caleb called them all together over coffee on the kitchen deck. He said it was very important that they determine a common sense of direction related to the area. A problem had arisen because half of them considered it common sense that the front of the main cabin was the lake side and the others were equally convinced that the front should be the sloped way down from the road. After all, that was the direction from which they approached the cabin. If Caleb suggested they go to the front, Izzy would head for the lake and Caleb for the driveway.

Their first resolution had been to drop the terms front and back and to refer to the four directions around the main cabin as the lake side, the road side, the north side – going over toward Bethany and Beulah's and the south side – going over to Liam's. Izzy refused to accept the terms south and north garden and suggested that the north garden be called the orchard garden as that was where all the apple trees were. The other garden would be called the greenhouse garden for obvious reasons. Everyone had agreed that there was enough common sense logic to these location names that they might just catch on.

Things still got confusing though. The kitchen deck was called the kitchen deck because it was right off the kitchen. The cliff deck was obviously on the cliff. But Izzy continued to call the deck that wrapped around the outside of the living room to overlook the lake, the front deck; and, for her, the door that led from the main cabin to the greenhouse garden would always be the back door.

Caleb had just sighed that day out on the kitchen deck. It seemed to Liam that Caleb found Izzy's inability to drop the words front and back as charming more than problematic. He said they would simply have to do their best to figure out which of the doors and decks people were talking about. He had winked at Izzy as he pulled her into his lap and snuggled her neck, "If you ask me to meet you on the front deck some moonlit night I won't be heading that way," he pointed toward the lake and laughed.

Izzy had relaxed into his embrace, her body fitting perfectly against his. "If I ask you to get your sorry ass out the back door I don't really care which door you use as long as you get out . . . OK?" Liam remembered the laughing that day more than anything else.

V.

Izzy quickly reviewed the established protocol for Lisa-Marie and Dan, turning gracefully as she pointed in each direction. "OK then . . . let's go inside," her smile easily held everyone as they followed her through the door and into the kitchen.

Beulah, Bethany and Cook went immediately to the kitchen counter and began getting things ready for dinner. Roland, who looked somewhat pinched after Liam delivered the news that he couldn't help with the power system maintenance, wandered away to straighten cushions in the living room and rearrange the wine glasses and cutlery on the dining room table. Justin flopped into one of the living room chairs and began to flip idly through a copy of *Gardening in the Pacific Northwest*. Liam leaned comfortably against the wall at the bottom of the three steps that separated the kitchen from the dining room. It was a spot that allowed him to hear what was being said in most of the cabin.

The tour began in the kitchen, a room dominated by windows. Potted geraniums with flowers in shades of salmon, pink and red spilled from the corners and the wide window ledges. The room narrowed into a galley-style kitchen and then opened to a pantry and utility room at the far end. The cedar ceilings were high in the galley section of the kitchen and light streamed in from the clerestory windows above.

Bethany pulled the foil tight around the chicken to keep it warm and turned to cut up a jar of pickles. She thought about how she loved this kitchen with its spacious counters and earth tones and the light falling everywhere around her no matter what she did or where she went. She remembered the last time they had all been together with Caleb. It was here in this kitchen – all of them sitting around the oak table for Bethany's birthday. It was right before Izzy had flown out to Montreal for a conference.

Caleb had leaned over and kissed Bethany on the cheek after she attempted to blow out her thirty-seven candles and said, "Happy Birthday Beth. Who would keep us all true if it wasn't for you?" Tears had sprung up in her eyes as she marvelled that Caleb would know what mattered most to her – loyalty and not letting each other down.

Beulah had her own memories of the last time she had been in this kitchen with Caleb. She had come over to check about what time they would head up to the woodlot the next day. Caleb and Liam were having a bachelor meal of sausages and beans with fried onions that was obviously turning Liam's stomach. He headed off home while Caleb pulled out the whiskey and two squat tumblers, their cut-glass design sparkling in the evening light of the cabin. The rich amber alcohol looked almost thick within them.

Caleb had been making his way steadily through his candy supply since Izzy had left for Montreal. When he tipped up the last jar, he looked guiltily over at Beulah, "You've got to help me replace this stuff before Izzy comes home . . . I mean it, don't laugh. She'll kill me if she sees I ate all of this." He held up the empty glass jar in his hand and swept his arm back to point to the row of empties on the nearby shelf.

They sat at the kitchen table, relaxed, drinking and playing a hand of Gin Rummy. Caleb was wearing a Stanfield wool shirt with dark-blue suspenders still attached to his jeans but slouched down off his shoulders. His work socks were hooked in the rungs under his chair. After a few drinks, Caleb sat back in the chair and stretched. "I can't really stomach this place much anymore when Izzy isn't here." He was quiet for a moment. "When we got together, I just figured we'd have a whole bunch of kids and they would run wild around here." He laughed and paused to glance over at Beulah, "Those kids would have kept you and Bethany and Liam on your toes for sure." He looked down to the deck of cards in his hands and shuffled them slowly, his fingers rhythmically caressing the worn edges. "You guys would have taught those kids a thing or two."

Beulah snorted over her drink. "I got nothing to teach a kid, Caleb."

He studied her carefully as he rocked his chair back on two legs, "You'd be surprised how wrong you are about that, Beulah." Finishing off his drink Caleb spoke with finality, "It wasn't meant to be. Kids just weren't in the cards.

I just hope to hell I'm long gone before Izzy because I don't find the thought of clunking around this place without her all that inspiring." He righted the chair with a bang and stretched his long muscular body to a standing position, rubbing his hand along his untrimmed beard. He smiled his crooked grin at Beulah, "We'd better pack it in if we want an early start tomorrow."

As Beulah watched Izzy move past her, beautiful in the red dress, she couldn't help thinking that at least Caleb had gotten his wish.

v i .

At the far end of the kitchen, stairs led to the lofts above or the main floor below. "Let's do the downstairs first." There was a lilt of enjoyment in Izzy's voice.

Through the dining room at the bottom of the stairs, French doors opened to a wide landing and two steps down to a sun porch overlooking the lake. Wicker furniture took up this space and a profusion of hanging and potted plants filled in the corners.

Beyond the dining room, with its table now laden with dishes and bottles of unopened wine, was the living room – the heart of the cabin. It boasted a twenty-three-foot ceiling where an upward sweep of the eye revealed railings to the lofts above. One wall was dominated by windows looking out towards the lake. A wood-burning stove with a burnished-coppery-gold pipe disappeared up into the cedar ceiling far above. Chairs and a sofa, all in overstuffed, dark-brown leather, were arranged invitingly around the room. Wall space was taken up with an eclectic mix of art, chosen more for personal appeal than with an eye to value or symmetry. Against one wall sat an upright piano, its highly-polished oak finish reflecting the light from the room in rippling waves of colour.

Dan went immediately to the piano. He pushed up the cover to reveal the ivory keys and pulled out the bench. He sat down with a flourish. Flexing his fingers over the keys, he was still for a moment, as if in deep thought. He glanced back at Izzy, "This is an old 19th century folk song." Without the faintest touch of self-consciousness, he began to play and sing.

I'm just a poor wayfarin stranger
I'm travelling through this world of woe.
Yet there's no sickness, toll nor danger

In that bright land to which I go.
I'm going there to see my father
I'm going there no more to roam.
I'm only going over Jordon
I'm only going over home.

In the moment of silence before the clapping started, Izzy felt totally delighted. She was happy to see the piano being played. It was her grandmother's and though Izzy didn't play at all herself, she asked for it when her grandmother died. Izzy had hauled the piano around with her for years before it found a home at Crater Lake. Dan was still smiling at her and before he got up he ran through a couple of quick scales. "I love to play the piano and this is a beautiful instrument."

"Then you should come over anytime and play. The piano just sits here." Izzy surprised herself by making the offer but as she continued the tour she thought, why not? He'll just be one more person wandering in and out of here.

As Izzy led Dan and Lisa-Marie across the living room towards a large foyer, Lisa-Marie let out a gasp. She was looking up the three stairs that led from the living room to the library. The window at the far end of the room was shaded by clematis vines, their deep-purple, trailing flowers dancing in the early evening breeze. The walls of the room were dominated by floor-to-ceiling book shelves.

Izzy remembered how stunned Caleb had been when he discovered she meant to move forty boxes of books in with her when she took up permanent residence in the main cabin. He always said those boxes of books had warmed him up for the shock of the piano. Over the years the collection of books had only grown.

Moving into the foyer from the living room, Izzy pointed at an exterior door to the left that opened out towards the lake and yet another deck. She waved her hand to the right where the doorway to her bedroom stood. The edge of a colourful patchwork quilt was just visible, folded neatly at the foot of an expanse of bed. Finally, she pointed straight ahead to a large, oak door flanked by stained glass panels that led out of the cabin to the greenhouse garden.

"I've counted five outside doors in this place. It must take you awhile to lock up every night," Dan was shaking his head as he made this observation.

Izzy was startled by the remark. Casting a glance at Liam through the doorway she caught his look of understanding. There was a running joke between all of them about the number of doors in and out of the cabin. Izzy never knew from which direction people were coming or in which direction they were going.

Izzy remembered – as if Caleb were still here – the way he had acted each evening – standing up and stretching, yawning and rubbing his beard with his open hand before saying, "Well, I guess I'll make the rounds."

This hadn't meant locking up because they never locked anything, but it was good practice to make sure all the doors were at least firmly closed. Neither Izzy nor Caleb had ever forgotten the shock of seeing a black bear emerge around the corner of the pantry, having walked in through an unlatched door. Izzy had dashed out of the kitchen to the deck screaming while Caleb had walked slowly backward through the living room and out the door towards the greenhouse garden with the bear ambling along in pursuit. Izzy remembered now that she would invariably reply to Caleb's comment about making the rounds by saying, "Well, if we didn't have so many damn doors around here it wouldn't be such a chore."

The tour continued to the upper floor of the cabin. A large loft that doubled as Izzy's office and a TV room opened off the top of the staircase. An antique, mahogany writing desk sat beneath a window that allowed a view all the way down the lake to the mountains in the distance. As Dan and Izzy admired this view, Lisa-Marie stared curiously at a silver-framed, wedding photo on the desk.

vii.

The only bright spot of grade ten had been the photography class Lisa-Marie managed to squeeze into when some timetable screw-up meant she had an empty block. The students were able to use high quality digital cameras and editing software. Lisa-Marie was a poor kid who could barely scrape together the cash from summer jobs and babysitting to buy cool clothes, let alone fancy electronics, so the class was a treat. Several lessons were devoted to understanding photo composition. The students analyzed dozens of pictures and Lisa-Marie had been fascinated by what she could find out from looking closely at a photograph. She took this knowledge with her when she got to go out, camera in hand to compose her own shots.

Lisa-Marie picked up the silver frame. Izzy was younger in the picture but not so different really. She still had the long, curling, black locks of hair, loose around her shoulders. They were adorned with a circlet of tiny white roses. She was wearing a white dress that seemed to shimmer. The silver medallion necklace, the very one she wore tonight, glinted and sparkled at her neck.

What really caught Lisa-Marie's eye was the man who stood beside Izzy. He had his arm wrapped snugly around her waist and the expression on his face, as he looked down at her, said that no one else existed for him in the whole, wide world. It must be Caleb, she thought. He was obviously older than Izzy, maybe more than ten years older. In the picture he was tall and muscular, really solid with long blonde hair and a wild-looking beard. He had a rugged, tanned look that reminding Lisa-Marie of Brad Pitt in, *Legends of the Fall.* Grannie loved to rent Brad Pitt movies.

They were all there in the photo, standing on the kitchen deck with the lake as a backdrop. Liam was on Caleb's left, looking stiff in a black jacket, his dark hair blown back from his lean and angular face. Beulah, in a matching jacket, stood to Izzy's right. Aunt Bethany was beside Beulah, wearing a totally knock-your-socks-off, black dress and matching spike heels. Her arms were heaped with flowers and her long blonde hair which was pulled to the side cascaded over one shoulder.

A barrage of impressions hit Lisa-Marie in the few short moments she studied the photo. Liam looked alone and she sensed that his solitude had nothing to do with the fact that he was the fifth person in a group of two couples. The way Beulah's arm was around Auntie Beth left no misunderstanding as to whom her aunt belonged. At the same time, Beulah's eyes were on Caleb, her free arm reaching behind Izzy to punch at his shoulder. Izzy was held snug in Caleb's embrace but some trick of shadow or light made it look as though she was standing in front of the others – like she was moving away from them in some way.

Lisa-Marie set the photo down carefully and stepped back from the desk. She caught Izzy's quizzical glance and smiled wordlessly as they both turned away and started back across the loft. The light streamed through the trees beyond the high windows creating a riot of rippling, leaf-like shadows over the sloped, cedar ceiling and down to the hardwood floor.

viii.

From the office loft they proceeded up another few stairs to a short hallway with built-in shelves overflowing with a large collection of CDs, cassettes and record albums. The other side of the hall was bordered by a railing that allowed a view of the living room from above. Lisa-Marie caught sight of the internet modem and wireless router tucked between the wall and the far side of the railing and did a doubt take before she asked, "You have internet?"

Izzy shrugged, "Have to, for work and stuff, satellite internet and phone. There's a laptop on the desk in the library. You're welcome to use it anytime you like."

The wall of built-in shelves almost obscured a sliding pocket door that provided entry to a small bedroom. It was lit by an angular window that looked over the orchard. Bright-yellow sunflowers danced along the duvet cover on the bed. Silver milk jugs on the desk and in the corners burst forth with a profusion of silk sunflowers. The main wall was painted a delicious buttery-yellow and a framed gallery poster of Van Gogh's, *Sunflowers*, hung in the center. "Oh wow," Lisa-Marie breathed out, "I love this."

Izzy smiled at Lisa-Marie's reaction. She had decorated this room especially for Caleb's mother, Lillian, who had visited from California at least three times a year, dropping in on them with crates of wine. At first Izzy wasn't a wine drinker; she hadn't really liked wine. Lillian said that was because Izzy had yet to try a decent wine and sure enough that was the case. Everyone loved Caleb's mom. Izzy was no exception. Lillian took one look at the sophisticated, grown-up woman Izzy was and saw right through to the motherless, little girl she had been. Having always wanted a daughter, she laid the mothering on thick and Izzy lapped up the attention.

Lillian had died three years ago after a diagnosis of breast cancer, quite suddenly and so quickly that Izzy was still stunned by the loss. She believed she experienced the emptiness of losing Caleb's mother even more keenly than he had. He had grown up in the light of Lillian's warmth and care so he tended to take her somewhat for granted. That was something Izzy never did. As she turned from the room she could still see Lillian with her blonde hair perfectly styled and her make-up on before eight in the morning. Izzy would bring up a coffee and find Lillian sitting at the little desk by the window, writing letters to various friends and relatives. When she stayed in the sunflower room she wrote a daily minimum of three letters that Beulah dutifully delivered to the Dearborn post office. Izzy and Caleb had received their own share of letters from Lillian and Izzy kept them in a special box and treasured every one of them.

Coming out of the guest room, Izzy said, "OK guys, we're almost done." The short hallway opened to another loft which was slightly wider than the queen-sized bed it contained. A railing at the end of the bed allowed a view from above to the library, soft-light filtering up from the window below. Three steps up from this loft led to the highest loft with its view of the greenhouse garden and glimpses of the back roadway.

What everyone commented on when they were taken through the cabin for the first time was the play of light in the various rooms. Changing with the seasons as the sun slanted at different angles in the sky and the trees gained and lost their leaves, the light was constantly shifting and playing elaborate patterns over the ceilings and floors. Sometimes it was diffuse and gentle, sometimes bright and cheery and at other times subdued and sombre. But always the light was a factor. Even though she had lived here for years, Izzy still fell in love every day with the light. It was as much a part of the cabin décor as any of the furnishings or artwork would ever be. It was the backdrop to everything else the cabin contained.

CHAPTER SIX

i.

As they completed the tour and returned to the first floor, Izzy drew Lisa-Marie aside, "I know this is right out of the blue, but I was wondering if you might like a small job cleaning the guest cabin once a week. It shouldn't take more than two hours." Izzy glanced at Dan on the other side of the kitchen. He was draining a beer while leaning casually against the wall talking to Beulah, "Let's just say two hours max. I'll pay you a dollar more than minimum wage because cleaning is a real pain. Think you might be interested?"

"That would be great." Lisa-Marie grinned at Izzy and shook her out-stretched hand to seal the deal.

Relieved that the guest cabin cleaning was taken care of, Izzy rounded everyone up and soon plates were being filled from the array of food on the dining room table – Bethany's fried chicken, cracked-wheat buns which were a signature product from Beulah and Bethany's bakery, the cheese and potato dish that Izzy brought steaming from the oven, various dishes of pickles and a fresh green salad dressed in a light balsamic vinaigrette. Lined up on the kitchen counter, for dessert, were Liam's box of Timbits and two large, golden-brown, cherry pies that Cook and Roland contributed.

Lisa-Marie manoeuvred her way towards a chair in the sun porch area. She was balancing a plate, a salad bowl and her can of Coke when she looked up and caught her breath. Justin was coming out to the sun porch too. "Mind if I share this table with you?" He was smiling in a warm and friendly way as he placed a napkin and his beer on a small table between the two chairs.

Justin dug into his plate heaped with food as if he hadn't eaten for a week. Lisa-Marie marvelled at the way guys could eat and eat in front of other people with no embarrassment at all. She was already regretting what she viewed as her own overflowing plate. She stared down helplessly at the small heap of potatoes sitting next to half a bun and the smallest piece of chicken she could find. The salad in her bowl barely reached the rim.

Justin stopped eating for a moment to look at her plate, "Wow, you'll have to go for seconds. You didn't take much of anything." He paused to take a huge bite out of one of the legs of fried chicken on his own plate, "That's good though . . . I hate to go back for seconds alone. And just a head's up . . . you won't wiggle out of pie and ice cream with Cook around." Lisa-Marie smiled back at Justin.

Dan ended up across from Bethany at the dining room table with Beulah sitting off to one side. Dan's laugh caught Bethany by surprise and she found herself smiling back at him and then laughing right along with a couple of his jokes. She had relaxed visibly when Justin had gone to sit with Lisa-Marie. She looked through the French doors to see the two of them below in the sun porch and she heard Lisa-Marie talking excitedly about working at the Camp. She could hear Justin's deeper voice interrupting and the two of them laughing.

She had felt emotionally overwhelmed since Lisa-Marie's arrival. No one could predict how or even if her time with them would work out. She and Beulah were not used to sharing their attention and space fulltime with anyone, let alone a troubled teenager. Bethany needed time to get to know her niece and to understand the haunted look in her eyes. For the moment, seeing Lisa-Marie smiling and laughing with Justin seemed like a hopeful sign.

She turned back to the table at the sound of Dan's questioning voice. She met his eyes and realized he had been watching her. Instead of her usual panicky feeling around a strange man, Bethany smiled back at Dan and told him in great detail exactly how she got the chicken so crispy. This conversation had Beulah howling and rolling her eyes.

Izzy rose gracefully from the edge of the sofa, her almost untouched plate of food in hand. She felt a nagging pain forming between her eyes. Roland had sat beside her and spoken at great length about an upcoming visit from one of the Board members. He ended his monologue with a suggestion, "I'm thinking, Izzy, that maybe we could co-facilitate a group session and our guest could sit in."

Izzy felt hard pressed to avoid a shudder. "You know, Roland, I'm pretty sure I'm tied up that day." She excused herself to see about getting the ice cream from the outside freezer.

From his vantage point in the corner of the living room, Liam could see Izzy up in the kitchen. He watched her drain her wine glass in a couple of quick gulps and then refill the glass from the open bottle on the counter. Glass in hand she disappeared out of sight around the corner towards the utility room.

Liam never drank now; but because he had drunk a lot in the past he was cursed with always taking notice of what and how much other people were drinking. He really didn't mean to or want to but he always noticed. Caleb had called Liam his drinking conscience, assigned the task of letting Caleb know when enough was enough. Caleb and Beulah had both honed the skill of drinking to a fine art and it was a rare occasion when either of them showed the effects. Their drink of choice was whiskey, neat; Beulah liked her beer too. Izzy was a wine drinker and lately she seemed to be drinking a lot more than she had when Caleb was alive. Dan was drinking beer. Liam noticed he had already had three.

i i .

Passing up the dessert course and earning a glare from Cook, Liam started washing the dishes. He had made his way through quite a stack before Roland and Bethany joined him. After the clean-up they all gathered in the living room for the book club portion of the evening. The wine and beer were still flowing and a pot of fresh coffee was also making the rounds. Liam opened the evening by introducing Alistair MacLeod's book, *No Great Mischief.*

Caleb had assigned this introductory portion of the book-club discussion to Liam. Given Liam's background, Caleb assumed this would be OK and though Liam had been reluctant at first, he grew to enjoy it. He would spend a good deal of time on his ten minute overview of both the author and the work in question, usually preparing what he hoped would be a couple of thought-provoking questions with which to conclude.

Izzy listened to Liam's voice. She was tucked into the recliner in the corner, her legs folded under her, holding the wine glass that seemed always to be half full. She tried to imagine Liam in another life than the one he had with them at Crater Lake. Maybe in a classroom teaching, perhaps with his own family – surely he must have family somewhere? She never heard him speak of whatever his life had been before he came to Crater Lake. She knew he had been a high-school English teacher only because Caleb had provided that tidbit of information as justification for choosing Liam to introduce the book-club selections. Liam wasn't in the habit of revealing personal details of his life related to the various novels they read together. The rest of them were constantly referring to how the monthly selection reminded them of this or that about their own lives. Liam stuck with character development and author's voice. Izzy couldn't imagine Liam anywhere else. He was just here, a part of the place now as surely as she was.

Lisa-Marie sat on the floor across from Izzy's chair. Justin was lounging to her left. His hair, dry now and raked back from his face, glowed golden in the evening light. She leaned toward him when Liam finished his introduction and whispered, "God, he sounds just like my grade ten English teacher." She delivered this comment with a roll of her eyes.

Justin looked intently at her, the light turning his eyes a darker-brown than usual. She sensed in that moment, in every small nuance of his facial expression, exactly what was different about Justin. He was a nice guy. He didn't make fun of people and he didn't get a kick out of jokes at someone else's expense. He wasn't sarcastic or nasty or needing to score points. Lisa-Marie hadn't known many nice guys before. She smiled and hoped with all her heart that he would think she was only kidding around and hadn't really meant to make fun of Liam. After an agonizing moment Justin grinned back at her. Close call, she thought and looking over at Liam she realized she really didn't want to laugh at him anyway.

In the lull that followed the end of Liam's introduction, while everyone got more comfortable, Cook piped up, "Halfway through I wanted to throw it against the wall but I managed to finish and it was good." Everyone started to laugh and she looked somewhat bemused. At every book-club discussion, Cook said at least once that she wanted to throw the book in question against the wall. The time they had read one of William Gibson's futuristic novels she went as far as to say she wanted to throw it right past the wall and out the door.

Lisa-Marie relaxed when she realized the discussion was going to be very casual. She began to get involved in what the others thought of the novel. She had enjoyed the book. The emotion of loss that pervaded the novel completely hooked her. She knew all about loss.

"The dogs were my favourite thing." Lisa-Marie dropped this comment into a brief lull in the conversation. She looked up to see Izzy watching her with a slight smile.

"Oh those dogs . . . they tried too hard and gave too much. You can't do more than that." Lisa-Marie was riveted by the sadness in Izzy's voice and how stunningly beautiful she was with a glint of what might have been tears in her large brown eyes. The evening light complemented her with just the right combination of shadow and slanting warmth. The way she curled into the chair presented a perfectly-constructed pose emphasizing the curves of her body and the soft-red fabric of her dress, which clung to her in a sensuous sweep. The play of emotion that raced across her face only increased her beauty with a haunting touch of vulnerability. Lisa-Marie could see in her mind's eye the photo she would take of Izzy at this moment and she would call it, *A Beautiful Sadness in Red*.

Lisa-Marie glanced over at Justin. She saw, with a dropping-in-the-pit-of-her-stomach feeling, the look on his face – the kind of look that screamed he was also noticing Izzy's beauty and not for the first time.

Izzy's gaze had also shifted to Justin and she didn't see Lisa-Marie's eyes turn from Justin's face to stare openly at her. All Izzy saw was the way she looked, reflected in the glow of Justin's eyes. She liked the way she felt – to be admired and to be thought that beautiful. She knew she was indulging herself at his expense. But despite that knowledge, she smiled into the warmth of Justin's eyes before looking down into the rich yellow of her wine. Only when Izzy looked up from her glass did she notice what might have been a glare as Lisa-Marie turned away. She was startled but the moment passed quickly; it was all too easily shrugged away.

Sipping from her coffee mug Bethany paused to smile at her niece, "The dogs were great. I liked them, too . . . especially the dog swimming out to the boat when the family left Scotland. It made me think of the way Gertrude and Alice act."

Beulah looked over at Dan's confused expression and explained, "Our dogs, two German Shepherds."

"Whenever I take the boat out to fish they follow me all the way around the point having a great time at the edge of the water . . . playing around and stuff. But if I let the boat go even a tiny bit past an invisible line they have drawn in their minds, just a fraction further from the shoreline towards the middle of the lake . . . oh my God. They jump right into the water and swim for the boat. The first time it happened I was so surprised and I yelled at them to go back to shore but they wouldn't listen. I started to row in and the minute I did they turned and swam back. I notice right away now if the boat is drifting out even a bit because they start barking and make for the water." Bethany laughed as she finished the story, "I'm not sure what they might do if I didn't turn back. Maybe drag me to shore or something."

Dan sat up straight in his chair as soon as Bethany said the word fishing and he listened impatiently to her story. As she finished speaking he cut in, "I came here especially for the fishing. I read up on Crater Lake and the travel brochure said it's a hidden gem . . . excellent fishing and underutilized."

He was talking with an animation that only another fishing enthusiast could understand and when he finally paused, Beulah piped up with, "I'm sure Bethany could give you some pointers, Dan. She's out on the lake fishing most afternoons."

Dan looked over at Bethany and smiled a wide grin. "Great . . . that would be great."

Bethany covered her resentment and gave Beulah a quick glare from under her eyelashes. Turning to Dan, she smiled politely.

The book discussion continued when Justin sat up from his lounging position on the floor and characteristically raked his hair out of his eyes, "The part where Grandfather makes sure Grandma and Grandpa get their big break . . . I really understood that part. Like how much it mattered to them and how grateful they were. It was like their one chance and Grandfather made it happen for them . . . committed himself one hundred percent to making sure Grandpa got that job." Justin paused and his gaze took in Roland and Izzy. "That's the way I'm feeling about the last year. Like I've got a real shot now . . . my chance, right?"

Lisa-Marie watched Justin as he laughed in the relaxed way that he seemed to do everything. She was trying desperately to rationalize the look she had seen on his face. He had been all deer-in-the-headlights – she couldn't deny that. Who could blame him? Izzy was gorgeous. But Justin was way too cool to fall for someone as old as Izzy. Even if she didn't look as old as she was, he had to know she was way too old for him. Justin was the nicest and best-looking guy Lisa-Marie had ever met and she wasn't going to let go of the way looking at him and thinking of him made her feel. Not without a fight and certainly not to someone old enough to be his mother.

i i i .

Roland and Cook were the first to make a move to leave. Brandishing a large flashlight, Roland called out, "Justin, want to walk back with us?"

Justin stretched and yawned as he got up off the floor, "I'll be along later. I'm going to start the fire out on the cliff deck for Izzy before I head back."

Izzy smiled her thanks over at him as she uncurled herself from the arm-chair and shook out her dress. A few small chunks of pie crust hit the floor and Liam grinned at her. She met his gaze with a warm smile on her face, "Well, as Caleb always said, he could dress me up but he couldn't take me out."

Lisa-Marie quickly stifled the urge to shove her fingers down her throat and make a gagging noise when she saw Izzy first flash her smile of thanks at Justin and then turn her attention to Liam. Izzy acted like every guy in the room should just naturally worship her. There was no doubt about the look on Liam's face. He was as taken by Izzy as everyone else seemed to be.

Dan looked somewhat bleary eyed as he rose from the rocking chair, "Any extra flashlights? I seem to have forgotten to bring one."

Liam called over his shoulder, "I'm going your way, Dan. You can walk with me."

Izzy refilled her glass and with the half-full wine bottle tucked under her arm and Dante rubbing against her leg, she asked, "Anyone want to join me out on the cliff deck for a bit?"

Beulah and Bethany agreed and Lisa-Marie tagged along with them. As they made their way across to the deck, which was cantilevered out over the water, Justin came toward them. "See you tomorrow, Izzy," he said quietly as he passed.

Seize the moment, Lisa-Marie told herself. She hoped her voice would come out with more confidence than she felt as she called after him, "Hey Justin, mind if I walk back with you? I think I'll head home now, OK Auntie Beth?" This question was directed over her shoulder to Bethany as Lisa-Marie was already moving towards Justin; she was determined to make it all a done deal.

Just past the fruit trees, Justin and Lisa-Marie entered the dark, evergreen-enclosed path. Justin shone his flashlight up and around making arcs of light through the branches of the towering trees that surrounded them. "Come on over to the Camp any evening, Leez." He had already found his own short-hand for her name and she loved the way that sounded. "A bunch of us are making our way through a few seasons of *Lost*. It's sort of a riot since some of the kids have seen the show and some haven't and you know, even if you have seen it you're still lost."

They were just coming in view of the A-Frame. Lisa-Marie tried not to gush, "Sure, I'd like that. Every evening with Beulah and Auntie Beth might be a bit of a strain for all of us." She was careful to keep her tone light and easy, no sarcasm or bite to her words. Justin smiled down at her and reached out to ruffle her hair, sending a shiver down to her toes. Waving a casual goodbye, he continued down the dark path to the Camp.

iv.

Justin moved quickly along the trail. The darkened silhouette of Micah Camp's main building came into sight. He veered off the path that went toward his resident cabin and moved toward a picnic table on the water's edge. He hopped onto the top of the table to sit and gaze down the lake to the black bulk of the mountains in the distance. This view of Crater Lake got to him every time he sat here. For a guy who had never lived outside of the city, the lake and surrounding wilderness were like nothing he could have imagined.

He was nearing the end of a year spent at Micah Camp. When he started the program he'd been an eighteen-year old with a big chip on his shoulder. He had been shunted from foster homes to group homes ever since he was eleven. His life trajectory wasn't exactly promising. But he knew he was smart enough to have options; he was different from the other foster kids he met. He was hurting and he was screwed up, that was for sure; but he wasn't broken on the level that some of those kids were.

He managed to squeak through his high school graduation with solid math marks but his English scores were too low to get him into most post-secondary institutions. His life seemed stuck in the rut of a minimum wage job working the counter at a self-serve gas bar. Then someone in the Ministry funneled the application papers for Micah Camp down some bureaucratic chute and they ended up in his hands. He made the first cut, went on to a couple of screening meetings and was accepted to the program. Now everything in Justin's life was different. He'd maxed out on the opportunities Micah Camp put before him. With his English marks upgraded he applied to several universities and was accepted to UBC to begin an undergrad degree in engineering. A comfortable amount of scholarship money from Micah Camp was thrown in for good measure.

Justin had a hard time explaining, even to himself, the degree to which his time at Micah Camp had changed him. The lake, the mountains, the feeling of space had grounded him right down into something in himself that was strong and vital – a quality he had always known he possessed. Justin had faced more than a few intense situations in his life. At those times it was as if everything slowed down. He knew he had forever to choose exactly what he had to do and he knew that when he did decide, he would make the right choice. Crater Lake had freed him to live in that quiet inner space where everything was so clear. But it was also Izzy. She had helped him talk about the strength he possessed. At first it had all seemed crazy but after a while everything made sense. Then she helped him stand firmly inside that strength. He found the courage to walk back into his past and deal with all the crap he never wanted to think about. And she had walked with him to a place where he believed enough in himself to reach for a different kind of future.

With her sitting across from him and walking along the lake trails beside him, he explored every dark and twisted thing that had happened to him over the years of his young life. He always started off saying he didn't give a shit and ended up crying like his heart was broken. Izzy kept her end of the bargain. He remembered the way she told him that if he could find his way to trusting her and talking about some of the things that were eating away at him, she would stick it out with him until things got better. And she had.

Justin knew his feelings for Izzy were all mixed up with painful memories of his past and the rush of warmth that came from knowing she had really been there for him. He remembered every time her hand had rested gently on his arm, when she would remind him to relax and just breathe; every time she looked at him with a compassion that filled her large dark eyes with emotion; every hour long session when no one existed for her but him.

But all that had changed. His formal counselling sessions had ended and now Izzy was his boss. God – it was so strange to think of her as his boss. There was no more talk of emotions, no more intimate sessions – no chance to talk at all about the messed up state of his feelings. He knew it was OK to care for Izzy but it couldn't be OK to think about her the way he had begun to think about her. And this seemed to be one area of his life completely resistant to any type of calm focus. Justin had tried enough times to breathe and get grounded to know that when it came to Izzy, it just didn't work.

All he could bear to tell himself was that he had a *thing* for her. As if that vague, non-descriptive word might take some of the emotional gut-punch out of falling for his counsellor, who just happened to be a beautiful, older woman. What he did know was that this *thing* was a big-time, going-nowhere-in-his-world-or-any-other-world *thing*. He knew that and yet the desire he felt wouldn't go away and it made him ache for something he wouldn't even let himself imagine.

V.

Dear Emma:

Justin walked me home from the potluck – just the two of us. Oh crap – I promised you the truth, didn't I? I sort of forced myself on him but he didn't mind at all. At the potluck he came and sat with me all on his own. And he invited me to go over to the Camp to watch DVD's. I think he likes me – oh, Emma – I want him to like me so much.

I met Izzy and she's beautiful – like a dark queen would be. She has this thick gold wedding ring on her hand and I can see her being like Galadriel in the Lord of the Rings – full of her own power. I could almost see her stretch out her hand with that ring on her finger. She could make all of us do exactly what she wanted us to do. I saw Justin looking at her and I could tell he sees how beautiful she is. He looked at her like he would die for her and I felt sick but I totally got it – I felt sort of like dying for her too. Crazy, right? She's not just beautiful. She's also really, really nice.

But I saw something else tonight too, Emma. Izzy looked back at Justin and I could tell she saw how gaga he was and she smiled at him all pretty and sexy and encouraging. She shouldn't have done that. I have to hate her for smiling at Justin that way but somehow I don't want to hate her. It's all so mixed up.

How can I hate her when she just gave me a really cool job? I'll be cleaning the guest cabin once a week for this funny guy named Dan who is renting it. To get there I have to walk right by Izzy's and then I can see Justin working. And I also have a job at the Camp every morning – I haven't even told you about that. I start in a couple of days. I just need to think of ways to run into Justin and be with him. I'm sure if I can be with him he will forget about looking at Izzy that way.

Auntie Beth says I should think about talking with Izzy. No – not just talk – talk to her like a counsellor because I'm all screwed up with problems. I'll tell you all about that soon, Emma. I promise. But how could I talk to Izzy that way? How could I ever trust her after seeing the way she looked at Justin? How could I tell her anything when I have to try so hard to hate her?

CHAPTER SEVEN

i.

Izzy sat on a wicker chair in one corner of the deck, her knees drawn up to her chin. She was cradling the bottle of wine. Bethany cuddled into the swing chair with a granny-square afghan wrapped around her shoulders. Beulah busied herself stirring the fire in the cast-iron, chimney stove Caleb had ordered especially for Izzy's birthday one year. Izzy wanted a swing chair for the cliff deck, so Caleb built her one. Izzy thought it would be nice to drink wine while swinging on the chair watching the water, the stars and the moon with a fire close by – so Caleb found the chimney stove.

Beulah flopped down beside Bethany. They enjoyed a companionable silence while the sound of the light chop on the water played around them. The wind was a pleasant relief from what had been a warm day and it brought with it a very unique summer smell as the lake released the day's heat. Izzy always loved that smell. She inhaled deeply and tried to will the tension out of the muscles of her neck and shoulders. It had been a very long day.

Looking over at Bethany cuddled into the afghan, Izzy wondered about Beulah's offhand remark that Bethany could show Dan her favourite fishing spots. "Beth, will you mind getting Dan started with the fishing?" Izzy knew that getting Dan settled in was her responsibility but she didn't have a clue about fishing. At the same time she had seen the look of resentment on Bethany's face when Beulah so freely offered her assistance.

Bethany took her time answering, her face a mixture of emotions in the shifting light provided by the fire. Finally it seemed she came to a tentative decision. "It feels like it could be OK . . . I guess." She paused to think for a moment, "Maybe I could take him out a couple of times in our boat and show him around and then he should be fine on his own."

"He's a decent enough guy, Beth . . . he's a priest for God's sake. Don't act as if I offered your fishing expertise to the Hell's Angels or something. He'll make you laugh if you let him. You might even enjoy yourself. Who knows? Maybe I'll have to get all jealous and drown him or something." Beulah laughed loudly – laughter that she could see gained no purchase with either Bethany or Izzy.

She shrugged and frowned into the flames. "I think those stale, hard-as-a-rock doughnuts have given me heartburn," she belched quietly. "Who brings stale doughnuts to a potluck?" Downing the rest of her beer, Beulah got up to add another piece of wood to the fire and muttered, "I wish you would learn to enjoy a good shot of whiskey, Izzy." Beulah watched Izzy's eyes scrunch in distaste. Whiskey was Caleb's drink. Izzy could never stomach it.

Beulah settled back on the swing-chair. Izzy had remained a mystery to her over the years. She had accepted her completely as the person Caleb was head over heels in love with. But Beulah had always thought that Izzy was not as satisfied and content with Caleb as he was with her. If Caleb could be seen to have a fault, in Beulah's opinion, it was the unrealistic way in which he chose to see Izzy. But the way Caleb had seen everyone was unrealistic so it wasn't really a fault – more like a character trait.

Beulah knew Izzy's grief over Caleb's death was real enough and she admired the way Izzy had managed herself and the place over the last two years. They all knew how hard Izzy worked to hold everything and everyone together. And then of course there was the matter of Bethany. Beulah was well aware that she owed Izzy more than she could ever repay because of the way Izzy had helped Bethany. Owing anything to anybody had never been a comfortable state of affairs for Beulah.

Bethany glanced over towards Beulah quickly and then back to Izzy, "I'm worried about Liam, Izzy. He's losing weight and this thing with his stomach doesn't seem to be getting any better."

Izzy felt her own stomach clench with tension and surprise to hear Bethany voice this concern in front of Beulah. Both of them were well aware Beulah had no use for Liam these days; though as far as Izzy could tell, Bethany had no more of a clue than she did as to what it could be about.

As if on cue, Beulah leaned forward and motioned in the direction of Liam's place, "He's going through the Pepto-Bismol like he has shares in the company. Maybe if he didn't swallow every second word he thought and just said what was on his bloody mind he wouldn't have such a gut ache. He's got something eating him. Probably thinks you'll give his job and cabin away to Justin, Izzy. He's already doing all of Liam's work."

Beulah had a quick wit and a sharp tongue but she wasn't a cruel person by nature and notwithstanding the lateness of the hour and the number of beers she had consumed, even she recognized the way the animosity in her voice had registered on both Bethany and Izzy. She tightened her gut and flexed her shoulders preparing herself for their response.

"You're too hard on Liam, Beulah –," Bethany readjusted the folds of the afghan to cover her exposed legs, "– you never seem to have anything good to say about him."

Izzy sat forward in her chair and contemplated her painted toenails. She directed her words nowhere in particular, "Liam's got more than enough on his plate with managing the woodlot and the sawmill." Izzy looking over at Beulah, "I know something hasn't been right between you and Liam since Caleb died but it's been two years, Beulah. Liam has a life here . . . he belongs here as much as any of us do."

Izzy knew as soon as the words were out of her mouth that she had crossed a line. It was the wine talking, spurred on by the accumulated drain of the entire day. She had forgotten that people don't appreciate having what they already know pointed out to them. To make matters worse, Bethany was nodding her head in agreement. Ganging up on Beulah was not a good idea at the best of times.

Beulah sat back quietly on the swing and stared out over the lake. The very mention of the woodlot and Caleb's death set her teeth on edge. She was not one to back down from a confrontation. This joint attack only stiffened her resolve. "Get this straight, Bethany – I didn't ask for your opinion on how I treat Liam and I sure as hell am not looking for your approval."

Looking over toward Izzy, Beulah spoke her next words slowly, "Maybe you should spend more time thinking about why you want that freeloader in your cabin, rather than preaching to me on things you know nothing about."

Bethany stared at Beulah in exasperation, "Oh my God, Beulah, really."

Beulah ignored her and kept her eyes on Izzy who had stood up from her chair. She rocked forward off the swing quickly. "You weren't there when Caleb died, Izzy . . . you don't know what you don't know and that's all I'm going to say to you."

What Izzy did know was that the worst thing she could do was give into Beulah's bullying. She had to stand up to her; she had to hold her ground. "I know I wasn't there, Beulah." Izzy had every intention of standing toe to toe with Beulah and staring her down. The tension hung taut in the air between them for what felt like forever to Bethany, who sat with two warm tracks of tears washing down her face.

As suddenly as Beulah's anger flared it was replaced by a smile as she threw up her hands, "OK . . . OK . . . I surrender. I've got to hand it to you, Izzy – you're tougher than you look." Throwing one arm around Izzy's shoulder, Beulah pulled her close and using her other hand she tugged Bethany up from the swing, "Come on Beth . . . dry your tears. Let's go home. I've got something in mind for you that should drive the thought of men out of both our minds." As they made their way off the deck and onto the path a large flashlight magically appeared from Beulah's pack. She called back over her shoulder, "Don't drink all that wine on your own Izzy. You'll regret it tomorrow."

i i .

Izzy moved over to the swing, wrapping the warm afghan around her shoulders. It still smelled of the light and somewhat intoxicating perfume Bethany favoured. She shivered as the wind shifted direction across the lake and washed over the cliff deck. The embers in the stove rose up the chimney and sparked. The fire would die out soon. She tipped the last of the wine into her glass.

No, she hadn't been there when Caleb died. Beulah and Liam had been there. Beulah's words brought back the memory of where she had been and what she had been contemplating – no doubt at the very moment of Caleb's death. While he was begging Liam and Beulah to watch out for her, Izzy had been considering infidelity. She was attending a conference in Montreal and enjoying the attentions of the handsome and way-too-young, keynote speaker – a man she had met over drinks in the hotel bar.

It wasn't the first time she had flirted with the idea of cheating on Caleb. And it wasn't about being dissatisfied with Caleb or falling for anyone else. It was just that it would never have occurred to Caleb that Izzy might contemplate such a thing. Caleb's sureness about her had grown, over the years, to be a gnawing irritant.

At first she was surprised that Caleb showed no real interest about her life before she met him. After all, she was twenty-eight when they got together; she had certainly been old enough to have a past worth delving into. She was consumed with curiosity and sorely tempted to demand that he reveal to her everything there was to tell about his past life. Caleb had been thirty-nine when she met him – he obviously had to have put some mileage on his love life. But she had controlled the urge to ask and he never said a single word. Caleb didn't seem to care at all who Izzy was before she met him and he acted like it was natural for her to feel the same way. It was as if the very fact that they agreed to be together erased the past as sure as a brush sweeps across a chalkboard. For Caleb, this one choice ensured a future of togetherness. She rankled at the thought that he assumed she could have chosen forever as easily as he did.

At times, like tonight, staring into the dying embers of the fire with the wind whistling past her and into the dark trees, she wanted to hate Caleb. Hate him with all her heart for dying with thoughts of only her, while she had been making no effort to fend off the sexual advances of another man. It was if she was trapped forever with the guilt of that juxtaposition of events pressing down on her like a huge fist.

Sometimes she could convince herself that she was actually relieved to be released from the way Caleb's love and acceptance made her into something she knew she wasn't. He had loved her with a complete and total trust she had never asked for or expected. She had done absolutely nothing to deserve what he gave. At the same time, she missed Caleb so much it was like an ache that went on and on, like an essential part of her own body was gone.

Raking through the jumble of her emotions, she knew she resented Caleb. She didn't think he worked hard enough to know her in a way that could justify the trust he bestowed on her so easily. Maybe it was the injustice of claiming something he hadn't really earned and in making such a claim taking something from her. But as her wine-weary thoughts came to this point she couldn't figure out what it was he could have taken that mattered so much to her; and hadn't he given her enough to even the score between them?

So she came back to her guilt and the ache of missing Caleb that made her stop to catch her breath while tears clouded her sight. In an unrealistically absurd fit of temper she found herself stamping her feet in anger and hissing through her sobs, "Why did you have to die then, of all times? Why then? Shit, shit, shit . . . why then, Caleb?"

A lone wolf howled in the distance as she rose from the swing and wove her way toward the cabin. She waited to hear the call taken up by the pack that must be gathered in the surrounding hills, but to no avail. As she closed the door she thought that the lonely voice of one wolf was a fitting way to end her day.

i i i .

Much later that night Lisa-Marie dreamed about the wedding photo. It was a crazy, mixed-up dream in which she looked away from the photo only for a second but when she looked back it was Justin with his arms wrapped around Izzy. Izzy had somehow traded her shimmering white for Bethany's black dress. All of this was plainly revealed as Izzy turned her body into Justin's arms; the photo had now become a tiny video screen.

Beulah seemed to smirk out at Lisa-Marie as she pulled Auntie Beth away. Liam stood by watching. At first Lisa-Marie thought he was stretching out a hand to her but when she looked closely – peering down at the tiny screen from what seemed a great distance – his dark eyes rested on Izzy's face and the hand outstretched was not for Lisa-Marie. Shivering, she rolled over in her loft bed and wrapped the quilt tightly around herself. She let the dream slip away and drifted back to sleep to the echoing sound of a howling wolf.

Chapter Eight

i.

Liam had come to the town of Dearborn chasing down Caleb's ad for a handyman, a jack-of-all-trades type of guy. A small cabin was offered rent free in exchange for two days of work per week. If interested, the successful applicant had the option of paid employment at the nearby woodlot and sawmill. Of course Liam was neither a handyman nor any kind of jack of all trades; his only work experience had been teaching high-school English. But Caleb didn't let that stand in their way. He took one look at Liam – thin-as-a-rail, barely thirty-two – and embraced him like a long-lost little brother. Back then Liam had been little in every way compared to Caleb who was ten years older and a good thirty pounds heavier. But it was more than that. Liam knew from the start that Caleb possessed a vastness – and not just on the outside. Caleb had a heart that was about as big as any heart could be. The only thing Liam remembered Caleb asking during their so-called interview was a question that had startled him. "Ever played any baseball, slow pitch maybe?"

ii.

"Liam, take a look at this . . . it's priceless to watch, really." Liam looked where Caleb was pointing but all he saw was Izzy out on the clothes-line platform Caleb had built for her. She was hanging out the wet laundry.

He cast a somewhat baffled look at his friend but Caleb just kept smiling through his words, "Look at how carefully she chooses each piece, Liam." Izzy did seem to search through the basket as if she were looking for something in particular.

"I used to think maybe she would hang only pants together . . . or shirts . . . or my stuff and then hers . . . or maybe there was a colour code or something. It never made any sense. It was the damnedest thing. And then one day I figured it out. It's because of those two lilac bushes. You see . . . look . . . first big pieces and then smaller pieces in the middle so they will clear that one bush and then some bigger pieces again but only small pieces at the end because if the wind comes up the bigger pieces would hit the lilac."

Liam was seeing the logic of this but Caleb's fascination with the whole process seemed odd. Izzy put the last piece on the line and reeled it out a ways. She turned, going quickly down the three steps from the platform and walking toward the kitchen door. Liam was about to head into the shop to do some task or another, he couldn't even remember what. He and Caleb were always working on something. But Caleb grabbed his arm to hold him back out of Izzy's sight, "No wait Liam, this is my favourite part . . . she'll stop," and as Caleb said those words, Izzy did indeed stop. "She'll turn back to the clothes-line –," this was exactly what Izzy did, "– and she'll survey her handiwork." Izzy stood gazing for a moment or two at the line and then turned and headed inside.

Caleb began to walk toward the shop door shaking his head, "It's always exactly the same . . . I have never seen that woman look as satisfied as she does when she turns back to that clothesline." He laughed out loud, pushed Liam in the arm and winked at him, "You know what I mean, Liam." Caleb paused for effect before he added, "Never seen her that satisfied." Then he had laughed even more. "Good thing I don't have a big ego, hey, Liam."

That was the essence of Caleb. Liam could still picture him, all these years later, leaning there against the workshop door – a big guy with shaggy blonde hair and a wild looking beard. He would often slouch a bit so he and Liam were on the same level. In Liam's memories, Caleb's dark-blue eyes always sparkling with humour. Caleb hadn't ever had anything to prove; he was sure of himself and his chosen friends.

iii.

The story of how Caleb came to settle at Crater Lake had achieved mythical proportions over the years. He was seen as everything from an American with trumped up dreams of manifest destiny to some sort of local folk hero. The truth, Liam came to realize from knowing Caleb, was neither. Caleb had simply been trying to recreate something of the sprawling estate life he knew growing up in the Sonoma Valley of California. He was certainly expansionist but it wasn't with a view to any type of money-making or investment. He just wanted the room and the freedom to do things his own way and he already had the money to make it happen.

Caleb had come to Crater Lake in the early seventies, escaping the US draft. He was the only son of a wealthy, wine-growing family. Before border hopping to Canada, he had been attending a class or two – now and then – at the University of Southern California in L.A. He was officially registered on a baseball scholarship and many people believed he had a real shot at the pros. The pressure of university-level ball didn't appeal to Caleb though. Practices, to say nothing of classes, cut into surfing time. One night his grandmother took him aside for a little reality check. It was obvious to everyone in the family that the university would soon give Caleb his walking papers and then he would become eligible for the draft. They had more than enough money to try to prevent that from happening but Caleb's grandmother had not wanted to take a chance. She urged him to go to Canada before current events could conspire to have him lying on his belly in a rice paddy in South-East Asia. All too soon after that, they might see him returning home in a body bag. Caleb's grandmother had never been one to mince words. His family freed up his trust fund early and it was substantial enough to mean he had never worried about money.

Caleb made his way up the coast of Vancouver Island to the Pacific waves off Tofino and then he had just kept heading north. Eventually he arrived in the Dearborn area. The back-to-the-land movement was in full swing and Caleb liked the idea of living out somewhere in the wilderness on a piece of land he owned. He was twenty when he purchased property on the relatively deserted east side of Crater Lake – a large chunk right in the middle of the only three pieces of lake-shore real-estate available. These properties were all in a row and nestled into a sandy-beached cove. The land consisted of a wide bench that dropped off a cliff to the lake below. It was accessible down a steep slope from the logging road. A nearby woodlot was for sale and this had also caught Caleb's eye.

i v .

It seemed to Liam that from the very beginning, Caleb must have had a vision for what his life at Crater Lake could be. He took his time and worked with a Vancouver architect to have plans drawn up for a large cabin that could be built in stages. A hydro-electric system that tapped into a stream up the mountain came next. A large workshop with attached greenhouse was built. Planting vegetables and eating produce straight out of the greenhouse had been a priority from the beginning. Caleb had lived in the workshop for a few years while construction went on for the main cabin. Over the years the rest of the main cabin came together, section by section, and due to the original architectural design, it escaped the fate of many places built up in stages – it never became a jumble of rooflines and awkwardly situated additions. Caleb had expanded the woodlot operation from selective logging to include a small sawmill. It made sense to generate lumber from the raw logs he was cutting.

When Izzy and Caleb got together most of the infrastructure around the place was complete. Caleb had nineteen years there to get the place ready for Izzy's arrival. The orchard had been planted years before and large areas were cleared and ready for the gardens. Izzy brought something special of her own. She was passionately interested in the gardening and had an eye for landscape architecture and design. What Caleb started, Izzy made complete; the place really became what Caleb had dreamed of from the start.

Liam remembered how Caleb had sung the words of Woody Guthrie's old tune, *Do Re Mi.* How those words described California as the Garden of Eden. Caleb had smiled and said, "It really is true. California is like that, it's so beautiful and the sun man . . . you can't believe how the sun shines. It's one big Golden State." Caleb's whimsical tone had given way to a shrug as he added, "You'd better have the bucks though or it's a real downer . . . places around LA, they make you wonder about the U.S.A." Then he grinned and thumped Liam on the back, "But now we have a piece of that California Garden of Eden right here at Crater Lake and I've got plenty of the *do re mi* so we don't need to worry about that."

Soon after Beulah and Bethany had taken over the A-Frame, the couple who owned the cabin Liam now occupied decided to sell. They came around giving Caleb first chance to buy them out. Years earlier, Caleb had picked up the A-Frame property in much the same way. Owning the pieces of property on both sides of his own had given him a type of security most could only dream of. He would have the luxury of choosing all his neighbours.

From the day Liam took up residence in the cabin next door, Caleb had always encouraged him to think of the place as his own. It was Caleb who had brushed aside Liam's lack of relevant job skills, "Heck, you can learn whatever you need from books – right? You're good with books. Like I always say, Liam, play to your strong suit." He presented Liam with his own battered, twelve-volume, Reader's Digest do-it-yourself series that gave detailed instructions on how to do everything from fixing a boat motor to building a chicken coop.

One of Caleb's proudest achievements had been what he and Liam both considered a perfectly-impenetrable-to-all-rodents chicken coop. They built it just up from Liam's at a point as far from the main cabin as was possible. Izzy hadn't bought the impenetrable part. She appreciated the idea that a small cottage industry for supplying fresh eggs to both the bakery and the nearby Camp could be a money maker for Liam, but she was no fan of rats.

Liam had learned what he needed to know but he sensed from the start that Caleb wanted a friend more than he needed a handyman. He and Caleb spent most of their days together. They managed the woodlot and the sawmill. They worked around the main cabin and the small place where Liam lived. There had always been lists of tasks to be completed with new things added daily. They never had a chance of catching up but that wasn't the point. Caleb had been uncharacteristically serious when he told Liam, "Confucius say: when man finish house – man die." With that in mind, neither one of them ever tried too hard to be done.

From the day Liam had arrived at Crater Lake, Caleb just took for granted that they would share a comfortable intimacy. It was a closeness that Liam hadn't expected and wasn't sure he wanted. In the early days he had wondered how on earth to respond to Caleb. Mostly Liam listened and he discovered that Caleb wasn't expecting anything else from him. All he ever wanted was for Liam just to be Liam.

V.

One afternoon when they were taking a break out on the woodlot, Caleb had told Liam that there had been a few women in his life before Izzy. Liam knew that this subject hadn't just popped out of nowhere. Past love lives had been a topic of conversation at dinner a few nights before. They had all been at the main cabin – Caleb and Izzy, Beulah and Bethany, and Liam – just digging into a rhubarb cobbler with vanilla ice cream on top. Izzy had told a story about backpacking in Europe with her boyfriend, when she was younger – something about missing a train and having to stay the night in an old barn. The next morning the two of them had been caught in that barn at a very awkward moment by an old man with a pitchfork in his hand. This man hadn't spoken any English but was quite able to get his point across. He had chased them out of the barn waving the pitchfork wildly, as they laughed and clutched their clothes and packs over their naked bodies.

Caleb had laughed along with the rest of them before commenting, "Oh Izzy . . . I know how irresistible you can be in the morning so I'm not surprised at the trouble you got yourself and your boyfriend into . . . and in a foreign country to boot . . . poor innocent guy."

"Hey, I'm at a disadvantage here," Izzy had snapped back, reaching over to punch Caleb in the arm. "How come you never talk about your past love life, Mr. Smart Guy?" She had paused for a moment before adding, "Maybe you didn't have one, though I find that hard to believe." An edge of something else had crept into her voice. "This place was probably a harem before I came along." It was clear to Liam that Izzy wasn't teasing anymore. Caleb had taken it the way he took most things – with an easy smile and a shrug. But it must have stayed on his mind.

Up on the woodlot that day, Caleb had pushed his long blonde hair out of his eyes and rubbed his hand along his beard before laughing in a self-deprecating way, "I was young when I came here, Liam. I had this place and money. I was here a long time and there were woman around who thought that made me interesting. I never had to go looking and courting if you know what I mean . . . well . . . not until Izzy." His smile seemed to indicate that everything he was saying was simply the way things would be – no surprises, nothing unusual.

Caleb told Liam some of these women even came out and lived at Crater Lake with him for a space of time, but none of these relationships had ever worked out. One didn't like the isolation. Bugs and wild animals didn't help endear the place to another. One liked it OK but was determined to change everything about the place and Caleb too. Another seemed to like Crater Lake and the isolation it provided for all the wrong reasons. So Caleb had stayed available until Izzy came along.

"When I brought Izzy here and she didn't care about being alone and she wasn't afraid of the dark or worried about bears or anything like that, I couldn't believe it. I already knew I was hopelessly in love with her and it seemed like unbelievably good luck that the place suited her. I asked her if she was sure none of that other stuff bothered her and she said the darkness she was worried about was of a different kind." Caleb laughed as he told Liam that part but Liam hadn't thought it was really funny. He knew exactly what Izzy was talking about.

Standing alongside Caleb, Liam had been able to enter a world where people got up every day and worked to build something that mattered. The past had settled into a place he could handle. He wasn't always at peace but most days he was able to be peaceful. He knew he bought this peace at the price of holding something of himself back, especially from Izzy.

Liam was aware of the kind of work Izzy did and how well she did it. The many young people who wandered in and out of their lives from Micah Camp made that obvious. Liam could see how those kids changed because of Izzy. He had known from the first time he shook Izzy's hand that if he let her get too close he would want to tell her everything. That knowing had been a shock that went through him like an electrical current. He believed down to the core of his being that if he gave into the invitation offered by her deep-brown eyes and the warmth of her hand in his – he would be lost. He had learned how to live with the past and he didn't want anything to threaten that.

Even deeper than the invitation to bare his soul, Liam had felt the darkness that swirled around Izzy. He didn't want a share of anyone else's demons; he had enough of his own. He wasn't going to take any chances on that score. Liam was no longer the type of man who took chances.

CHAPTER NINE

i.

Izzy finished her morning walk with the dogs and was heading to the fork in the trail to send Liam's dog, Pearl, home. As she rounded the corner from the greenhouse garden and came in view of the guest cabin, she saw Dan. He was sitting comfortably in the old rocker on the porch drinking a coffee, the steam rising in thin curls from the thick white mug. He smiled and waved her cheerily up onto the deck.

Dante quickly settled under Izzy's chair while Pearl stared up at her from the trail, tail wagging. "Go on home now, Pearl. See what Liam is up to," Izzy pointed down the trail and the dog dutifully trotted off.

Through the open door of the guest cabin, Izzy noticed that Dan had moved a small table close to the window. His laptop sat on the table flanked by a stack of paper and several books. Leaning against the edge of the veranda railing were two fishing rods and on the deck near Dan's chair, an open tackle box. It was filled with various objects Izzy was at a lost to identify. "So, I see you've settled in."

"Yes, indeedy –," Dan's smile was wide and inviting and his cheeriness somewhat infectious, "– it doesn't get any better than this." He raised his coffee cup in a salute to the view of the lake. "Can I get you a cup of coffee, Izzy?"

Izzy declined and chatted with Dan for a few minutes before asking, "Would this be a good time to show you around the place?" Rising, with

Dante scrambling out from under her chair as if he knew exactly what she was going to do before she did, Izzy moved toward the stairs.

Dan rose quickly in Izzy's wake and slipped on his joggers, "Okey Dokey, let's go," he chimed and met her on the path.

The Y in the trail in front of the guest cabin seemed a good spot to start. "If you head in that direction –," Izzy pointed to the trail down which Pearl had so recently disappeared, "– you'll walk along the cliff for a bit, then downhill to a bridge and across to Liam's place." She then pointed to the fork that headed back toward the main cabin. "If you go the other way, you'll pass the south stairway down to the beach. If you keep on that path you'll reach the cliff deck." Izzy paused to look over at Dan who was staring back and forth between the paths.

"Past the cliff deck you can follow the path beyond the main cabin to another set of stairs that lead to the beach on the north side. I'll take you around that way later from the other side." Izzy turned her back to the lake and moved up the trail past the guest cabin in the direction of the greenhouse garden, "I guess this is the way you walked back with Liam the other night, right?" Dan nodded but the look on his face seemed to say he really didn't remember it all that well.

Izzy caught her breath whenever she came at the greenhouse garden from this direction. Around a tight, tree-enclosed corner, on a narrow bark-chip trail the garden opened up in front of Izzy and Dan. It ran one hundred metres from where they were standing at the bend in the trail to the main cabin entry. Flowers, shrubs, vines and vegetables grew in a wild profusion, overflowing raised beds, trailing up and around arbours and trellises, pushing through outcroppings of rocks, climbing past the few stumps that had resisted all attempts to be removed and surrounding strategically placed benches and garden art.

The garden was flanked on the lake side by a wide row of raspberry canes that stopped just short of a small rectangular-shaped building. The garden house was no more than one large room, its four sides encircled with glass. The only pieces of furniture were a large desk and chair placed right in the middle of the room. The décor was kept rustic – the dark roof rafters exposed and the planked floor unadorned. Climbing roses twined around the outside of the building's four corners, winding up to the sloping, cedar-shake roof. Izzy thought of the garden house as a sanctuary – a place where she could shelter from the elements but still be in the midst of the garden.

The garden was about half as wide as it was long. It was bordered on the roadside by a large greenhouse that backed onto an attached workshop. The workshop opened onto the driveway. A low, narrow building cut in at a right angle from the greenhouse into the garden. It contained covered compost bins with a tool shed and a potting shed on either side of them.

Izzy was passionate about the garden in much the same way Caleb and Beulah had been passionate about baseball. She checked quickly for a look of appreciation on Dan's face. Izzy knew right away that he had no idea of the perfection stretching out in front of him. Well, Izzy thought, trying to be fair, I suppose I had the same look gazing into his tackle box.

Izzy moved up one of the paths that traversed the garden. "Let's go this way through here and up around the greenhouse." The interior of the greenhouse, clearly visible through the high glass panels, was lush with climbing nasturtiums and brightly-coloured yellow and orange marigolds interspersed among cucumber vines, bunches of dark-purple and emerald-green basil, and tomato plants. Izzy could see Justin inside the greenhouse. He was watering with one hand while reaching up with his other for something on the shelf above his head. As he moved his tanned skin and firm muscles showed below his raised T-shirt. Momentarily distracted, Izzy shook her head and thought, whew – that is a sight to take one's breath away.

She and Dan walked past the greenhouse along a paving-stone path, crossed in front of the attached workshop and entered the gravel turnaround at the bottom of the driveway. "I recognize this for sure," Dan was pointing up the road and making the Sign of the Cross. "In the name of the Father, the Son, and the Holy Spirit – Amen," he intoned. "May God have mercy on my soul if I ever again fall victim to a ride down that road with Beulah."

Izzy laughed right out loud and decided that Dan, despite all evidence to the contrary, really must be a priest. Only a cleric could make the Sign of the Cross and pray in public, even in a humorous way, with that much ease.

Liam came out from the small office at the far end of the workshop and stopped in his tracks when he heard Izzy laugh. He had been doing the month-end books for the sawmill accounts. He stood quietly watching Izzy with Dan and he remembered how she had invited Dan to come by any time to play the piano.

Caleb and Izzy were consistent in a doors-always-open policy around their cabin. In fact, Liam never heard either of them refer to the place as their cabin.

It was always the main cabin. Liam, Bethany and Beulah came and went at will, calling out before entering just to be polite. The thought that this privilege was now to be extended to Dan caused Liam's stomach to twist painfully. It was as if the ground was tilting slightly under his feet. Liam's dark eyes narrowed and he frowned. Coming to the conclusion that he probably wasn't going to warm up much to Dan, Liam returned to the workshop.

Dan followed Izzy as she walked up a few stone steps to a point behind the main cabin. Further back among the tall evergreens, tiered into the slope was yet another patio space. The sound of water was clear and comforting as it cascaded down a mossy, rock-covered slope and into a pond. Coming around the cabin to the orchard side, Izzy cut across the wide expanse of the kitchen deck and stopped at the railing. "You can see the north stair just below here." She pointed out the top landing and railing in the shadow of a large Mountain Ash tree.

"There's the trail coming across from the cliff deck. It carries on past the stairs and up the hill through the apple trees. It levels off and then if you walk along for a few minutes you'll come to Beulah and Bethany's A-Frame. Beyond their place the trail goes on to Micah Camp." Izzy looked over at Dan and said, "I guess that's that . . . I suppose I should ask if you have any questions?"

Dan glanced back at Izzy from the maze of paths, decks and gardens he was trying to sort out and smiled, "Coffee?" He was looking hopefully toward the main cabin.

She shrugged and returned Dan's smile, "Why not?"

There were students' papers to mark and a group session to plan, but Izzy could afford to take a break. Dan followed her inside and around the kitchen as she prepared the coffee, asking her one question after another. How had she come to be working at Micah Camp? How long had she been at Crater Lake? How long was it since her husband had died? What kind of a guy had he been? Dan had a way of popping out questions with such innocence that Izzy found herself answering before she had time to think of telling him to mind his own damn business.

They settled down with the coffee out on the kitchen deck. "I love sitting on this deck when the lilies are in bloom." Izzy breathed in deeply the scent carried on the morning breeze.

"The smell of lilies always reminds me of funerals." Dan laughed and Izzy smiled but she wondered if his comment meant he liked the smell or not.

Sipping a coffee and enjoying a piece of left-over pie, Dan spoke comfortably of his work. "Being a hospital chaplain suits me. I don't get to do it as much as I'd like . . . parish stuff really eats up the time . . . but it's good work, satisfying."

Izzy sat back in her chair observing Dan as she listened. He was the type of person who just naturally put other people at ease. He seemed so comfortable himself that he actually slowed people down. Not a bad thing, she thought, as she relaxed into her chair and sipped her own coffee.

"The work is mostly just listening to people. Right before I left I sat with a young guy who had been driving drunk on his grad night. There was a terrible accident and he was responsible for the death of his girlfriend and his best friend. He was messed up physically but he was going to live. It was just one of those things. That kid made one stupid choice and his whole life is changed. He had everything going for him until that moment when he didn't." Putting his empty plate down on the table between them, Dan studied Izzy's face for a moment, "Well, you know how it is, right? The stories get to you sometimes."

"Yes, they certainly can." Izzy paused for a moment and considered the invitation Dan's smile seemed to issue. Once again she found herself thinking, why not? "I work with young people over at Micah Camp. We get them when they've come out of the foster care system and with one thing and another . . . well . . . most of them have gone through their share of traumatic events."

Dan sat forward, quietly attentive, while Izzy continued, "The counselling work is complicated. Building up trust is a challenge. Just trying to find a way to get close to a young person who has no reason to trust anyone because most adults have let the kid down . . . it takes time, for sure." Izzy sipped her coffee and spoke, almost as if to herself, "I saw a new client yesterday. We just didn't click. Of course the first session is a testing-the-water sort of thing but I do usually come away with a sense of where I might start to build up a relationship." Izzy went on to sketch her impressions of the session with Jesse. Like a light bulb going on over her head she found the answer, "He was playing me." She sat back in her chair with a sense of relief. Obviously she couldn't allow Jesse to take control of their sessions together if it meant he kept things superficial; it was a waste of time for both of them. But at least she now had an idea of what was going on.

Izzy sipped her coffee before adding, "It's common enough, I suppose. Many of the kids I work with have learned to survive by manipulating others the way they were manipulated. You can't really blame them." She looked quickly at Dan, "The truth is I often admire the ways they've found to cope." Dan nodded his understanding.

Izzy wasn't surprised that talking to Dan was effective in bringing about her own insights. She missed George and the easy way she could toss around ideas and thoughts about her client sessions with him. She had taken a few months leave when Caleb died and by the time she got back into the stream of work, George was on his way out – busy with his retirement plans. Izzy had enough experience as a counsellor to do a lot of what she did by instinct, but this last year she definitely felt off balance – like a picture hanging slightly askew on the wall. Because she was busy she couldn't stop to straighten the picture but she shook her head in irritation every time she became aware of the tilt.

Dan's ability to listen and not offer advice was exactly what Izzy needed. She wasn't comfortable working with Roland in the way she had worked with George and other counselling peers were hard to come by in an isolated community like Dearborn.

Dan began to speak of another experience he had with a young girl who ran away to Toronto, to a hotel to meet a guy she met in some internet chatroom. She got beat up pretty bad and was lucky to have survived. He talked about how the girl's mother stormed around the hospital room crying and demanding that the police, the doctors and even Dan do something. "What were any of us supposed to do after the fact?"

"Right, no easy answers there for sure," Izzy replied.

After a comfortable silence in which they both seemed lost in thoughts of how, at times, their ability to help seemed small and ineffective, Dan sat forward in his chair and looked down the orchard path toward Bethany and Beulah's. "I want to talk to Bethany about the fishing. When do you think would be a good time to go over?"

"They're usually tied up with the bread all morning. I suppose any time after that would work," Izzy replied as she looked at her watch. She was startled by how late it was. Dan took the hint and strolled off in the direction of the guest cabin as though he had all the time in the world. The truth was, Izzy told herself somewhat resentfully, the lucky guy probably did.

ii.

Armed with a stack of papers, Izzy walked up behind the kitchen to the cool shade of the patio. Seated near the pond with the tumbling waterfall splashing down behind her, she attempted to make a start on the marking. Her eyes kept flitting from the paper in front of her to the stone pagoda nestled among the ferns and the lazy koi fish drifting in and out of the brightly-coloured water plants. She was having a difficult time getting focused. Her attention seemed scattered like the ripples blowing softly over the surface of the pond.

Dan's questions had brought up a flood of memories. He had asked at one point about how she came to be here, living at Crater Lake and working at the Camp. She had given a highly abridged version of the truth. The way in which these things had all come about was like the pool – dropping down into coolness, a quiet stillness beneath the turbulent times of her life.

Her name was Isabella, Izzy for short – always Montgomery. She kept her maiden name even after she and Caleb were married. By the time she met Caleb she'd finished a graduate degree and had already been working for a few years as a counsellor in the field of psychological trauma. She had a natural gift for the work and she was a fast learner. Her resume indicated much more experience than usual for someone her age.

She came to Dearborn to interview for a counselling position at their newly opened crisis centre. She would have got the job too; no one else with her qualifications had applied. The hiring committee told her as much. But later that day, in the small motel room she rented for the night, she found herself having doubts. Frontline trauma work had introduced Izzy to a certain worldview. She was well versed in the many ways that the wrong types of intimacy and violence could destroy people – especially women. She didn't think that she was jaded or burnt out. However, she had developed a belief about how the world worked and because she saw this belief confirmed again and again, it wasn't likely she would develop a new perspective. The job she had just interviewed for was looking like it would only strengthen, rather than challenge her worldview. Izzy found herself thinking that maybe challenges might be more important than confirmations.

While eating her dinner at the café attached to the motel, Izzy had glanced through the local paper and noticed an ad for a counselling position at Micah Camp. The next morning she called the Camp and they sent someone into town to pick her up. She liked what she saw and they liked her qualifications. The place was beautiful and although she was well aware that it would not be a picnic to work with young people coming out of years in care, it might be a chance for her to make a difference in her clients' lives at an earlier age. It was most definitely a change. She said yes and was hired that day.

A number of times over the years, Izzy heard Caleb tell the story of how they met. How he had seen her standing on the gravel road with at least eight kilometers still to go to Micah Camp. He liked to say she was staring at the flat tire on her car like it was a personal insult. How he had thought, at that moment, this is the woman I want to marry. That was Caleb's story. What happened to Izzy out on the logging road that day had a much deeper impact on her than Caleb ever imagined.

He had driven up, jumped out of his truck and walked around to the side of her car. He stood beside her, his arms folded. Both of them just stared at the tire. She remembered it quite clearly even now, that sensation of standing shoulder to shoulder with him facing the same way. Finally he said, "Looks like you could use a hand."

She turned to get a good look at him and he was smiling that crooked smile of his. At that moment, the sun flashed through the clouds and sifted down through a break in the tall firs that lined the road and he was awash in sunlight. It would have been impossible for Izzy to articulate or explain what that image of Caleb did to her. It was why she said yes when he asked her down to his cabin for dinner later that day; why she slept with him not even a week later; and why she moved out to Crater Lake to live with him that very month.

Though many other things happened over the years to cement their relationship, it was always that sensation of standing shoulder to shoulder looking in the same direction, and then turning to see Caleb in the light, that bound her to him. Sometimes the complicated twists and turns of life, the endless questions of why this choice and not that one, could be understood and answered that easily.

As it turned out, Izzy needed a partner like Caleb. He was as smart and quick as she was, though he didn't feel the need to show that off to others as much as she did. His physicality freed her up in ways she couldn't have imagined. And if all of that wasn't enough, he presented her with a home. It wasn't until she was totally in love with this piece of land perched over Crater Lake that she realized how much she had been longing for a home.

Over the years Caleb taught Izzy something else that was very important to her. Her life and work experience had shown her that many people were moving about the world stuck in really bad stories, unable to rewrite the past or move forward. Getting to know Caleb meant Izzy was confronted with a different reality. While there were people who were carting a shitload of darkness from relationship to relationship, there were also some people, like Caleb, who had always walked in the light. Nothing really bad had ever happened to them. She had been pretty sceptical about that for a long time and looked closely for the crack in Caleb's equanimity. But she couldn't find the kind of shadow she was looking for. Caleb really was the golden boy from the Golden State. He had been a happy kid and as an adult he continued to be content with himself and his life. Leaving his family and his country when he was young had been a challenge but he had taken it all in stride, drawing on the resiliency and strength that his upbringing had fostered. At any given moment in his life, it seemed he was where he wanted to be and doing what he wanted to do. The light he radiated drew people to him like moths to a flame.

Being with Caleb made Izzy a better counsellor because he was a constant testament to the fact that no matter how many dark stories she heard, the light was still there, always possible. The dark pulled at Izzy but with Caleb beside her it never gained a hold on her. He became her solid point of reference in a world that seemed at times to spin out of control.

Izzy thought suddenly of Lillian and her tactful but obvious disappointment that over time, grandchildren didn't start to make an appearance. Izzy and Caleb were both open to the idea of having kids but it hadn't happened and after a time they conceded that parenthood wasn't going to be a part of their lives. Izzy knew Caleb had worked hard to accept this reality and she felt compassion for him. She suspected it was Caleb who couldn't father a child. She had been pregnant in her early twenties. It hadn't been a good time for her to have a child so she had ended the pregnancy. Sometimes now she was sorry she didn't decide to have the child and cart it to Crater Lake with her, since no other children were in the offing. Maybe she and Caleb should have explored adoption with a bit more energy. Children would have been something to keep her going. But that was probably just the loneliness talking.

Gathering up her papers, Izzy walked over to the railing of the kitchen deck to stare out across the lake. She noticed the late morning wind pushing the fluffy-white clouds quickly across the sky. The moving clouds caused dark shadows to rush over the cabins that marched along the opposite shore. It looked as if the sun singled out each cabin, like a spotlight, and then the clouds passed over and all was shadow once again. Izzy shivered. The play of light to darkness made her feel empty.

CHAPTER TEN

i.

Dear Emma:

Here is my plan – I'm calling it Operation Justin. Step one – I have to be where Justin is. If I leave to go over to the Camp around the time he goes to Izzy's, I might run into him. Step two – whenever I see Justin I have to try to be really nice – no more being bitchy to be funny. I'm not sure what Step three should be. I'll think about it. Maybe – look hot all the time. I've got to go now though – it's my first day of work at the Camp and I'm so nervous.

ii.

"Hey, you have a real knack for this," Josie told Lisa-Marie as she checked the large drying tray filled with bright blue cornflowers. "Just pop it back in its slot and I'll get you started on the next one." She pointed back through the workshop to one of the large wooden flower presses.

Lisa-Marie took a moment to look around the workshop. Josie's tour had been a bit of a whirlwind and before Lisa-Marie knew it she was tucked up on a stool carefully arranging flowers on a tray. There were five other kids working at various tasks in the shop that boasted a vaulted ceiling and huge windows. The solid, butcher-block worktables and high stools were oriented to the view of the lake wherever possible. The soap and paper-making vats filled most of the back area and the two kids working there were garbed in thick, black aprons and gloves.

Everyone had smiled when Josie introduced her. The friendliness caught Lisa-Marie by surprise. One of the girls – Maddy – wore her short, brightly-coloured, purple hair in a spiky style. She was knocking finished bars of soap from a form in one area of the shop and she grinned at Lisa-Marie with a sparkle in her eye – the kind of sparkle that said Maddy might jump up and pull Lisa-Marie's hair or chase her around the room, just for the fun of it.

Josie seemed to be everywhere in the shop at once and Lisa-Marie took right away to her friendly, up-beat way of running things. She had been nervous earlier that morning walking over to the Camp. Even running into Justin on the path hadn't helped. Lisa-Marie had stood inside the large doors of the workshop not knowing what to do or where to go. She felt like it was the first day of high school all over again and she did not have good memories of that time. But thankfully none of those feelings lasted for long. Josie had met her at the door and before Lisa-Marie knew it she was working away like everyone else.

She watched Josie now as she was waylaid by Roland. He was coming through the doors of the shop with a young man behind him. Lisa-Marie resumed her perch on the stool and began to pick through the bin of fragrant green parsley in front of her while checking out the guy standing beside Roland – shorter than her idea of a really good looking guy. He was dressed in a pair of slouchy jeans belted low on his hips and what looked to her like a bowling shirt, hanging loose over his solid body. His hair wasn't too bad – a coppery-brown colour and curly around a face that sported a small, neatly-trimmed goatee of the same colour. The *goat* was pretty cool.

As he moved across the shop, Lisa-Marie noticed the way he walked – with a bit of a swagger. And she noticed the way he looked around him – with a smirky, phoney smile playing around the corners of his wide mouth. Taking in this information, she narrowed her eyes and thought, what a jerk. He obviously thought he was something special but he didn't look like anything special to her. More like a Mr. A-S-S-O.

At that moment, Roland spotted Lisa-Marie and made his way over to her. "Hello, Lisa-Marie. I hope you're settling in well to the new job. This is Jesse," Roland pointed over his shoulder. "He's our newest resident."

Jesse gave Lisa-Marie a long, evaluating look that made her want to squirm on her stool. Under his scrutiny she became overly aware of how her shorts were riding up her thigh and how the second undone button on her shirt revealed her skin beneath. When Jesse finally met her eyes she gave him a look that she hoped said in no uncertain terms – as if, asshole – while what she did say was, "Hi," in a completely neutral tone.

iii.

Strolling back to the A-Frame at noon, her first shift at the Camp completed, Lisa-Marie felt great. She passed the now deserted bakery shed nestled against the backdrop of the tumbling stream. The smell of fresh-baked bread was still in the air as she banged open the screen door at the back of the A-Frame. Bethany was placing cold cuts on a plate to go with the pickles, buns and sliced cheese already on the table. Beulah was at the counter shuffling through a stack of invoices – a pair of half-moon, black-framed glasses perched low on her nose.

Beulah watched Lisa-Marie as she made her way to the table. Catching Bethany's eye for a moment in a pointed stare, Beulah looked back at her invoices. "I assume, from someone's cheery state that things went well on the first day of paid employment."

"You know what they say about assuming, right Beulah?" Lisa-Marie was layering cheese and honey ham on a bun already thick with mayonnaise, "It can make an ass out of you and me . . . hee-hee. But in this case you would be right on the money . . . get it . . . money . . . paid employment." Lisa-Marie grinned before she bit into the loaded bun.

Bethany moved across the room to give Lisa-Marie a quick hug, "That's just great, sweetie," she said as she looked up to smile brightly at Beulah.

Cramming the invoices into a worn, brown-leather briefcase, Beulah shook her head as she came to the table. She was thinking about the incongruity of Bethany at times. Judging from Bethany's self-satisfied smile, you'd think that it had been her idea for Lisa-Marie to get a job at Micah Camp. Like maybe Beulah had imagined the angry tirade from Bethany the night that she learned her niece had gone over to the Camp looking for a job; that it had been someone else telling Beulah in no uncertain terms, "You are not to bully her like you are always bullying everyone, Beulah, I mean it."

With the lunch dishes dried and put away, Lisa-Marie noticed a small loaf of bread on the counter. Izzy's name was scribbled on the label. "I could take this over to Izzy's for you, Auntie Beth, if you like?" Lisa-Marie's heart was already thudding at the possibility of seeing Justin again; her opportunity lay right before her in a plastic wrapper adorned with a plain brown label that said, *Crater Lake Organic Bakery.*

Bethany was heading out the door with her fishing tackle box in hand; smiling back at Lisa-Marie she said, "Sure, sweetie." She put the box down suddenly and returned for a hug. "It's so wonderful to have you here, Lisa. I love the way you're always helping out. See you later."

Lisa-Marie watched her Auntie Beth cross the wide deck and almost skip down the stairs in front of the A-Frame on her way to the beach and her rowboat. I do love to be helpful, she told herself as she ran up the stairs to the loft to put on a bathing suit under her shirt and shorts. It was getting warm and she knew she would want to go swimming at some point that afternoon.

As Lisa-Marie rounded the corner of the path, the main cabin came into sight. She couldn't believe her luck. She could see Izzy, Justin and Liam through the window, standing in the galley portion of the kitchen. Izzy looked up as Lisa-Marie came across the kitchen deck. She hurried over to the screen door to let her in.

Taking the bread bag with a smile of thanks she said, "It's great that you're here right now because I really need a female opinion." She gestured back into the kitchen where Liam and Justin were standing at the counter near several gleaming, glass jars of the brightest red jam Lisa-Marie had ever seen. The gold-toned rings and lids on the jars shone and a knife was sticking out of the one jar left unsealed. Justin was munching into a large bun smothered in jam.

Liam, spoon in hand was leaning a hip into the counter and smiling over at Lisa-Marie, "Oh, you're in for it now, kiddo."

Izzy frowned at Liam and Justin and shook her head, pulling Lisa-Marie over into the narrow kitchen area, "These two are useless. They taste anything sweet and their brains go to mush." Izzy reached for a clean teaspoon from the drawer and dipping it into the jam she held the spoon out to Lisa-Marie, "This is the last batch of this year's strawberry jam and I think it's off somehow."

Izzy's face was a portrait of concern as she looked from the row of glistening, sealed jars to her tattered, old recipe book lying open on the counter. Streaks of jam ran down her apron and she had what looked like more of it in her hair. Justin was quickly spreading a second bun with jam. Lisa-Marie's knees felt weak standing so close to him in his T-shirt streaked with fresh dirt and grass stains. As she caught a hint of his clean sweat smell, she reached for the spoon from Izzy's hand.

"It's good . . . really good," she said after a moment, with a serious look on her face. Glancing over to Izzy she added, "Really strawberry tasting, but what is that other flavour?"

Liam rolled his eyes and looked up to the ceiling while Izzy punched him lightly in the arm and said, "Watch it, you."

Turning to Lisa-Marie she said, "That's my secret ingredient. A little something I came up with to make the jam interesting."

"Watch what you say, kiddo," Liam scooted back away from the threat of Izzy's raised spoon. "Izzy takes this jam thing way too seriously. It's the same every year."

Izzy's frown deepened as she looked from the cookbook page to Lisa-Marie, "But you shouldn't actually be able to taste another flavour. Hmmm . . ." Izzy grabbed a spoon and tried the jam again. She cast a thoughtful look at Lisa-Marie, "You're exactly right though. These last strawberries of the season were super sweet and I thought I might get away with just a smidgen more of the secret ingredient." Dropping the spoon she grabbed a pen to make a notation in the cookbook – *extra sweet berries don't need extra Red Chili Sauce – stick with regular amount.* Still looking down at the book she said, "OK, you guys, scat – get back to work or something."

Liam was walking away down the stairs to the living room. Lisa-Marie was disappointed to see Justin wave goodbye to her with the last of the jam bun in his mouth, as he headed out through the pantry towards the utility room. She seemed to be left with little choice except to leave the way she had arrived.

Looking up suddenly, Izzy called to Lisa-Marie, "I didn't mean you Lisa. Is it OK if I call you Lisa? Lisa-Marie is a bit of a mouthful. I was wondering if you would like a tour of the garden. I was on my way out there right now."

Lisa-Marie considered her options for a split-second. With Justin working in the garden, the invitation fit perfectly with *Operation Justin*. "Sure. Maybe while we're out there you can show me the way to the guest cabin. I talked to Dan the other day when he was over at the A-Frame for lunch and he says I can do the cleaning on Friday afternoons."

Izzy pulled her apron over her head and hung it on a hook near the stove. She walked down the stairs to the living room, calling over her shoulder, "That sounds great. I'm glad you could get that worked out on your own. Make yourself comfortable while I get changed, I'll be ready in a few minutes."

Lisa-Marie watched Izzy disappear into the bedroom off the entry and heard the door shut. She wandered over toward the three steps that led up to the library and was surprised to see Liam sitting at the desk at the far end of the room, hunched over the laptop. "Oh sorry," she said halfway up the stairs, "I didn't know you were still here."

"No problem, kiddo." Liam spun his chair away from the desk so he could see Lisa-Marie. "If you're interested in just about anything, I bet you can find a book here on the subject," his hand made a sweeping gesture toward the bookshelves.

"Don't stop what you're doing, I'll be quiet." Lisa-Marie came up the last stair, already engrossed in scanning the shelves. On a shelf just below eye level she found a small section of books on photography. Pulling them out one by one she knew she had discovered real treasure. She had seen almost all of these books in the library at school. Written in small, neat script on the front fly page of each book was the name, *Edward Montgomery*. Hearing Izzy's door open, Lisa-Marie slipped the book in her hand back onto the shelf. She called out a hasty goodbye to Liam and followed Izzy out the door to the garden.

iv.

Lisa-Marie trailed Izzy around the garden as she pinched a shoot here, pulled out hand-clippers to trim this or that, deadheaded flowers and talked nonstop about the names and varieties of the plants. Justin was nearby, working in a bed of flowers, their dark-purple, spiked petals dancing in the breeze all around him. His presence didn't hurt, but the truth was that Lisa-Marie was charmed completely by the garden. Izzy regaled her with the origin of each statue, bench and piece of sculptured art and she took it all in the spirit it was offered – Izzy's passion for the garden was contagious. Lisa-Marie's conflicted emotions battled away inside of her – she was drawn to Izzy and repelled by her all at the same time.

After the meandering tour, Izzy went over to an outdoor tap to get them both a drink, telling Lisa-Marie that the cold water came straight from the stream up the mountain. Lisa-Marie stood alone for a moment taking in what was all around her – exposed rock surrounded by dry-stack stone walls, random stumps acting as mother logs to bunches of huckleberry and salal, many trellis structures with climbing peas, beans, nasturtiums and morning glory, mounds of perennial herbs like golden oregano and lemon balm and raised beds filled with a variety of brightly-coloured plants. The delightful smell of peppermint rose all around her as she shuffled her feet over the profusion of small plants that grew along the edge of the garden path. Her hands itched for a really good camera and she longed to see the garden in the early morning light or in the golden hour of dusk. The way it was surrounded in the distance by tall evergreens, a garden in the midst of the forest, meant that the light filtered through high branches with amazing effects. If ever a place screamed to be photographed it was this garden.

With the two glasses of water in hand, Izzy led Lisa-Marie to a shaded bench across from the garden house. Lisa-Marie studied the headless, winged statue standing to the side of the small building's French doors. "Once you look at her you can't seem to stop," she said and her hands itched again for a camera.

"*The Winged Nike of Samothrace.* She is beautiful," Izzy paused to take in the beauty of the white statue, which was five feet tall on its concrete base. "The original is in the Louvre in Paris. I saw it there when I travelled to Europe in my early twenties and I never got the image out of my head."

Izzy glanced over to see Lisa-Marie studying the statue carefully. She tried not to sound like a tour guide as she continued, "She was discovered on the Greek Island of Samothrace in the mid-eighteen hundreds, but she was sculpted long before that, around two-hundred years before Christ. They think she might have sat in a corner of an open-air theatre on a marble pedestal that was shaped like the front of a ship. Apparently she was meant to look like she had just come down from the sky, like she was leading a triumphant fleet of ships."

"Did she have a head or her arms when they found her?" Lisa-Marie's head was tilted to one side, her long brown hair sweeping down to the bench she and Izzy shared.

"Good question," Izzy said as she sat back on the bench stretching out her legs. She sipped slowly from the plastic glass of cool water and focused her attention on the statue, only stopping briefly to pluck a leaf of lemon balm from the outcropping by her end of the bench and crush it lightly between her fingers. The fragrant leaf released its pungent, lemon smell. "They found her just the way you see her. It seems to me like she is more fascinating because of what is missing. I'm not sure, but there is something about the way she is straining forward and how her dress has been sculpted to look as if it is blowing back in the wind. You can almost imagine how the wind would shake the feathers on her wings. I find her totally compelling."

Lisa-Marie nodded silently, she could see exactly what Izzy meant.

"I had a poster of the Nike for years and when we finished the garden house I wanted to find it again and have it framed for that wall," Izzy gestured to the wall behind the statue. "Caleb said it would fade and moisture would get behind the glass and stuff like that." She shrugged at Lisa-Marie as if to say, men know that kind of thing, but it sure is irritating.

"Anyway, Caleb said why not get a statue; and who knew it was so easy to order a statue online?" Izzy laughed and then continued in a quiet tone, "When we had her here, I felt like the garden was complete somehow, maybe a bit like my victory."

Lisa-Marie pondered the statue's fluid sense of movement and considered an angle shot from the bottom of the stairs looking up. "You know what? I don't even care what her face was like. She's perfect just the way she is."

Izzy nodded her agreement. "There are lots of good replicas in museums and galleries but you know what is really odd?" Izzy paused, "The best replica is supposedly outside of Caesars Palace in Las Vegas," she laughed and added, "Celebrating another type of victory, I guess."

The sound of a door shutting turned Lisa-Marie's attention to the main cabin where she could see Liam walk down the stairs and head off toward the workshop. "I thought my Auntie Beth said Liam lived somewhere past your place?"

"Oh, he does – right down the trail past the guest cabin. Liam's in and out and around here all the time. He manages the woodlot and sawmill so he needs access to the phone and the internet." Izzy was still holding the crushed lemon balm. She brought it close to her nose and inhaled as she spoke, almost to herself, "Everyone is always in and out of the main cabin. Caleb was just the kind of guy who had permeable boundaries." Izzy looked over and caught Lisa-Marie's blank stare, "He just let everyone in. When I first came here I thought it might bug me but it didn't. Now I hardly think twice about it."

"Of course when Caleb was around there were embarrassing moments . . . the man could never get dressed in just one room." Izzy remembered the way Caleb would wander from room to room half-dressed; his socks might go on in the bedroom, his shirt in the office, and his pants somewhere between the living room and the kitchen. "Now I, on the other hand, having been raised in a somewhat uptight and prudish home, have never once run into such a dilemma. Let's just say people got into the habit of calling out well in advance of going into any room when Caleb was around. Not that it helped at all." Izzy was quiet for a moment. "Well –," she continued, "– as you can see, Caleb's open door policy is still in place. So remember what I said about the computer in the office or if you want to phone anyone back home . . . you're welcome anytime."

Lisa-Marie relaxed next to Izzy. Attraction was winning out over revulsion. It was nice to be sitting here on this bench listening to Izzy talk. She tried to imagine what it would be like to travel to Europe, go to Paris and visit a museum like the Louvre. The sadness in Izzy's voice when she talked about Caleb brought a lump to Lisa-Marie's throat.

Justin came into view on the garden path. He was raking his hand through his hair, lank from the day's work and the heat. "Quitting time, boss," he called out to Izzy as he came towards them. Stopping short of the bench, Justin glanced at Lisa-Marie's outfit – her bikini top was just visible beneath her low-necked T-shirt. "Hey, want to go for a swim, Leez? Izzy's got the best beach with a raft for diving and she hardly ever uses it." Lisa-Marie was up in a flash, almost wanting to pinch herself with glee at her foresight in having put on her bathing suit. She had never been a girl guide but she had the motto down pat – be prepared.

Izzy shaded her eyes from the slanting rays of the afternoon sun. She looked up at Justin, "Yes, go, go, have fun. Swim, enjoy yourselves." As she watched them walk away together, Izzy stood up and called out to Justin, "Stop by before you go back to the Camp, OK? I want to talk about what you'll be working on the next few days."

Izzy entered the garden house and sat down at the desk in the cool interior. She opened the top drawer and took out a heavy journal bound in deep-green leather. She began to make quick notes. I do need to talk to him. He works for me. Things aren't going to get done around here without a plan, are they?

V.

Dear Emma:

Justin asked me to swim with him today! We had such a riot. He raced me to the raft and of course he won. He looked so great in his work shorts with his hair dripping from the water. I wore my pink bikini and I'm sure I looked pretty good.

I wanted Justin to walk me home but Izzy asked him to go back and talk to her about work. I saw them on her deck. From far away they looked perfect together – Justin was drinking a beer and she had a glass of wine. I heard them laughing. I can't see what could be so funny about gardening. I don't think they would have noticed me if I was standing right in front of them with my hair on fire. Crap, crap, crap – why does he have to work for her?

Izzy's garden is magical. I felt like Mary Lennox in that book, The Secret Garden. If I could be in Izzy's garden every day then I wouldn't care or mind about all the things I never had. Izzy told me about this awesome statue – she called it the Nike of something or other. I just wanted to take a million pictures of it.

My life would be perfect if only Izzy could be a really ugly, old woman – maybe fat with way more grey hair. Then I could like being with her in the garden every day and Justin would never look at her at all.

CHAPTER ELEVEN

i.

Caleb had turned out to be a force hitherto unknown in Beulah's life. She had marched with a firm step through her world dividing everyone she met into two distinct groups – those she might need to rescue and those she would need to fight. Caleb resisted landing in either group. Beulah could see from the start that Caleb didn't need rescuing and he had an annoying habit of standing solid in the face of all her early attempts to get one up on him. She couldn't fight the guy no matter what she did. With an easy grin he'd offer her a drink from his flask, or whip out the deck of cards he always carried and invite her to play a quick game of Gin Rummy. He brushed Beulah's bristling, I-can-take-you-down attitude right off the table. She could still see him relaxed in a chair shuffling that deck of cards with a look of ease and contentment on his face.

Beulah had come from Edmonton – fifteen years ago now – looking for Crater Lake. A guy she worked with at the Safeway raved about spending his holidays there every summer and showed her some great pictures of the area. One October morning she found herself wandering around the deserted campsite on the other side of the lake. She knew right away the area she was exploring was wrong for what she wanted. Come summer it would be crawling with people because of its easy access from the road, sandy beaches, camp grounds and costly private cabins. Sitting on a picnic table in the campground, she raised her binoculars to scan the obviously inhabited cove in the distance. Micah Camp, across the choppy water of the lake, was easy to identify and she had already heard in Dearborn that it was some sort of a place for foster kids. Her eyeglasses swept past the Camp to a small A-Frame sitting up from the beach, then further on to an extensive cleared area of gardens and fruit trees with a large cabin in the middle. Finally her gaze ended where the cove ended – with a view of a small place seemingly perched right out over the cliff.

Moving her focus back to the A-Frame she could see it was unoccupied. No smoke from the chimney on that cold October morning years ago. No signs of life at all. It looked perfect. She asked around for directions and drove out on the deserted gravel road. As luck would have it, she ran right into Caleb.

When Beulah pulled off the logging road she spotted a man hopping effortlessly across a ditch to the roadway from a large open shed stacked with lumber. The fresh smell of cut wood was in the air and the whining sound of a large saw provided a steady background drone. Chain saw in hand, this man was calling out instructions to a couple of younger guys behind him. He walked over to Beulah who was getting out of the new four-by-four she had purchased before leaving Edmonton. He extended his hand and said, "Hi . . . Caleb Jenkins . . . are you looking for someone or something?" He awaited her reply with a smile that she came to know as his characteristic, twisted-slightly-at-one-corner grin. To her amazement, she found that grin a disarming combination of vulnerability and charm.

"I noticed from across the lake that the A-Frame down below seems unoccupied. I'm interested in buying something out here and want to take a look at it. Got any idea who I should talk to?" Beulah believed in the direct approach and she delivered her request in a clipped tone, staring Caleb right in the eye.

"Well, you're looking at him but I'll tell you right off, I'm not particularly interested in selling." Caleb pulled a flask from his back pocket and took a long, slow drink. He screwed the cap back on and shrugged. Studying Beulah casually he said, "What the hell, I guess I've got nothing better to do and you've driven all the way out here." He gestured to the narrow path that disappeared into the bush to his left, "It's a pretty steep hike. If you're up for it, follow me."

Even further back than this October afternoon, before Micah Camp had been built, rumours had mysteriously started to swarm over the town of Dearborn. Some type of large building was going in at the end of the cove on Caleb's side of the lake. No one knew for sure what was happening but speculation ran rampant as it was apt to do in a small town. Everything from a fancy lodge to a prison facility was discussed. Weedy Wendell, Caleb's neighbour in the A-Frame, began to get antsy. His nickname was well deserved. Somewhat of a lonely and morose guy, he used the cabin and the falling-down, plastic-covered greenhouse built along the side almost exclusively for growing and smoking dope. Thinking that the privacy he had always enjoyed might be at risk, he offered Caleb first chance to buy him out. Caleb purchased the A-Frame to act as a buffer between his property and whatever was going to be built next door He had the vague idea he might turn it into a guest place. The cabin had ended up sitting empty most of time since he bought it.

After a quick tour of the place, Caleb and Beulah sat on a couple of old lawn chairs on the veranda of the A-Frame, the weak but welcome fall sun touching their faces. Caleb asked Beulah why she was interested in purchasing property on Crater Lake. She was abrupt to the point of rudeness as she laid out her plans for the outdoor wood-burning oven and the organic bread business.

Something strange happened to Beulah that day as she sat on the veranda looking out over the gently rippling water of the lake. An aching want opened inside of her for this place. It was an overwhelming need that would make hardball negotiating painful, if not impossible. She could already see, just out back of the A-Frame, where the oven should go. She had checked Dearborn out carefully and the whole area had great potential. The shop owners she talked to had shown much more than polite interest.

Beulah was no fool when it came to reading people. She could tell Caleb was curious about her, but the curiosity had nothing to do with her business plans. He was the type of guy who got curious about people and all the contradictions they could present. He had insisted she come over to what he referred to as the main cabin and meet his partner, Izzy. The three of them discussed Beulah's plans over coffee with Izzy drawing out detail after detail. Beulah saw from the very start that Izzy would be the deciding factor in any decision Caleb made.

Izzy turned to Caleb and said, "Sell her the place for whatever she can pay." Then she smiled at Beulah and turned back to Caleb with a twinkle in her eye as she reached over to push him lightly on the shoulder, "We all know you're going to anyway."

Izzy and Caleb had been together for a couple of years by then. Later when Beulah knew both of them better she heard Izzy say that she never understood how Caleb could be such a people person and yet hang onto all these buildings and have no one living in them. Izzy liked her privacy but she also liked having neighbours and she hated to see anything go to waste.

The details of the sale had followed easily enough. Caleb had already run power lines from his place to the A-Frame. The size of Caleb's power-generating system along with his land holdings had been the talk of Dearborn for years. He had almost doubled over with laughter the first time he heard that he was nicknamed, Don Caleb, the Godfather of Crater Lake. He had practically begged Beulah to accept his offer of free power, "I'm just spending hours trying to figure out how to use the bloody power anyway, so help me out here, woman."

Caleb had insisted on a composting toilet as a condition of the sale. He explained to Beulah, in more detail than she wanted to hear, the relative advantages of composting human manure as opposed to fussing around with a septic field. He went on a rant about Wendell's option for the A-Frame – a stinking outhouse up the hill which Wendell had considered quite adequate for anything more time consuming than stumbling out to the edge of the veranda to take a leak. Caleb was planning to purchase and install the toilet. Upon hearing that, Beulah cracked a smile for the first time during the negotiations and agreed.

Soon after Beulah had settled into the A-Frame she strolled down the path to the main cabin with a very young and, at least to Izzy's already practiced eye, fragile-looking Bethany. Caleb and Izzy became regular consultants and active helpers as Beulah planned and built up the organic bakery business and renovated the A-Frame to its present level of comfort.

ii.

Beulah liked being around men. She supposed it made her a bit of a stereotype – a lesbian woman who identified with male energy, but that energy was something she understood. It had always been that way, all the way back to when she was little. Beulah's real dad had never been in evidence, not even in a picture. Her mom married Jack Johnson when Beulah was two. The relationship lasted for the long haul and Beulah ended up with two step-brothers into the bargain. She could remember hanging out with Jack when he worked around the house or on the car. She loved chumming around with her step-brothers and their friends, playing street hockey and shooting hoops in the driveway – until they crossed some invisible line that said having your sister around was crap and they stopped hanging out with her.

Jack treated Beulah OK, but there was always an underlying text in the family story that ran something like – Beulah wasn't Jack's real daughter and naturally, she occupied a rung down from his boys. When it became obvious in her senior-year of high school that Beulah liked girls, Jack's attitude became more pronounced and his disapproval was clear. Beulah's mom worked hard to run interference for her and the family life ticked along on somewhat of an even keel. At least everyone was willing to keep up appearances.

After Beulah graduated from high school she drifted into community college for a couple of years with no real idea what she wanted to do with her life. The summer she turned twenty she went along to a big Johnson family reunion. There she was reacquainted with Jack's real daughter, Cassie. Beulah and Cassie were the same age but hadn't seen each other since they were in grade school. Cassie's mom wanted as little to do with Jack as possible and had actively done all she could to keep Cassie away from her father and his new family.

The chemistry between Beulah and Cassie was immediate and it wasn't just sex, which Cassie was pretty free and easy with when it came to girls and guys alike. It was something about the way Cassie wanted to do so many of the things Beulah wanted to do but couldn't muster the wherewithal to do them on her own. Cassie wanted to travel and Beulah could make it happen for both of them. With Beulah you didn't just talk about doing things – you actually got off your ass and did them.

From the reunion they embarked on a whirlwind relationship that took almost three years to burn itself completely out. They travelled all over Canada, the States and even spent time in Europe – working jobs to get from one stop to the next. They were on a layover in Edmonton with Cassie working at a Burger King and Beulah working part-time in the bakery at Safeway, saving to head out to the West Coast. Beulah came home from work one day to find Cassie packed and ready to leave, this time solo. They parted amicably enough though Cassie was at pains to point out to Beulah that she didn't want to be looked after or managed anymore. She had taken a page from Beulah's book and wanted to be her own boss. She planned to go back to school and finish her degree.

Beulah stayed on in Edmonton. Her time with Cassie made her very unpopular in her mother and stepfather's home. Going back there was not an option. Her mother had given up trying to run interference for Beulah and her lifestyle. She continued for years to refer to what had happened as Beulah's shenanigans with Cassie. She demanded, in a tone of disbelief, every time the subject came up, "Aren't there enough women in the world? Why did she have to take up with Jack's daughter?"

Jack parked Cassie's fall from grace clearly on Beulah's shoulders and that ended even any attempt at cordial relations between the two of them. Since Beulah had spent more time hanging out with Jack than with her mother she actually missed the loss of her relationship with him the most.

By the time Beulah was thirty she had made a good life for herself in Edmonton. She moved steadily up the chain at the Safeway bakery and was in line for a promotion to assistant head baker. She bought a nice house. She played on the store slow-pitch and bowling teams. She had a few lightweight relationships under her belt. They were relationships that hadn't seemed to go anywhere but they did pass the time. Things were OK. It was a life.

Then Beulah met Julie. Julie started working at Safeway as a cashier. She had twin ten year olds named Erwin and Darcy and she had recently separated from her husband Mark. The relationship went from zero to a hundred in a matter of weeks and Beulah found herself setting up a life with Julie and the boys – an instant family. She moved them into her house and she took on the lion's share of the financial burden so Julie could work part time and be with the kids.

For six years they made a life together, what Beulah thought was a good life. She got Erwin and Darcy from ten to sixteen, which weren't easy years for a couple of rambunctious boys. And she lived through a lot of fallout due to the crap Mark was always pulling on Julie. He fought and badgered her on every single aspect of the twin's lives, from the big issues like visitations, to the inconsequential things like how many cavities they might have, why their school marks dropped even slightly, or whether the boys would play hockey or soccer or both. Mark was like a pit bull taking on a mouse when it came to giving Julie a divorce or a cent of the money she had coming to her. Every time he bullied her, Julie would end up sobbing, giving in, and taking to their bed with a migraine for a day or two.

Then came the morning Erwin and Darcy were to fly out to spend the summer with Mark. Beulah waved goodbye and headed for her shift at Safeway. She had nothing against the boys, but she always looked forward to the times they visited their dad. She didn't want to get rid of them – she just wanted to be assured that for a period of time there wouldn't be any bullshit phone calls from Mark to upset Julie. Coming home later to an empty house, she found a short note from Julie pinned to the fridge with a magnet that advertised take-out pizza.

I just can't do this anymore, Beulah. It's too hard all the time. I'm not as strong as you. I'm going back to Mark. It's better for the boys and Mark has agreed to take me back, mostly because I haven't been with another guy. Sorry. I know the way I'm doing this is all wrong. I know you'll hate me forever, but I just can't face you.

Looking at that note, Beulah had not been able to believe her eyes, or the emptiness of the house, or the level of Julie's betrayal – going back to Mark after six fucking years. In those first days after Julie left, Beulah could not make sense of what had happened to her. The line in Julie's note about Mark's reason for taking her back seemed like the biggest slap in the face of all; as if what they had together in the bedroom didn't mean anything because she didn't have a dick. So it was instant family, instantly gone. Beulah knew she wasn't always the easiest person to live with and she knew she could have done some things differently, but she didn't think for a second she deserved to be treated the way Julie had treated her and she took the whole thing hard.

A lot of alcohol went under the bridge the next year. Beulah had a work ethic that wouldn't allow missed shifts or screw-ups, but she ended up looking pretty haggard before she got her feet under her again. It was in those days, moving through her life, that Beulah felt something essential about her had disappeared. To be more accurate, something had been stolen from her and she didn't really think she would ever get it back.

Beulah recovered to a degree, just in time to learn that her mother and Jack had been killed in a car accident. She was surprised by the grief she felt. She thought she was used to being orphaned but facing the reality of death was much different than living away from people who she knew were still out there, even if they didn't want to see her.

Then the fight for her third of the estate got underway. Jack had done all he could to make sure she would get nothing and her step-brothers were not so much against her as they were greedy. It took some hard slogging over a couple of years to work it through the courts, but Beulah persevered and got her third. She found herself with a fair amount of capital and wanting a change. So she came to Dearborn and Crater Lake.

Beulah met Bethany the very day she had signed the deal to buy the A-Frame. She had been on an incredible high that late afternoon in the Fields store in Dearborn. And there, down a long aisle folding towels was Bethany. She had given Beulah a shy smile and asked if she could help her with anything. Those incredible blue eyes and that long, blonde hair swinging around her face stopped Beulah in her tracks. She simply wanted Bethany almost as much as she had wanted the A-Frame and the dream of the organic bakery. And despite Beulah's suspicions about why Bethany chose to be in her bed, she had a way, from their first night together, of leaving Beulah gasping and thinking about the next time, before she even caught her breath. She didn't think she would fall for anyone ever again after Julie and her betrayal. But she fell for Bethany and if it was mostly about protecting her and sleeping with her, so what? The fall had landed her in love.

Chapter Twelve

i.

Bethany busied herself about the kitchen. Her mind kept going back over Dan's visit two days before. He had appeared on the veranda as if he dropped by all the time and Beulah invited him in for lunch. All he could talk about was fishing and arranging a time when Bethany could take him out. Beulah left the table when Dan's questioning about where and when they should meet got so direct that Bethany was left with no choice but to make up her mind one way or the other.

Lisa-Marie had been cleaning up the dishes and casting curious looks at Dan, her aunt and Beulah in turn. Bethany knew the tension in the room must be obvious to Lisa-Marie. Only Dan seemed unaware of any problem. Bethany had given in to the inevitable. She had said that Thursday would be good . . . and here it was, Thursday. Dan would be here any minute. Bethany found herself dreading the thought of fishing for the first time in years.

Bethany hadn't fished before coming to Crater Lake. She had never even been in a boat. Beulah didn't fish; she got the small rowboat because she thought it might be relaxing to row around a bit and explore the lake. Izzy and Caleb had no interest in fishing either. Three years after Bethany moved in with Beulah, Caleb's aunt and uncle had stayed at the guest cabin and rowed out past the A-Frame, fishing practically every day. One morning when Bethany was down on the shore the woman rowed up on her own and asked Bethany to join her. Bethany got hooked – funny to put it that way – but there was something about the boat's movement and all the pretty lures lined up in the tackle box that was soothing.

Bethany started going out on her own to fish. She had been seeing Izzy for a couple of years by then. Izzy said fishing could be a way for Bethany to ground herself. Izzy said it was a good thing.

ii.

Bethany had left home when she was barely seventeen and she'd been back only once — for her younger sister's funeral. She held her new-born niece, so soon orphaned and already in the care of Bethany's own mother. She snorted at the suggestion they call the baby Lisa-Marie. Her mother's obsession with Elvis was always good for a laugh. She ignored the pleading looks for help her mother threw her way. Bethany had a life and she wasn't about to move back to Kingston to help raise her junkie sister's child.

She certainly did have a life. She had shown up for the funeral in a pair of oversized, dark glasses to hide the black eye Chantelle had given her as a going away gift. Bethany's mom tried to get her to talk about what had happened but Bethany shrugged her off. She was used to Chantelle's temper and the idea of her mother suddenly caring about her was a good one.

Several months after her trip to Ontario, Bethany left the apartment in Victoria she shared with Chantelle, carrying only what she could stuff in her back-pack. She thought it made sense to get as far away as the Island offered, so she made her way north. With a bulky cast still on her broken arm she applied for a job working evenings at a convenience store in Cedar Falls.

One night after work Bethany came home to the dumpy little motel that she rented by the month and Chantelle was there. It was amazing to Bethany that Chantelle actually came after her. The hitting started almost immediately. Bethany remembered feeling as though she had been walking through a dream in slow motion. It was like disappearing in plain sight. She went to work each day in various states of disarray and no one said anything. One night the police showed up in answer to a call from the neighbours. Bethany was bleeding profusely from a head wound and Chantelle was nowhere to be found. She had hit Bethany with the bat Bethany kept behind the bedroom door as some sort of security. That bat had sent Chantelle into spasms of laughter on a number of occasions. The thought of Bethany using it on anyone was simply impossible to imagine. Clearly Chantelle didn't have the same scruples.

After being stitched up at the local hospital, Bethany was advised to go to a safe house in the nearby town of Dearborn. She went and didn't look back. A couple of months later she moved into a small apartment over the Ship Shape Laundromat and got a job working in the local Fields store. Dearborn seemed as good a place to live as anywhere else. Then one Friday night Beulah came through the double-glass doors of the store. She seemed to need an unusual amount of assistance. She ended up asking Bethany to go for a drink and one thing led to another. Bethany invited Beulah back to her place. She was surprised the next morning when Beulah asked her to come out to Crater Lake and see the cabin she had bought.

Bethany had sat with Beulah on the veranda of the A-Frame. She had fallen in love, not with Beulah since they had just met, but with the view. She had stared down the lake towards the mountains that formed a series of wonderfully, overlapping valleys highlighted by the slanting rays of sun through the clouds. It had been like a watercolour with everything draped in delicate tones of purple and blue washing out to multiple shades of grey.

Beulah looked at her and asked, "What's your story Bethy? What are you running from?"

Bethany was used to telling people the story of all the shitty things that had happened to her, all the way back to when she was thirteen and being forced into the closet of the neighbour's house. It was dark in that closet. The smell of Lysol coming off the mop in the corner was overwhelming. Bethany was terrified every single time that closet door closed her in. Each time was like the first time and it was strange to her how she would feel the darkness and smell the Lysol, then come back to herself in her neighbour's kitchen doing something mundane like washing dishes or sitting on a chair and hearing the kids wake up. She knew what had happened. She could tell herself what had happened. Still, she felt like she hadn't really been there.

It had all started when she began babysitting on the weekends for Mrs. Malone who was busting her ass working twelve-hour shifts cooking at the local hospital. Bethany was supposed to keep the kids quiet so Mr. Malone could sleep – he was a prison guard and he worked graveyard shift, Friday through Tuesday at Kingston's federal penitentiary.

There was always a time when Mr. Malone wasn't sleeping. He would come home in the early morning hours – right after his wife went to work but before the kids woke up. He would come in with a big smile on his face and ask Bethany how she was doing. He would hang up his coat and place his heavy, black, prison-guard shoes on the mat. Then Mr. Malone would pad quietly over to where Bethany stood with her back against the kitchen counter and push her slowly but forcefully across the room towards the closet door. The first couple of times she had tried to stop him but each time she resisted he had held his hand over her mouth and whispered in her ear that he would make things much, much worse for her if she kept up that little game; and she believed him. In the dark closet Mr. Malone touched her and made her touch him and he pried her mouth open as he pushed her head down into an even darker space.

The closet episodes lasted forever. Time moved on and what Mr. Malone did to her moved on as well. When she was sixteen, Bethany discovered that she was pregnant.

The really terrible thing, at least in Bethany's mind, was that Mr. Malone acted as if they had been in it together all along. He said he loved her. He would kick Mrs. Malone out and look after Bethany and their baby. He had actually seemed pleased at the prospect. Bethany knew she couldn't look after a baby. She was mouth-dry, hands-shaking, heart-thumping-in-her-chest ter-rified every time she looked at Mr. Malone. She certainly couldn't live in the same house with him and a baby.

Her mom said maybe she should leave. It was too late for Bethany to have an abortion but she could give the baby up and move on with her life. Bethany jumped at the idea of getting away from Kingston. Mrs. Malone had been spreading rumours about how Bethany was a tramp who had chased after her husband from the start. Bethany wasn't able to show her face at school or anywhere else in town for that matter. She felt overwhelmed with the fear of going, but she was so scared all the time, of everything, that one more fear didn't really matter that much.

Her mother found a place for her to stay in Toronto – a place where other girls like her were also waiting for unwanted babies to be born. Bethany didn't even think about why she was the one who had to leave; why she was having a baby all by herself, afraid and alone and way too young to understand any-thing that was happening to her.

She remembered that when the extreme pain of giving birth was finally over she had turned her face to the wall and refused even to look at the screaming baby. She covered her ears tightly when the nurse asked, "Don't you want to know if it's a boy or a girl?"

After Toronto, a string of relationships followed Bethany all the way to BC. The women she chose had their own shitty stories and were filled with a rage that seemed to find a natural outlet on Bethany's soft frame. She usually went on automatic pilot when she told what the counsellors called her *trauma story*. She said the words and that didn't hurt at all.

On that day, sitting on the veranda of the A-Frame, Bethany had finally wound down to silence. Beulah looked at her for a long time before straightening her shoulders and saying, "If you stay here with me, Bethany, I will look after you. I will never hit you, and no one else will ever lay a hand on you either. I promise you those three things."

The look on Beulah's face shook Bethany out of the stupor in which the telling of her story always left her. Most of the women she had been with had made promises of one sort or another but nothing like this. There was no doubt in Bethany's mind, at that moment or at any time since then, that Beulah had the strength of character and purpose to carry out every single word she said.

Over the years that followed, Bethany slowly came to understand that Beulah counted her among the lost causes of the world. Bethany put two and two together and concluded that it was because she was such a lost cause that Beulah had made those three promises. Beulah liked to manage people. But in the final analysis, Beulah's motivations didn't matter to Bethany one way or the other. All she had wanted was to be safe and Beulah gave her that safety. Beulah kept her promises.

CHAPTER THIRTEEN

i.

Dear Emma:

I said I would tell the truth, the whole truth, and nothing but the truth. Here is the biggest truth, Emma – the biggest secret I don't want anyone to know. Of course Grannie told Auntie Beth but I made Auntie Beth promise not to tell Beulah. Exactly one month ago I tried to kill myself. Sorry to shock you, but there it is – the truth. I can hardly believe it either. I took a whole bunch of T3's that Grannie had hanging around in the medicine cabinet forever – she was supposed to use them last summer for her broken ankle but she said they made her constipated. Then I drank a whole bunch of vodka from an old bottle at the back of the china cabinet. But Grannie got home from Bingo early. She couldn't stay for the second set because her leg was all puffed up. She called 911 and I had to go to the hospital and get my stomach pumped. The nurse was so horrible to me, Emma – you wouldn't have believed it. And I'll tell you this – getting your stomach pumped makes you wish you really did die.

But I didn't cry – not even once. Another truth about me is that I never cry – no matter what. I feel like I would rather die than cry. Anyway – now my grannie thinks I'm crazy or something and she begged Auntie Beth to take me for the summer, so here I am. Auntie Beth is worried about me all the time and Beulah hates me because I worry Auntie Beth. I don't want everyone to worry about me or think I'm crazy. And I'm glad I didn't die because then I never would have met Justin!!!

No one believes me when I say it won't happen again. It won't happen again – I don't want it to happen again – I don't want to die. You're probably thinking – why did you ever do such a stupid thing, Lisa-Marie? I don't know – I just don't know. It all feels so unreal now – like it happened to someone else. I know it was a crazy thing to do but I don't feel like I'm crazy. Does that sound crazy too?

i i .

Lisa-Marie had been waiting in the gravel drive at Izzy's for about five minutes when Liam came into view heading for the Dodge. Feeling lake-bound, Lisa-Marie had decided she'd better find a way to get to town. She wanted to check out her Facebook page. She remembered Izzy's invitation to stop by and use the office laptop but Lisa-Marie didn't want to take the chance that anyone would see what she wanted to look at. Izzy's revolving door policy made real privacy a challenge.

Thinking neither she nor Beulah would enjoy a trip together, she asked her aunt if there was any other way to get into town. Bethany laughed and replied, "Liam goes every Thursday afternoon at two – you can set your clock by him."

Lisa-Marie sauntered casually up to the passenger side of the truck, "Hi Liam, mind if I catch a ride to town?"

Liam was already getting into the truck and replied, "Sure, no problem."

As they headed up the steep drive to the logging road, Lisa-Marie was surprised and relieved that Liam hadn't questioned her at all. No suspicious adult voice had asked, "Why do you want to go to town and does your aunt know where you are?"

As they rounded the end of the drive and started out on the gravel road, Liam turned to Lisa-Marie and said, "You're sixteen. You can drive, right?"

"Well, I had my learner's in Ontario for a month or so before . . . before I came out here but I've only ever driven my grannie's old Honda Civic."

Liam pulled the truck to the shoulder, put it in park and hopped out. He came around the front of the truck to the passenger side and opened her door, "Come on and give it a try then. This old truck isn't much different than a Honda Civic."

Lisa-Marie walked slowly over to the driver's side of the truck and got in as Liam settled in the passenger side. Her heart pounded as she put the truck in gear and tentatively gave it gas. She looked over to see Liam resting his head against the passenger window. His eyes were starting to close.

"I hardly got any sleep last night. Pearl ate something she shouldn't have and she was up howling and moaning like a baby half the night. Wake me up before we hit the pavement – OK?" After a moment's pause he mumbled, "Just watch the blind corners and keep to your own side of the road. Oh, Pearl is my dog if you were wondering," he added as he closed his eyes. Later Lisa-Marie would think Liam's letting her drive the truck was one of the coolest things she had ever seen an adult do.

When they got to town Liam pulled the truck over at an internet café place on the main street. He drove off telling her he would see her back there at five. Lisa-Marie went in, ordered a latte and found an empty computer. Pulling up the Facebook site she entered her password: cinnamon-girl. The guy she gave her virginity to – that pig Jason as she now always thought of him – had called her cinnamon-girl a couple of times when he was flirting with her over the veggie counter at Subway. She had been working there part-time – a summer job. The nickname stuck. She remembered everyone had been into retro-music that summer and the lyrics of Neil Young's song, by the same name, could still make her cringe.

Jason-the-pig was her shift supervisor. The whole first-time-sex-thing had been a letdown which was probably the understatement of the year. After closing one night, he had coaxed her into the walk-in storage locker. A few minutes of heavy petting found her sprawled out on a stack of pallets with her bra unhooked and her panties down around her ankles. The rest is history, as the saying goes. When it was over he looked pretty pleased with himself but he didn't look at her like she imagined a boyfriend would. That was what she thought the discomfort in the storage locker would mean – that he would be her boyfriend. Turned out he already had a girlfriend and Lisa-Marie came away from the encounter branded as the fifteen-year-old-trashy-little-lay-from-Subway.

Popping up to her home page, Lisa-Marie scanned through the status updates. She had a list of friends who had probably accepted her friend request by mistake and just hadn't bothered to drop her. She checked out comments made by friends of friends because most of the kids didn't bother with any privacy settings. She was looking for anything to do with her botched suicide. What she found were wildly exaggerated accounts containing totally false details. She had no idea where people got this stuff. She was relieved to see that the references to her were tapering off, the last one was posted over a week ago: *Too bad the slutty little skank didn't try a bit harder – LOL.*

Oh nice, real nice, Lisa-Marie thought. On the bright side, she guessed what people said about a person having only fifteen minutes of fame was really true. With school out now everyone was onto other topics of interest, the latest party or beach event, things more interesting than her failure to rid the earth of her useless self.

She spent the rest of her time in town wandering through the drugstore which carried an amazing assortment of stuff, browsing in a couple of tourist shops that displayed gorgeous things way out of Lisa-Marie's price range and ending at the thrift shop where she bought a flouncy peasant blouse – circa 1973 – for fifty cents. She was back at the cafe to meet Liam at five.

Lisa-Marie was far more comfortable driving the truck back on the logging road. Liam was awake this time and she was able to manage casual conversation as she manoeuvred around the curves. They switched over again for Liam to take the truck down the driveway. As Lisa-Marie hopped out and prepared to head back to the A-Frame she watched Liam load the chicken feed into the nearby wheel-barrow and then try to balance three bags of groceries on top of that. She walked over, wordlessly grabbed the groceries and nodded her head in the direction of his place. Liam smiled and started down the trail through the garden pushing the wheelbarrow.

"You didn't drink at the potluck thing the other night. How come?"

"I don't drink."

"How come?"

Liam shook his head slowly and shrugged, "Oh you know the old saying – one is never enough and two is always too many." Faced with Lisa-Marie's blank look, Liam added, "I've done my share of drinking – enough to last me a lifetime."

Lisa-Marie was quiet for a moment as she followed Liam on the trail and then she called out, "How come Beulah has such a crappy-ass attitude about you? She always calls you that freeloader who lives in Izzy's cabin."

Liam glanced back at her for a moment. He wondered if she was planning to rip open every wound he might have before they even got to the bridge. "I guess I saw something about her one time that she didn't want me to see."

Liam's answer reminded Lisa-Marie so powerfully of something that once happened to her that she stopped right in her tracks. They were coming down the hill to the bridge and Liam slowed down to pull back on the heavy wheelbarrow. If he hadn't almost stopped he would have been over the bridge and around the tree-enclosed corner on the other side, maybe wondering if she had decided to run away with his groceries or jump off the bridge. She got her footing and hurried to catch up. "Something like that happened to me once," she blurted out as she slowed down behind Liam.

Liam stopped halfway across the bridge and edged the wheelbarrow close to the side. He parked it and leaned casually on the rail looking up at the tumbling stream. There had been rain the night before and the stream was summer-swollen. Lisa-Marie stopped beside him. "It's a nice view from here," Liam commented quietly, then he went on, "So?"

"So what?"

Liam continued to look up at the rushing water, "So what happened to you."

Lisa-Marie was surprised that he would want to know, taken aback again as she had been in the truck earlier when Liam didn't ask her any questions about wanting to go to town and when he offered to let her drive the truck and then fell asleep. Liam was not like other adults she had known. "Ya, well, OK . . . are you sure?"

"I wouldn't ask if I didn't want to hear and I guess you wouldn't have mentioned it if you didn't want to say."

iii.

The summer before Lisa-Marie started grade eight, the taxes and upkeep on Grannie's old house got to be too much for her. They had moved to a small trailer in a crappy trailer park in an equally crappy part of the city. Lisa-Marie ended up in a high school where she didn't know anyone. The first day of classes she was hopelessly lost in every way that a kid could possibly be lost. She was in the crowded, second-floor hallway trying to juggle books, binders, a time table and map. The bell rang and the hallway emptied rapidly with her no closer to finding her way.

She was standing in a small alcove by the water fountain when she heard voices just across the hall. It quickly became obvious to her that a girl, who looked about her age, was in the process of being dumped by an older guy and she was taking it hard – crying and clutching onto his sleeve. Lisa-Marie saw the guy jerk his arm away. As he walked down the hall she heard him tell the girl in a cold tone to grow up.

Lisa-Marie stood staring like she was watching a train wreck; she couldn't drag her eyes away from the carnage. It was the moment when the girl, alone now, her mascara tracking down her cheeks in two blackened rivulets, looked up and locked eyes with Lisa-Marie that was the powerful memory Liam's words had evoked. Lisa-Marie knew in that moment she would live to regret hearing what she heard and seeing what she saw.

iv.

Lisa-Marie watched the water tumbling down the hill and rushing under the small bridge and whooshed out her breath in resignation before wrapping up her story, "Well . . . that girl turned out to be one of the really popular girls. From that day on her and her friends made my life pure hell."

Liam's eyes had been on the stream the whole time Lisa-Marie was telling her story. He glanced sideways when she was silent for a moment, "It wasn't really about you at all though, was it?" These words, said so simply and with such compassion, caused Lisa-Marie's throat to go dry and she swallowed painfully.

A few minutes later, toting the grocery bags into Liam's place, Lisa-Marie met Pearl and it was love at first sight. Throwing herself on the worn-smooth boards that made up Liam's floor she buried her face in the warmth of Pearl's golden coat and Pearl responded by writhing about like a pup, finally showing her belly for a rub.

Lisa-Marie refused Liam's offer of tea – only old people drank tea – and wandered through the garden on her way back to the A-Frame for dinner. The late afternoon sun was creating wonderful shadow effects and deepening the colours that ran riot throughout the garden, spilling out and overflowing the beds and planters like so many cans of paint tipped over at random. Once again Lisa-Marie wished she could capture the photos she was composing in her mind.

She wandered close by the vegetable bed where Justin had been working earlier that afternoon. The ground was freshly dug around the plants and the smell of the rich, dark soil was everywhere. At that moment the automatically timed sprinkler flipped on and Lisa-Marie was caught in the garden path with the fine spray of water falling down all around her. Standing with her arms outstretched she twirled around and around, caught in the garden's spell. She lifted her head and let the water fall on her face. Liam's words came back to her as she spun with carefree joy on the garden path. She wondered if what he said could be true. Could all of it really not have been about her at all?

V.

Coming out of the tool shed, dusting the dirt from her gloves, Izzy saw Lisa-Marie twirling under the shower of the sprinkler and she moved back into the dark, cool interior of the shed. She caught her breath at the sight of Lisa-Marie's uninhibited joy. She was young and beautiful and all of a sudden Izzy felt old and worn out. Long after Lisa-Marie whirled around a final time, laughing with her head thrown back in the cool spray, Izzy stood leaning against the door jamb lost in a memory of the past.

She remembered how she and Caleb were caught out here in the garden in a pelting summer rain storm. She was on her knees weeding and Caleb was digging over a bed getting it ready for a successive planting of something. The dark clouds rolled in quickly and a powerful clap of thunder barely preceded the downpour. Izzy jumped up, tearing off her gloves, ready to make a dash for the main cabin but Caleb hung back revelling in the sudden storm.

He grabbed her playfully and twirled her around in the drenching rain. "Izzy, do you know how sexy you look in the rain?"

She pushed him away, laughing now too. He chased her up and down the garden paths and grabbed her at last in a strong embrace. Caleb kissed her with a passion that weakened her knees and set her entire body trembling. He carried her to the shelter of the tool shed and leaning back against the door jamb where she now stood, she had pulled frantically at the front of his pants and shimmied out of her own.

Afterwards, Caleb held her up gently against the door frame gasping slightly to get his breath, "I don't know how you do this to me, Izzy, but promise you'll never stop, OK?"

Her face was buried in the collar of his work shirt and at that moment she knew, with an overwhelming clarity, that she loved Caleb completely. A thousand things she wanted to say to him raced through her mind – Can't you see? You do the same thing to me. Do you know how much I love you? I've never loved anyone like this before. Don't ever leave me. But she didn't say anything. She just held onto Caleb tightly while her tears slowly and steadily soaked into the collar of his shirt and he simply accepted whatever that homage might mean.

Izzy closed the door of the tool shed and walked through the garden to the main cabin. For all its open-door-policy it was often, like now, empty. She wondered how she could ever have wanted more than what she had.

CHAPTER FOURTEEN

i.

Dear Emma:

Here is another truth about me. I was the most unpopular girl in my whole high school. I didn't have one single friend. Maybe you think I'm exaggerating, but I'm not. There was a girl in my class who chewed her hair and wore old-lady, flowered dresses that came right down to her ankles. Even she had one friend.

It was mostly the other girls. They called me crappy names every single time they saw me. My hair was stringy or greasy; my clothes were always wrong – too loose, too tight, too old, too new. I was fat, I was ugly, I had a pimply face, I looked like a slut – you name it, they said it.

They were always pushing me around – in the hallways, on the stairs, waiting for the bus – I can't even bear to tell you what the bus rides were like. They stole my stuff, they wrote horrible things on my locker, they wrote awful comments on my Facebook page, and sometimes they even phoned me at home to call me names. And they got the guys to do awful stuff too. But worst of all – they made sure no one ever talked to me. Everyone told lies about me until I started making the lies come true. But like I told you, Emma – I never cried – not even once. They never made me cry.

I told Liam a bit about this. He said – It was never really about you at all, was it? I felt like crying when he said that, but of course I didn't. I get feeling way too sad when I think about this stuff.

Liam let me drive his truck – can you believe that? It was so cool! He says I can go to town with him every Thursday and drive the truck on the gravel road. I helped him carry his groceries to his cabin and he has the best dog ever – her name is Pearl. I don't get why Beulah hates Liam – he's really nice. He listens to me when I talk – not in a worried way like Auntie Beth. He listens like he really cares about what I have to say.

i i .

Justin looked up from spreading bark mulch over a bed of rose bushes. He was being careful to avoid the thorns as he reached under with the rake, pushing the thick mulch around the base of each bush. He heard Lisa-Marie calling out hello and saw her waving as she cut across the garden. She was carrying a large blue bucket in one hand with bright yellow rubber gloves draped over the edge and a variety of spray-top, plastic bottles peeking out from within. She had an iPod in the other hand, its thin cord around her neck. He hoped she wouldn't want to talk because he had a lot of things to do before Liam came over to help repair the wisteria trellis. After his swim with Lisa-Marie the other day he knew she could really fill up time talking.

Thankfully she stopped for only a moment, "Want to swim later when I finish the cleaning at Dan's?"

He had been able to manage a simple nod and get back to work. As he swivelled around to the wheelbarrow for another shovel of mulch, Justin's thoughts were all of Izzy and how she had looked the other afternoon relaxing in a deck chair with a glass of wine in hand, talking about one garden chore after another. Her loose shirt, open at the neck, revealed the top edge of her tanned breasts whenever she leaned forward and the steady clinking and movement of the silver medallions around her neck drew his eye exactly where he wanted and didn't want to look. He was stretched out on the lounge chair with a cold beer in his hand, his arm thrown back to shade his eyes as he listened to Izzy speak. Every moment he spent with her had been a painful combination of pleasure and longing edged with discomfort.

He missed being close to Izzy so he couldn't pass up an invitation to stop by and share a drink with her and talk, even if it was about the garden and work – even though the jumbled mess of his feelings kept him wound-up in a knot of anxiety whenever he was alone with her. She seemed to want them to chat together like equals. But she was his boss and even if she weren't, they could never be equals after what had happened in the counselling sessions.

She had seen him when he was drowning in painful memories of the past and feeling so raw it was as if he had to regrow his own skin. He had needed her acceptance so desperately then; he knew that he could never see them as equals now.

He shoveled and spread the mulch with quick, aggressive movements. All he had to do was hang on a few more weeks. When he left here the fucking, emotional roller-coaster he was on would grind to a halt – distance would solve everything. But for now, there was one thing he did know – laughing and joking with Izzy like a friend was only making things worse for him.

iii.

Arriving at Dan's cabin, still congratulating herself on arranging the swimming time with Justin, Lisa-Marie tried the sliding-glass door and found it open. Going in she took a look around and quickly opened all the windows to counteract the gathering heat. She didn't think the cleaning was going to take two hours. Dan seemed like a tidy guy. The kitchen looked like it hadn't been used at all. The flashlight collection on the counter seemed a bit odd. Why did one guy need so many flashlights? A quick wipe around, a bit more time with the bathroom, a small amount of dusting, a sweep of the broom over the hardwood floor and that would be that.

As she ran the dusting cloth over the small bookshelf in the living room, Lisa-Marie noticed a box on the top shelf. She pulled it down to dust around it and her eyes widened. The box, which looked brand new, appeared to contain a digital camera. She turned the box slowly, reading about the features of the camera and her fingers were actually twitching. She peeked carefully under the flap to make sure something else had not been packed in the box for safekeeping.

What she saw was a digital camera to take her breath away. She had used a slightly older model of this very camera in school and it was a dream to work with. Anyone could manage to take good shots on the automatic setting, while the programmable features offered a bit more of a challenge and the opportunity to do semi-professional photography.

Lisa-Marie couldn't figure out why Dan hadn't taken the camera out. Taped to the top side of the box was an envelope, the flap facing out and wide

114

open. Lisa-Marie looked out the window quickly to make sure no one else was around and then she removed the small card.

To Father Dan: enjoy your sabbatical. We hope this camera will come in handy to record your travels. Best wishes. We can't wait to have you back and really get to know you. St. Michael's Parish.

Sliding the card back in the envelope, Lisa-Marie dusted the shelf where the box had sat and returned it to its place. The note answered one of her questions. The camera did belong to Dan, but why on earth wasn't he using it?

Hanging out in the garden waiting for Justin and Liam to finish working on a broken trellis that contained a mass of twisted vines, Lisa-Marie couldn't get the camera out of her mind. Everywhere she looked she saw angles and shots she would love to have captured.

iv.

Dear Emma:

Justin asked me to come over to the Camp tonight to watch a movie. That's almost like a real date – don't you think? I've got to wash my hair and straighten it and find something hot to wear, something to make me look older and cool. He's sure to walk me home – maybe he will hold my hand. Anything could happen – maybe he will kiss me goodnight. Oh my God – my hand is shaking – I'd better go. Wish me luck, Emma.

v.

Dan and Beulah were lounging on the veranda of the A-Frame, beer cans in hand, waiting for Bethany to call them in for dinner. When he and Bethany came in from their second time out fishing together in as many days, Beulah invited Dan to eat with them and he readily agreed. He grabbed the local paper Beulah had brought home from town and was casually flipping through the pages.

Sitting forward suddenly he spread the paper on the table in front of Beulah and said, "Hey, look at this." He was pointing to a half-page spread of the local ball field's summer schedule. The ball field was in use most nights of the week – men's fast ball, mixed leagues, women's softball, little league and even t-ball for preschoolers. "Let's go to town one night and see a game," Dan urged Beulah. He studied the schedule and pointed at random to the following Tuesday night when the men's fastball team, the Desert Rats, was playing the Beer Belly Sluggers. "How about this one?"

Beulah frowned, "It's just the local beer league. Are you sure?"

Dan waved her comment away with his hand, "Any baseball game is worth the effort. What do you say?"

"Well, I suppose it's doable." As she agreed, Beulah found herself thinking it might be good to see the old ball diamond again.

Inside the A-Frame, Lisa-Marie was dishing up squares of thick, cheese-filled lasagne while her Auntie Beth heaped caesar salad into bowls and pulled garlic bread from the oven. As they all gathered around the kitchen table, Dan chatted comfortably about how great the fishing was. He also asked Lisa-Marie all kinds of questions about her work at the Camp. He acted like he had known all of them forever and his relaxed demeanour made everyone comfortable. Dan was super easy to have around.

He covered his disappointment well when he tried to convince Bethany to come to town for the ball game and she refused, "I can't go on Tuesday, that's the night Izzy, Liam and I play Scrabble." Beulah rolled her eyes when Liam's name was mentioned. Dan cursed his luck for randomly picking a Tuesday.

After dinner, Dan helped Lisa-Marie dry the dishes that Beulah was washing and rinsing in what looked like boiling water. On her first day at the A-Frame, Lisa-Marie had innocently grabbed a towel from a bar near the counter and started drying dishes only to have Beulah pull the cloth quickly from her hand. "That is a hand towel. We do not dry dishes with a hand towel. Tea-towels are in the drawer. Use a new one every time and change to a second before you do the pots." Beulah had a real thing for how the dishes should be done.

"Hey Dan," Lisa-Marie said as she reached around him to grab a plate from the dish drainer, "While I was cleaning at your place this afternoon . . . dusting the book shelves . . . I noticed you have a great digital camera that you haven't even taken out of the box. How come?"

Dan was completely distracted by Bethany as she bent over to dig in a lower cupboard for a plastic, leftover container. He had raved about the lasagna so much during dinner that of course Bethany had offered to parcel it up for his lunch the following day.

Lisa-Marie punched him lightly on the arm and said, "Earth calling Dan, Earth calling Dan." When she finally got his attention, she repeated her query about the camera.

Dan shrugged, "Oh right, the camera –," he grimaced slightly, "– it was a gift from my parish when I left."

Lisa-Marie tried to act surprised about the gift part while regaling Dan about all the great features of the camera, how it was a breeze to use and how it took the best pictures. She told him he really should get it out of the box and give it a try.

"I looked at the box and the camera seems pretty complicated. I don't suppose I'll get much use out of it. I'm not that interested in taking pictures."

Before she could stop herself Lisa-Marie asked Dan in a rush of words, "Could I use it if you aren't going to?"

Beulah frowned at Lisa-Marie and turned to Bethany to ask, "Do you think Dan should lend a brand new, expensive camera to this irresponsible teenager who has been rude enough to put him on the spot by asking?"

Bethany looked up and appeared startled by Beulah's question. Lisa-Marie couldn't figure out if Beulah was serious or just trying to give her a hard time. She couldn't always tell the difference with Beulah.

Bethany glared over at Beulah, "Don't call Lisa irresponsible and she isn't rude either."

Wanting to be on the same side as Bethany and having no attachment to the camera, Dan told Lisa-Marie he had no problem letting her borrow it for as long as she wanted.

Beulah shook her head and walked away from the sparkling sink she had just scoured within an inch of its stainless steel life. "A fool and his expensive toys are soon parted, Dan old buddy."

CHAPTER FIFTEEN

i.

Jesse was waiting for the dinner bell to sound. He had started to enjoy himself at Micah Camp. If what he had seen so far was any indication, the next year was going to be like an extended vacation for him. He had open access to the computer lab with machines high-powered enough to enable him to work on any project he might imagine. He was trying to get the last few glitches out of a computer game module he had designed. He wanted to send it along as an example of what he could do when he applied to some undergrad programs in Computing Science. He hoped to let some companies in the States see it, as well. If he could skip right over the whole post-secondary step it would be all the better for him.

Open access to the computers also allowed Jesse time to download, crack and copy to his heart's content. That certainly increased his popularity with the other residents. The sessions with Izzy were a joke. She was a pushover and pretty easy on the eyes with her older woman, dark-haired, good looks. It wouldn't be much of a challenge to string her along through as many little walks on the Camp trails as she wanted to take. Caging a few random looks at her tits now and then was an added bonus. She had a great set of tits.

Today she had asked if he was interested in any part-time work – maybe something on the woodlot above the Camp or at the sawmill. He turned that down flat. What did she take him for anyway – a labourer? He had no intention of working any harder than he had to and tromping around the woods with a chainsaw, under the direction of that Indian dude, was not his idea of a good time. If he actually had to do any work outside the computer lab he would stick with the paper and soap business. Josie was another pushover and he already had Maddy figured out; with that glint in her eye she had to know a thing or two that would be worth exploring. And that cute chick from next door, Lisa-Marie, with her tight tops and skimpy shorts was a real sweet little piece. She'd been around the block more than once or twice. He could always tell that sort of thing.

ii.

Izzy was not a fan of having dinner at the Camp but with a session booked for six o'clock and the staff meeting running late, she wouldn't be able to get home to eat. The meeting ran late because Roland bogged things down endlessly with his trivial nitpicking. He had actually asked for a show of hands as to whether people preferred flat or textured paper clips. She couldn't even bear to think about how dull his power point presentation had been – an overview of his binder on trackable, counselling outcomes – the unopened binder she had hidden in the lower drawer of her desk.

Leaving her office with a tension headache, she saw Justin coming down the hall toward the dining room in answer to the dinner bell. As they fell into step together, Izzy asked anxiously, "How did the work on the trellis go?"

A trellis in the greenhouse garden had collapsed under the weight of one of the older wisteria vines. Izzy had discovered it just that morning and had waylaid Justin before he started work to tell him that Liam would help him with the repairs that afternoon. The trellis had to be rebuilt and strengthened but Izzy wanted it done with no risk to the wisteria. She knew the job was a challenging one.

Justin smiled down at her tousled black curls and her concern. God, he thought, how can she always look so perfect? "Well, it was a bit tricky at times but I think we steered clear of any real damage to the main stock. We lost a few side branches but you said you thought that might happen. I'll probably have nightmares about being strangled by the monster but it will live to bloom another day. Are you staying for dinner?"

Izzy had turned down the hall toward the dining room with him. She smiled at the nightmare comment but was grateful Justin took the whole thing seriously. She loved the wisteria and it had taken years to get it to bloom. "Yes, I've got an appointment at six."

Justin moved ahead to open the dining room door for Izzy. "Roland says the maintenance guys saw a bear with a couple of cubs the other day. I'll meet you at your office when you're done and walk you back."

Izzy smiled her thanks. She knew she should tell Justin that walking her home wasn't necessary. She had walked the trail between the Camp and the main cabin for years without any kind of an escort – at all times of the day and night, through all seasons of the year and she'd never thought twice about it. But she didn't say anything.

The afternoon light from the upper windows in the dining room was filtering in and Izzy laughed and chatted easily with Justin as they moved along the food line toward the huge pans of meatloaf, home fries and corn on the cob. The honey-blonde of his hair was glowing and the warmth of his eyes, when he smiled at her, lit up his face. Her headache had vanished.

Jesse was already at his table. His loaded tray had drawn a sharp glance from Cook. She had gone as far as to point at her own eyes with two fingers of her right hand and then point those same fingers at him, as if to say that she had her eyes on him. He snorted as he walked away. As if he was afraid of her five-feet-nothing; she could keep her eyes on him all she wanted. Jesse dug into his extra-large helping of meatloaf and fries. He had to admit – the food here was good.

He glanced up and saw Izzy in the food line laughing in response to something Justin was saying to her. He watched both of them for a moment before he returned his attention to his plate. Jesse had survived much of his life by being extremely observant. Vigilance was second nature to him and many times he had only well-honed observations to help him side-step being slammed against a wall, pushed down a staircase or thumped in the head. It was important to know what other people wanted even before they knew it themselves. That way he could stay one step ahead of the game.

It was clear from day one that Justin was the resident star at Micah Camp, the big success story; it seemed everything the guy did turned to gold. He saw the way golden boy's attention was drawn to Izzy. Justin's face and his drooling-dog look were worth noting. It brought Justin down to where Jesse wanted him. But of much more interest, was how much Izzy liked the way golden boy grovelled at the foot of her pedestal. Well, well, well, he thought, that is worth keeping in mind. Careful observation often exposed another person's weakness and knowing a thing like that, in Jesse's opinion, was always helpful.

Dipping a large forkful of home fries into the ketchup that smeared the side of his plate, Jesse saw Maddy coming across the dining area and he smiled broadly and motioned her over to the spot across from him.

"God, Jesse . . . are you in training for something?" She gestured toward his overflowing plate as she slid her own tray onto the table and pulled out a chair.

"Have to keep my strength up," he winked at her and casually pulled a DVD from his pack on the chair beside him, "Here's the movie you were talking about the other day."

"Wow, thanks." Maddy's eyes were wide as she studied the carefully printed black letters on the DVD. "I seriously didn't think you could get this. You're the real thing, hey – computer geek and all that," Maddy raked her long fingers through her purple hair and studied Jesse carefully.

"I prefer the word genius to geek, but ya . . . I'm the real thing. It's just one of my talents," he added as he reached across the table, brushed his fingers lightly down the edge of Maddy's shirt and lifted the gold chain she was wearing around her neck. He inspected the tiny cross that dangled at the end. "What do we have here, Maddy –," he teased, "– are you a good little Christian girl or do you like to come out and play sometimes? I could show you the other talents I have . . . if you're interested."

He dropped the chain and let his fingers linger on her neck for a moment. Maddy knocked his hand away and said, "I'm really sure you get laid every day with that line." The feel of Jesse's touch had made her shiver down to her toes and when her eyes met his she could tell he knew it. She wasn't sure whether to throw her dinner plate at his smirking face or arrange then and there to hook up with him later.

i i i .

Dear Emma:

Oh my God – Emma – I have three huge things to tell you. OK – first – movie night at the Camp with Justin – it was so much fun. Justin came here to get me – just like a real date! We walked to the Camp and he sat right beside me for the whole movie!! He was so close I could feel his arm brushing against mine. I thought I would die every time that happened. He got me a Coke and we shared a bowl of popcorn. And then he walked me home and said goodnight in such a sweet way – he ruffled my hair and said – see you, Leez. He always calls me Leez. Cute – hey? I like him so much – I just can't believe a guy like him wants to be around me.

I know you can hardly believe things are so great for me but listen to the second thing – I think I've made a friend. I'll have to wait a bit to see if it's really true. Her name is Maddy and she lives at Micah Camp. She works in the paper and soap shop with me. She's funny – always telling jokes and stuff.

Here is my last big piece of news for the night, Emma. Dan is going to let me use his camera. He says I can borrow it for as long as I want. I'm going to go over and pick it up tomorrow. I can hardly wait to be taking pictures again.

CHAPTER SIXTEEN

i.

Calling out Liam's name as she knocked, Izzy opened the door to his cabin and went in. Pearl was on her feet, tail wagging the moment she heard Izzy's voice. Dante rushed through the door past Izzy. In her attempts to get out of Dante and Pearl's way, amid their frisking and barking, she didn't see the bathroom door open. She caught sight of Liam emerging from the tiny room in the back. His hands were working to wrap a towel snugly around his naked hips. Izzy recognized the towel as an old one she had gotten rid of and it was more threadbare now. He was shaking water out of his left ear and his straight, black hair was hanging free and wet over his shoulder. "Pearl, what in the hell are you barking like that for," he said before he noticed Izzy standing in the doorway with the two dogs circling her wildly.

Izzy was not particularly embarrassed by half-naked men. Years of living with Caleb, who lacked even the most rudimentary form of inhibition, had worn her down. He would prance around the cabin in a state of undress with an abundance of blonde, curly hair on display. But the sight of Liam's almost hairless, deep-brown chest had Izzy staring a moment longer than was comfortable. A thin line of the darkest black hair twisted and ran down from his navel to disappear below the knotted towel. She raised her eyes to meet Liam's a second before she threw her hands up and turned away, "Oh my God . . . Liam . . . sorry . . . sorry. I should have called out sooner."

Liam shrugged and smiled slightly at Izzy's discomfort. "No worries, Izzy. Stay, sit down. Give me a minute here to throw on some clothes and then we can have some tea."

Izzy sat down at the kitchen table. It was hard to believe that this was the first time she had been to Liam's cabin since Caleb died. She and Caleb used to stop by and have tea with Liam all the time. She would sit back in the rocker by the fire, drink her tea and watch Caleb and Liam at the table. She enjoyed the way Liam's dark silence provided such an excellent foil to Caleb's easy-going bravado. Odd as it seemed, there was a bond between them from the very start. At one time, Izzy thought she had it figured out – Liam was like all of the movie-star Indians she'd ever seen, rolled neatly into one darkly proud and brooding package; Caleb was the US Calvary, blazing ahead with colours flying. Caleb dragged Liam forward and Liam held Caleb back and the push and pull fit the two of them perfectly.

An eagle swooping down towards the rippling surface of the lake caught Izzy's attention and brought her back to a world where Caleb's presence no longer held sway. She sighed. As she watched the eagle's progress, its talons scraping along the edge of the water, she remembered how she had always enjoyed the view from Liam's kitchen table. His cabin was perched further out on the cliff than any of the other places and when she sat at the table in front of the large window it seemed almost as though she was floating above the water.

The rest of the cabin was mostly one big room. A small kitchen area wrapped around one corner where a window looked out onto the boardwalk and up the path to the road. A wood-burning stove stood near the back of the room with an old wooden rocker pulled up in front – another castoff from the main cabin. A small sofa sat against the back wall between two doors, one of which led to the bathroom and the other to a storage area. In the far corner Izzy could see the bottom step of the steep staircase that led to the sleeping loft above. The cabin was not fancy, by any means, but Liam's place was tidy and pleasant.

Liam came out of the storage room buckling his belt with his hair still wet and loose down his back. Izzy ran her gaze over him and she realized that Bethany was right; Liam was losing weight. His belt was cinched to a tighter notch.

Liam filled the kettle and set it on the small stove. Izzy saw him reach for the worn tin of Earl Grey tea from the same spot on the counter where it had always sat. Though she hadn't been here in almost two years, the simple fact that *her* tin of tea was still in the same place made a lump rise in her throat and she swallowed hard. The first couple of times she had been to Liam's cabin she had accepted cups of his home-brewed, herbal teas. But no matter what she had sampled, they had all smelled slightly of compost and tasted like hay. On her third visit Izzy had brought over the tin of Earl Grey.

As soon as the tea was poured, Izzy broached her reason for stopping by, "I've been thinking, Liam, that I want to go through the boxes of stuff we packed away after –," her voice suddenly caught and she took a deep breath before continuing, "– the accident . . . Caleb's stuff." She looked over in time to see a stab of pain pass over Liam's face. Caleb's death was still a deep wound for all of them. It had scabbed over in various ways but it still hurt like hell. They couldn't talk to each other about how they felt so the wound festered and the poison worked its way around and around.

Gripping her mug with both hands and staring down into the amber liquid, Izzy continued, "I just thought maybe it was time. I couldn't face it before but it's been almost two years now. I was thinking that I might give Caleb's old gold watch to Justin as a going away, good luck gift." She looked up at Liam suddenly, "Remember how Caleb always said that watch brought him luck?" Liam's face was touched again with a sadness that hit Izzy like a physical blow. She inhaled sharply, stared back down at the table and blinked her eyes rapidly to stem the sudden rise of tears.

Liam was caught up in a skein of thoughts related to Caleb's watch; by pulling one string, Izzy had set the ball in motion. Now it was unravelling wildly all around him. Caleb had told him once that he got the watch – a Rolex – for a graduation gift from his family. He had joked to Liam about how much the watch was worth on the current market. "The thing turned into some sort of special edition model because Steve McQueen had one."

Liam had raised his eyebrows in disbelief that anyone would pay that much money for a watch and Caleb had warned him sternly, "Not a word to Izzy about this. If she had any idea we could buy a mid-sized car for what this watch is worth, she'd tell me not to wear it to work . . . and that's just ridiculous. A watch is for telling time, not for show . . . besides, this watch is lucky." Caleb had grinned over at Liam. "I was wearing this watch one night when I walked away from a serious car crash on the coast highway." Caleb had stared at the watch for a moment and then said, "Rites of passage, man. Sure makes for a good story to tell your grandkids someday. If you survive, that is."

Yes, Liam thought now, glancing up at Izzy sitting across from him; survival was the thing. He certainly did remember how Caleb always said that old watch brought him luck. But it hadn't brought him any luck that last day on the woodlot. It was on his left wrist the way it always was when they took him away.

Izzy was about to leave with both dogs to continue her walk. She and Liam had arranged a time to meet at the workshop to haul out the boxes. She stopped at the door to turn back to Liam for a moment, "Do you ever hear that one wolf howling at night, Liam?" He shook his head and Izzy pulled a face, "It's driving me crazy. There's something spooky about the sound of a single wolf howling." With a shrug she called the two dogs to her and headed off down the path.

i i .

Liam sat in the chair in front of the cold stove, rocking back and forth, lost in thought. Liam, Beulah and Caleb had been up at the woodlot with a friend of Caleb's from town – Johnny Walker. "I swear to God, that's his real name," Caleb told people, laughing every time he introduced Johnny.

It was a clear, crisp day in early October. They worked steadily, chainsaws whining loudly and spewing clouds of white exhaust into the fall air. The trees snapped as they fell to the forest floor. The only time they stopped was to eat a quick lunch.

Around three o'clock a wind started up in the hills and came whistling and whipping over the woodlot. Caleb hollered to them to get moving; it was time to head out of the trees. Liam remembered clearly that Caleb was out ahead on the trail packing two of the chainsaws. He could still see Caleb's particular gait – a sort of rolling-the-shoulder-forward walk – as he made his way in the lead, laughing and shouting back at them to pick up the pace. That was Caleb, always out in front, drawing them all forward, blazing the way.

The cracking sound of a huge snag on the hill brought everyone up short. What came next took place faster than Liam could remember anything in his life ever happening. The snag hit a large rock scree and dislodged a boulder that came tumbling out of nowhere down the hill. It slammed into Caleb, pinning him against a tree trunk on the other side of the narrow trail. Johnny made a dash for the ATV to get down to the cabin and a phone but they all knew they were at least fifteen minutes from where it was parked.

It was obvious to Liam, from the moment he took a close look at Caleb that he wasn't going to make it. He had to have sustained massive internal injuries and most of his body was crushed up against the tree to which the boulder had pinned him. They couldn't move it and they couldn't move him. His face was untouched by injury and though he was still conscious, Caleb was in shock. In the short time he had left to live he was probably spared most of the pain and he was more lucid than Liam thought possible.

For the first few minutes Caleb wanted to review with Liam various emergency measures from the first-aid course they had recently taken together. He asked several times about who was going for help, forgetting each time what Liam told him. Then he became very focused on Liam's face and asked, "I'm not going to make it, am I man?" Liam shook his head wordlessly and Caleb clutched hard to his hand.

Beulah was behind Caleb stabilizing his head, mostly because she needed to be doing something. Caleb wasn't going anywhere. At Liam's gesture she cursed loudly, "Fuck sakes, Liam, don't tell him that. Listen to me Caleb, listen . . . you are going to hang on and you are going to stay alive until they get a chopper in here, do you hear me? You stay with us, Caleb. Do you hear me? You keep your eyes open and you stay with us." It was as if Beulah thought she could keep Caleb alive by the very force and tone of her voice.

Caleb smiled, trying to look back and up at her, "Ya . . . OK Beulah . . . whatever you say, woman. A wee shot would go down good now, hey? Did either of you see my flask?" He looked as if he might try to reach his one good arm toward the place where his back pocket must have been. "Ah shit . . . forget it," he sighed.

Beulah let go of his head and slid into his line of vision beside Liam. Caleb caught sight of her and said, "You've been a fine friend, Beulah . . . I thank you for that." His voice was fading and he struggled to get the next words out, "The Timber Wolves wouldn't have been much of anything without your pitching."

His gaze turned to Liam and he held tight to his hand. "You're my brother, man. Remember that. Never leave this place . . . Liam. Like I told you before . . . you belong here. Promise me that." Caleb waited to see Liam nod before gasping out, "Take care of Izzy . . . she won't think she needs it but you guys will know what to do."

Caleb's breath was laboured for a moment or two and his eyes were far way. He sucked in air with a gurgling sound, then in a low, strained voice he whispered, "I still remember exactly how she looked the first time I saw her on the road. I feel pretty tired . . . think I'll just rest a bit. God . . . what I wouldn't give to hold Izzy just one more time."

They waited a few more moments in silence but Caleb hadn't said anything else. His passing seemed peaceful enough considering the wreck his body had become. When Beulah was hit by the realization that Caleb was gone, she tried to push Liam aside. "Get the hell out of my way, Liam. We've got to try something else. Do some CPR, for God sakes, Liam . . . you're wasting time, Jesus Christ . . . let me go," she was pushing wildly and struggling to release Liam's hold on her. "Try to move the rock again; Liam . . . come on . . . we've got to try." Liam just held her back.

Then Beulah, who never showed a sign of weakness, buckled over and began to sob in a way that was unbearable to witness. Liam had not said a single word the whole time and though pain was in every line of his face, Beulah didn't see it as pain. She saw someone who had given up, someone who didn't break down. She needed to hate someone very badly at that moment. The fact that Liam had witnessed Beulah's breakdown was only more fuel for the fire.

She looked at Liam with a coldness he remembered now even more than the agony of watching Caleb slip away from them, "You bastard, you let him die." She turned her back on Liam that day and had not spoken a kind word to him since.

Liam rocked slowly back and forth. The morning sunlight sparkled off the white caps on the lake making it seem like a sea of diamonds. He closed his eyes against the glare and he could see the white sheet drawn up over Caleb's face, the gold watch gleaming on his exposed wrist as the air ambulance guys lifted the stretcher into the helicopter.

CHAPTER SEVENTEEN

i.

"OK Maddy, tell me five things you can see right now." Izzy watched Maddy shake her head a bit and start to look around the office.

"I see the flowers," she began. Her voice came out small and tremulous. "I see the candlelight," she added with more control. "I see out the window to the lake," she was leaning forward in her chair now. "Someone's swimming out there. I see the smiling Buddha statue on your book shelf." Maddy sat up a bit straighter and her voice was no longer shaking, "And I see you Izzy, right where you always are."

"Great Maddy, tell me five things you can hear right now." Izzy was leading Maddy gently through a grounding exercise. Maddy had already listed five things she could see. After identifying five things she could hear, she would be asked to describe five things she could feel. Before the exercise finished, Izzy would guide Maddy through the same sequence of seeing, hearing and feeling things in sets of four, three, two and one.

"I see you Izzy. I hear your voice. I feel my feet on the ground," Maddy sat back in her chair and continued quietly, "I always knew I hated him ... nothing new there for sure. But I never knew how angry I've been with her. I feel like I hate her too and she's my own mother for frig sakes. But she should have believed me; she should have kept him away from me. She should have kept me safe ... that was her job."

The session had begun with Maddy choosing an image from the large tray of cut-out magazine pictures Izzy kept in her office; it was an almost pornographic shot of a nearly naked young woman bound and gagged on the floor with a man standing over her. Izzy remembered the image being used in an advertisement for perfume. Maddy laid the picture on the table in front of her. After reviewing all of the strategies she and Izzy had devised for not becoming overwhelmed while working with trauma memories, Maddy spoke of a time in her life when she was twelve. Her Grandfather was sexually abusing her on a regular basis and she tried and tried to tell her mother, all to no avail.

The work Izzy did was a delicate dance. She carefully guided clients to a place where they could touch on a painful memory from the vantage point of distance and strength. The intention of the work was to have a client come back to their present reality without being re-traumatized or overwhelmed by the memory; to come back to the present with insight or a resolution of some kind. This type of trauma work meant not only ensuring Maddy's emotional safety in the session but afterwards as well.

Izzy could see now, watching the play of emotions across Maddy's face, that though she was sad and angry, the insight she had gained about her feelings toward her mother was an important discovery. Maddy could now begin to explore how that resentment might be guiding some of her current behaviours.

"You've had the courage to talk about a painful time in your life, Maddy. It's normal to resent and even hate the actual abuser . . . but for a child there is always another question. Where were the people who should have kept me safe?" Izzy reached out to rub Maddy's arm, "Could you imagine having the kind of courage it takes to ask that question when we first started working together?"

"No. I never thought I'd be able to even think about any of this stuff let alone talk about it, but I can handle more and more now. I get that my anger toward my mom is probably more important than how I'd like to kick that dirty old goat's balls half way up his throat." Maddy made a face and then glanced nervously up at the clock, "I know the session is just about over but, Izzy . . . how will I ever be able to have kids of my own and be normal like other people? I'm bound to end up just like her, aren't I? Isn't that how things work out in this shitty world? Didn't she act that way to me because he had abused her, too? Probably her mom didn't care or protect her either." Tears appeared in Maddy's eyes and spilled down her cheeks. She reached for the magazine photo that sat on the table and tore it into tiny pieces.

"Maddy take a deep breath, OK?" Izzy waited for Maddy to respond, "And again, and one more." Maddy's shoulders slumped and she sat back in the chair, calming down. As the tears slowed, Izzy reached across the space between them and placed her hands over Maddy's, which were still clutching the ripped bits of the picture.

"Those are normal questions Maddy . . . good questions and it's OK to be afraid. I don't believe that any of our lives are so completely dictated by the past. Each and every day we have a chance to write a new chapter of our story. I don't think for a second that you have to turn out just like your mother." It was Izzy's job to hold out hope for her clients when they weren't quite there themselves and she did it with sincerity and conviction.

Maddy nodded, wiped the tears from her face and glanced at the clock again. She straightened in her chair, "OK – my grounding stuff review." She held up her hand and ticked off her fingers as she recalled her strategies, "Do five, four, three, two, one if I feel like I am falling back into the memories, do it again if the first time doesn't help. If that doesn't work, I'll use the relaxation tape you made me. If that doesn't do it – come straight to your office – if you're here – if not, go to Cook."

Izzy nodded her approval at Maddy's efficient check list. Cook, who had lived at Micah Camp for years, often agreed to be disturbed at all hours by kids who needed the distraction of a glass of milk, a cookie or a grilled cheese sandwich.

Shame and sadness flitted over Maddy's face for a moment, "And if nothing works and I think I have to cut – I'll do it safely." She straightened her shoulders and walked with purpose over to the garbage can to toss away the bits of the shredded picture. "I don't think that's going to happen though. I really feel like I can handle this."

Izzy could see Maddy was still shaken but she knew there was a time when she had to let her client leave the office and get on with life. Kids like Maddy were often far more resourceful than they were given credit for.

i i .

Lisa-Marie left the workshop for her break after Josie approved the way she had wrapped several bars of soap and stuck on the Micah Camp Soap Company label. She stopped at her locker to get Dan's camera and walked through the covered breezeway watching the sunlight glinting off the waves on the lake. Some of the kids had canoes out and the red and yellow hulls sped across the water. Instinctively she had turned on the camera and was shooting the progress of the boats over the rippling surface. Moving on, she pushed open the heavy, wooden door of Micah Camp's main building and headed for the kitchen.

Calling out hello to Cook, she was given her choice of the large oatmeal cookies fresh off the baking sheet. Lisa-Marie had some social capital with Cook – mostly because she was Bethany's niece, but Cook had also smiled with approval when Lisa-Marie went for seconds of her cherry pie at the book club night. Now Cook slipped her a treat whenever she came through the kitchen. Lisa-Marie quickly raised the camera and caught Cook up to her elbows in flour, making yet another batch of cinnamon buns, her strong hands punching and working the mound of dough in front of her.

"Girl, you get along out of my kitchen right now with that damn camera," Cook howled at Lisa-Marie who scooted off down the hallway, stopping just long enough to raise the camera and snap one more shot of Cook with her flour-covered fist raised in the air.

Lisa-Marie represented an anomaly for the adults working at Micah Camp. Her youth put her as much in the category of resident as it did in that of co-worker and because of that she was able to cash in on the advantages of each. It meant everyone treated her like she was someone special and that was an unusual experience for Lisa-Marie. The second time she came to the kitchen at coffee time, Roland had presented her with a coffee mug. It was the insulated kind with a tight fitting lid and the Micah Camp logo on the front. Only the staff had these coffee mugs and she supposed it was Roland's way of keeping her status straight in his own mind. The day before he gave her the mug she had been walking out of the kitchen and he had come out of his office and said, "Aren't you supposed to be somewhere right now, Miss –," he had paused, at a loss as to what her name could be. She turned and he recognized her. With an awkward, startled expression on his face he added, "Oh . . . sorry, I didn't realize it was you, Lisa-Marie."

Sipping coffee from her staff mug, Lisa-Marie wandered down the hallway toward Izzy's office. As she rounded the corner she saw Izzy standing in the doorway with her arm around Maddy's shoulder.

Maddy was smiling though it was obvious she had been crying. Lisa-Marie could hear Izzy telling her, "I'll see you the day after tomorrow. If things feel rocky you know what to do and if it doesn't all go the way you would like, don't be too hard on yourself." Maddy nodded quietly and then smiled at Lisa-Marie as she passed her in the hall.

"Hey, Lisa, how is everything going?" Izzy whistled softly under her breath at the sight of the camera around Lisa-Marie's neck, "Wow, that is some nice piece of equipment."

"Oh good, working here is great." Lisa-Marie stopped outside of Izzy's door. Holding up the camera she said, "Ya it's a beauty isn't it? It belongs to Dan. He's letting me use it."

Izzy's eyebrows went up as she studied the camera, "Pretty generous of him."

Shifting her weight from one foot to the other, Lisa-Marie looked past Izzy into her office, "I don't want to interrupt or anything but I was wondering if I could ask you something?"

"Sure, come on in. I don't have another session booked this morning . . . just paperwork." Izzy frowned over at the stack of files on her desk. "Sit down," she pointed to the comfortable chairs in the corner while going behind her desk to store Maddy's file, "I'll just run and grab a coffee for myself and we can chat."

While Izzy was gone Lisa-Marie studied the room around her. The sound of water flowing down into a round stone bowl was relaxing. The smell of lavender that came from the candle in the corner was nice. Yellow and pink roses interspersed with delicate fern drew her eye forward and then past the table to the view of the lake out the large windows. Lisa-Marie had never been to a counsellor before and she had never thought of what a counsellor's office would look like. It seemed OK.

Izzy came back through the door cradling a large, white mug in her two hands. The logo on the front proclaimed, *Worship me like the Goddess I am.* She took the chair near Lisa-Marie's and sipped her coffee, savouring the full-bodied flavour. The coffee pot in the main area of the kitchen was always full but Cook and Izzy kept a smaller pot on a counter in the back corner. There they brewed a special organic blend of freshly-ground beans.

"What did you want to ask me?"

Stroking the camera in her lap, Lisa-Marie explained, "I want to take some pictures of your garden if that's OK with you? But I need to be there at different times of the day . . . like early in the morning or right before dusk . . . to get the light just right." Looking quickly up at Izzy's face and then back down to the camera, Lisa-Marie added, "I guess I'd be sort of hanging around. Would you mind that?"

Izzy was surprised at the request but also delighted that she hadn't misread Lisa-Marie's interest in the garden. "Sure, I meant it when I said you were welcome at the main cabin anytime and that includes the garden." As she leaned forward with her coffee cup warming her hands, Izzy asked, "How did you get interested in photography?"

Lisa-Marie relaxed in her chair and told Izzy, "I took this photography class last year in school and it was so awesome. Near the end we got to go out with the cameras and take any kind of pictures we wanted. I went downtown and I took a shot of this old lady dumpster diving. The photo turned out so good the teacher wanted to enter it in this magazine contest but first I had to go back and find the old lady and show her the picture. Then I had to get her to sign something saying I could use the photo," Lisa-Marie laughed at the memory.

"And did she sign?"

"Oh ya, for sure . . . once I found her again and she got what I was trying to say. She didn't understand English very well – I think she was Chinese."

"What happened with the contest?"

"Oh . . . I came out here so I never heard what happened," Lisa-Marie shrugged before she shook her head and quickly changed the subject, "I've already got lots of ideas for shots in the garden . . . especially the Nike statue."

Without conscious effort, Izzy processed the shadow that had passed like lightening across Lisa-Marie's face. Her gut told her to pursue that shadow. "Was it hard to leave all your friends and come out here for the whole summer?"

Lisa-Marie stiffened in the chair. Looking up at the clock on Izzy's wall, she hurriedly stood up, "Oh jeez, I'm way over my break time and Josie has stacks of soap for me to wrap. I better go. Thanks for saying I can hang out in the garden; I'll try not to get in anyone's way." Moving quickly she was out of the office and down the hall.

Well, Izzy thought, a tense body, hurried speech and a rapid exit. It didn't take a whole lot of insight to figure out that Lisa-Marie did not want to discuss how she felt about leaving her friends behind in Ontario for the summer.

iii.

Pulling Maddy's file back out of the locked drawer, Izzy made a few hasty notes and returned it to its place. She frowned at the rest of the paperwork on her desk and then swivelled her chair so she could see out the window to the lake. She thought of the session with Maddy, what she had said about the past not being destiny. She believed it was true; Maddy didn't have to become her mother, but it would take a hell of a lot of work not to fall into that trap.

Izzy's mother had been a university professor who had clawed her way to the top of her profession at a time when a woman in the upper ranks of the ivory tower was common enough but still not an easy position. And let no one be misled, her mother often told Izzy, the halls of academia are populated by packs of slavering wolves. She was made full professor with tenure and ended up the Dean of an entire faculty before Izzy finished elementary school.

Izzy's mother was beautiful – tall and fashion-model-thin. Izzy had described her to Lillian as the kind of woman who would put you in mind of Audrey Hepburn in, *Breakfast at Tiffany's*. She had deep hollows at the base of her throat and a long, graceful neck that was almost always adorned with a choker of pearls. Matching ear bobs were visible below her dark hair which was piled on top of her head. Her skin was alabaster pale and she was cold and contained and controlled in a way that would have made Machiavelli proud. When she looked down her nose over the top of her glasses, with one eyebrow raised, she could intimidate anyone into silence – from her students clear on up to the university President.

The problem was that Izzy's mother never left that look at work. She was able to bring Izzy into line with the mere hint of a raised eyebrow before Izzy even knew she was out of line. Her mother's rigid restraint contributed to a home that was a veritable waste ground when it came to expressing emotions.

An absent father didn't help. Edward Montgomery was a photo-journalist and he travelled extensively. Izzy hadn't seen much of him even before her parents agreed to live apart on a permanent basis. After that she hadn't seen him at all. Over the years, he kept in touch with brief notes mailed from odd sounding places. The year Izzy graduated from her Master's program he came home to Canada to help her settle her mother's affairs.

Her mother had died quite suddenly during what was meant to be a very simple and straightforward gallbladder surgery. She had been violently allergic to the anesthetic and that was that. Izzy's parents had never been divorced or remarried so her father, who still owned the house and was listed as her mother's beneficiary, dealt with all the legal matters while Izzy was left to sift through her mother's papers.

Izzy sobbed her heart out reading the journals her mother had kept over the years. They were all arranged meticulously by date on a shelf at the back of a closet. The content was so uncharacteristic that Izzy was hard pressed to believe the woman she had known could have written them . . . rants and ramblings filled with sarcastic tirades about colleagues and departmental struggles, professional slights and triumphs . . . pages where the pen had practically ripped through the paper with the intensity of the writing. Then there were pages of jealous invective and raging insecurity related to her parent's married life . . . pages where the writing tipped wildly between intense passion and unbelievable sorrow . . . where whole passages were scored through with thick black ink and stained with tears. But by far, the hardest pages to read were the ones on which her mother wrote about her feelings for Izzy; her overwhelming sense of being a failure as a mother and endless recitations of her concerns and fears. All of that was juxtaposed with description after description of even the smallest of Izzy's accomplishments. Her mother's pride in her jumped off the pages.

The fact that her mother had never shared any of these feelings with her, made Izzy boil with anger amid her grief. Over time she developed an intellectual understanding of how her mother could have compartmentalized her life in such a way – living emotionally in one place and physically in another. But at the time of her mother's death she had been too young and too close to her own situation to forgive her.

A few years later her father had sent her a short note to say he had settled fulltime in London. They weren't close and she didn't suppose they ever would be. He was still out there though and if anything happened to him she knew she would hear about it; he had sent her the name of a lawyer who would inform her of accident or death.

The truth was, she reflected, watching the clouds build-up at the end of the lake – her parents should never have had a child. Neither of them were suited for or inclined to parenting. Maddy's words came back to her now and Izzy doubted her belief about writing a new chapter. Maybe it was for the best that she and Caleb had never had kids. Maybe she would have been a parent every bit as cold as her own mother. Maybe she wouldn't have been able to help herself.

Izzy shook her head and remembered Caleb's smile and his easygoing personality – Caleb with the rays of the sun falling all around him. Caleb had made her a better person and he would have helped her be a good mother, too. And there would have been kids in the plural, never just one. Those kids would have had Beulah and Bethany and Liam too. It wouldn't have been like it was for her.

iv.

Dear Emma:

I love taking pictures so much. It feel like I'm in a different world – I look through the lens of the camera and I disappear. It's so weird. When the camera is in my hand I feel glued down to something – like that big chain that holds the raft in front of Izzy's beach. I can't float away. I'm here but I'm not here. Oh geez – you must think I'm really nutty, Emma. Today I took the most awesome photo of the Nike statue. I waited and waited for the sun to just touch the ends of her wings – and then the moment came – I knew when I started shooting that the photos would be perfect.

CHAPTER EIGHTEEN

i.

Izzy, Liam and Bethany were seated around the kitchen table at the main cabin with the Scrabble board spread out between them. As usual, Liam was far away in the lead. Izzy wondered if he had some kind of personal rule about not playing any word that didn't gain him at least thirty points.

Laying her *Z* alongside the word *any*, Bethany hooted when Liam totalled up her score. As she reached her hand into the bag of tiles, she said, "I think Lisa-Marie is really settling in well." Rolling her eyes at the letter on the tile she had chosen, Bethany continued, "Justin came and got her to go over to the Camp on Friday night to watch a movie. They looked so sweet going out together. He's such a nice young guy, isn't he?" Bethany looked to Izzy for agreement.

Justin had mentioned to Izzy that he had invited Lisa-Marie to join the kids at the Camp for movie night. She wasn't surprised by Bethany's gushing story and she told herself that it made perfect sense for Lisa-Marie to hang out with Justin. They were close to the same age and Justin was a nice guy, just like Bethany said.

Puzzling over her six vowels and a *K*, Izzy rearranged her tiles and scanned the board as she spoke to Bethany, "It must be kind of hard for Lisa-Marie being here for the whole summer. Kids can't seem to go a week away from their friends at that age."

"Well, I haven't seen her for so long," Bethany's voice was rushed. "I want her to stay and now that she has the job at the Camp and is making friends . . . I'm sure it will be OK."

i i .

Beulah sat in the passenger seat of the cab as Dan drove the truck back from the ballgame in Dearborn. She was two beers, maybe three at the most, over her set limit for driving. She had thoroughly enjoyed watching the ball game with Dan. They put five bucks on the line and flipped a coin to see who would root for the Beer Belly Sluggers and who for the Desert Rats. They had bounced up and down on the bleacher seats and screamed out advice and heckles in turn, while eating concession-stand hotdogs dripping with fried onions and mustard. Beulah talked with people she hadn't run into forever.

One of the Beer Belly Sluggers, a guy who had played for the Crater Lake Timber Wolves, called Beulah down to the dugout after the game and she and Dan squeezed in to share a beer. Then they tagged along to the Legion with both teams when the beer in the dugouts ran out.

Dan slowed the truck to ease around a tight corner before he glanced over at Beulah and commented, "Everyone seemed to have a lot to say about Caleb. He must have been one hell of a guy, hey?"

The beer and the enjoyable evening at the ball park loosened Beulah's tongue. "Ya, Caleb was one hell of a guy alright; one in a million." Dan kept his eyes on the dark curves of the gravel road ahead. "The thing about Caleb – he was the real deal, Dan. He didn't have to work. His family was rolling in dough. But he worked his tail off here with the sawmill and the woodlot. He could have gone anywhere and done anything but he lived here. He was such a damn good ball player he could have been a pro, but he played here in a mixed, slow-pitch league and it was all he wanted. This place, Izzy, friends – he had everything and he knew it."

Dan glanced back at Beulah with a look she interpreted to mean – *OK, if you say so.* Beulah sat up straighter and shrugged, "I know it's hard to get if you weren't there, if you didn't know him. Look, I'll tell you a story about Caleb," and with Dan driving the road much slower than Beulah could have believed possible, she began to talk.

iii.

Bill and Lila played ball with us on the Crater Lake Timber Wolves for years. God, we watched their little girls grow up – cutest couple of kids you'll ever see. The oldest was maybe ten that last season we all played together. Bethany kept score for the team so she wasn't on the ball field all the time like the rest of us. She was up in the score shed where she kept an eye on everyone's kids. She knew them all and they loved her. Why not, right? She always had money for a kid to grab an ice cream or a bag of chips from the concession.

One night when we got home after a game, Bethany told me that Bill was hurting Meghan, his oldest daughter – sexually abusing her, to be specific and Bethany seemed to have no problem being that specific. I told her she was nuts, crazy or something – this was Bill we were talking about. It was hard to take Bethany seriously; she tends to see the boogie-man wherever she looks. We had a huge fight and I remember I screamed at her – Did the kid say exactly that it was Bill? Bethany said, no – not in so many words, but that she knew it was Bill. She said she had thought something wasn't right between Bill and Meghan for a long time and when Meghan told her what was happening she believed her. She knew it was Bill, though Meghan refused to come right out and say it was her Dad. I flat out refused to believe it and I still remember Bethany shrugging her shoulders like it didn't really matter what the hell I believed; she knew what she knew.

The next day, after I went to town with the bread, Bethany walked over to the main cabin to find Caleb. She was more than willing to give me all the details later when everything came out and it was pretty clear how right she had been and how wrong I was for not listening to her. Anyway, Caleb and Liam were in the office of the workshop and Bethany looked at Caleb and said it straight out – Bill is sexually abusing Meghan and I think it's been going on for a long time. Caleb just looked back at her for a minute, nodded and then said he would go and get Izzy. That afternoon Caleb and Izzy drove into town to Lila and Bill's place. Bill was out of town working and by that evening Lila and the girls were set up in the guest cabin and that heavy steel gate that is always wide open at the top of the drive . . . well, it was closed and padlocked. Lila told Izzy and Caleb she wanted a couple of days alone with the girls to talk before they got anyone else involved.

The next afternoon, when I was up at the truck loading the bread, I noticed that Caleb and Liam were working out in the sawmill yard close to the road. I'll never forget what it was like when Bill drove up. His truck was spinning wildly out of control on the gravel. He jumped out of the cab with a shot gun and was waving it all around the place and screaming and swearing. All I could think was that this guy couldn't be serious, and surely to God, that bloody shotgun couldn't really be loaded. I've never seen anyone move as fast as Caleb did that day. He was in the open space between my truck and Bill's and he never took his eyes off Bill.

I remember he held his hands up telling Bill, "Calm down man, calm down."

Bill pointed the gun right at Caleb's chest, "Don't give me that shit about calming down. You get your fucking ass down that driveway, Caleb and you bring Lila and the girls up here, right now."

"That isn't going to happen, man . . . no way is that going to happen," I remember being sure Bill was going to shoot Caleb right then and there. Then the bastard would probably turn the gun on me and Liam for good measure.

But Caleb just walked right up to Bill, walked right up with that shotgun leveled at him. Bill was shaking like a leaf by the time Caleb took the gun out of his hand and cracked open the breach to drop the bullets on the ground at their feet. I almost buckled when I realized the gun really was loaded. You always think a guy acting that way must be bluffing . . . full of shit, you know.

Bill crumbled down on the gravel in a pathetic heap after Caleb took the gun from him. He was sobbing and blubbering down in the dirt and Caleb pulled him up and said, "Come on man, I'll drive you home." He grabbed Bill's keys and loaded him into the passenger seat of his truck. Caleb told Liam to pick him up later at the gas station in Dearborn.

I was so angry I couldn't see straight and Liam was no help at all – nodding and acting as if he understood what the hell had just happened – all calm like we hadn't dodged a fucking massacre. That low-life Bill came here waving a loaded shotgun at us and Caleb was driving him home like he was his best friend. I can tell you, Liam might not have had a problem with that but I sure as hell did. When I saw that pervert crumple up in a heap on the gravel you can bet your ass I didn't feel a bit of sympathy. I wanted to kick the shit out of him the second Caleb had the gun away. Ya . . . he was down but I didn't see how that guy deserved anything else after what he did to his own kid; his own kid for God's sake.

I didn't speak to Caleb for a week. One night Izzy showed up at the A-Frame and asked me, "Why are you mad at Caleb?"

I ranted and raved around the kitchen going on about what an animal Bill was, how Caleb should have decked the guy and how we should be protecting kids from creeps like him. I admit, it was a stretch with Bethany sitting right there accusing me with those damn eyes of hers for not believing what she had told me about Bill in the first place.

Anyway, I remember Izzy asked me if I had ever seen Caleb angry at anyone and I told her sure I had, of course. Caleb wasn't a freaking saint or anything. Izzy should have figured that out. Just that week he was supremely pissed when his credit card wouldn't work at the gas station. He went on and on about global collapse due to everyone's bloody dependence on technology.

Izzy laughed and said, "So he wasn't angry at the kid who worked there, right?"

I told her of course not, it wasn't the kid's fault.

I remember the way she looked at me when she said, "Caleb doesn't get angry at people, only things. Look, Beulah, Caleb believes people are good at the core but that sometimes they do shitty things. That doesn't stop him from believing people are good. You and I both know that's crap, right Beulah? People are not, as a general rule, good. A lot of people are bad. We know that but Caleb doesn't. And guess what, Beulah? I don't want Caleb to change. My life is better for knowing there is at least one person who believes in the good. I don't want to live in a world where everyone believes in the shitty, dark side of things like you and I do."

She got up and walked to the door but before she went out she said to me, "I'm not going to tell you what to do Beulah, but I am going to ask you to think about the way you're treating Caleb. It's breaking his heart."

The next day I walked over with his favourite bottle of whiskey and things went back to how they had always been between us. That's another thing about Caleb – you never had to hash over the past with a million words and apologies – it was the here and now that mattered to him.

Beulah sat up straight in the passenger seat and glanced over at Dan. She unclenched her fists and flexed her fingers before tucking her hands firmly under her thighs. She stared hard at Dan before she went on, "What I want you to get, Dan, is that Caleb believed Bethany without a moment of doubt. Caleb was the one who protected Lila and the kids. He figured Bill might pull a stunt like the one he did and Caleb was ready. And I guess he knew Bill a hell of a lot better than I did when he took the chance of walking right up to the guy with a loaded shotgun pointed at his chest. Caleb wasn't angry at Bill. He didn't feel like Bill had betrayed all of us or that he needed to be strung up and fed his own balls on a platter."

Beulah paused for a moment and frowned before she went on, "I couldn't believe that a guy I had trusted could do what Bill had done. I was so shit-kicking angry I could have killed him . . . I was totally useless. Caleb always had his priorities straight. He didn't need to get angry to get the right things done. He could see through the crap about Bill – right down to the guy we had all been close to for years. Ya . . . like Izzy said . . . Caleb always believed in the good but it didn't blind him to reality either." Letting out a sigh that seemed to shake her thin frame, Beulah nodded to Dan, "Sure, Caleb was human like all of us but he was a hell of a lot bigger than life too."

Beulah stretched out her arms and locked her hands behind her head. Staring straight ahead, she was quiet for a moment before adding, "I guess that's why everyone had a lot to say about Caleb."

iv.

Having won the weekly Scrabble game by an embarrassing margin, Liam walked Bethany home and then stopped back at the main cabin to make a few phone calls. A large lumber order was going out the next day and Liam needed to make sure he had a full crew lined up. He could hear the CBC evening news broadcast coming from the radio in Izzy's upstairs office when he called out to say he needed to use the phone. As he hung up after his last call he heard the radio click off and the sound of her steps on the stairs.

"God, it's really hot isn't it, Liam," Izzy paused in the kitchen, holding her thick hair up and off her neck. She looked down the three stairs to where Liam stood beside the phone, "I don't remember it ever being this hot so early in the summer."

Liam nodded in agreement as he shoved a note into his shirt pocket. He started to turn away, just glancing up to say goodnight. It was getting late and he had an early morning coming up.

Izzy stopped him in his tracks by asking him a question in a very odd tone – a mixture of supplication and jittery anxiety – a very unlike-Izzy tone. "What about a swim? Would you like to go for a swim with me, Liam?"

This question, to say nothing of the way it was delivered, took Liam completely by surprise. He had rarely seen Izzy go into the water and he knew for sure that he had never been swimming with her. He and Caleb had often stripped down and jumped into the lake. It was a great way to cool down after a day's work. And when Caleb was alive, he and Izzy had guests over and people were always down at the beach swimming. But Izzy had played the hostess then and he never saw her running down to the lake for a swim.

Although he was pretty sure his face had already given him away, Liam tried to keep the surprise out of his voice. "Sure, sounds like a great idea. I'll grab a pair of trunks from over at the workshop and meet you on the stairway."

"Shall we swim out to the raft?" Izzy sounded doubtful as she stood up to her knees in the lake.

"Why not, I'll race you," Liam called as he dived cleanly under the dark water and emerged several feet ahead, swimming strongly toward the raft and gasping at the cold. Touching the wood surface moments later he turned to see where Izzy was and found to his surprise that she was still hugging her arms around herself near the shore. "What's up," he called, "You lost the race."

"Just stay there, Liam. I didn't want to race. I'll swim out now but watch that I don't go under or anything, OK?"

Liam laughed before he realized this was not a joke. He kept his eyes on Izzy as she swam slowly to the raft. Side by side they steadied themselves with their arms folded on the worn wooden boards, their bodies floating freely. Izzy seemed to relax slightly now that she was safely at the raft. She stretched out under the blanket of dark water. Liam floated silently beside her and watched the path of the crescent moon ripple on the lake surface. Across the water at the public campground a huge bonfire was visible; the chording of a guitar was carried quite clearly across the lake.

"You OK, Izzy?"

"Yes. I just haven't come down here to swim in a long time."

Izzy and Caleb used to swim out in the lake after dark, leaving their clothes on the shore, the cold water almost painful against their naked skin. She hadn't attempted to swim out to the raft at night, or any other time for that matter, since Caleb died and only now did she realize how much she missed the refreshing feel of the spine-chilling water at night. Crater Lake was almost always a cold lake but it usually warmed up slightly in the late weeks of August. This year's unexpected string of hot weather had made a night dip possible in July, but a quick swim out to the raft, a breather and then back to the shore was enough for most people.

Liam lit a small blaze in the fire pit on the beach. With thick towels wrapped around themselves, they sat side by side listening to the music coming from across the lake. Izzy turned to Liam and spoke quietly, "I guess you could tell I was scared." She laughed a bit ruefully, shaking her wet hair out of her face, "More like scared shitless –," she paused for a moment to gesture out to the lake, "– of the water."

"How come?"

Izzy turned her large eyes to Liam in the dark, the firelight glinting off the skin of her shoulders. Her towel was wrapped tightly around her chest so only the straps of her bathing suit were visible. The rest of the towel was tucked between her legs as she dug her bare toes into the sand. Liam thought she looked like a scared, little kid.

Izzy hugged her arms around herself and stared out over the lake. Beside her, there in the darkness, Liam wanted to know what Caleb had never asked her. She had been afraid of the water ever since she was a kid. The summer after she turned ten she had been invited on a camping trip to a lake in the Okanagan with a girlfriend's family. She was with a bunch of kids, jumping off a raft into the warm water. She loved swimming and because she had never been tested, she felt the supreme confidence in her ability that only a child could feel. She dove into the water without a care in the world and became disoriented. With her eyes closed tight against the silt, she had swum under the raft rather than away from it. She would never forget the feeling of coming up for air, only to hit her head on the underside of the raft where she couldn't get above the water at all. She still wondered to this day why she hadn't gone into a complete panic. She marvelled at how she had opened her eyes and thinking her lungs would burst, got herself turned around and out from under the raft.

She came up gasping for air. When she told everyone what had happened to her, no one seemed to think much of it and by the time she got home it didn't even seem important enough to mention to her own parents. But Izzy always thought that was the moment she could have disappeared in plain sight of everyone and everything and life would have gone on its merry way without her.

It had taken some convincing on Caleb's part to have Izzy participate in the night swims but he persevered, staying close to her. Eventually the extreme fear backed off but she would never go to the beach at night by herself and even during the day she did little more than dip in the lake to cool off.

Liam could actually feel waves of fear coming off Izzy as she described how she felt surfacing under the raft and not being able to breathe. But what really got to him, like a punch in the gut, was her saying that no one seemed to think it was that big a deal. No one saw the little girl who was terrified she could have drowned that day. It was easy for others to say – *what's the big deal – it didn't happen, did it? You didn't drown.* As if they thought pointing that fact out could make things OK.

But those words never helped. Liam knew that what could have happened was as powerful as what actually did happen. If Caleb hadn't been out in front walking so quickly that day on the woodlot, he never would have died and he would be here with Izzy right now. Liam understood why Izzy couldn't help thinking about what might have happened that afternoon so many years ago on the raft. He could never help thinking that way either.

Walking back to his cabin later, Liam knew he was in way over his head. It was one thing to desire Izzy when she was confident and in charge, giving orders and behaving as if she had all the answers. That Izzy was distant and cool, just the kind of woman one could dream about from afar. It was quite another thing to desire her when she was vulnerable and afraid and willing to let him see that side of her. Izzy, like that, was as close to irresistible as any woman Liam had ever known.

V.

Dan walked down the twisting gravel drive brandishing a flashlight he had borrowed from Beulah. He couldn't ever seem to remember to bring one from the guest cabin and he now had quite a collection of borrowed ones on the shelf there. He reminded himself to ask Lisa-Marie to return all the flashlights the next time she came over to clean.

The workshop and the main cabin were dark and the sliver moon had slid behind the mountains. As Dan walked along the cliff path the embers of the bonfire across the water glowed low to the ground. He was pondering the story Beulah had told him about Caleb – a story that was as much about her and Bethany and Izzy as it had been about Caleb. It must have been difficult for Bethany to forgive Beulah for not believing her. Something like that would be hard to get over. He bet Bethany still thought about it. Dan was always surprised how one person could so easily overlook what really mattered to the other. He had seen more than a few relationships dissolve because of one partner's resentment – usually about something the other person considered a trivial detail from the past.

vi.

Dear Emma:

I lie in my bed at night and I think about what it would be like if Justin kissed me – if Justin and I were really together – not like when I was with the other guys. It wouldn't be anything like that. Oh this is so dumb, Emma – but I when I think about it – it's like being wrapped up tight in the softest blanket ever and my heart starts to beat so fast and I feel all warm and I want – well – I don't even know how to say what I want. I just want him.

CHAPTER NINETEEN

i.

Lisa-Marie saw Justin coming around the corner from behind the work-shop. She and Liam had just returned from their Thursday afternoon trip to Dearborn. Even before getting out of the truck, she was thinking about how she could arrange to have Justin by-pass Izzy's deck to walk her home instead.

But as soon as Justin spotted them he called out, "Izzy said to watch for you guys. She has some big thing she wants to talk to everyone about."

Izzy was waiting for them, her wine glass in hand. A pitcher of iced tea and two frosted glasses sat on the table and she handed Justin a cold beer. Picking up a small stack of books, she turned to Lisa-Marie, "Before I forget, I was wondering if you might find something of interest in these; they belonged to my father."

Lisa-Marie held out her hands for the books she recognized immediately. She shuffled through them quickly. "Wow, thanks. I saw these in your library the other day and I was dying to borrow them. I've looked at some of them before . . . at school . . . they're great for technique."

"My father was a photo-journalist. I never saw much of him when I was growing up because he was always away somewhere on assignment and then he was away, period. I've never thought much about photography myself but I took those books when I left home." Brushing her past off with a shrug, Izzy didn't notice Liam looking at her intently as she continued, "You're welcome to borrow them."

Justin took one of the books from the table and flipped through it, "They're kind of dated though, right? The camera you're using is pretty new isn't it Leez?"

"The camera you use doesn't matter as much as how you use it. That's what our teacher always used to say." Lisa-Marie turned to the contents page of the book she took out of Justin's hand, "These books are about technique and composition – and how you make use of the light. That's what really matters in photography and I guess the basics of those things haven't changed much." For once Justin was far from Lisa-Marie's thoughts as she sipped her iced tea and studied the book in her hand. She didn't look up until Izzy sat forward and clapped her hands to get everyone's attention.

Izzy took a quick sip of wine, paused for dramatic effect and then said, "I've been meaning to run something by you three –," she glanced quickly over at Liam, "– the end of the year Garden Club Gala."

Liam's eyebrows went up and he whistled softly, "Are you thinking of hosting it?" Over the years Izzy and Caleb had hosted the event a couple of times.

"They asked me if I would consider taking it on. It was almost as if I was expecting them to ask – Justin and I have been dividing and potting up plants since early spring."

Lisa-Marie was looking from Justin's smiling nod, to Liam's shaking head, to Izzy's look of pleasure mixed with indecision. Feeling totally out of the loop she asked, "What is the Garden Club Gala?"

"Just Dearborn's social event of the year, kiddo," Liam said. "Nothing much at all," he added with a pained expression on his face.

Izzy finished her wine and placed her glass on the small table beside her chair. "The Gala is an annual gathering. It's always held in the evening in some-one's garden around the time of the August full moon. It's a big competition to outdo whoever hosted it the year before –,"

"You can say that again." Liam looked up to the sky as if he hoped some help might be at hand.

Izzy laughed and shrugged her shoulders. "People decorate their gardens and serve fancy desserts and drinks and there's always a dress-up theme. Everyone who attends gets a gift from the host's garden and there are raffles for plants and door prizes." She paused and looked at the three of them in turn, "The garden is looking the best it has in years –," she flashed a smile over at Justin before continuing, "– I'm seriously considering accepting the invitation to host the event but I would need help and lots and lots of ideas."

Lisa-Marie's eyes shone with enthusiasm and she began to make rapid-fire suggestions, "I know what would be so awesome! What about a fairy-tale theme? You could serve fancy fruit tarts like the one's from *Alice in Wonderland* and we could do invitations on paper from the workshop. They have some beautiful blank cards with spots for photos on the front and I have a ton of great pictures of the garden we could use."

"This is exactly why I wanted to talk to all of you about this. I never seem to have imaginative ideas like that. A fairy-tale theme . . . I like it." Izzy looked thoughtful and mischievous all at once, "Who should I be?" She went on, only half joking, "I'm the hostess so my costume is obviously very important. I'd have to set the tone."

Lisa-Marie gave Izzy an appraising look before saying, "You could be the fairy-tale Queen, the Queen of the Night." Izzy's eyebrows shot up at the idea.

"Good Queen or bad Queen . . . that's the question," Izzy mused more to herself than to the others.

"Liam would make a great dark prince of some kind –," looking over at Justin, Lisa-Marie became tongue-tied. Her breath ran out and she stopped talking abruptly.

He reached over to shove her playfully in the arm. "You were probably going to say I would be perfect as one of the three little pigs or something. No way, forget that. I'll be Robin Hood," he declared, "I'll have a bow and arrows and wear a sword so I can steal from the rich to give to the poor." Justin chuckled and set his half-finished beer down. He looked at his watch and whistled. "Gotta go. I don't want to miss first helpings on pizza night." Lisa-Marie got up quickly to join him.

Izzy stretched her arms over her head and smiled. "OK, it's settled then. We'll do it . . . but what about you Lisa, what will you be?"

Staying close to Justin, Lisa-Marie called back, "Oh, I'll think of something."

i i .

Earlier that afternoon, Beulah turned out of the IGA parking lot with Dan's two litres of ice-cream packed into the cooler and his large bag of dill-pickle chips on the front seat. She saw Caleb's Dodge pull off the highway across from her and into the Petro Canada station. For her, it would always be Caleb's Dodge and seeing Liam drive the truck made her jaw clench painfully. As she made her turn and drove by the gas station she caught a glimpse of Liam jumping out and heading for the pump while Lisa-Marie scooted into the station's convenience store.

Driving back out to Crater Lake, Beulah remembered the day Caleb died. In the early years after she bought the A-Frame, when the bakery was just starting up and money was tight, she had worked on the woodlot with Caleb and Liam many times. Those had been good days spent traipsing through the bush, selecting the trees to fall, skidding the logs out along the primitive roads Caleb had pushed through with the bulldozer. Not like work at all. Beulah went less and less over the years. The bakery kept her busy. That Sunday in October there was no bread to deliver and Caleb had asked her if she could help out. One of the kids from the Camp had cancelled. So she had gone.

What Beulah believed, when she thought about that afternoon and Caleb dying, was that they should have been able to do something. When Caleb was lying there so broken up they should have been able to help him. And she blamed Liam for the fact that they hadn't. You don't tell a guy in the kind of shape Caleb was in that he isn't going to make it; you might as well tell him to give up. Liam sat and watched Caleb die. He sat there with his stony face and let Caleb die. There must have been something he could have done. She had gone along with Caleb and Liam for the Level One First Aid course. She and Caleb mostly fooled around, but Liam was the star student. He knew all the first aid stuff. He had even gone on to take several more levels. There had to have been something he could have done. He gave up because he was weak and she would be damned if she would forgive him for that.

Thinking of Liam as the bad guy helped Beulah deal with her grief and her overwhelming sense that the center of her life had dropped out when Caleb died. His death put her in mind of how she had felt coming home to that empty house in Edmonton so many years ago. But always, even when she was at her most hostile toward Liam, there was a little voice of common sense in the back of Beulah's head. That voice told her Caleb was a goner from the moment the rock hit him. She simply didn't want to accept the fact that there was nothing anyone could have done to change the course of events that October day. It was too hard to know they were powerless to change anything that mattered so much.

151

iii.

Dear Emma:

Izzy is planning a big garden party and we're all going to help. I had tons of ideas and she liked all of them. Everyone is going to dress up in fairy-tale costumes – that was one of my ideas. Justin's going to be Robin Hood. Oh Emma – I need to think of the best costume ever. It has to make me look beautiful and sexy and grown-up so Justin will look at me the way he looks at Izzy. I try not to think about that, but it's still happening – I'm not blind.

Last night when Justin walked me home, I thought for a minute he might kiss me goodnight instead of ruffling my hair the way he always does – but he didn't. For just a second, he didn't move – he was so still. I wanted to throw myself into his arms, but I didn't have the nerve.

Justin's not like the other guys – I said I would tell you the truth about them. Don't hate me, Emma, when you hear what a slut I've been. It's very hard to write about this stuff, even when I know only you will see these words. You better be the only one – this journal is rigged to blow-up if touched by spies! I'm only kidding, Emma. But snoops will be punished. (That means you, Beulah.) But I don't really think Beulah would snoop on me – she's a big bully, but she isn't a snoop. It is just you and me – I know that.

I'm sitting on my bed – it's very dark outside. I like to be awake when Auntie Beth and Beulah are asleep – it's so quiet here sometimes I can hear my own heart beating. I get to have the whole top of the A-Frame to myself – I sleep in the bigger loft at the back so I can see the baking shed and oven and the waterfall. I love to listen to the waterfall at night. And I can see the oven glowing in the dark.

You've probably guessed I'm only telling you all of this so I don't have to tell you the truth about how stupid and slutty I've been. I did it with five different guys. The first was Jason the pig. I won't say any more about that time – except that I was so stupid I thought he would be my boyfriend if I said yes.

Next was Barry. He always ordered a tuna sub – who orders tuna at a Subway? He was Jason's friend. Jason must have told him about me. I don't think Barry ever had a girlfriend before because there was something weird about him. You're probably thinking – why did you go with a weird guy? I don't know – I didn't get that he was strange at first.

Then there was Conrad – I recognized him from school. He would pick me up after work and drive down to the waterfront. Conrad always wanted to watch porn stuff on his computer before we did it. He wanted me to do what the girls in the videos did. One night he told me his girlfriend was coming home from her holidays so he wouldn't be able to see me anymore. I thought I was his girlfriend. Every day that summer I got stupider and stupider.

Mr. Duthie owned the gas station near the trailer park. He offered to give me a ride home one day. He always seemed really nice – like someone's dad. He didn't drive me home though – he drove down a dead-end road. He said he could guess what I had been up to with the guys. He wanted me to give him a blow-job. You probably think I should have punched him in his fat face and jumped out of the car. But I was scared. So I did it. The whole thing made me want to puke. Afterwards he said I better not tell anyone – as if I would ever tell anyone about something so totally gross.

What happened with Andrew will tell you how really stupid I was. I thought he was so cool. He played hockey and he was from out of town. Then one night, after we did it, he said the next time he wanted me to go to his friend's house with him. He said his friend had some video equipment. He said it would be great to do it in front of the camera. What a creep. I told him I would think about it, but the only thing I ever thought about Andrew after that was what a total sicko.

That's the whole horrible story of my sex life so far. I was a total slut – I was stupid – I was all the things the girls called me when I went back to school after that summer. I never even liked one of those guys. I wanted them to like me but I never liked any of them. Since I met Justin I know how it feels to really like someone. I know why everything was so awful before. You have to be with a guy you like – a guy who is nice and sweet. That's the only way you won't feel like a slut. If Justin kissed me even once I think it would be like fairy-tale magic – you know when the beast turns into a prince or the girl wakes up from sleeping for a hundred years – all the bad stuff would just disappear like it had never been at all.

CHAPTER TWENTY

i.

Izzy was waiting outside the workshop doors when Liam came into sight. Together they went inside and Liam grabbed a small step-ladder from the corner. He brought it over to a wall of two-by-four shelving. Near the ceiling, Izzy could see several boxes set onto the shelf in a row, her handwriting in black ink running diagonally across the side of each. Liam pulled the boxes down one after another and handed them to Izzy.

Izzy opened the box labelled *dress clothes* to reveal the black suit jacket that Caleb had worn at their wedding. She trailed her fingers over the lapel of the jacket, the satin piping running along the edge, cool and smooth to the touch. She and Caleb had been married on the kitchen deck almost fourteen years ago. They had been living together for a while and Lillian was after Caleb to make things official. She would often say, "Don't let this one slip away, Caleb."

Izzy had asked for a small gathering but the guest list mushroomed to what seemed to include half the population of Dearborn. Liam was Caleb's best man and Izzy remembered the night that Caleb had asked Liam to do him the honour. They had been over at Beulah and Bethany's for the second-year anniversary of the bakery. Caleb had announced that he and Izzy were going to get married in July. He had casually thrown an arm around Liam's shoulder and said, "Liam will be my best man, because he is the best man I've come across in a long, long while."

Izzy had seen the emotion on Liam's face and she had saved the moment from becoming overly maudlin when she turned to Beulah and said, "Not to be outdone here, Beulah, I would appreciate it if you would be my best man."

Beulah had tried, unsuccessfully, to hide a loud guffaw of laughter. Then she nodded her head and said, "Happy to do my part. If ever two people deserved to get married, it's the two of you." She had paused to pull Bethany towards her, "I have only one condition. Bethany must be the flower girl," and on that note they had all dissolved into peals of laughter.

"Do you remember how the justice of the peace looked when I introduced her to our two best men?" Izzy asked as she glanced up at Liam. He was leaning against the shop's workbench, his eyes on the jacket in her hands. That jacket stirred Liam's own memories of the wedding. He, Caleb and Beulah had stood in front of the frail and elderly justice of the peace, waiting for Izzy to make her entrance. Beulah had whispered to Caleb, "It's going to be a miracle if this old lady makes it through the ceremony . . . the sun is beating down like the furnaces of hell."

Liam and Beulah were wearing matching black jackets and he remem-bered thinking Beulah should have saved her concern for them. Bethany had appeared first, her arms brimming with flowers and Izzy followed beside Lillian. Izzy had worn a beautiful dress, form fitting with thin straps. As Liam recalled her on that day she was all shimmering white fabric and bare, brown skin. Her hair had shone like the feathers of the raven that often preened itself on Liam's porch railing.

Liam smiled over at Izzy as she pushed the clothing box aside and opened another to reveal a number of baseball trophies, "Oh Liam, remember how insane Caleb and Beulah always got about the slow pitch."

Liam reached down for one of the engraved trophies, "Who could ever forget the Crater Lake Timber Wolves' howl?"

"That is one thing I am glad to forget."

Izzy pulled a team photo out of the box and they both stared at it for a moment. She ran her fingers slowly along the edge of the frame, "I sure loved those uniforms." The Crater Lake Timber Wolves had sharp uniforms – dark burgundy shirts and white pants with a matching burgundy stripe up the side, burgundy baseball socks and white ball caps. Izzy laughed softly as she looked at them all, tidied up for the photo and ready to march out onto the field to get the evening game going. In a couple of hours those beautiful uniforms would be grass stained and ripped in spots. The ball caps would be thrown off sweat-drenched hair, shirts once so carefully tucked in would be in disarray. Grouped together in the dugout the Timber Wolves would be wildly congratulating one another for a win or commiserating about a loss.

What Izzy remembered most, as she looked at Caleb in the photo, was the perfect way he had looked playing baseball. She could see him standing up behind the plate and flinging back his catcher's mask to wind-up and throw the ball – whizzing it right past Beulah to Liam on third base or Cook on first. He would bounce out of the dugout when it was his turn at bat and plant himself firmly in front of home plate. His body would twist and the bat would swing out behind him. Then he would give a wiggle of his butt as he scrunched down and adjusted his stance – he was always totally focused and ready to hit the ball out of the park.

Liam was also looking at Caleb in the picture and he knew that in those times, playing ball for the Crater Lake Timber Wolves, he had come close to worshipping the ground Caleb walked on. Caleb had the ability to make people feel part of a team magic that was hard to describe to anyone who hadn't shared the experience. Liam never realized, until he was on the team, just how desperately he wanted to belong. In his own way he was every bit as crazy about baseball as Beulah and Caleb. The camaraderie was heady stuff.

The memory of one night at the Dearborn Legion stayed with Liam for a long time and he still recalled the way his emotions had run wild that night. They had taken a tournament trophy, trouncing a hotshot team from down Island in the final. That was the night he got really angry at Caleb – for the first time and the last time. He learned something that night – getting angry with Caleb was an exercise in futility.

Liam's recollection was so thick with sensory impressions that he felt like it had happened yesterday. The smoke-filled bar was over-crowded and spilt beer was sticky underfoot. The band played music at a level that was decibels beyond deafening. Standing at the bar, Liam overheard a big, redneck guy from the other team talking to Caleb. Beulah had just headed to the wash-room and Liam was a couple of stools down sitting with Josie. The redneck guy was half-way to drunk and that hadn't looked like a good thing. He was body-builder big with blonde, going-to-grey hair in a close, brush cut. He was still wearing his grass-stained ball uniform as he leaned on the bar to get right in Caleb's face.

"Hey Caleb . . . that's you right? I hear they call you the Godfather of some fucking lake around here." The guy was all smiling aggression.

Caleb laughed easily enough and moved slightly away. His laid back attitude wasn't cutting it with old redneck though; the guy's voice began to rise along with his colour. "Hey, listen up –," he grabbed hold of Caleb's arm, "– the way I see it the only Godfather you could be is to some butch dike and her blond sidekick there . . . what a waste hey?" The guy laughed in a nasty way, staring at Bethany who had just come off the dance floor looking gorgeous. "Oh ya, better not leave out that wagon-burner you chum around with –," his hand pointed toward Liam dismissively, "– I figure the only thing you got going for you is that hot, little number you came in here with. Does all your money make her forget you're a draft dodging coward from the U.S. of A.?"

Caleb simply shook off the guy's grip and said, 'Hey man, chill out –," and with a gesture to the bartender at the guy's empty glass he added, "– have a beer on me." He strolled away toward the table where Izzy and Bethany sat.

The redneck wasn't finished though. He pointed after Caleb and told the rest of the guys at the bar, "This time around we don't let his kind in . . . my own brother is on the ground right now in Afghanistan and I can tell you we don't need any fucking US cowards up here in Canada." Liam saw Caleb stop for just a moment. Though his shoulders stiffened, he didn't turn around. He only rubbed his beard in a puzzled way and continued walking.

The redneck banged his hand on the bar with a satisfied smirk on his face and guzzled the beer the bartender set in front of him. He turned to Liam, "Like I thought, chicken shit," pointing Caleb's way and laughing loudly.

Liam knew the guy was yanking Caleb's chain, trying to get him to fight and he also knew that fighting with a moron like that wouldn't solve anything; but he wanted Caleb to fight the guy. He wanted it so bad that when he followed Caleb out to the parking lot he dragged him away from the others, over to the back of the Dodge. He was so pissed off he thought he might fight Caleb himself. "How could you let that bastard talk to you like that? How could you let him say those things about all of us? For Christ's sake Caleb . . . where's your pride?"

Caleb hunkered down in the gravel of the parking lot, pulling Liam down with him so they were eye to eye. "My pride? That's a funny one, Liam." Caleb put a hand on Liam's shoulder. "Listen man, when I made the decision to be a draft dodger, I knew I was telling the whole world I was the kind of guy who would turn his back on his own country, the kind of guy who would run away from a fight . . . a fight other guys were willing to die for, Liam."

"Come on Caleb . . . everyone knows the Vietnam War was just bullshit. Anyone with half the sense he was born with would have left like you did."

"That's irrelevant man . . . you don't understand what it's like to be American." The way Caleb drew out the word American made Liam wince. "When you've done what I've done and everyone knows it . . . well, it frees you man, it totally frees you from ever having to prove anything again in your whole, long life. And when you've got nothing to prove, pride isn't really an issue. There's no reason to get angry." Grabbing Liam's shoulder tightly, Caleb stared intensely into his eyes, "That freedom is about the best damn thing that ever happened to me."

Beulah came along then jingling her truck keys and whistling. She asked if they were praying or puking and all three of them laughed. Liam's anger at Caleb dissolved away like it had never been. Pulling his far away thoughts back to the workshop, Liam noticed that Izzy had opened another box that contained a pile of paper.

"Thanks for getting these down for me, Liam. I'll be awhile with all of this –," Izzy waved to indicate the other unopened boxes, "– you don't have to stay."

i i .

"Just what the hell do you think you're doing?"

"I'm practicing my strip-tease act for the Dearborn talent night . . . what the hell does it look like I'm doing?" Lisa-Marie stared at Beulah. "I'm downloading my pictures onto the laptop, for frig sakes and you can take that look off your face . . . I'm not smearing jam all over your precious computer."

"Who the hell said you could touch my laptop in the first place?" Beulah was glaring past Lisa-Marie to Bethany who was stirring dressing into a large bowl of potato salad.

Bethany's stirring hand stopped in mid-motion. She pulled the wooden spoon out of the salad and threw it full force toward the sliding glass doors that looked out to the lake. Lisa-Marie and Beulah stared at the flight of the spoon as it arced over and over in the air. Their eyes widened in unison with the thunking sound that came when the spoon made contact with the glass doors. They both watched the trail of potato salad that hit the window in the spoon's wake and slid slowly down to the floor. The A-Frame was dead silent.

Bethany never even glanced toward the glass doors. "I want you to tell me where you get off, Beulah, walking around here every single day saying things like that . . . your truck and your cabin and your bakery and your laptop. I work in that bakery, too. Did you ever notice that? I work around this cabin. Did you even consider that? I think I've bloody well earned the right to tell my niece she can use the laptop." Bethany wiped her hands deliberately on a tea-towel which she flung at Beulah. "And I'll use a tea-towel to wipe my hands any time I want." She walked into the bathroom and slammed the door.

Lisa-Marie sat in front of the laptop, her fingers still poised over the keys, her eyes going from Beulah to the closed bathroom door.

"Don't smirk," Beulah warned.

"I wasn't going to . . . honest to God . . . I wasn't going to."

"I guess you'll be using the laptop to download your pictures." Beulah looked over at the potato salad on the floor in front of the window for a moment, "Did you want some lunch – potato salad, maybe?"

Lisa-Marie could feel an uncontrollable giggle start in her chest. She glanced over at Beulah who was trying not to smile. Then the two of them started to laugh until tears rolled down their faces. They kept pointing to the stained tea-towel, the pile of potato salad on the floor and the wooden spoon. With each gesture the laughing became more uncontrolled and hysterical.

Finally, Bethany emerged from the bathroom. She took in the scene before her – Beulah doubled over on the coach and Lisa-Marie in tears of laughter, trying to clean the window. She shook her head and returned to the kitchen to finish getting the lunch on the table.

iii.

Caleb's gold watch, his wallet and a worn deck of playing cards were lying on the workbench. Izzy remembered, as soon as she saw the Ziploc bag that contained these items, how Caleb's personal things had come back to her. She was amazed to find a hundred dollar bill and three twenties in a compartment of what had once been a beautifully crafted, black leather wallet – a Christmas gift from Liam the first year he had been at Crater Lake.

She chuckled her way through the wallet's contents – there were strangely obscure bits of paper with odd notes only Caleb could have written or later deciphered – there was a ridiculous picture of Izzy and Lillian out on the cliff deck; the blue of the lake spread out behind them and they were raising amber-coloured glasses of wine while kicking their left legs in the air, can-can style.

Izzy grabbed a handful of papers from the bottom of the last box and spread them out on the old desk in front of her. Going through the box of papers was like stepping back in time. A month after Caleb died, in the agony of thinking she had to do something concrete to make herself believe he was really gone, she had gone into the library, to Caleb's file cabinet. It contained piles of stuff Caleb thought he might need someday. Izzy had pulled out each drawer and simply tipped the contents into one large box – the things that had been on the top were buried under the past.

Izzy's sorting revealed a thick cream-coloured envelope with her name on the front. Turning it over slowly, she pulled up the flap and slid out a card. It was a print of a watercolour done by a local artist – a view of the cove from the other side of the lake. She remembered Caleb was amused when the artist in question dropped by and offered to sell him the original. He told the woman it made no sense to hang a picture on the wall when all he had to do was look out a window to see the real thing. But he bought boxes of the cards when they came out in the Dearborn tourist places. Izzy opened the card and read the words, written in Caleb's slanted handwriting.

Isabella Montgomery: I am grateful beyond all the words I could ever think to write, that I am able to share this life and place with you. Even though you are far away right now, halfway across this huge country, I feel as though you're right beside me. From that first moment we met on the logging road you have been a gift in my life. I never feel apart from you. My only wish is that I can continue to tell you this over many, many Happy Birthdays. All my love forever, Caleb.

Izzy's birthday was October tenth, three days after she was due to come back from Montreal, four days after Caleb died. Izzy was overcome with a feeling of grief and regret so powerful she could hardly breathe. Two years allowed her time to get used to the idea of Caleb's death, to adjust to living alone. She guessed time did that; but really accepting that Caleb was gone and she would never hear his voice or feel his arms around her again was a differ-ent type of reality. Her grief seemed stronger at that moment than at any other time she could remember. Dropping her head onto her folded arms she began to cry, the tears coming in what seemed like an unstoppable flow.

Caleb had given himself to her freely and completely. In many ways, over the years, he had invited Izzy to reciprocate. But she hadn't been able to get past the feeling that what Caleb offered was an invitation to dissolve into him. She couldn't risk losing herself that way. She needed to feel there was a part of her that was separate. She hung back from making the final commitment. Now it was too late and she would never have another chance. Now she was really alone.

When he came back to the workshop hours later, Liam found Izzy with the boxes spread out around her and the card lying open on the desk. Caleb's gold watch, wallet and deck of playing cards were beside it. The wallet made Liam's stomach knot, as did the sight of the other items that were so much a part of Caleb's everyday presence in the world.

Izzy's head was down and turned to the side, her tears spent. As she raised her eyes to meet his they contained such a look of sadness that Liam moved without thought across the room to stand behind her. He placed his hands on her shoulders and gently moved them back and forth. He could read Caleb's words on the card over Izzy's bent head and nodding slightly, he thought, that's exactly how I always believed that Caleb loved you.

Liam felt Izzy lean back into him and the moments stretched out slowly, endlessly. He caught a slight hitch in her breathing every few seconds. Standing so close to her made his heart thud painfully loud in his ears. Then suddenly Liam understood something about the resignation in Izzy's slumped body leaning into his. She wasn't going to move away from him. It wasn't because she wanted him so close to her. She simply didn't have the strength of will one way or the other. He didn't want to be close to her in that way. Slowly he backed up, a step, then another, finally gently pulling his hand away. "I'll move these for you," he said, pointing to the finished boxes on the floor and she nodded wordlessly.

iv.

Dear Emma:

You know what is really weird? Before I came here I don't think any grown-ups ever talked to me. At home it was always just me and Grannie. Sometimes I babysat, but the people never really talked to me – just told me what they wanted me to do. Teachers – it was like they didn't see me, or they didn't want to see me, because then maybe they would have to do something and who wants to try and do anything for the kid everyone hates. I went to the school counsellor last year but she was so busy and then I was supposed to go back but my timetable didn't fit with hers – so that was that.

So now I'm here and a whole bunch of grown-ups are talking to me all the time. And they seem interested in me, too. There's Auntie Beth and Beulah – well, you have to admit, Beulah does notice me for sure. There's Liam and Josie and Cook and Roland. And Izzy – even though I want to hate her, I have to tell you the truth, Emma – it's hard. I can't help but want Izzy to notice me. At first all the attention was weird – but now, I'm getting to like it.

CHAPTER TWENTY-ONE

i.

Bethany was amazed to find that the afternoon fishing trips with Dan had gone from being a dread to an out and out pleasure – something she looked forward to. She had been painfully self-conscious that first afternoon. Every move she made, from the second she met Dan at the door of the A-Frame to head down to the boat, seemed like a slow motion agony. She felt awkward in her body and the actions she performed daily with no effort at all seemed like unendurable chores – pulling the boat down to the water's edge, stowing her gear, getting into the boat with the life jackets and tossing them carelessly under the seats – all of it a painful drawn out process. But once the boat was in the water, Dan's enthusiasm for fishing and interest in their surroundings took over. Before she knew it she was caught in the flow of her own passion and the awkwardness of Dan's presence vanished.

Bethany found it intoxicating to share the flow experience of fishing. The only thing she could compare it to was sex and she shook her head when that thought occurred to her, blushing even though she was alone. But the comparison was valid. With Beulah she experienced intimate moments that seemed to make time stand still and the world disappear. Fishing with Dan had become like that.

She was surprised when Dan kept showing up at her boat each afternoon rather than using the one Izzy provided. On their second trip, Dan mentioned that he wished he had thought to bring a thermos, so Bethany started packing a thermos of steaming coffee. The next day, as they shared a coffee from the thermos top, Dan said he should have brought along a snack to go with the coffee, so Bethany started to bring along snacks. Their rituals quickly became established.

Talking was usually reserved for the times spent rowing to their favourite spots and then making the return trip around the point. If anyone had trained their binoculars on Bethany and Dan sitting together in the boat, they would have seen two heads bent over tackle boxes, lost to the rest of the world in an intricate web of lures, weights and flashers. Or maybe two people sitting almost motionless in the gentle, bobbing slip-stream, thinking their own thoughts as their lines played out over the water. They favoured the small hidden coves along the cliff faces that were overhung with thick trees and always cool; the afternoon heat never penetrated these secret spots.

Gertrude and Alice were already anticipating the end of the afternoon's fishing trip and Bethany could see them running along the shore heading for the point. She was rowing, and though her mind was no longer on fishing, she was preoccupied with a problem.

"A penny for your thoughts," Dan said as he smiled over at Bethany, watching her body move forward and back in the rhythmic motion of rowing.

Bethany looked up startled, "Oh, I was just thinking about Beulah's birthday, day after tomorrow. You're coming for dinner and cake, right?" Dan nodded.

"I usually order a gift for Beulah on the internet and then get Liam to pick it up for me. I try to make it a bit of a surprise." She paused and frowned before adding, "– with Beulah that can be a challenge."

Bethany looked over her shoulder for a moment and readjusted her course, "Beulah has this annoying habit –," Bethany grinned, "– well, just one of many. She'll wait until a couple of days before her birthday and then guess out loud what I got for her." Bethany shrugged in frustration, "It makes wrapping up the gift and giving it to her a real let down." Dan laughed as if he could imagine exactly how Beulah would do such a thing.

"Well, last night it happened again. She was going to take the dogs out and check the fire when she turned back and said she was sure looking forward to getting the latest season of 24 for her birthday. Of course that's what is hidden in my sock drawer." Bethany ended her story with a shake of her head. "I'm so bugged by the whole thing."

"No problem," Dan said, "I know what we'll do. I'll borrow Izzy's Jeep tomorrow and you and I will go to Dearborn together and get her a gift that will be a real surprise."

Bethany's hands suddenly froze. She stared at Dan before letting the oars drop down into the locks. She looked out over the water towards the shore and the boat started to turn in the flow of the current.

"What's up . . . what's wrong, Beth?"

"Oh . . . this is probably going to sound crazy to you, but I don't go to town."

"What do you mean you don't go to town?"

"I don't go. Everyone else goes to town and I don't."

Dan was frowning, "You mean, never. You never leave here," he gestured up towards the A-Frame that was now coming into sight around the point.

Bethany looked over her shoulder and then leaned forward to take up the oars again. It was quiet for a moment as she concentrated on getting the boat headed back in the right direction. "Well it's not that I never have. I used to. In the beginning when I first moved here I went to town now and then. We all went together, for the slow pitch games and the Legion dances, too. Then things changed . . . I didn't want to go to town anymore."

Dan was quiet – watching Bethany. She spoke into the space his silence created between them. "Everything changed when Caleb died. I don't know how to explain this, how to say what it was like when we were all together." Bethany continued to row, tears gathering under her lashes and falling silently down her cheeks. "It was as if the five of us were having a private party all the time. There was a circle around us – like no one else could get in. Caleb and Izzy and Beulah and Liam . . . they were all so powerful. It was like magic. But everything changed when Caleb died." Bethany could see them now, all whirling around in their own little worlds. The magic had blown away in a million directions. It had disappeared like Caleb's ashes had done two years ago when Izzy had stood on the edge of the cliff deck, leaned way out over the railing and flung them into the wind.

Dan was quiet for most of the return trip. They were almost at the shore when he said, "Come to town with me tomorrow, Beth. It'll be fun and I promise you, it'll be OK. I'll be there with you the whole time."

Bethany looked over at him. He was very close to her in the boat and she saw the way his green eyes picked up the light on the water. There was a look of acceptance and invitation on his face. Before she could stop herself she said, "OK, I will," as if responding to a dare of some sort.

That night she lay awake in the bed next to Beulah. She couldn't believe she had said yes to Dan's invitation. She ruthlessly searched her feelings for a hint that she wasn't actually OK with saying yes or for any suggestion that she should tell Dan she couldn't go. But she could find no trace of panic. She was actually looking forward to going to town with Dan.

ii.

Cutting through the garden on her way over to do the cleaning at Dan's, Lisa-Marie almost walked right past Izzy. She saw her at the last moment, knee deep in a huge patch of rhubarb. Justin was nearby, shirtless in the afternoon heat, weeding a vegetable bed in front of the greenhouse. Lisa-Marie felt a jolt of nauseating jealousy and a wave of resentment directed at Izzy. It wasn't fair that Izzy was able to share so much of Justin's time and see him like this – looking so hot and sexy.

Izzy stood up with a dozen of the deeply-red stalks cradled in her arms. Lisa-Marie covered her resentment as best she could by directing her attention to the rhubarb. "Wow, that's awesome rhubarb. Are you going to bake pies?" She relaxed and laughed at a sudden memory of her grandmother. "My Grannie was always raiding people's gardens back home for rhubarb. She called it the best pie-plant ever."

"Pies would be fantastic, but you know what?" Izzy frowned, "I can't make piecrust to save my soul. I've tried about a dozen recipes and it always turns out the same – a bunch of falling apart chunks. Then if I do actually get the mess into a pie plate it always bakes up like a slab of concrete." She shrugged helplessly, "I've just given up on pies."

Lisa-Marie looked puzzled for a moment before she said, "Ya? That's funny. Grannie taught me to make piecrust when I was a kid. I know a recipe that's super easy."

"Will you show me how?"

Izzy's sincerity caught Lisa-Marie off guard. She did a quick mental calculation – an hour of cleaning at Dan's, maybe two hours to get the pies made – she would be done before Justin finished work and right on hand to go swimming with him. As she told Izzy yes, she could already see herself handing Justin a home-baked rhubarb pie.

i i i .

Dear Emma:

I made pies with Izzy today and it was a blast – I know it's so crazy because I want to hate her and sometimes I really do hate her but then we end up doing something fun together. How can I have fun with someone I hate? She asked me and Justin to stay for supper with her and Dan. We had yummy barbecued steaks and veggies. Everyone loved my piecrust. I had a glass of wine like a real grown-up and afterwards we all played cards together.

I spent hours with Justin today – from 4:00 when we went swimming all the way to 11:00 when he walked me home. That is seven whole hours, Emma – but here's the thing – after all that time together all he did was walk me home, ruffle my hair and smile that smile that makes me want to throw myself into his arms. Then he walked away. Why doesn't he kiss me? Or maybe put his arm around me? I know he likes me, I know he does. I thought all I had to do was spend more time with him and everything else would just happen.

I know Justin is a nice guy – but he's still a guy. Why would he want to spend all this time with me if he isn't thinking of me as a girl?

i v .

The angel-food birthday cake, covered with gooey frosting was a big hit. Beulah was surprised that after unwrapping the DVD set, she received a second gift from Bethany. Something soft, tucked into a gift bag, with pretty pink tissue and ribbons overflowing the top. Beulah slowly drew from the bag a beautifully, handcrafted, fair-isle pullover in rich fall shades, the browns and russet colours blending in an intricate pattern around the neck and borders.

Beulah had admired this very sweater. It was hanging outside a small shop that catered to American tourists off the occasional cruise boat. No one but Bethany could have known that Beulah would like this sweater. No one could have described it to Bethany as a possible gift for Beulah and then offered to pick it up. Beulah was pretty sure the little shop didn't have a website or online shopping. How did Bethany manage to get a hold of this sweater?

She looked up to see Dan and Bethany exchange a conspiratorial grin and then Bethany announced, "I went into town with Dan a couple of days ago and when I saw this hanging in the shop I knew it was perfect for you."

Beulah had not survived to this point in her life without realizing that a steely control over her emotions could come in handy at times. She put on her best poker face and said, "Do tell."

CHAPTER TWENTY-TWO

i.

On the Wednesday afternoon of Lisa-Marie's third week at the A-Frame, Justin cut short their time on the raft and delivered a message from Izzy – Lisa-Marie was to come back to the garden after she went home and changed.

She looked suspiciously at Justin's grinning face and said, "Changed for what?"

"Izzy says to say – a fancy dinner – nothing else."

Lisa-Marie arrived back in the garden about an hour later clad in the only thing she had that she thought might be suitable – a short black spandex skirt and the white peasant blouse she had bought on her first trip to Dearborn with Liam. She wore a black bra under the flouncy-white fabric for effect. She barely applied any make-up at all – a bit of lip gloss and a light dusting of mascara had to do. Her time-consuming makeup rituals were now a thing of the past. She certainly didn't want mascara running all over her face when she climbed up on the raft with Justin after a swim in the lake.

Lisa-Marie saw Liam setting up a portable table in the garden house, just the right size for the four chairs he placed around it. Justin was waiting for Liam to get the table set up so he could cover it with a white linen tablecloth. Izzy was coming out of the cabin with a large basket.

"Oh, Lisa, you look pretty and your timing is perfect. We're almost ready. The first salsa cruda feast of the season is being served tonight and we are going to enjoy it."

She beckoned Lisa-Marie over and together they set the richly-draped table with pasta bowls and heavy, silver cutlery. Wine goblets, their deep-blue, glazed finish matching the bowls, came next. Izzy set a center-piece on the table – red roses in a black bowl with tiny, white floating-candles, winking and sparkling between the flowers.

Izzy and Liam returned to the main cabin and emerged moments later carrying wine, a huge covered bowl of pasta, a basket of fresh bread, and the salsa cruda – a cold pasta topping made from the first ripe tomatoes of the season mixed with garlic, red onion, black olives, fresh basil, balsamic vinegar and a light olive oil. Lots of cracked pepper was thrown in for good measure and a block of pungent parmesan cheese lay nearby, to be grated on top.

Izzy waved them all forward, "Everyone sit – let's get started." She smiled at Justin before adding, "We've been looking forward to this all day."

Lisa-Marie stiffened at the sound of the word *we* that so clearly referred to Izzy and Justin. She was wildly glad she and Liam had been invited to share the meal. The thought of Justin looking forward all day to anything alone in the garden house with Izzy, made Lisa-Marie feel sick.

Liam sat down and clutched at his stomach, "I'm going to pay for this. But it'll be worth it."

The wine Izzy chose to go with the dinner was a Zinfandel, glittering pink as it was poured from the bottle. All the windows in the garden house were open wide. Together they savored the cold freshness of the tomato dish ladled onto the hot pasta. The early-evening songs of the birds and the cooling smells of the garden made for a meal that was pure magic.

Izzy's dark, twisting curls were piled high on her head and they tumbled down around her face. A large pair of silver hoop-earrings danced and sparkled whenever she turned. She wore an off-the-shoulder, white dress. Lisa-Marie sat right beside Justin and he often turned to smile at her, seeming to include her in everything he said. Still, she saw that his eyes were at least as often on Izzy. A painful lump lodged in Lisa-Marie's throat.

Izzy pushed back her chair and hastily began to clear the table while tipping the last of the Zinfandel into her own glass. "Don't any of you move," she warned them. "A full meeting of the garden gala planning committee is well overdue."

With the dishes off the table she opened the desk drawer to extract a pen and an old tattered notebook. Flipping it open she sipped at the wine, referred to her notes and glanced around the table. "Lisa and I finalized the menu the other day," Izzy announced.

"Fresh raspberry tarts with dollops of whipped cream and plenty of champagne," Lisa-Marie told Liam and Justin.

"You'll pick the raspberries Justin, and Lisa-Marie and I will bake the tarts first thing on the morning of the big day," Izzy looked down to make a hurried note. "The champagne is on order and will be here next week sometime and I've arranged to borrow the champagne flutes and a bunch of silver trays from the Concert Series group in town. Apparently they store stuff like that for their own events." Izzy shrugged, "Who knew, right?"

Lisa-Marie sipped the last of her wine, feeling a bit light-headed. She hadn't developed a taste for wine but she liked being included, so she took what she was served. Shaking her head to gather her thoughts she looked over at Izzy, "The invitations are all done. Beulah picked up the photos yesterday afternoon and Justin and I put them together last night at the Camp."

Izzy ticked off something in her notebook and nodded, "Great . . . I might get you to help me tomorrow afternoon, if you have time Lisa, to get them ready to send out in the mail. I've got address labels but I love your idea of including a dried flower from the garden with each invitation."

"OK . . . decorating the garden is the next thing. What have you and Justin come up with, Liam?" Izzy turned to Liam to ask this question with a smile in her sparkling eyes, her pen poised over the notebook.

Liam lowered his own eyes for a moment and cleared his throat before speaking, "Well, lots of lights, strings of little white lights all over the place. And Justin has a good idea about setting up a welcoming arch to greet everyone before they get to the garden." Liam nodded toward Justin as he spoke and then shrugged his shoulders before adding, "I really don't think we'll need much more than that . . . the garden will speak for itself."

Izzy nodded her agreement and looked over at Justin, "I've got an idea for the arrival gifts that you and Lisa can take care of." Lisa-Marie nodded enthusiastically at any job she and Justin could do together. "Take all those lavender slips we potted up last week and put them in the clay pots I found in town. I'll maybe wrap some type of ribbon around them later."

"The raffia we use to wrap the soap over at the Camp would be perfect. I'll ask Josie if I can have a hunk of it," Lisa-Marie offered.

Again Izzy was jotting in her book and she raised her eyes to say, "Great idea. Make up about three dozen just to be on the safe side." She turned to Justin to add, "Are the raffle prize plants all ready?"

Justin had pushed his chair back to stretch out his legs. "Yup, boss . . . they're all set out in a corner of the greenhouse and ready to go."

Izzy closed her book with a satisfied look, "Well, I guess the last thing we need to discuss is how the costumes are coming along."

Lisa-Marie smirked with pleasure before telling everyone, "Mine is still a secret but it's coming along great."

i i .

Frantic for just the right costume idea, Lisa-Marie had been rescued by Beulah of all people. She had been tossing out and rejecting idea after idea over a sink full of dirty dishes, when Beulah had looked up from the newspaper, her black, half-moon glasses sliding low on her nose, and said, "You seem the Tinkerbell type, what about that?"

Lisa-Marie wrinkled her nose, "Thanks, but no thanks." But the more she thought about it the more Beulah's off-the-cuff suggestion grew on her. Not exactly Tinkerbell but maybe a garden sprite dressed a bit like Tinkerbell.

When Josie heard her idea she offered Lisa-Marie a figure-skating costume her daughter had used in her last year of competition – a white spandex leotard, high-cut in the leg with a sheer skirt attached; the hemline barely fell to Lisa-Marie's upper thigh.

"How on earth does anyone go into an ice rink dressed in this?" Lisa-Marie was holding the skimpy costume up against her own body and shivering at the thought.

Josie rolled her eyes and said, "The whole sport is turning into one third talent and two thirds *Victoria's Secret* lingerie act. You can do whatever you want with the thing. Angie's off at SFU now. She's going to be a teacher." Auntie Beth was working on a beautiful set of gossamer thin wings to attach to the back of the dress.

One day at the workshop, with Maddy's help, Lisa-Marie tie-dyed the outfit in multiple shades of green. Later, while sitting at the worktable wrapping and labelling innumerable bars of soap, they talked about the look Lisa-Marie was after. Maddy smiled with sudden inspiration. "You'll need make-up for sure, but what you're really going to want is body paint." Maddy stopped talking to sweep her hand like a paint-brush over Lisa-Marie. "I see green vines and leaves everywhere on your arms and legs and across your top as well. Yup – body paint will be just the sexiest thing," Maddy winked, while running her hand suggestively along Lisa-Marie's leg to pinch her on the upper thigh where her shorts were riding up. Loving the idea, Lisa-Marie giggled while she slapped at Maddy's hand.

iii.

Turning her attention away from thoughts of her own costume, Lisa-Marie nudged Liam lightly on the arm to get his attention, "Justin and I went over to the Church in town with Dan the other night, before the ball game. In the back of the church they have all these robes and stuff. I borrowed a long black thing for you –," she paused to think for a moment and then continued, "– Dan called it a cassock. Auntie Beth says it will make the perfect dark-prince costume for you." Liam groaned and stared up at the exposed beams and rough wood that made up the ceiling of the garden house.

Lisa-Marie turned to Justin, "Auntie Beth is coming along great with your Robin Hood tunic, too."

Izzy looked up from her notebook and said, "The dress she's making for me is really something. I think she's putting way too much work into it but she says she's enjoying it." Izzy added the last bit in a doubtful tone.

iv.

The day the decision was made to host the Garden Club Gala, Izzy sat Bethany down in front of the computer and put a credit card in her hand. Making it clear that money was no object, Izzy told her to order whatever she needed to sew a *Fairytale Queen* dress. Bethany chose a pattern that featured a high-collar combined with a plunging neckline. The tight bodice ended in a point of fabric at the waist and gave way to the flouncing, rich folds of a floor-length skirt. Fitted sleeves belled out just past the elbow to drape gracefully over the lower arms and hands. The fabric Bethany ordered was satin, midnight-blue and shot through with silver thread. She also requested several yards of a thin black thread to which tiny silver stars were attached. She planned to weave these through Izzy's hair.

After Bethany had pushed the send button on the computer she sat back with a frown on her face. "What would really finish off this outfit would be the perfect piece of jewelry – something like a crown."

Izzy burst out laughing and grabbed Bethany by the hand to drag her out of the back library and into the bedroom. She threw open the wooden box on the dresser and pointed triumphantly to the contents. A silver tiara and matching necklace, both studded and sparkling with small stones, lay nestled on the green velvet fabric.

"Are these real?" Bethany sucked in her breath as her fingers traced the ruby red, emerald green and sapphire blue of the stones.

"Oh yes, they're real," Izzy said. "Lillian gave me these to wear at the wedding. Caleb and I couldn't believe our eyes. We tried to explain to her that these would be way over the top for a wedding on the kitchen deck."

Lillian had laughed and said, "Well, keep them just the same. You never know when expensive jewelry will come in handy." On the actual day of the wedding she had presented Izzy with the necklace of pounded silver medallions she often wore, even all these years later. Lillian had explained, "I picked this up at the Taos Pueblo when Caleb's grandmother and I were traveling in New Mexico. I hope it suits you better than the tiara." It had indeed, and Izzy treasured it.

V.

"You guys aren't going to believe the costumes Auntie Beth is working on for her and Beulah. She's made me swear not to say a word."

Izzy turned to put away her notebook and rose from the table, "Whew, we're finishing just in time; I can hardly see the last few things I wrote." She wrapped a black silk shawl around her bare shoulders. "Let's walk in the garden for a bit."

Liam and Justin said they would be back after taking care of the clean-up. With her camera in hand, Lisa-Marie joined Izzy in the garden. She would have preferred to share the clean-up with Justin but since Liam had insisted, she was stuck with Izzy. But at least that meant Justin wasn't.

vi.

Dear Emma:

I'm happy but totally pissed off – how can I be both at once? Happy because Justin talked to me all the time tonight and when he walked me home we just stood out on the path and talked and talked before he finally said goodbye. But I'm pissed off because Justin also stared at Izzy so much tonight I wanted to die or throw up or both. He tries to hide it – I know he doesn't want anyone to notice – but I'm not blind and Izzy isn't either. She saw how Liam and Justin acted like they were sitting with a movie star or something. She loves it – everyone just worshipping her – like that mug she has in her office – worship me like a Goddess. What an ego maniac.

Well – I promised to tell the truth – right Emma? I couldn't take my eyes of her either! I can't even bear to describe to you how perfect her hair and dress were. After we ate and talked about all the planning for the garden party, I had to walk around the garden with her and of course I had to take pictures of her – the light was just right. A few minutes ago I looked at how the pictures had turned out and I knew before I did what I would see – the camera loves her as much as everyone else does. Even if I live to be as old as her – I'll never look that good. I'll never be that perfect and Justin will never look at me the way he looks at her. Every single day I want to hate her but I just can't seem to do it.

vii.

Without conscious thought, Justin found himself sitting on a picnic table staring out at the dark lake. He had made a complete fool of himself tonight – he was sure of that. He wasn't used to drinking wine and it had broken down his defenses more than a beer would have done. He knew he had stared at Izzy like a love-sick puppy. He could swear he had caught a glint of something in Liam's eye – like Liam felt sorry for him, like he understood how Justin couldn't help staring at Izzy. And though he had tried to pay as much attention to Lisa-Marie as possible, he thought she had looked oddly at him a few times. Only Izzy hadn't seemed to notice anything strange about his behaviour.

He thought about Lisa-Marie – how she stood on the trail and held him there with her chattering and her smile and those eyes looking up at him with something close to hero-worship. He knew she wanted him to kiss her and his hand had lingered for a moment longer than usual when he reached out to ruffle her soft-brown hair. He could have slid his hand down her face and pulled her close. Part of him had wanted to. What a complicated, fucking mess his whole life was turning into – just a few more weeks until he would walk away from all of these people.

Justin pushed himself off the table and walked down to the edge of the dark water. He stripped of his clothes and quickly moved into the lake. His arms reached out in a strong, front stroke and he swam until he began to feel tired. Floating on his back, he let himself drop into that quiet space inside himself where everything slowed down. He knew what he had to do. Take things very, very cool – his obsession with Izzy would pass – it had to. Lisa-Marie was only sixteen and she didn't deserve to end up as his consolation prize. He wouldn't let the way she idolized him make him do something he knew he would regret. Cool and slow and quiet – that was the way to deal with both of them. He turned then and leisurely made his way back to the shore.

v i i i .

Liam's desire for Izzy was a slow-burning pile of embers. He watched her laugh out loud during the meal at the near misses of the bright-red, tomato sauce on the front of her white dress. The little-girl dress didn't go with her wildly, sexy hair tumbling over her shoulders; nor did it match the wine-sparkled glint in her eye as she peppered him with questions about the garden decorations. As he rocked quietly in the chair by the cold stove, Liam pictured Izzy wrapped in the sensuous black silk shawl, the white dress outlining the curves of her body. She had walked barefoot along the garden path with him, to the curve near the guest cabin, before saying goodbye. Leaving her there like that was too much. He had returned alone to his cabin where his longing for Izzy was a painful sentence that he did not want to serve any longer.

i x .

Izzy, the object of such powerful emotions on the part of her three dinner guests, suffered too. The first salsa cruda of the season had always been her and Caleb's secret delight. Growing tomatoes was one of Caleb's frustrations and joys. He would often say that any fool could grow a tomato in California. Simply toss a seed in the dirt by the side of the road, give it a bit of water, and lo and behold big, juicy tomatoes eventually appear. But here, on Northern Vancouver Island, growing tomatoes was a different story. Every year he carefully chose seeds, nurtured the little seedlings, set them out in the greenhouse and kept a watchful eye on their progress. Caleb cherished every small success and in the end he had gotten the growing of tomatoes down to a fine art. So, the first tomato harvest was something he and Izzy shared with ceremony befitting the labour that had gone into the whole tomato-growing endeavour.

Ensconced in the glass house they had relished every bite of that first meal of salsa cruda. Later, she and Caleb wandered the garden trails and only returned to the outside sheltered space to make love in a tantalizingly slow and luxurious twining of their bodies. Izzy could remember looking down at Caleb, outlined in the thin light of the moon, his eyes wandering down from her face and over her body. She could recall how it felt as she moved oh so slowly against him. Afterwards, they cuddled together in a sleeping bag and fell asleep to the night sounds of the garden.

CHAPTER TWENTY-THREE

i.

Lisa-Marie dropped the heavy novel she was reading into the sand beside her and flopped over onto her side. Stretched out on the towel, she was trying to even out her tan. She had been reading Anne Marie MacDonald's, *The Way the Crow Flies*, the August book club selection and it was heavy going at times. She shaded her eyes to gaze up at the clear, blue cloudlessness of the sky. The recreational season was in full swing as the month of July was coming to an end and Lisa-Marie could hear kids screaming gleefully across the water. Miniature bodies capered about and colourful air-mattresses dotted the cork-enclosed swimming area of the camp site. At night, on the beaches in front of the summer cabins, she often saw the lights of camp fires and heard music and voices drifting across the water. The beach where she now lay was quite the contrast – deserted and quiet.

The best part of the beach lay between the north and south staircases. Here the small rocks strewing the water's edge in front of the A-Frame gave way to sand. Lisa-Marie had gotten into the habit of spreading her towel out near the bottom of the north stair. She had the whole area to herself most afternoons. Occasionally Izzy appeared. She didn't swim. Lisa-Marie didn't count a quick dip in the water to cool off as swimming. Izzy didn't come down to the beach to socialize either; she was always carrying papers, or files, or books; she barely gave Lisa-Marie more than a quick wave.

Closer to the south stair, Lisa-Marie could see a fire pit surrounded by log seating, a mini version of what was over at the Camp. She had been at the Camp the other night for a bonfire on the beach when Justin brought out his guitar and played, *You are my Sunshine*, and every time he sang the chorus – *You'll never know dear, how much I love you* – she thought she would slip off her seat on the log and run like a stream of hot oil over the rocks of the beach to float on top of the water like one big slick. When Justin looked up at her and smiled a wave of longing left her legs weak and trembling. The evening had ended with Justin walking her home on the darkened path and leaving her moments later, alone with her wildly beating heart. It just went on and on, the wanting and the wishing and the growing frustration.

As if the thought of Justin had in fact conjured him, Lisa-Marie looked up to see him coming down the south stairs two at a time, calling out to her, "Race you to the raft, Leez." He tugged his sweat-stained T-shirt over his head and kicked off his dirt-encrusted shoes as he hit the beach running.

Lisa-Marie was up off her towel in a flash and dashing at an angle along the beach to splash into the water with a clean dive before Justin came off the stairs. As her head cleared the surface she swam hard for the raft. Justin won the daily race, as usual, hauling himself onto the raft's surface with enough time left over to offer her a hand. Moments later they were both stretched out on the raft as it swayed and moved gently with the water. Lisa-Marie was amazed that there were times like this, lying beside Justin in her skimpy bikini, that she felt perfectly comfortable – like he was her best friend. Then there were times, like the other night, when she was so self-conscious and aware of every movement he made that she couldn't think straight.

ii.

Lisa-Marie's life had settled into a comfortable routine over the last month. Most mornings she was up by eight with the A-Frame to herself. Other days she would scramble out of bed before six and make her way over to Izzy's garden to take pictures, just as the morning light peeked over the mountains. She would get back from her job at the Camp in time to have lunch with Auntie Beth and Beulah. She helped her aunt out with a few things around the cabin before Bethany headed out to fish, lately in the company of Dan, or hauled out the sewing machine to work on the garden party costumes.

In the early afternoon Lisa-Marie spent her time downloading and editing the scads of photos she had taken. One day, as she poured through the pictures – many of Justin working in the garden – Lisa-Marie had what she felt was an idea bordering on genius. It was obvious to her that Justin took his gardening work seriously. She would give him a gift, something that would let him know that she understood how much pride he took in the garden. She would choose some of her best garden photos, have them printed and make him a special album. The more she thought of the idea the bigger and better it got.

She asked Liam if he would help her make a leather cover for the album. She got permission from Josie to prepare a special batch of paper that she could use as inserts between the matted photos. She pinched little pieces of plants from Izzy's garden every time she walked through; she hand pressed these artefacts in the heavy Funk & Wagnall's dictionary Beulah kept on the living room shelf. One day she stayed at the Camp and spent the whole afternoon placing the bits of dried plants into her paper.

Early in the afternoons, Lisa-Marie would close up the laptop and make her way down to the beach to work on her tan, swim, read, write in her journal and wile away the sunny afternoon hours. Justin regularly made his appearance when he finished working. The daily race, the hour spent lying in the sun and diving off the raft, became a Lisa-Marie and Justin *thing*. The afternoon usually ended with Justin heading up to the outdoor shower at Izzy's and Lisa-Marie making her way back to the A-Frame to help with dinner.

She had her weekly trips to town with Liam and she was getting good at driving the truck. She had also taken to visiting with Liam a couple of nights a week. He started keeping a Coke in the fridge for when she stopped by. She would flop on the floor of his cabin and play with Pearl. Liam was very easy to be with and she didn't have to say anything at all if she didn't feel like talking. If she did talk, he never made her feel like what she had to say was stupid, or that he didn't have time to listen. He didn't give advice or tell her what she should do.

i i i.

"What do you think of the *Crow Flies* book", she asked Justin as she swung over from her back to lie on her stomach. She raised her head up to look at him, hoping that he might be at least a bit interested in the way the top of her bust pushed out of her bikini top.

Justin was sitting on the dock picking at a sliver embedded in the palm of his hand, "I haven't even started it. I don't have time to read a book that thick. I don't suppose I'll go at all."

That settles that, Lisa-Marie decided to herself. I won't be going either.

Looking up from the work on his sliver, Justin did glance idly down the front of Lisa-Marie's bikini top while she was looking out over the lake, chatting on about what had happened with a batch of soap earlier in the day. He noticed she was hot looking in her bikini with her summer tan and sun-bleached, long hair drying in the wind. At the same time he reminded himself of his resolve to keep things cool with her.

Justin was used to girls having crushes on him and a lot of those girls were pretty screwed up in one way or another. Lisa-Marie was not a kid from the Camp or from a group home but there was something about her that she was hiding. Justin had seen enough of her body in her skimpy clothes to know she wasn't a cutter and that was good. The cutters and their game playing had led to some of Justin's worst experiences. But still, there was something about Lisa-Marie – a look in her eyes sometimes – that kept him on guard. His radar for stuff like that was pretty well-tuned.

He felt protective towards her and the truth was he liked hanging out with her, despite the need for caution. She was funny and cute and above all, she was not one of the kids from the Camp. At times, the we-are-on-big-happy-family feeling around the Camp made Justin antsy. He had been through this experience many times in group homes and all he wanted to do was find anyone or anything that was out of the circle. It was OK to be friends with Lisa-Marie. OK if he kept his distance. So he averted his eyes and told himself that enjoying the way Lisa-Marie's body looked swelling out of her bikini top was definitely not a stellar example of keeping it cool.

i v .

Dear Emma:

Do you sort of wonder why my grannie didn't do something to help me out when things were so bad at high school? She must have noticed something was wrong. Like why didn't I ever have any friends come over or get invited to anyone's house?

Why did I just hang-up the phone whenever anyone called me? Why did I come home with my clothes ripped and my face scratched or bruises all over my arms? Why did I never have my gym strip? I was always super careful with my things and she knew that. Why were my textbooks always ripped up and scribbled on? Why did I come home so late on so many nights when I was working at the Subway? I could go on and on but what's the point?

In the beginning I wanted her to figure out something was wrong but after a while I started to get that she couldn't let herself see how messed-up I was. I don't blame Grannie – she did her best. She didn't want to get stuck with me – she was old even when I was little. But she didn't dump me or anything. She just had a hard time noticing things or keeping up with stuff – she liked the bingo and her movies. Poor Grannie – does she ever think about how screwed up everyone she ever looked after got? Not a great track record, Grannie – Auntie Beth, my mom, and now me.

CHAPTER TWENTY-FOUR

i.

Izzy awoke the morning of what would have been her and Caleb's wedding anniversary with a splitting headache that persisted throughout the day. A go-no-where session with Jesse, a pile of paperwork to finish and a forty-minute phone conversation about the loss of Maddy's high-school transcripts did not improve Izzy's mood. She managed to dodge an encounter with Roland by leaving a few minutes early, only to be scared half out of her wits by a bear dashing across the path – the animal was no more than a couple of metres in front of her. That close encounter seemed like the icing on the cake of a thoroughly crappy day. Izzy wasn't afraid of bears. The area was as much their home as hers and seeing a bear was a common occurrence. But she didn't like being startled any more than she imagined the bears did.

With her heart still thumping she came through the kitchen door into a silent cabin. Apparently it wasn't Dan's night to share dinner with her and that was for the best. She had no appetite. A cold shower to try to relieve the pounding in her head and a glass of chilled Chardonnay would do the trick.

Liam called out hello as he came in from the greenhouse garden; he stopped in his tracks half-way across the living room. He saw Izzy emerge from the bathroom, her dark hair piled haphazardly on her head, one hand holding a towel barely wrapped around her body and the other balancing a large glass of wine. She clutched at the towel and gasped, "Good God, Liam, you startled the hell out of me."

Izzy could not believe that she had been caught in such a Caleb-like indiscretion. Regaining her composure, she took a quick sip of her wine, set it down on the table and tightened the towel around herself. She reached up to pull the clip from her hair allowing the curls to fall around her bare shoulders. Raising an inquisitive eyebrow at Liam, who still stood rooted in place, she said, "Don't let me stop you from whatever you're here to do, Liam."

Liam cleared his throat and set his eyes firmly on Izzy's face, "I was going to ask if you felt like going into town for dinner."

Izzy looked at Liam with stunned surprise. She left her wine glass on the table and padded across the living room towards him. She rose on her tiptoes to kiss him lightly on the cheek. "I have had a shitty day, Liam. Going out for dinner tonight would be a real treat. I'll go and get dressed and be with you in a few minutes."

With that, she was out of the living room and Liam heard her bedroom door shut behind her. He let out a whoosh of breath and sat down heavily on the sofa. He had known all day it was Caleb and Izzy's anniversary and he also knew they usually hadn't done much to celebrate the day. Caleb often joked that Izzy's lack of sentiment would be a relief for any guy. Liam had come into the cabin planning to do an online check of the company bank account. He needed to know if a large deposit had cleared before doing the payroll. The sight of Izzy coming out of the bathroom wrapped in a towel, letting her hair down the way she had, rattled him to such a degree he had simply blurted out the dinner invitation. As soon as the words were out of his mouth he was amazed at himself. He had no idea where on earth the idea had come from. Watching the look of shocked surprise on Izzy's face, he had been certain she would say – no thanks – in a tone of voice that indicated Liam should not pity her in this way. What had happened next – the kiss on the cheek, the smiling acceptance – had left him in shock.

The Sea Shed, an old house on the Dearborn waterfront, had been repurposed as an upscale restaurant. It specialized in the fresh catch of the day accompanied by organic side-dishes. The targeted market was the summer tourist trade but it was also a great stop for locals who desired a special night out. The wine list was as impressive as any place in the city. The restaurant was quiet on a week night. Liam and Izzy were seated beside a large window in what had once been the living room. The sun was setting over the ocean waves and the horizon had turned a brilliant, dark gold. The nearby dock and fishing boats were outlined in black and the boats were swaying with the tide.

Izzy was sipping a glass of wine and they were sharing a basket of fresh bread. Izzy dipped hers in olive oil and balsamic vinegar while Liam opted for the whipped, chive butter. He spread each small piece of bread thinly with the green-flecked mixture. He sipped his water slowly and watched Izzy who was gobbling up the bread like she hadn't eaten in a week. She was wearing what he would describe as the quintessential little black dress – form-fitting, with a plunging neckline and a slit high on one leg. Her silver medallion necklace glinted in the candle light and everything about her glowed.

"Do you want to hear about my rotten day, Liam?" Izzy asked this question as she leaned forward to avoid the possibility that drops of balsamic vinegar would spill down the front of her dress.

Liam reached across the small table to brush a lock of her hair away from her mouth, "I would like to hear about your rotten day –," he held his hand up to stop her from speaking, "– but first you have to let me torture you with ten uninterrupted minutes of talk about the sawmill."

He watched Izzy grimace, frown, shrug and then smile, "It's a deal," she conceded as the waitress brought a fresh basket of bread and refilled her wine glass. She sat back in her chair with a sigh of pure pleasure as she sipped the wine.

"I got a phone call this morning . . . from the reserve up at Cedar Falls." Liam took a small bite of his bread and chewed slowly. "They want a huge order of lumber . . . they've got some government money for housing and it sounds like they plan to rebuild half the village." He picked up his glass, took a sip of water and then buttered another piece of bread. "To get the contract they want us to train a few of their young guys. We'd need the extra guys to fill an order that size . . . but training people is a big obligation." Liam set the bread down uneaten and stared out the window for a moment. "We could turn the whole contract down but an order this size would go a way towards building back the equity in the business." He shrugged and finally looked over to meet Izzy's eyes, "The money coming in lately is not what it could be. Shit . . . I know you already know that."

Izzy felt a sudden rush of compassion for Liam. He was doing the best he could but he really wasn't the type of guy who was suited to run the woodlot and sawmill on his own; they both knew it. She reached over to cover his hands with her own, "Look, Liam . . . the money doesn't matter at all, OK? We wanted to keep the business going for Caleb and for the sake of the guys who work there . . . right?" Liam nodded silently. "Well, you've done that and we haven't lost any money so don't worry about it. Take the job if you think it's worth it for the guys who'll get trained or turn it down. Do whatever you think you can handle. Just don't worry about the money."

Liam stared down at Izzy's hand over his – her long graceful fingers with their soft-pink nails glowed against the darker brown of his own hand and her gold wedding band shone softly in the candle light. He raised his eyes to hers with a smile of relief on his face. In that moment Izzy withdrew her hand, smiling back at him. He felt cut off, bereft and lost, but he hid his disappointment well under a soft tone, "Your turn. Tell me about your bad day."

Izzy studied Liam's face over the bowls of seafood-stuffed tortellini smothered in rich béchamel sauce, now steaming between them. Salad plates of ruby-red beetroot and onion wedge salad, smelling sharp and tangy with orange zest, flanked the pasta. Suddenly, she couldn't think of one thing that seemed all that bad. Her headache was gone; the minor irritations of the day seemed trivial. "You know what, Liam? Everything is perfect right now. Let's enjoy this wonderful meal and talk about something else."

Through the rest of the main course, coffee and a shared piece of apple and hazelnut shortcake, they chatted like old friends. The conversation moved easily from talk about their day-to-day lives, the chickens, the garden, Izzy's work and Micah Camp. They spoke of people they knew and hadn't seen for a while, things that needed to be done around the main cabin, news and politics, books they had read or were thinking of reading.

Izzy stopped Liam from reaching for his wallet by tucking her credit card inside the flap of the leather cover that held the bill. She threw the black silk wrap over her sleeveless dress and linked her arm casually through Liam's as they walked toward her Jeep. Halfway across the parking lot she stopped, "What about a walk on the boardwalk for a bit, Liam? I don't know about you, but I'm way too stuffed to get in the car just yet."

Dearborn's historical boardwalk ran a half a kilometer in either direction along the ocean front. The waves were lapping quietly against the rocky shore and the sky was a dark shade of midnight-blue, the last of the day's light giving way to stars. Walking in comfortable silence, Izzy cast a discreet, sideways glance at Liam and she found she liked what she saw. Liam had a look that had always appealed to Izzy. Until she met Caleb, she had never been attracted to a guy with blonde hair. She caught herself wondering about Liam's being alone for as long as she had known him.

"Today would have been my wedding anniversary. Did you know that, Liam?" As they turned at the end of the boardwalk and headed back toward town, she added, "Some days I find it hard to be alone –," her voice broke slightly, "– but I can't imagine moving on from everything Caleb and I had, either." Liam was so quiet beside her she wondered if he had heard her. "How do you do it, Liam? Being alone, I mean." Izzy was suddenly overwhelmed with curiosity about all the things she had never been in a position to ask Liam.

Liam thought that his entire future depended on his answer to this one question. He hoped that someday Izzy might love him the way he knew he was falling in love with her. She couldn't see him in that way right now. She didn't even realize that she and Liam could be a possibility and he thought he understood why. He and Caleb had been so close there wasn't any room for Izzy to think of him as anything but Caleb's friend. He also knew she was only now starting to feel again. Her grief at Caleb's death had wrapped her in a cloak of distance from everyone and everything. The fact that she had functioned as well as she had was a testament to her strength. The way she had broken down sorting Caleb's things, the way she had opened up to Liam on the beach, these moments seemed to say the distance between them was contracting. In time, she might love him. All the right pieces were there between them, he was sure of that. All they had to do was connect the dots. What he said now might be the line that ran from A to B; then all the rest of the alphabet would stretch out in front of them.

Liam stopped at the railing and looked out over the moving body of water, across the expanse of waves and up at the stars. He inhaled the sea salt smell so different from the lake. He could feel her beside him leaning into the railing and hear her breathing in deeply. He began to talk.

"When I was little my grandmother lived with us. She had a weak heart for a long time and she mostly just lay on the sofa in the living room. I remember coming home from school and sitting on the floor by the sofa. I'd hold her hand and rattle on and on about every little thing that had happened to me. I would drive my cars up and down and around her or build forts in the blankets. She hardly spoke a word of English but she understood everything I said.

My mom was away a lot, so when I was little my grandmother was my whole world, all my people," Liam glanced over at Izzy for a moment and saw her watching him intently.

"She died when I was eight and I stopped eating. My mom got worried about me and then out of the blue, my dad showed up. He wasn't around much, so for him to make an appearance meant something serious was going on. He took me out on the land one day and I remember we were sitting sideways on the snowmobile sharing a thermos of tea."

Liam paused as if he wanted to get the words exactly right, "He told me – you loved your grandma. You're sad she's gone and that's good. It honours her memory. You love people and you lose them one way or the other. It hurts – you maybe start to think that loving people isn't worth that kind of hurt. But remember this, Liam, without other people we die. Then my dad laughed and said – but something else is true too, son. Look at this land. It seems very empty, right? In some ways we need to be empty and alone like this land. We come into this world alone and we leave alone. To be with others we need to know how to be alone."

Liam looked over and held Izzy's gaze for a moment. "Later in university I read about duality but it never seemed like anyone said it better than my old man." He shrugged and pushed away from the railing to begin walking again. After a long silence, when they were almost back to the parking lot, he said, "When I found you and Caleb and Bethany and Beulah there hadn't been any people in my life for a long time. I did figure out how to be alone though. Since coming here, I've never felt alone."

With tears in her eyes, Izzy sniffed quietly and got in the passenger side of the Jeep. She was grateful for the dark and the quiet drive back to the lake. Before she fell asleep that night, she thought of what Liam's dad had told him. She knew that throughout her life, in every attempt she had made to keep a part of herself separate, she had never learned to be alone. If she had, she wouldn't have clung to her need for space; she would have opened herself completely to Caleb. She would have taken the intimacy he offered.

She fell asleep with tears of regret slipping down her cheeks to wet her pillow and she dreamt that she was swimming. She thought she was in the lake but suddenly realized it was the ocean. She was so tired and the waves were getting bigger and bigger; there was no shoreline in any direction. In a panic she tried to scream for help but no sound came out of her mouth. She was terrified. Just when she thought she couldn't swim anymore she saw the raft in front of her and she was swimming in the lake towards it. An arm reached out to pull her out of the water and though she was cold and naked, she was shaking with relief as she climbed up on the raft. The last thing Izzy remembered of the tatters of her dream, when she woke up to the familiar numbers on her digital clock, was that the arm that had reached for her had belonged to Liam.

CHAPTER TWENTY-FIVE

i.

The recreational areas on the other side of the lake were going full tilt throughout the entire August long-weekend. Motor boats zipped up and down the lake pulling water skiers and kids on tubes. Sea doos, shooting huge plumes of water behind them, bounced over the waves. Bon fires glowed from the camp site and the sound of voices drifted across the water. One night, Bethany, Izzy and Liam sat out on the cliff deck to watch the fireworks spiralling up into the sky in a rainbow of snapping and screaming whirs of colour – all courtesy of one of the recreational places on the other side of the lake.

Justin watched the same display, sitting close to Lisa-Marie at the fire pit in front of Micah Camp with a bunch of the kids. He threw his arm casually around her shoulder; the atmosphere and her cute body pressed close to him weakened his resolve. Moments later he noticed Jesse sitting on the other side of the fire, giving him a leering, thumbs-up. That gave Justin just the reminder he needed. He withdrew his arm to pick up his guitar. But he was careful to make sure Jesse didn't get within touching distance of Lisa-Marie. Like that had a chance in hell of happening, he told himself angrily.

ii.

Dear Emma:

Justin put his arm around me at the fire pit tonight – right in front of everyone. I was snuggled up close to him. I could hardly breathe – my heart was thumping so loud I thought everyone could hear it. But then he just moved away to pick up his guitar and that was that. I thought maybe tonight when he walked me home it would finally happen – the kiss. But he just walked away – like every other night – he just walked away. I don't know what to do, Emma – I feel like screaming and pulling my hair. I just wish I could figure out what to do.

iii.

Late one morning, Izzy came to the workshop door and asked to speak to Lisa-Marie in the hall. "Sorry to interrupt," she began, "Mrs. Clayburn, the social worker from Dearborn, is here. She has appointments with a couple of the residents and she asked if she could see you at 11:30." Izzy paused for a second to gauge Lisa-Marie's reaction – a nod of acknowledgment and nothing else. "Last week, I gave your aunt the message to call Mrs. Clayburn." Izzy was waiting for Lisa-Marie to indicate that she was prepared for this meeting with the social worker, that she had some idea of what was going on. For her own part, Izzy was in the dark about the whole situation.

"Ya, Auntie Beth told me."

iv.

Bethany had been taken completely by surprise when she got the message to call the social worker. She went to Izzy's to make the call and Mrs. Clayburn had practically demanded that a time be arranged for her to see Lisa-Marie. Bethany had hung up the phone and stood very still in the quiet emptiness of the main cabin. Then she had picked up the phone again and dialed her mother's number in Kingston. When she came back to the A-Frame the look on her face had Beulah up off the sofa and pacing.

"What is it Beth, what the hell's going on?"

Bethany had sat down for a moment and glanced over nervously at Lisa-Marie who was sitting at the kitchen table sorting through a large stack of printed photos. Turning back to Beulah's pacing figure, she spoke quickly, "Mom's not doing so well. She's decided to sell her trailer and go into one of those supported living places. She talked to social services back home about Lisa-Marie. They called the Ministry out here and now a social worker wants to see her –," after a shaky pause, Bethany added, "– and us."

Beulah had stopped dead in her tracks. As the full realization of what she was hearing sunk in she narrowed her eyes and glanced quickly from Lisa-Marie to Bethany before she said, "Jesus H. Christ."

Lisa-Marie had become very still, staring down at the pictures spread on the table in front of her. Bethany rose quickly and walked over to the table to put her arms around Lisa-Marie. "Your grannie has written you a letter explaining everything. She says she mailed it a couple of days ago."

V.

Norma Clayburn met with Lisa-Marie in a small room next to Roland's office. Lisa-Marie's file, forwarded to her from social services in Ontario, was in front of her. She had scanned it quickly and it was pretty straightforward – mother dead, no father listed, her grandmother was her legal guardian. The school records indicated OK grades. A report from a school counsellor noted that Lisa-Marie had been victimized by several of the other girls – the word *bullied* wasn't used but it was clearly meant. The counsellor wrote that Lisa-Marie was responding to the situation by acting out. Norma frowned and thought, what the hell is that supposed to mean? A comment like that was a waste of the paper it was written on. Another form, written by a social worker in Kingston, described Lisa-Marie's suicide attempt and recommended follow-up. The final notation in the file stated that the grandmother was requesting a change in Lisa-Marie's guardianship.

"I get that my grannie can't look after me anymore," Lisa-Marie blurted out.

"You're right, that doesn't seem to be in the cards," Mrs. Clayburn looked up from the file at Lisa-Marie, "I'm thinking it's not in your best interests to go back, even if you could. Sometimes a fresh start is the best option; make a new beginning."

Lisa-Marie was stunned and she kept repeating the words – *make a new beginning* – over and over in her mind as the woman in front of her continued to talk.

"We can look at your options when we meet with your aunt. But, frankly, since she's your only other relative ... let's hope she can step up to the plate."

Lisa-Marie would have had to be blind and deaf not to notice the tension between Beulah and her Auntie Beth since they had learned of Grannie's plans. She'd also seen the lights on late in the bakery shed every night and she suspected that Beulah had been sleeping out there. She could see her Auntie Beth stepping up to the plate out of guilt. Whether Beulah would allow that was another question entirely.

Mrs. Clayburn's voice intruded on Lisa-Marie's thoughts with a thud, "Your living situation aside, I'd like to talk about the suicide attempt." She looked straight at Lisa-Marie, "For example, are you thinking of trying that again?"

The whole topic was introduced so suddenly that Lisa-Marie didn't even have a chance to resent the implication. The question was there in the space between her and Mrs. Clayburn and it was clear neither of them was going anywhere until Lisa-Marie answered.

"No, absolutely not," she was surprised at the conviction in her own voice.

Mrs. Clayburn nodded and looked back at the file, "You're going to need to talk this over with someone. It doesn't look like you saw anyone back in Kingston." Lisa-Marie shook her head. "Well – I can't take you on right now. My calendar is full and I'm going on leave soon." The social worker stopped talking for a moment. She suddenly pointed her pen at Lisa-Marie and smiled, "This is what we'll do. Izzy Montgomery is an excellent counsellor. I'm sure she would have no problem fitting you in. I don't want to leave this suicide thing as a loose end. I'm going to make a note on your file that you'll book a few sessions with her, talk things through a bit," Mrs. Clayburn was already scribbling in the file and though Lisa-Marie was thinking, fat chance, she just nodded.

vi.

Norma Clayburn set her coffee cup down firmly on the kitchen table and quickly took the measure of the women seated around her. Beulah, with her arms folded tightly and eyes darting hostile glances around the table was an easy read. The other two were also transparent as far as Norma was concerned – Bethany with eyes cast down at her clutched hands and Lisa-Marie trying, quite unsuccessfully, to appear uninterested in what anyone had to say, as she stared out the A-Frame's front window to the lake.

"I'm just going to spell this out for the three of you without any frills, how does that sound?"

Beulah sat forward in her chair, "That's how I'd like it Norma – straight-up. Tell us exactly where we stand in respect to this sudden turn of events." Bethany dodged Beulah's accusatory stare and nodded silently toward Norma. Lisa-Marie continued to study the lake, her mouth set in a firm line and her eyes narrowed.

"Bethany, your mother can't provide care for Lisa-Marie any longer and since you are her only other relative, the responsibility could fall to you – if you were willing." Norma paused for effect. "Mind you, this is all subject to a decision by a judge, but as I see it, you and your partner –," she nodded toward Beulah, "– might be a good choice for Lisa-Marie right now. However, if there are reasons you can't make a home for her, she will be sent back to Ontario to be placed in the foster-care system there." Bethany's eyes widened as Beulah's fists tightened on the table and Lisa-Marie's bottom lip started to tremble.

Norma frowned, "I'll be honest with you . . . going into the system at Lisa-Marie's age is a bit of a pig-in-a-poke, so to speak. She could get great foster parents, they're out there for sure; but even then, going into care with total strangers when she's sixteen and has always lived with family . . . well, it wouldn't be easy. She might end up going through a lot of short-term place-ments and that can make school difficult. There are issues of neglect, too – the system is what it is." Norma shrugged and then added, "Whatever the arrange-ment, it will only be for a couple of years, anyway."

Bethany could read a change coming over Beulah in the shifting emotions that raced across her face. Lisa-Marie was morphing from a pain-in-the-ass burden to a rescue mission. Bethany allowed herself to feel hopeful, though she kept this to herself. She knew it was only a matter of time before Beulah would give in, but not without some kind of fight. Appearances had to be preserved.

Beulah locked eyes in a staring match with Norma and stabbed a finger toward Bethany, "What about the issue of our same sex relationship, Norma? You don't anticipate that being a barrier to our being seen as appropriate care-givers for a sixteen-year-old girl?"

Norma gave a dismissive shrug and said, "Come on Beulah, we aren't living in the dark ages here. Bethany is the girl's aunt – family. That matters much more than who she shares a bed with."

Beulah shook her head and played her last card, "You will admit that we live in an isolated area here and there is the issue of schooling to consider."

Norma was prepared, "It's not as if you're living in Timbuktu, Beulah. I got out here in less than forty minutes. School can be managed. Someone can drive Lisa-Marie into the Dearborn high school every day; or you can get her a little car and she can drive herself. You might even want to think about boarding her in a bigger center down island, like Nanaimo or Victoria. She could come home for the longer holidays. Lots of the local teens do that."

Lisa-Marie took careful note of the look on Beulah's face as Norma made what seemed like outlandish suggestions for transportation and living arrangements. The silence around the table was unbearable, "Don't I even get a say in any of this?" She was biting her lip and looking from her Auntie Beth's impassive face to Mrs. Clayburn's all-in-a-day's-work expression.

"Of course a judge would want to take your preferences into account, but you are a minor and those in charge will make decisions in your best interest." Mrs. Clayburn shrugged her shoulders.

"I would rather be with you Auntie Beth, than go into foster care with strangers," Lisa-Marie bit down firmly on her lower lip to stop from crying and looked away quickly from the tears forming in her aunt's eyes.

"I'm going to leave the three of you to discuss this on your own." Norma drained her cup, "Excellent coffee, by the way." She handed Bethany her card as she got up, "Just call me at the office in Dearborn when you've come to a decision."

"That won't be necessary, Norma," Beulah was on her feet now as well. "Clearly Bethany and I have a responsibility for Lisa-Marie's care and we have no intention of shifting that onto anyone else. Go ahead and prepare the paperwork. We'll jump through whatever hoops we need to." Turning to Bethany, Beulah gave her a tight-lipped smile, "Isn't that right, Bethany?"

Tears washed down Bethany's face as she jumped up to hug Lisa-Marie and then holding her tightly, she smiled at Beulah and turned to Norma, "Yes, yes. We'll do whatever you need us to do."

As Bethany saw the social worker out and onto the trail back to the Camp, Beulah and Lisa-Marie sized each other up across the table. Lisa-Marie shrugged her shoulders and said, "I guess you're stuck with me."

Beulah rose from the table and looked down at Lisa-Marie for a moment, shaking her head. "Think on that again missy, more likely you're stuck with me."

Norma Clayburn picked up the inter-office phone at Micah Camp and dialed Izzy's extension. She got an automated message reporting Izzy wasn't available. She went by Izzy's office and knocked on the door but no one answered. She looked with irritation at her watch; she really couldn't hang around here anymore. She had told Beulah it wasn't like they lived in Timbuktu but it felt like that to her now as she contemplated the drive back to Dearborn. She made her way to Roland's office but no one was there either. Tearing a piece of paper from the pad at the main desk, she quickly scribbled a note to Izzy and walked back down the hall to push it under her door. She planned to follow up the note with a phone call when she got back into the office the next day – a professional courtesy. She should make sure Izzy had no objection to taking Lisa-Marie on. Unfortunately, Norma never got around to making the call.

v i i .

Lisa-Marie gathered her things from the beach and made her way up the stairs and onto the path toward home. She was still on shaky ground after the meetings with the social worker. At the Camp that morning it was possible to push the whole thing out of her mind and while she was with Justin she didn't think of anything else. Now that she was alone it all flooded back. Everything she had ever known of her life was up for grabs and she was scared. Lost in her own thoughts, she was startled when she almost ran right into Izzy at a curve in the path.

"Lisa . . . hello . . . I'm glad to see you. I've just been talking with your aunt and Beulah and they told me about your grandmother. I'm really sorry. I imagine the whole thing is a bit of a shock," Izzy paused to give Lisa-Marie a chance to talk. Nodding silently, Lisa-Marie simply lowered her eyes to study the ferns along the side of the trail. Izzy went on, "They mentioned the meeting with Mrs. Clayburn yesterday and their decision to have you stay here."

"There weren't exactly that many options," Lisa-Marie said quietly and Izzy nodded, waiting once again for Lisa-Marie to talk; but her silent study of the ferns went on.

"We talked a bit about school and I wanted you to know that if you decide to board down island, Caleb and I know –," Izzy stopped talking for a moment and then shook her head and went on, "– I know a few families, good people in Nanaimo and Victoria too, that you might be able to board with. Since it's already August, Bethany said it's OK for me to ask around. I might be able to line up something if that's what you decide you want to do."

"I just need some time to think, everything is happening so fast," Lisa-Marie barely looked up.

Izzy waited patiently, a sympathetic look on her face, but it was soon obvious to her that she wasn't getting anywhere in her attempts to get Lisa-Marie to talk. The few lines Norma Clayburn had scribbled and slid under her door, saying Lisa-Marie would be coming to her for some counselling sessions, surprised Izzy. She hadn't been able to get an explanation because Norma was out of her office all day. Izzy felt frustrated not knowing what the hell was going on. That had been the motivation behind her unannounced visit to the A-Frame. She was hoping she might pick up some hint as to why Norma would have written such a note.

Izzy was in a difficult spot. Ethically, she couldn't ask Bethany what Norma's note meant, in case Bethany knew nothing about it. Norma's idea had to have come out of the meeting she'd had with Lisa-Marie and that meeting was confidential. Izzy couldn't ask Lisa-Marie either – nor could she issue an invitation to counselling. She had no right to push herself into Lisa-Marie's life in such a way. She didn't like being placed in such a position.

Bethany and Beulah had been very open about their decision to take on the responsibility for Lisa-Marie's care. But Bethany had quickly steered the conversation to the issue of high school. By the time Izzy left the A-Frame, she was no closer to understanding why Norma thought Lisa-Marie would come to her for counselling than she had been when she arrived a half-hour earlier.

It was obvious that nothing more than a silent nod was forthcoming from Lisa-Marie. Izzy gave up, "OK then . . . well . . . have a nice evening." As if released from a cage, Lisa-Marie shot past Izzy to move quickly along the path toward the A-Frame. Izzy continued on the trail in the opposite direction.

viii.

Izzy walked through the kitchen door and realized she was starving. She had missed lunch and the smell of trout frying in garlic butter was intoxicating. She smiled to see Dan, clad in her poppy-strewn apron, busy at the stove with a metal flipper in one hand and an open beer in the other.

"I didn't think you would mind if I just came in and got dinner started. I've opened a bottle of wine for you."

Izzy found she didn't mind at all, "There are new potatoes that Justin dug earlier and fresh green beans, too." Izzy moved past Dan to the pantry, taking the glass of wine he poured for her. "But you're going to have to fight me for that apron," she told him.

Later, she sat reading in the armchair in the living room while Dan played the piano. Izzy thought of all the times she and Caleb had sat comfortably together in the evenings, music in the background, each doing separate things – she reading or marking and he doing a nightly crossword or Sudoku. Caleb had been mad for puzzles of all types – puzzles and cards.

Izzy and Dan had gotten used to having dinner together a couple of nights a week and ironically, having Dan around only brought home to Izzy how alone she really was. It was strange, because she hadn't thought of being alone when she was alone. She realized that she didn't enjoy eating by herself as much as she thought she did.

Suddenly she remembered her dinner out with Liam and what he had told her about learning to be alone. She shrugged and found herself feeling irritated at Liam. It's all well and fine for him to say he never feels alone. He doesn't know what it's like to live with someone day in and day out for years and then have it all come to an end. She wasn't sure how she knew this about Liam but she didn't care if she was right or wrong.

As Izzy saw Dan out the back door later, he turned at the last moment to ask, "I guess Bethany and Beulah have been together for a while, hey?"

"Well, all the time I've known them. But they got together very soon after Beulah bought the place, must be fifteen years now." Izzy looked closely at Dan. "It doesn't bother you at all, Beulah and Bethany?" Dan was obviously startled by her question and Izzy rushed a bit to finish her thought, "I mean the whole Church thing, same sex relationships, you being a priest?"

Dan looked thoughtful for a moment, "No. I've never thought being a priest meant I had to sit in judgment on people's private lives. When you get right down to it, most couples . . . same sex or not . . . have similar challenges. It's always just people trying to make sense of things day by day. I try not to draw too many lines. The Church will catch up – but probably not fast enough to please most people." With that he was out the door waving a cheery bye.

i x .

Pearl raised her head and got up to pad over to the back door of the workshop. She had been lying under the desk with her paws over Liam's feet. Liam heard Dan stop briefly by the screen door and call out, "Hey there, Liam," as he passed by.

Over the last few weeks, Liam had begun to experience more than a passing dislike for Dan. He couldn't help but watch and notice things about the guy. He noticed that Dan didn't exert himself much at all and since Liam was running himself ragged, that kind of inaction was irksome. Dan liked to sleep in and he liked to fish most afternoons if he could. Besides that, he mostly sat in the rocker on the veranda of the guest house chatting with whoever came by or dozing in the nearby hammock. The neatly stacked piles of papers and books, which sat prominently on the table in front of his main window, never seemed to be disturbed. In the time that Dan had been there, Liam had yet to see him ever sitting at that table.

Liam knew that Beulah made regular afternoon stops with deliveries for Dan. As far as he could see, she didn't seem to resent it in the least – beer, bags of potato chips, bakery cakes and cookies, fishing magazines – you name it. It seemed that whenever Dan had a whim for something, he would simply order it up from the request box at the top of the trail like it was take-out pizza.

Dan also seemed to have a knack for never staying at the guest cabin to cook his own dinner. It was like he expected to make the rounds eating at other people's places. He could be seen over at the Camp for dinner at least three times a week. Dan had charmed Cook the first night they met at the potluck when he lavishly praised her pie. Cook did like a man who enjoyed a good pie. Dan was welcome at Bethany and Beulah's whenever he wanted and he was regularly at Izzy's. When Liam came over to the shop to work on the accounts, over two hours ago, he had heard Dan playing the piano.

Liam was jealous, plain and simple. He didn't want Dan sitting with Izzy, laughing and enjoying himself. Liam had known enough priests and heard about others during his growing up time on the reserve to realize that priestly celibacy was no barrier to anything. On top of that, Dan didn't act like a priest at all; there was no praying, or quoting scripture, no collar and Liam caught him on more than one occasion looking at Bethany, Izzy and even Lisa-Marie in a way that was far from priestly. He marvelled that Beulah wasn't more concerned with the time Bethany was spending out in the boat with this guy every afternoon. Not that he thought Dan was Bethany's type, even beyond the obvious fact that he was male. Liam didn't trust Dan as far as he could throw him.

X.

Izzy took a drink of what she promised herself would be her last glass of wine for the night. She was sitting on the swing chair on the cliff deck, her mind still puzzled over Norma's note. Why would Norma think that Lisa-Marie wanted to have counselling sessions with Izzy? Could Lisa-Marie have told her this? And if so, then why didn't Lisa-Marie say something to Izzy?

Izzy understood that Lisa-Marie must be upset about her grandmother's decision and suddenly finding out she had no home to go back to, but that didn't seem like something Norma would judge as requiring Izzy's professional skills. Norma dealt with kids who had serious issues. Surely she would tell Lisa-Marie that her aunt was the logical person to support her through this transition. *Family first* was definitely Norma's motto. With her thoughts chasing each other around the way Dante and Pearl would spin about after one another's tails, Izzy couldn't shake the idea that something wasn't right about Lisa-Marie's visit here this summer. Something was going on.

It was after midnight and the thin moon was slipping behind the mountains, its razor-sharp path on the lake becoming shorter and shorter. Izzy felt cold for the first time that day and was glad of the chill. The surprising heat of July was rolling into August. Izzy stretched up from the swing chair, calling Dante softly. As he rose to trot after her the lone wolf call in the hills sounded and Dante's ears perked up as he growled low in his throat. Izzy reached down to pat him, "I know boy, it's driving me crazy too."

CHAPTER TWENTY-SIX

i.

The late afternoon sun was slanting through small cracks in the closed blinds of Micah Camp's TV room. Jesse was lounging on the sofa making his way crunch after crunch through a bag of potato chips. Justin came through the door and walked over to check the TV schedule. He watched Jesse out of the corner of his eye. The guy was a pain in the ass – friendly enough, with a quick smile and an even quicker joke, but he was always eating. Justin had no idea why that should be a source of irritation. He remembered the way Jesse had watched Lisa-Marie down at the fire pit – watching was hardly the way to describe it. He had looked at her the way Justin imagined a fat kid on a diet would look at a display of doughnuts in the window of a Tim Horton's. But what bothered Justin most was the smirk that Jesse usually had on his face. It was like he knew something that Justin wouldn't want him to know.

Justin looked up to see Izzy walk past the open door heading down the hall to her office. She was dressed in a simple, sleeveless dress, her medallion necklace clicking against her neck, her bare arms and legs flashing brown as she walked. Justin wasn't the only person watching Izzy. Jesse winked at him and at the other two guys in the room and said, "I sure wouldn't mind bagging that, hey."

Justin moved swiftly across the room to grab Jesse by the collar of his T-shirt, haul him up off the sofa and push him against the wall. "It wouldn't hurt . . . to have a bit of respect . . . now would it?" Justin spoke quietly and close to Jesse's face. The two stood there like that for a moment, Jesse clearly bowing to the fact that Justin was taller and stronger than him. Justin pushed Jesse again as he let go of the T-shirt. He shook his head in disgust and walked out of the room.

Jesse watched Justin go and a small smile lifted the corners of his mouth. He whistled softly under his breath. Shrugging to the two other guys, he returned to the couch and dug back into the potato chips with single mindedness.

i i .

Later that evening, in the TV room, an episode of *Lost* was in full swing. Justin was sitting on the couch and Lisa-Marie was sitting cross legged on the floor in front of him. He looked at his watch and got up quickly. Placing a hand on the back of the sofa, he swung himself over it and was on his way out of the room. Lisa-Marie turned in surprise to hear him say, "Don't leave before I get back. I'll be here before the show ends to walk you home."

Lisa-Marie slid into Justin's vacant spot on the sofa; the warmth of his body and the smell of his soap still lingered in the space. Jesse was sitting across from her and he winked. Scowling she turned back to the TV. A few minutes later there were voices and the sound of laughter coming from the hall. Jesse caught Lisa-Marie's eye and gestured with his head for her to turn around and take a look. She glanced over her shoulder and saw Justin strolling down the hall with Izzy; he looked as if no one else in the world would ever matter to him. Lisa-Marie turned back to the TV hoping she had been able to conceal the pathetic look that had crossed her face. Someone suggested they stop the show for a bathroom break and as people began to stretch and move around, Jesse slid onto the arm of the sofa next to her.

He leaned in close to her ear to whisper, "She's here for group every Wednesday night and just like clockwork golden boy jumps up to walk her home at nine. Sort of like a well-trained dog when you think about it. I guess you haven't been here on a Wednesday night before, have you? Otherwise you would have noticed how golden boy can't wait to run out and be with her."

No, she hadn't been at the Camp on a Wednesday night because she had gotten in the habit of going to Liam's on Wednesdays. He was letting her help with the leather cover she wanted for Justin's album and they usually worked on it then. Liam was busy with some sawmill accounting stuff so he'd had to cancel on her tonight. Coming over to the Camp had been a last minute decision.

Lisa-Marie yanked her body away from Jesse, "You're a real asshole . . . you know that? Justin's just being nice. Something you clearly wouldn't have a clue about." She got up from the sofa quickly, "Leave me alone, OK . . . get it?" She stomped off to the washroom and when she got back she sat as far away from Jesse as possible.

Justin, true to his word, was back before the program finished and as the final credits rolled he asked, "Ready Leez?"

She got up, ignoring the way Jesse was trying to catch her eye, "Ya sure, let's go."

Justin was quiet on the walk down the trail and Lisa-Marie was feeling too down in the dumps to manage any type of romantic fantasy about what could happen on the dark path. They stopped within view of the A-Frame. Noticing how quiet Lisa-Marie was, Justin reached out to ruffle her hair, "Anything wrong, Leez?"

He leaned back against a large fir tree and Lisa-Marie felt tears welling up in her eyes. She blinked rapidly, swallowed hard and shook her head. She looked up to see the concern on Justin's face and before she could stop herself she blurted out, "I keep thinking about how I might never see my grannie again or go home. One minute I think it's good and I'm all excited about staying here with Auntie Beth or maybe going away to school down island; then the next minute I feel scared and sad." Her voice broke slightly and to her total horror, the tears gathering under her eyelashes ran down her face.

Justin reached over and tipped her face up, "Hey Leez, don't cry. It's all going to work out OK, you'll see." Lisa-Marie looked into his eyes and she was sure she read an invitation there. She stepped forward into Justin arms.

He held her and looked down at her head resting against his chest. He could so easily tip her face to his, kiss her tears away and just not stop. Justin knew she wouldn't want him to stop and his body wanted what she seemed determined to offer. He knew it would feel great to take the edge off – lately he was tied up in a knot so tight he had trouble breathing. But that kind of behaviour could definitely not be listed under the heading of keeping things cool. Slowly, gently, Justin moved Lisa-Marie away from him. He saw the confusion in her eyes and a hint of something else – something that made him feel cold inside. But he reached out and ruffled her hair like always and said goodbye.

"See you tomorrow Leez," he began to walk away but turned at the last second and called out to her, "Hey, maybe tomorrow you'll beat me to the raft, you were close today. Things will be OK, Leez."

i i i .

Dear Emma:

Oh crap, crap, crap. I burst out crying in front of Justin. I feel so humiliated and stupid. And when he asked me what was wrong I threw myself into his arms. It felt so good – he was holding me and it felt so good. But then he sort of pushed me away. I know he wanted to kiss me when I was in his arms, I know it. But he didn't. Why? Why wouldn't he kiss me when the moment was so perfect? For a second I thought I hated him. How could I feel like that, Emma? How could I feel like that about Justin for even one second?

Jesse says Justin walks Izzy home every Wednesday night – you should have seen how cosy they looked together. What if – I can't bear to write it – what if he kisses her goodnight? What if he doesn't want to kiss me because he's already been kissing her – and maybe even more than kissing? Maybe they laugh together about what a total fool I am for throwing myself at Justin. I really do hate Izzy now.

i v .

Back on the path headed to the Camp, Justin's thoughts were all of Izzy – her grateful smile when he showed up as he did every Wednesday to walk her home. How she looked wrapping her sweater around her body, hugging herself into it when the wind came up off the lake. He thought of her going alone into her cabin, sleeping alone in the big four-poster bed under the white duvet he saw often enough through her bedroom window. Some days he thought he must have walked by that window a dozen times and every single time he fought off the image of Izzy stretched out on that white duvet.

Snap out of it, Justin told himself. If he kept this up he would end up as bad as Jesse. He could still feel his fists bunching up and the anger rising in him when he thought of Jesse's comment about Izzy. To say nothing of the way Jesse was always looking at Lisa-Marie. Where the hell did that guy get off thinking he could act like that? As he neared the Camp and turned toward his cabin the thought crossed Justin's mind that at least Jesse had the guts to say out loud what he would like to get from Izzy. He might be a smirking, crude, over-eater, but he was honest. Justin, who would have given a lot for any piece of Izzy at all, kept his fantasies to himself. And he certainly had no right to say who should or shouldn't look at Lisa-Marie. I'm a fucking idiot, he told himself. Maybe I should just pack it in early – leave for Vancouver before the end of the month. He shook his head. He knew he wouldn't seriously consider that idea. He wasn't going to give up a single minute he could spend with Izzy. It was that simple and that hopeless.

CHAPTER TWENTY-SEVEN

i.

Dan strolled along the tree-lined trail, his thoughts bouncing around comfortably in his head as he loudly sang the words to an old tune. He had been told singing was a good way to stay clear of the bears. He thought about the last ball game he and Beulah had gone to. The regular Tuesday night baseball outings meant cheering at whatever event happened to be booked for the ball diamond that night. This past Tuesday they had watched a T-ball tournament with a bunch of preschoolers running around the field. Dan had to admit some of those little kids could really whack the ball. He thought about the trout he had cooked at Izzy's the other night – it was delicious. He hoped that Beulah would remember he had asked her to get him a big can of Tim Horton's coffee – he was running low. Dan kept walking, singing and feeling pretty good about his life.

Dan knew he wasn't the type of person to spend a lot of time dwelling on his own motives, right or wrong, good or bad. He had never really seen the point of too much self-reflection. It just seemed to lead to confusion. There was really no sense in getting wound up in a knot dwelling on past events that couldn't be changed or in thinking too much about problems that didn't have solutions. It was better to take each day as it came and relax. Dan thought that if more people adopted his way of thinking, fewer people would suffer from depression and anxiety related disorders.

He was enjoying his time at Crater Lake. He liked going over to the Camp for dinner, joking around with Cook and talking with Roland. He was happy to borrow Izzy's Jeep and fill-in for an occasional Mass at the Church in Dearborn. He'd already performed a wedding and danced through the night at the reception, leaving with a fat stipend envelope in his pocket. He was enjoying his friendship with Beulah, drinking beer and watching baseball. He was comfortable talking with Izzy about the helping work they were both committed to doing. He liked spending time with her in her beautiful cabin, playing her piano and eating the wonderful meals she threw together with ease. He was ecstatic about the fishing – Crater Lake truly was the hidden gem he had read about. And Dan was thrilled to be able to spend most afternoons with a woman as pretty as Bethany.

Dan wanted to have an affair with Bethany. He knew this part of himself well and he didn't fight it. He had chosen her the first night at the book club gathering. Granted, the selection of women within the vicinity was not as diverse as your average parish. Beulah was off the romance list for sure. Lisa-Marie, though possessing ample charms in the body department, was typical of so many young women these days – she seemed to enjoy putting it all on display. He would take discreet looks now and then. What red-blooded male worth his salt wouldn't? But he was definitely not interested in more. Dan didn't want to babysit. Izzy was very attractive but he suspected she was far too self-assured in the bedroom for his taste.

Dan would have picked Bethany even if the crowd had been much bigger. She was his type. He could hardly believe his good fortunate that she happened to be the only person around who cared about fishing. He had a golden opportunity from that first week to be alone with her. He was not in the least fazed by the sex of Bethany's current partner. Dan believed that physical desire isn't really as cut and dried as most people think. It is more a shifting and turning phenomenon. It depends a lot on circumstances. His instincts had led him to Bethany right from the start and his track record had been pretty good so far when it came to choosing women.

As he strolled along the shady path to the A-Frame, Dan's only issue was why things were moving along so slowly. It was into August now and he had endured a number of restless nights, ending in yet another area of sin, with images of Bethany on his mind. They had already spent what seemed to Dan like endless afternoons in the boat together and he was unsure why things hadn't progressed beyond their sitting knee to knee for so many hours.

He concluded it must be the fishing. He had never met a woman who shared the same passion for fishing that he experienced, a woman who could disappear into the activity while the entire world faded away for a portion of time. Every afternoon was the same. Dan would come down the path to the A-Frame absolutely resolved that today he would make a move. He and Bethany would be in the boat, talking for the first bit and then the spell of the fishing would take over. Before he knew it he would be sitting on the veranda of the A-Frame having a beer with Beulah while Bethany prepared dinner, or on his way to Izzy's or to Micah Camp for a meal. But never where he wanted to be – tangled up naked with Bethany somewhere, his hands entwined in the long rope of her blond hair.

ii.

Before leaving for his sabbatical, Dan had been summoned to a meeting with the bishop. The diocesan chancellor had delivered this request via telephone in the high pitched nasal tone that always got on Dan's nerves. Seated in the bishop's office, Dan was told of three letters that had been received regarding his activities in several adjacent parishes over the last year. Dan had recently left that particular area to take over a parish at the other end of the diocese.

According to the chancellor, these letters were of a disturbing nature. Dan glanced casually between the chancellor and the bishop and then studied his fingernails carefully. He certainly wasn't going to get worked up about a few letters. Surely the bishop shared his opinion of the chancellor – a guy overly convinced of his own importance who had clearly let the nitpicking details of his job destroy any sense of humour he might have had. As the chancellor read each of the letters out loud in his nasal tone, Dan had to admit that the picture painted of him didn't sound great. But then again the letters told only one side of the story.

An older, female parishioner at St. Mark's wrote about the number of times Dan's car was parked in the driveway of the home of a certain married woman when her husband was out of town. The new priest at St. Anthony's reported that a parishioner had gotten drunk and parked his truck on the lawn of the church demanding to know where that wife-stealing priest Patterson had gone. In his anger, the drunken man had thrown beer bottles at the stained glass windows. Dan shuddered when he heard that – they had fund-raised forever to pay for those windows. The liturgical director at St. Jude's penned a particularly vicious letter. Dan had served as one of three priests at St. Jude's before his most recent move. He had been good friends with the liturgical director – they had played on the same parish baseball team. His letter accused his own wife and Dan of sharing a room at a religious education conference in Quebec.

The bishop folded his hands on the large oak desk in front of him and looked steadily at Dan, "We aren't asking you to defend yourself. You've done good work here in the diocese . . . in the parishes and with your hospital chaplaincy commitments. Both the chancellor and I know the reality of parish life."

Dan seriously doubted that, especially in the case of the chancellor. He imagined the chancellor's only reality consisted of knowing where to buy cheap black suits that Dan wouldn't have been caught dead in and shoes an undertaker would have been embarrassed to wear.

The bishop paused to look out the window of the second-floor office to the busy street below. "The women are the only ones doing anything in the Church these days." He folded his hands together on the desk as he laid out his perspective on this reality, "The parish council, liturgy, catechism, adult religious education – it's all women. As a parish priest it's your job to work with them on a daily basis. That can present challenges." The bishop looked past Dan to the wooden crucifix over the door and shook his head, "It's a lot more complicated now than when we were giving spiritual guidance to the ladies in the Catholic Women's League – all of the old dears baking pies to get to heaven." The bishop flipped open a calendar on his desk and continued, "What I need you to do, Dan, is spend some time in serious reflection."

The chancellor nodded emphatically, "It's not just the occasion of sin we are to be vigilant about, Father Patterson. We must always be on guard against the appearance of sin."

The bishop frowned over at the small, delicate looking man in his early thirties dressed in a dark-black suit, black clerical shirt and a white Roman collar tight around his neck. The chancellor's appearance was a stark contrast to the bishop's own blue shirt topped by a navy cardigan or Dan's sports slacks and golf shirt.

"Yes, well, I think that will do," he stated firmly and then turned back to Dan. "I see you're booked to start your sabbatical next month. There's a ten-day silent retreat for priests being held just outside Toronto. It's scheduled to start right at the beginning of the month. I know the spiritual director running things there and the center has a couple of very good counsellors on staff."

The bishop made a couple of notes on his calendar and rose to shake Dan's hand, "It's been really good to touch base with you, Dan. Go to that retreat . . . get yourself on track. Come back from your sabbatical rested and ready to work. We need priests like you in the diocese." Ten days out of his sabbatical, though not seeming like a lot of time when he had a whole year, was a serious inconvenience to Dan. And he knew full well that the mention of counsellors on staff meant he would be required to see one.

When Dan got to the retreat center he booked a session with one of the resident counsellors, a fellow priest with enough credentials displayed on the wall of his office to indicate he had done a lot more schooling than preaching. He advised Dan to speak openly and to understand that he was being offered strict confidence in their sessions together. Dan had to be totally honest if they were going to get anywhere.

Dan had no problem being honest. Everything was easy to explain. He enjoyed being a priest, the lifestyle suited him and for the most part he found the work he did rewarding. He thought he did a good job, too. At the same time, he was a man who found the vow of celibacy a difficult thing and he didn't believe that God cared if a couple of consenting adults stole a few moments of pleasure together here and there. The women he chose were willing partners and he imagined they went right on with their lives just as he did when the affairs ended. He certainly wasn't forcing anyone into anything. Being a priest was a vocation – yes, he understood that – but it was also his career and he wasn't going to throw his career away and start again because he had a problem with the company line. He had over twenty years in the priesthood and a pension to think about. He attended enough conferences and various gatherings where he could always find a fellow priest willing to exchange a quick confession with him. Dan believed people made things far more complicated than they needed to be and he told the counsellor that.

On the last day of the retreat the counsellor spoke to Dan about compartmentalizing his life and acting as if he could just parcel out bits and pieces of himself into little boxes and try to pretend none of them were connected.

The counsellor leaned forward in his chair to tick off on his fingers all of Dan's so-called boxes: Dan the priest, Dan the hospital chaplain, Dan who was everyone's buddy, going as far as to have an affair with the wife of one of his buddies. The counsellor added this bit with a slight frown. Dan the man who found a life without sex too much of a burden, who broke his vows of celibacy and encouraged married women to break their wedding vows in bed with him.

Dan stared out the window at a beautiful Japanese Maple, its branches bowed over in a shower of blood-red leaves and he thought what a bunch of clap-trap, mumbo-jumbo. Little boxes indeed; he was hard pressed to keep from laughing right out loud. But the counsellor was not finished. He leveled a stern glance at Dan and peppered him with questions to consider.

What was going to happen, he asked Dan, when the walls of those boxes came down? What about how the women felt when he left them to move onto the next parish and yet another affair? These kinds of things were not as secret as Dan might imagine, so what about how his parishioners felt? He talked about levels of denial and personal responsibility and challenged Dan's argument that being a priest in the Roman Catholic Church was a career. He asked Dan to seriously think about what being a priest meant to him. He stated quite firmly that the Catholic sacrament of Holy Orders was much more than a set of work policy guidelines.

Dan had no interest in pursuing the answers to any of these questions or getting too wound up about the difference between a career and a vocation, but he knew enough about getting on with his life to nod his head and agree to journal and seek regular spiritual guidance when he got home. These were things easily set on the back burner as he continued on with his sabbatical. By the time he did return, all would be forgotten. Priests were in too great of a demand to make a big deal of his affairs. It wasn't like he was a pedophile or something. Dan didn't flatter himself. Regardless of how he chose to live his life – whether it was within the strict confines of canonical law, or if he chose to bend certain rules he found overly repressive – it wouldn't have much of an effect on the whole grand scheme of Catholicism.

Chapter Twenty-Eight

i.

Maddy and Lisa-Marie were sitting together at the worktable trimming bars of soap. "How are the plans for the garden party coming along?" Maddy asked as she dropped a bar of *citrus splash* into a tub marked *Ready for Wrapping* and grabbed for the next bar that needed trimming.

"Great . . . my costume is done and I helped Izzy get the invitations ready . . . my photos look really professional. That's what Izzy said." Lisa-Marie's knife scraped deeply along the edge of a bar of *orange zest*, "Oh crap," she muttered, "I can't ever seem to do as neat a job as you do."

Maddy grabbed the bar from Lisa-Marie and smoothed the ragged edge. "You're lucky to get so much time to spend with Izzy. She's great isn't she?" Maddy leaned toward Lisa-Marie, "She had this gorgeous husband who died. She showed me his picture." In an elaborate pantomime, Maddy clutched at her heart, gave a couple of heavy breaths and fanned herself as if she were burning up. "He was really hot . . . like Brad Pitt in –,"

"*Legends of the Fall* . . . right?" Lisa-Marie chimed in, "I saw a picture of him over at Izzy's." They both started laughing and Lisa-Marie added, "My grannie made me watch it."

Maddy hooted with laughter. "Oh ya, mine too. Anyway, Izzy told me that when her husband died she thought she would never be able to breathe properly again, but she did. She said time heals stuff."

Lisa-Marie nodded in agreement. Maddy looked over at her with twinkling eyes as she tossed the bar of *orange zest* into the bin. "Sometimes I wish I could have been Caleb. I would have been able to kiss Izzy and make passionate love to her all night. She's so beautiful and so perfect and I would love to be that close to her." Maddy's mischievous grin widened as she raked her hands through her hair and stretched on her stool in a sensuous way.

Lisa-Marie frowned and stared at Maddy for a moment, unsure about how to respond. Maddy was always joking around and saying crazy things and she could carry on a joke long after it stopped being funny. To be on the safe side, Lisa-Marie decided to slide her stool back and move slightly away from Maddy at the workbench.

Maddy watched Lisa-Marie's retreat and threw her head back laughing, "I'm not a lesbian or anything, Leez. I like guys. In fact, I happen to have a little something set up with Jesse in the boat shed later tonight." She pulled Lisa-Marie's stool back towards the table. "I don't go after girls and even if I did, I wouldn't go after a little girl like you."

Lisa-Marie shrugged but she still wasn't sure if Maddy was joking around or being serious. Lisa-Marie wasn't used to having a friend. There were times, talking to Maddy in the workshop or chumming around with her in the evenings, when she felt tongue-tied and couldn't figure out how to do this friend thing.

"I'm just saying Izzy is so nice –," Maddy caught Lisa-Marie's look of scepticism, "– no really, Leez, believe me. When you sit with her in her office she makes you feel like you matter . . . like for that one hour you're the most important person in the whole world. Everybody wants more of that kind of feeling." Maddy completed trimming a bar of *peach punch*.

After working silently for a few minutes, Lisa-Marie looked quickly over at Maddy and then back to her bar of *raspberry riot*. "Are you serious about Jesse?"

Maddy kept working, "Well, I wouldn't say I'm serious about him but I'm serious about meeting him in the boat shed. Why not? He's not so bad and if you weren't so hot for Justin, you could see that."

"Hey . . . we aren't talking about me. It's just that Jesse seems like such a jerk. You know he's always coming onto all the other girls, right?"

"I'm going to screw him Leez, not marry his sorry ass." Maddy locked eyes with Lisa-Marie and said, "He's messed up just like the rest of us, you know.

He's OK. You should give him a bit of a chance. He can fill your iPod with the best music."

Lisa-Marie worked away quietly on a bar of *chocolate-vanilla*. "Maddy, do you think all the kids who see Izzy feel the same way you do about her?"

"How could they not?" Maddy answered in a matter-of-fact tone that made Lisa-Marie's stomach hurt.

"Did you ever think of going after Justin?" Lisa-Marie didn't even attempt to hide the insecurity in her tone.

"He's way out of my league and he's not interested in fun times in the boat shed. Believe me, every girl here has tried to hook up with him at one time or another."

"Has anyone had any luck?"

Maddy shook her head, "Nope – no one that I know of."

Lisa-Marie was relieved but she frowned all the same because she was afraid she knew exactly why Justin had no time for any of the girls at the Camp.

"Justin has bigger and better things ahead of him and he knows it," Maddy said, leaning back and stretching her arms over her head. She looked around the workshop and nodded in the direction of the soap vats where Jesse was working, "You know Jesse always calls Justin, golden boy, right? What bugs Jesse is that Justin really is golden." Maddy shrugged, "He's definitely one of the nicest guys I've ever met."

Lisa-Marie nodded, "Ya, me too."

Keeping her voice low, Maddy told Lisa-Marie, "I did do a stupid, let's-hook-up routine with him when I first got here. Had to take a shot, right? He wasn't interested but he was super nice about it. He didn't make me feel like a loser or a slut or anything. He's been a good friend. He understands me – what I do." Maddy was silent for a minute, trimming with more attention than usual, "I cut. You know what I mean, Leez? I'm one of those slasher chicks."

Lisa-Marie nodded silently. She knew what cutting was.

"Way less now for sure than when I was younger . . . but sometimes I still feel like I have to do it. Izzy says I shouldn't be too hard on myself. It takes a long time to get over the kind of stuff that makes you cut." Maddy's hands were still for a moment.

Lisa-Marie understood, all of a sudden, that this friend thing required telling as well as listening. She took a deep breath and with her eyes on her own work, she said, "Before I came here I tried to kill myself. My grannie can't look after me anymore so she sent me here. Now I can't even go back and maybe I'll have to stay here or go somewhere else for school. I don't think anyone really wants me and I don't know what I want either." Lisa-Marie bit her lip hard to hold back the tears, "Don't tell anyone, OK?"

Maddy nodded, "You know what I like about you, Leez?" She paused and Lisa-Marie shook her head. The fact that Maddy had been so nice to her from the first day in the workshop surprised the hell out of her. She couldn't think of a single thing that Maddy could have seen in her to like.

"Remember when Roland brought Jesse in to meet everyone?" Lisa-Marie nodded and Maddy said, "He sidled up to you with that come-on-I'm-a-really-big-stud routine of his. I was watching both of you and you gave him a look that said crawl under a rock you asshole . . . remember?" Lisa-Marie smiled and when she looked up, Maddy's eyes were sparkling.

"That's what I liked about you right away. I thought to myself, this girl is a real firecracker and she's not going to take crap from anybody." Maddy quickly grabbed for the last bar of soap in the bin, *lime pie*, "It's nice to be able to hang out with someone who doesn't already know every shitty thing about me from some group session. I know how to keep a secret, Leez."

Lisa-Marie shook her head in disbelief at Maddy's assessment of her. She had taken so much crap from kids for the last three years that she was surprised she could raise her head above the shit line. Now Maddy had seen a spark of something in her that Lisa-Marie didn't even know she had. She liked the way Maddy saw her; she liked it a lot.

i i .

Later that evening, Lisa-Marie was sitting at the end of the couch in the Camp's TV room, her stomach tight with anxiety. She was practically holding her breath and trying to will Justin to make his way over to the sofa to sit beside her before the movie started. He was across the room hunched over his laptop finishing an important email about course registration. It didn't look as though he had any interest in the upcoming movie or her. Jesse plopped onto the couch next to Lisa-Marie. She looked at him with irritation. He was sitting too close and his grin always seemed to set her teeth on edge. Even if Justin got up and came over he wouldn't be able to sit beside her now, not with Jesse slobbering over her shoulder.

"Want to come into town with us on Friday? A bunch of us are going to that ghetto movie theatre," Jesse ripped open a chocolate-bar and bit off a big chunk. He offered her a corner but she shook her head.

"No thanks," she said, to both invitations.

Jesse followed Lisa-Marie's gaze over to where Justin was sitting and he whistled slow and low under his breath, "So, still have your sights set on the golden boy, hey?"

Lisa-Marie looked sharply at him, "So what if I do? Mind your own business, Jesse."

"He isn't for you . . . give it up. He really has his hands full with someone else – someone else who's a bit more mature than you."

"Shut up Jesse. What the hell do you know? You're pissing me off. I'm going."

Jesse grinned and said, "I could be a good second choice, Lisa. Give it some thought. I have scads of free time."

Lisa-Marie made her way across the room. She wasn't interested in the movie now that she realized Justin wouldn't be sitting beside her. She waved a casual goodbye to him and left the Camp to head back to the A-Frame. She hoped Justin might leave the computer to walk her home, but he didn't.

iii.

Dear Emma:

I have two things to tell you – one is great and the other sucks. Justin was too busy tonight to even look at me. He didn't want to watch a movie and he didn't walk me home. Jesse says I'm wasting my time. He says Justin is with Izzy – I know what he meant. He doesn't mean Justin spends time with Izzy or just likes her. He means Justin is with Izzy. I hate Jesse – what a big, fat liar. I don't get how Maddy can have anything to do with him.

Here's the great thing and it's about Maddy. She is my friend – she really is! I can't believe I have a friend. Today in the workshop she told me that she cuts – you know – cuts herself. Scary – but she said she doesn't do it so much now because Izzy has helped her. She is just over the moon on Izzy. She says everyone who sees Izzy feels that way. Maybe that's all it is with Justin, too – maybe he looks at Izzy the way he does because of counselling stuff.

I knew when Maddy told me about cutting that I would have to tell her some-
thing too – so I told her about trying to kill myself. She didn't even flinch or laugh at
me or anything like that – she totally understood. She said she likes me – she's says
I'm a little firecracker who doesn't stand for any crap. How can she think that about
me, Emma?

i v .

The next morning Izzy was in her office glaring with frustration at the email screen on her laptop. She had played telephone tag with Norma Clayburn for well over a week and now her email asking for a meeting bounced back with a message saying Norma was out of the office, on leave until mid-September. Turning from her in-box, Izzy opened a document she was preparing for an upcoming group session.

Roland appeared in her doorway tapping a client file against his hand. "Do you have a minute, Izzy?" He came in, shut the door behind him and took the chair across from her desk. Izzy closed the lid of her laptop with a snap; it might be nice, she thought, if just once, Roland would actually wait for her to answer.

"Last night I intercepted a resident exiting the boat shed with his clothes in quite a state of disarray." He tapped the file against his hand, waiting for Izzy to respond.

Izzy got up and walked over to the window. She opened it wide and inhaled the fresh air for a moment. It had rained the night before and every-thing smelled green and alive. "If there's something you think I need to know, Roland, please just tell me, OK?"

"At 1:45 a.m.," Roland emphasized the time dramatically, "I caught Mr. McAlister coming out of the boat shed with his pants unzipped and I think I spotted Ms. Sinclair heading around the corner trying to pull her shirt on. It was dark so I can't be positive but I'm pretty sure I recognized her spiky, purple hair. I suggest you speak to her about her choice of after hour activi-ties. I'll handle Mr. McAlister." Roland stopped talking, crossed his legs and continued to tap the file against his hand.

"What on earth were you doing down by the boat shed after midnight?"

Roland shrugged, "I was doing my job, Izzy. As I've told you before – living on-site is not always a pleasant experience."

Sexual relations between residents at the Camp were discouraged. It inevitably got in the way of what the residents were at the Camp to achieve. Most of the young people Izzy worked with understood that. At the same time, she and George had always taken a pragmatic approach. If one of her clients brought up the issue, Izzy preferred to explore what this type of a relationship meant in the big picture of the person's overall goals. She also stressed such things as respecting personal boundaries and practicing safe sex rather than preaching rules and regulations. The reality was that all the residents were close to nineteen or over – they were adults.

"I can't bring this up with Maddy. You're not even sure it was her and even if I knew you were sure, I still wouldn't confront her with such an accusation. It takes a long time to win these kids' trust. I won't take a chance on losing that with Maddy by poking my nose in what is obviously her private life."

Roland leaned forward, "She's your border line personality disorder, right?" Without waiting for Izzy to reply, he added, "I could do some screening with her. I've been reading about a couple of good assessment tools. As you know, I'm certified to do testing and assessment. There are also some really effective pharmaceutical measures available."

Izzy shook her head, trying to keep the impatience and the mounting anger out of her voice, "You know what, Roland? The DSM labels just don't work for me. Maddy's a young woman who has experienced a lot of trauma in her life and she's developing skills to deal with her past. I won't risk slowing down that progress, even if she is having sex with Jesse in the boat shed. If she needs to talk to me about that, she'll bring it up in session."

Roland backed off and Izzy was relieved. The last thing she wanted was a confrontation with him over anyone's care. Maddy was a brilliant kid on the verge of breaking through to a really exciting future. She certainly did not need to be tested, labeled or drugged; nor should she be lectured about her sexual choices.

Sitting back in his chair Roland picked up the file again to tap it against his leg, "I think I will talk to Mr. McAlister. I'll book a couple of sessions with him and get to the bottom of this."

"Get to the bottom of what, Roland? They were having sex – what more is there to find out. He'll deny it all. Say he was out there for a smoke or something." Izzy was confident that Roland would get no further in a session with

Jesse than she had and that he was quite capable of making the whole situation worse.

"That would be difficult. I caught him red handed, shall we say, about to throw what appeared to be a very full condom into the lake."

"Did you stop him?"

Roland sniffed, "Of course I stopped him. I marched him right into the nurse's office and had him deposit it in the bin for used needles and hazardous waste."

Just before Roland opened her door to leave, Izzy said, "At least they used a condom, Roland."

Chapter Twenty-Nine

i.

The day of the garden gala arrived. Tarts were baked, laid on the kitchen counters and covered with thin layers of wax paper. Whipped cream was being kept cool on ice. Champagne was chilling and glass flutes were set out on silver trays in the garden house. Lights were strung and a welcome arch was erected and woven with strands of greenery, flowers and yet more lights. Small lavender plants in their clay pots sat carefully arranged on a table near the welcome arch. Raffle gifts were adorned with brightly coloured bows. Citronella candles in fancy holders graced the edges of the garden paths.

Izzy stood in front of her mirror in the bedroom turning this way and that at Bethany's insistence. She had to admit that she did look the part of a *fairytale queen.* The fabric of the dress clung and flowed in all the right places. Her bust, in a wired push-up bra, made her look like the kind of woman who is sometimes pictured on the cover of a romance paperback. Her breasts seemed about to burst from the confines of her dress.

"Are you sure about this Bethany?" Izzy was frowning into the mirror and pulling at the top of the dress, trying to cover herself up.

Bethany slapped her hands away, "Stop it, for God's sake, Izzy. Of course I'm sure. I sewed the bloody dress exactly to your measurements." Bethany was losing patience after spending twenty minutes winding silver stars through Izzy's hair while Izzy fidgeted and fussed over the dress.

"Enough already, I mean it," Bethany commanded as she placed the tiara on Izzy's head and fastened the matching necklace at her throat. As Bethany turned to leave the room, she looked back over her shoulder to warn Izzy, "Don't eat anything. You're bound to get crumbs all over yourself."

Izzy pouted, "Can I drink?"

Bethany laughed, "Like I could stop you."

Bethany passed Maddy coming down the stairs. Maddy smiled and called back up the stairs to Lisa-Marie, "Don't smear that paint up in any hot, sticky embraces with you-know-who." Bethany heard Lisa-Marie hoot with laugher at Maddy's remark.

Lisa-Marie was standing in the sunflower decorated room and Bethany caught her breath at how magical she looked. The costume appeared only slightly less revealing than it actually was because of the profusion of twining vines and leaves that ran over Lisa-Marie's arms and legs, across the top of her breasts and even up the sides of her neck.

Maddy had helped Lisa-Marie twist her hair into thick spiralling curls pinned up on the sides and loose in the back. Lisa-Marie was just placing a circlet of leaves and bright red berries on her head when she saw her aunt in the doorway. "What do you think?" She had a nervous smile on her face, spinning slowly so Bethany could get the full effect of the body paint, the sheer, flouncy skirt and the gossamer wings.

Bethany smiled and walked behind Lisa-Marie to adjust the headpiece and straighten the wings slightly, "You look like a bit of fairytale magic, sweetie. Away you go now; Izzy is downstairs driving everyone crazy with the last minute details."

Lisa-Marie ran down the stairs to join Izzy in the living room. They spun around and preened for each other and then Izzy put her hands on Lisa-Marie's shoulders. She gave her an intense look, "OK, Lisa, show time. Are you ready?" Lisa-Marie nodded with excitement; before she knew it they were out the door and into the garden.

Justin was already at the welcome arch. He was dressed in a dark-green tunic layered over a black T-shirt and jeans. Over one shoulder he carried a quiver of arrows and a bow borrowed from an archery guy in Dearborn. A green hat with a Stellar Jay's feather sticking out of the brim, sat atop his blonde hair. He had grown a scruffy beard to complete his look. When Izzy and Lisa-Marie approached him, he bowed low and said to Izzy, "Robin of

Locksley at your service, my lady." Then he glanced at Lisa-Marie. A long wolf whistle included her in his greeting.

Izzy laughed and pulled Justin up by the arm. She looked around the garden. In the low light of dusk everything was breathtaking. Strings of lights glittered and twinkled from the edges of all the buildings, along the trellis structures and through the branches of the trees. The light of several lanterns softly lit the garden house and sparkled on the array of shining glasses and silver trays within.

Just three days before, Marjorie, the president of the garden club had called to ask Izzy if she could use a couple of harp players. Marjorie had explained that her son was home from U of T for the summer with his girlfriend and one of her friends. The girls had both arrived with their harps. As music majors they would love the chance to perform in public. Izzy saw the two girls setting up their harps and chairs in front of a bed of flowers. They wore matching white dresses with gold belts slung low on their thin hips. Gold headbands encircled their long, straight hair. They looked like medieval, court musicians.

Izzy turned, trying to take in everything at once and she caught sight of Liam coming from the main cabin. A black robe was cinched in at Liam's slim waist by a thick, black belt. A surprisingly lethal looking sword was at his side. A number of strands of gold-tone chain hung around his neck. With his long, dark hair and angular face, Liam looked the part of a dark prince to perfection.

Liam approached Izzy feeling like a total fool. Bethany had insisted on the ridiculous chains around his neck and he's had to stop her, with some force, from painting a drooping mustache over his upper lip. Izzy began to shoot last minute detail questions at Liam the second he was within hearing range. She was completely oblivious to the impact her outfit might be having on him. He had caught sight of her standing by the welcome arch with Lisa-Marie and Justin. She had spun around suddenly to face him. Liam would not soon forget the silver stars twinkling in her dark hair, the jeweled tiara sparkling among them and the matching gems glittering at her throat. All of this, combined with the way her most attractive assets were on full display, had him almost tripping over the ridiculous gown he was wearing.

"Everything is ready, Izzy, relax. The guests are starting to arrive," he gestured to the people coming down the drive towards the welcome arch. Liam shook his head at the sight of Jack carrying his beanstalk, Little Boy Blue, Mary with a stuffed lamb, the Lion King, several women dressed up as Snow White, a few Cinderellas, a couple who made an amazing Beauty and the Beast, two or three Little Red Riding Hood's and even a Goldilocks with a stuffed baby bear. They were all strolling through the arch and into the garden, laughing and chatting.

Dan had borrowed a brown cassock and matching rope belt from the parish in Dearborn. He strolled into the garden as St. Francis. His costume was completed by a wooden cross on a chain around his neck and a staff he had found among the walking sticks propped against the back door of the main cabin.

He arrived in time to see Bethany make her entrance as Glinda, the good witch from the Wizard of Oz. She wore a floor-length gown with puffy, short sleeves. The dress was a bridesmaid's cast-off that Beulah had picked up at the thrift store. Bethany had snipped it here and there, letting out the waist a bit and cutting down the neckline. She added sequins and trim. With a crown and a magic wand from the Dollar Store and with her hair done up in thick ringlets, she looked quite glamorous.

Dan took two champagne flutes from a tray Liam was holding. He stopped for only a moment to laugh at the black cassock turned dark prince costume and then headed straight for Bethany. Liam frowned as he returned to the garden house to refill the tray with brimming glasses. With a glint like the one Dan had in his eye, Liam suspected that the Big Bad Wolf had come to the party dressed as St. Francis.

Lisa-Marie, showing miles of body-painted skin, flitted from one place to another among the twinkling strings of light. She helped Justin serve the raspberry tarts by dropping a spoonful of thick, whipped cream on each one. She helped present raffle gifts to delighted guests when Izzy called out their names. She danced away just out of reach of a jokingly lecherous St. Francis who was joined by a wildly funny pirate. The pirate was dressed in tight, black pants, and a white ruffled shirt. An eye-patch and a black handkerchief wrapped around Beulah's porcupine-bristled, grey hair completed the look. Lisa-Marie stood by giggling when Justin and Liam drew their fake swords to defend her honour, chasing both St. Francis and the pirate around the garden. Whenever she had a free second she dashed back to the garden house where she had stashed Dan's camera. She snapped picture after picture.

Izzy stood back against the vine-covered wisteria trellis and looked with awe over the garden. The harp players plucked gracefully at their instruments. A light breeze caught the flowers and the blossoms seemed to dance in time to the haunting music. Costumed people wandered the paths, champagne glasses in hand, admiring the various plants and stopping to chat together in small groups. The garden gala was a huge success and already people were moaning that no one would want to take on the challenge next year and have to compete with what was obviously a *tour de force*.

Toward the end of the evening, with the full August moon lighting the garden, Dan spotted Bethany standing alone on the path in the shadow of the greenhouse. He came over and in a playfully serious way raised his heavy cross to offer her a blessing.

"Thank you, Father."

Dan warmed to the role play and standing quite close to her, he whispered, "Would you be willing to grant me one wish?"

Bethany raised her magic wand, "Perhaps, but what could St. Francis wish for?"

Dan moved even closer, "A small wish really; one simple kiss for a lonely cleric."

Bethany blushed, a pink glow rising slowly up across her exposed breasts to spread in a lovely mist of colour over her neck and across her cheeks. She stood very still and then leaned forward quickly and kissed Dan ever-so-lightly on the lips. The next instant she was gone down the path.

i i .

"Come on, garden sprite . . . I'll walk you home," Justin called out to Lisa-Marie when the last of the champagne flutes had been brought in. Waving goodbye to Izzy at the kitchen door they strolled away together. On the dark path, Lisa-Marie reached out for Justin's hand. She was flushed with confidence from the admiration in the eyes of so many of the male guests. Her costume had been a hit. She felt beautiful and desirable and couldn't imagine that Justin didn't see her that way as well.

When she reached for Justin's hand he didn't seem surprised and he didn't pull away. Her heart beat loudly against the painted vines that twined over the top of her breast. She and Justin stopped by the turn in the path to the A-Frame and the ferns that grew so profusely there brushed her bare legs. She leaned into him and tipped her face up, "A kiss goodnight, Sir Robin?"

Justin smiled down at her and leaned close to brush his lips against her cheek. He slipped his hand from hers and moved away down the path. Lisa-Marie was left alone with the painful thudding of her heart blocking the night sounds around her and tears of disappointment gathering at the edges of her darkly fringed lashes.

i i i .

Dear Emma:

I asked Justin to kiss me tonight and he did – on the cheek – and it was all wrong. You can't believe how beautiful I looked – my costume was so perfect. Oh shit, why did I do something so stupid and embarrassing like asking him to kiss me? Anyway – he leaned down to me and I could smell the soap he uses – sort of like fresh cut grass – and I felt like my legs would give out and I would fall to the ground. But he was holding my arm and everything was perfect and all he did was kiss me on the cheek and say goodbye.

The tears are staining your pages, Emma – I'm sorry – you know how much I hate to cry. Shit, shit, shit – all he did was kiss me on the cheek because of Izzy. She really did look like a fairytale queen. Why did I ever give her such a great idea for a costume? I should have told her to dress up as one of the ugly step-sisters from Cinderella – a fat, ugly step-sister with a big wart right on the end of her nose. But no – she was the dark queen and if she had pulled a poisoned apple out of her pocket and made me eat it she couldn't have ruined my life any more.

i v .

Justin walked down the trail to the Camp. He knew he had moved away from Lisa-Marie too quickly, he saw the hurt in her eyes. But what the hell was he supposed to do? He wasn't blind and he wasn't some kind of monk. She had looked very sexy and cute tonight and he could easily imagine a different ending to that moment just now on the trail – really kissing her and dragging her off to the boat shed to get a lot more serious. But the way her eyes shone up at him made it all wrong. He wasn't going to play the part of her Prince Charming, no matter how available she made herself. She was just a kid. And why the freaking hell was a kid looking at a guy the way she looked at him tonight? He guessed he'd soon have to be on the watch for girls in elementary school.

Justin's thoughts turned from Lisa-Marie to Izzy – what a fucking gong show – Izzy in that dress, smiling that smile at him – what next? She was obviously pleased by the way everything had turned out and flushed with the praise heaped on the garden. Her excitement had been like an electrical connection between them making him vibrate with desire every time he looked at her.

V.

Izzy walked with Liam through the garden, under the still twinkling lights, as far as the turn in the path. They chatted about how well everything had gone. "Thank you for all your help, Liam." She smiled playfully at him, "You make an attractive dark prince."

Liam reached across the small space that separated them and took Izzy's hand. He bowed low and kissed it just below where the silver threaded fabric ended. Looking up at her he said very slowly and softly, "I am your servant in all things my queen, but be cautious. Praise can easily turn the head of a dark prince such as I."

Izzy bowed her head slightly, "I stand warned. Goodnight my dark prince."

vi.

Liam dreamed of Izzy that night. At least it started out as a dream about Izzy, before it turned into a nightmare about something else completely. He was in the garden trying to catch-up to Izzy as she moved quickly along the path. But with every step Liam took the way ahead became more choked and overgrown and twisted. No matter how fast he went she was always just ahead of him, her silver-threaded dress disappearing around yet another bend in the trail. He grew more and more frantic as he scrambled over stumps and clawed through underbrush that appeared out of nowhere. All he knew was that he had to get to Izzy.

He came around a corner and quite unexpectedly a huge field of wildflowers opened up in front of him. Liam caught his breath at the beauty of it. He could see her in the distance. She was almost at the door of a building. Liam started to run, desperate to get to that door before Izzy did. Something was terribly wrong. Then as suddenly as he had come to the field of wildflowers he was right in front of the door. He stumbled in shock, his feet scrambling to stop his forward motion.

It wasn't Izzy standing in the doorway. It was Lisa-Marie, wearing the revealing costume she had worn earlier that evening. She looked at him for a moment that seemed to go on forever, shaking her head as if to deny whatever he would say. Then she opened the door and went inside the building. Liam's mouth opened in a silent, dreaming scream. He knew exactly what was going to happen – the entire building burst into flames, fire leaping and licking wildly towards the sky. Liam stood there with the hot blast of the fire in his face and screamed and screamed and screamed.

He woke up suddenly, moaning with his head thrashing wildly back and forth on the pillow. He was drenched in sweat. Blood pounded in his ears and throbbed intensely in his groin. He groaned in an anguish of fear and a lingering lust that his mind refused to acknowledge. Curling into a fetal position he tried desperately to shake off the dream. He knew what he had to do. He looked up to the small window beyond the bed and the view of the few stars that outlined the handle of the big dipper. The stars were crystal-clear and sharp in the night sky. He focused all his attention on those stars and willed himself to take long, slow, deep breaths. In a mantra chant he repeated, with each breath, it's just a dream – it's just a dream – it's just a dream. Eventually his breathing became deep and regular. His eyes began to close and for a few moments he fought the darkness, afraid the dream fire might come back. But he couldn't stop the pull into unconsciousness, so he let go and slept like a dead man until the sun was already bright in the morning sky.

CHAPTER THIRTY

i.

Lisa-Marie drove the truck along the logging road with Liam beside her. Suddenly he sat up straight in the passenger seat and told her to pull over, "Right there, OK? I haven't seen those plants in bloom like that for years." Lisa-Marie dutifully parked the truck in the gravel space Liam had pointed to.

While Liam gathered flower tops, Lisa-Marie scrambled down a steep path to find a vantage point on a mound of rocks overlooking the expanse of Crater Lake. She had never seen the lake from above. Camera in hand she began capturing the way the dark clouds and threatening raindrops provided a display of multiple shades of grey over the water and around the surrounding mountains. Hearing the sound of the truck door slam she looked up from the camera to see Liam side-stepping down the path towards her. He was carrying two small cartons of chocolate milk.

He plopped down on a rock. "Quite the view, hey?"

Lisa-Marie fiddled with the camera in her lap, snapping the lens cover on and off. She stopped for a moment to break open a carton of chocolate milk and take a drink. Then she resumed the snapping. Liam sat silently beside her.

"Liam, did my aunt tell you the reason why I'm here?"

Liam glanced sideways at her and shook his head, "Bethany isn't the type to talk about other people's stuff." Lisa-Marie was quiet for a couple of minutes before Liam asked her, "Why are you here, kiddo?"

Looking down at the toes of her joggers, Lisa-Marie took a deep breath and slowly exhaled the words, "I tried to kill myself."

The first hint of rain was coming as the dark clouds gathered overhead. Liam sat very still beside Lisa-Marie, his legs bent and his forearms resting on his knees.

"When I think back to that Friday on the bus . . . the way the other girls were at me, saying stuff and pushing me around . . . it was the way it always was . . . sort of blah, blah, blah, you know?" She glanced over at Liam, who was nodding silently as he looked at the ground. "But then I got into the trailer and Grannie was at Bingo and –," Lisa-Marie paused to catch her breath; it was beginning to hitch and she hated that. She didn't want to cry, "– I'm no candy ass, Liam. I mean, I'm pretty tough. I would have been OK . . . but at the end the crap was coming at me too fast . . . for some reason on that day, I couldn't stop hearing their words . . . like there wasn't anything else in the whole world but their words."

As she pushed her hands down firmly on the rock in front of her, Lisa-Marie's voice was barely audible, "I don't remember ever thinking I wanted to be dead. I only remember wanting to stop the sound of their voices in my head." Two large tears fell directly from her eyes onto the back of her hands.

In the silence that stretched out between them they were linked together inexplicably by Lisa-Marie's memories, her tears and Liam's quiet understanding. He reached out his hand and rested it gently in the middle of her back for a moment. He let his hand drop back to his knee and sat beside her, staring down at the lake, the rain now falling steadily. Then he spoke. "A long time ago something really bad happened and it was my fault. I tried to kill myself twice. I'm not surprised you didn't think about what it was like to die; you've hardly had a chance to be alive yet, kiddo."

Lisa-Marie was shocked away from her own memories by Liam's confession. She stumbled over her words in her desire to know more, "What came next, Liam? I mean, you made it, right? How did you know you would live, that it wouldn't happen again . . . that you would be OK?"

A quick look of anguish crossed Liam's face. How was he going to answer that question when the truth was so brutal? How could anyone ever know it wouldn't happen again – that things would be OK? But he couldn't spell out that reality to a kid sitting there with her whole life in front of her – a kid so goddamn vulnerable and hurt because of things that had been said and done to her; things that had nothing to do with who she really was.

"I joined a group of guys and we got together and just sat around and I stopped drinking. I came here and after a while I knew I would keep trying to live. You've heard of Caleb, Izzy's husband, who died a couple of years ago?" Liam glanced at Lisa-Marie and she was nodding, "Well, he helped me a lot. He was a good friend. It isn't always easy, for sure." He looked right at Lisa-Marie then, his dark eyes holding hers, "Maybe try to think every day, kiddo, every single day, about what it's like to be alive. Because, when you get right down to it, there isn't much else that matters."

This was about as close as Liam would ever get to giving advice. After a few more moments of silence, as the wind picked up and the rain showed no sign of abating, Liam gathered up the empty milk cartons and he and Lisa-Marie headed up to the truck.

ii.

Liam sat in his rocker that night, slowly going back and forth, thinking about Lisa-Marie's words. The summer storm blew rain steadily against the cabin windows. The lone wolf that Izzy mentioned to Liam was howling in the hills and it was an eerie sound. He sipped slowly from a cup of tea, a new special brew he was trying. The taste was unpleasant to say the least – bitter but he was used to that.

Liam's thoughts skittered away from Lisa-Marie to his father – Alexander Collins. A man part Mi'kmaq on his mom's side with a dad who was Scottish. He had come from Nova Scotia. He used to tell Liam, "Don't forget, kid, you're part Highlander too."

Liam's strongest childhood memory of his father was of him sitting in an old recliner, surrounded by piles of books, reading one paperback novel after another. The way Liam remembered things, his father had always been the kind of dad who dropped into Liam's life without warning. Whenever he did appear, Alexander Collins seemed to be on some sort of vacation from his real life elsewhere.

Liam had grown up on a small reserve in Northern Manitoba. He was a smart kid. It was decided when he was still in elementary school that he would go away to complete his education. He would be one of those native kids who got a post-secondary degree and then came home to help his people. When he was thirteen he was packed up and sent to board down south. He remembered being scared and lonely beyond belief those first few years, living only for the summer holidays when he could go home. But he survived and stuck it out all the way through to getting his Bachelor of Education at the University of Manitoba. He hadn't gone home at all while he was at the university. He returned to the reserve when his mother was slipping away – arriving in time for her last few agonizing days of life. If his mom hadn't been dying he wouldn't have gone back at all – the south had made him feel completely separate from everything he had ever known.

Liam found he was a rare commodity on the reserve in those days, with his fancy degree and his high school teaching diploma. They needed him but that didn't mean they particularly cared to have him around. It was as if he gave off a bad odor – like someone who worked in the sewer all day or sorted thrift store clothes for a living. Something clung to him and no one stood too close for too long.

He was offered a position teaching at the newly-opened, band-run high school. He was told he would be the principal in no time. He was doing what he had been handpicked to do. He had the education and now he was paying it all forward. But fitting back into the life of the reserve was much harder than Liam had imagined, as agonizing an adjustment as what he remembered going through when he first went down south. His years away were a runaway train that had taken him further and further from everyone and everything – most of the time he felt he wasn't a part of anything. When people talked or gathered he simply disappeared. The only time he felt even slightly confident was when he was in the classroom teaching. Even then, he felt that what he knew of teaching literature was not really relevant to the reserve kids who were forced into the desks in front of him. His day-to-day life started to become an unbelievable struggle.

The loneliness and apartness and disappearing started to get to him and he began to drink in order to feel more solid. At first he drank to get through the weekends, then after school to survive the lonely evenings, then in the morning to get started and finally at lunch to keep going. He started hanging out with his cousin and her husband and friends who all drank heavily for their own reasons; and for little bits of time, Liam no longer felt apart.

One cold, Northern Manitoba Saturday, the drinking started early in the ramshackle house where his cousin lived. Liam was going strong on a bottle of Canadian Club. He supposed that the rest of them thought it would be OK to go out and leave the three-week old baby upstairs asleep in her crib. After all, Liam was there – on the couch, passed out cold.

The fire started in the baby's room. Someone had plugged a space heater into an overloaded circuit; the door was shut tight to keep the heat in and the baby warm. They were all just doing the best they could. Liam awoke to a house filled with smoke, still more than half-drunk. He barely managed to stumble to a window where someone pulled him through. He had no idea then, or for many hours afterwards – not until he sobered up – that there had been anyone else in the house with him.

Of course there was the inevitable round of inquiries and a coroner's inquest to get through. Liam's cousin and her husband testified that there was no drinking at their house that day. They said Liam volunteered to babysit while they went out to the Legion. He must have gotten drunk after they left and passed out on the couch. Liam hadn't seen much point in challenging the version of the truth they needed to get on with their lives.

The coroner was a white guy claiming to be a First Nations advocate. He talked about how he had written and spoken about many issues related to reserve life. He was more than willing to take into account the shoddy wiring and overcrowding of band housing as extenuating circumstances in the baby's death. He ruled that the fire was not deliberately set. But he wasn't inclined to look on Liam with any mercy. In the coroner's opinion, Liam had been given every opportunity that a kid from the reserve could get and he had pissed it all away. The coroner made sure he let everyone know that even though he couldn't recommend that Liam be considered criminally negligent in the baby's death, he certainly felt Liam was morally responsible.

Other recommendations were made; an initiative to upgrade band housing was promised, but no one believed any of it. Liam knew he was responsible and he didn't need any Indian-judging, white guy to make him feel guilty. He didn't need any formal charges to convict himself. He was moving into a prison of his own making and the sentence he imposed on himself was harsher than any of the people gathered at the inquest could have imagined.

In the days following the inquest, when Liam looked into people's eyes, he saw emptiness reflected back. He didn't belong. He left the reserve for good.

He drank his way through two years of savings, drifting south and west until he hit Vancouver. He spent one winter on the streets there and it was in those days that the idea of ending his life took serious hold. His sense of simply disappearing became so strong he remembered some days feeling confused about whether he was still alive or not. It was as if he walked the streets as a ghost.

He had tried to kill himself twice – bumbling, amateur attempts at shaking off the earthly coil. The first time he meant to use a knife on his wrists, in a flop hotel. The hotel desk guy had knocked on the door because Liam was making a racket trying to get the window open. Liam was so drunk he actually opened the door. The desk guy saw the knife, took it and kicked Liam out onto the street. The next time, Liam pawned his watch to buy a shotgun off an old guy who had just arrived from a reserve up north. The gun was all broken down and in his pack. But when the old guy put it together for Liam they found the firing mechanism was hopelessly jammed. He was a good old guy though. He gave Liam the money back and they both went on quite a bender with the cash. It seemed Liam was no better at dying than he was at living. He couldn't pull off a total disappearing act.

One day when he walked into the local Native Friendship Center for a coffee, someone asked him if he would like to join a men's group that was start-ing. Liam would never forget the times he and five other guys spent sitting in a circle in the back room of the Center. The first few sessions they had a facilita-tor, Lionel. He let them all know, on the first night, that he had credentials and extensive experience facilitating groups. Lionel left after three sessions when none of them had said a single word in response to his many prompts. Liam guessed the silence had freaked Lionel out. The rest of them seemed to like it. Jake, the oldest guy in the group, asked if they could keep on meeting without Lionel, so they had. That first night when it was just the six of them, Jake had commented sadly that it was too bad they couldn't have been a better group for Lionel. All of them had nodded in unison. When Liam thought about the group he remembered he did a lot of nodding and staring at his hands.

One time he said, "There was a fire. A baby died." Just those seven words as he stared down at his hands and he knew without looking up the other guys were nodding. They really saw each other. Somehow it helped. He knew he would try to live.

After a while the Center got him into a residential addiction program on the Island and he spent a year there. Near the end of that time, when Liam had no idea what he was going to do with his life or where he might go, one of the other guys showed him Caleb's ad. Liam had taken one look at the photo with its view of Crater Lake and the small cabin perched on the cliff edge among the trees and he felt like he was going home. The feeling had been a mystery to him. The pristine lake nestled between the mountains was as far from home as he could imagine. Living at the lake these past years had helped the gaping wound of his guilt knit over somewhat. But he never shook the conviction that if only he had been different, if only he hadn't been drunk that day, he could have saved the baby.

i i i .

Dear Emma:

Today I told Liam about trying to kill myself and you would not believe what he told me! Something really awful happened in his life and he tried to kill himself – twice! I couldn't even believe my ears. Liam is so nice. He's a good person and how can something really awful happen to such a good person? How could anything have made him feel so bad? I wanted to throw myself into his arms and cry and cry when he told me – it's like we're the same somehow. But of course, I didn't do anything like that, Emma – you know I try never, never to cry.

Liam said – try to think every single day about what it feels like to be alive. I am thinking about that – you know what I'll do, Emma? Every time I write in this journal I'll write about one great reason to be alive. Oh – I know what you're think-ing – Justin, Justin, Justin. OK – I promise to make it something other than Justin.

Today I am glad to be alive because Maddy is my friend and if I wasn't around who would get to use Dan's great camera? That's two things. So there!

CHAPTER THIRTY-ONE

i.

Izzy was relieved that Justin and Lisa-Marie had decided not to attend the August book club. The sight of the two of them out on the raft, afternoon after warm summer afternoon, made her uneasy. She knew her discomfort was caused by more than their youth and apparent ease together, diving and swimming and laughing, or lying out on the raft, their tanned bodies almost touching. But what that *more* might be was something she didn't want to think about.

She looked around the living room and saw Bethany sitting on the floor with her back to the chair Beulah was stretched out in. Dan was in the rocker with the best view of the lake. Liam, Cook and Roland were seated on the sofa. It was good to be in the company of adults. Tonight she wouldn't even let her ongoing irritation with Roland bother her.

Liam began the novel's introduction and Izzy relaxed into the sound of his slow and easy voice. She leaned forward in her chair to catch the soft cadence of his speech as his expressive hands moved and gestured. Izzy had always found a man's hands and arms to be subtly arousing. She liked the way a man moved his hands, how tanned forearms gave way at the elbows to well defined biceps, especially if a man had those arms bent and resting casually behind his head, like when he was lying in bed after – Izzy jerked her thoughts back to Liam's voice with a twinge of discomfort. She watched the play of the evening light across his face, sipped her wine and settled more comfortably into her chair, not quite able to shake the memory of the way Liam had looked up at her after kissing her hand, the night of the garden party.

"Well, I wouldn't be pitching this novel anywhere," Cook stated while brandishing the seven-hundred and twenty page, hard-cover edition of Anne Marie MacDonald's novel, *As The Crow Flies*. "Afraid I would bust a wall or something."

Everyone laughed. They had all enjoyed the book and comments ranged from drawing parallels to the true life experiences of Steven Truscott through to admiring the stunningly realistic depiction of life on a Canadian Forces base in the early 1960's. When they touched on the sexual abuse experienced by Madeleine, MacDonald's main character, Bethany began to speak.

"It's very real . . . the way the author describes it," she paused for a moment and looked around at the people in the circle. She met Izzy's eyes last and saw there an understanding she remembered well. She could feel the warmth of Beulah's leg behind her. "I mean, the way Madeleine simply isn't there when the abuse is happening. That is very real." Bethany took a deep breath, "Something like that happened to me when I was young." Once again she scanned the faces around her, "I mean the sexual abuse," she added for clarification. "The sense of just disappearing . . . well, it really is the way she describes it."

Tears ran slowly down Bethany's cheeks and Roland reached for the box of Kleenex on the nearby table and passed it down to her. She said, "Thank you, Roland. I'm OK, really . . . it was a long time ago." She wiped the tears away and continued in a stronger voice, "What I wanted to say is that reading that part of the novel made me think of the amazing power of the mind – to know exactly when we can't handle something and to allow us a space, a time away." She looked over at Izzy for a moment and shrugged, "I realize that type of coping can become a problem in life, but I find it comforting to know that there is a part of me that watches and tries to protect me when the going gets tough."

There was silence around the circle until Roland began to comment on how adept the author was at conveying the emotion of all the characters. Bethany dutifully turned to the page Roland indicated to illustrate his example. The discussion moved on but the effect of Bethany's words on those gathered around her was a revelation for some and a jolt for others.

Liam had watched Bethany's face as she spoke and he finally understood this woman who had become such a good friend over the years. It was as if a piece of a puzzle suddenly clicked into place. He now understood why it had taken Bethany almost three years of relieving him of the eggs at the sliding-glass door before she ever offered him a coffee. And he knew why two more years went by before she seemed comfortable sitting out on the veranda or inside the A-Frame, alone with him, drinking that cup of coffee.

Izzy listened to Bethany and thought back to the day Caleb had come to her saying, "Maybe Bethany could talk to you about some stuff." Izzy remembered listening to Bethany, session after session, as she recited her long list of abuses – her voice emotionless and her eyes vacant, staring ahead of her as if she were a zombie. After the recitations had gone on for a while, Izzy had felt despair herself. Any attempt to pluck Bethany out of her monologue and into a discussion of how she felt when these things had actually happened to her, always resulted in Bethany simply vacating the session – not physically, of course. She would sit there and disappear – one time she actually fell asleep right in the chair.

When the breakthrough came, it came suddenly and took Izzy completely by surprise. As Bethany went over, for the umpteenth time, the story of how she had first gone into the closet with Mr. Malone, Izzy had burst into tears. She had felt so stupid and angry at herself for losing control in that way. She had hurriedly wiped her eyes and tried to apologize. The stunned look on Bethany's face stopped her words.

"Izzy, why are you crying?" Bethany had asked in a voice laced with shock.

Izzy remembered struggling to come up with an explanation and then simply telling the truth, "I guess I just can't stand how sad it is anymore, Beth . . . you keep telling me these horrible things and you don't cry. You act like you're telling me what you had for dinner last night. But what he did to you was so unfair." Tears started to spill out of Izzy's eyes again. She saw Bethany shake her head and grab onto the seat of her chair with both hands as if a strong wind was blowing through the room and there was a very real danger she would be swept away.

"I want to stay here with you, Izzy . . . I don't want you to cry by yourself."

"Tell me how you felt Beth . . . tell me how you felt that first time he forced you into the closet?"

And Bethany stayed and she cried and she started to uncover those feelings from the past. From that day the work they did together began to help Bethany. Now Bethany was sharing a painful and traumatic moment out of her past with a group of friends. She was fully present and feeling the emotion that went with her words – emotions that had now been dealt with and were definitely a part of her past. It was an amazing testament to how far she had come in her healing journey. As a counsellor, Izzy heard only a small portion of a client's story. It was a privilege to witness another chapter of Bethany's story unfolding as it was actually being written.

Beulah went through a gamut of emotions that was wide-ranging and left her feeling completely off balance – a state of affairs she didn't much appreciate. At first, when she realized where Bethany's comments were headed, she was shocked – a deep-down shock that left her scrambling to believe her ears. Then she mobilized for an emergency rescue as a real fear for Bethany's well-being hit her like a wave. But the rescue hadn't been necessary. Beulah was thrown into a state of confusion and then she felt plain-old, pissed off.

It was fortunate for Dan that Izzy, Liam and Beulah were so focused on Bethany. If any of them had looked over at him, as Bethany spoke, they would have seen a man leaning forward in his chair with a look of unguarded emotion on his face. Everything he felt for Bethany would have been clear to all of them. Dan was shocked to find that his desire for this woman, with her beautiful, blue eyes – eyes that spoke so much when they chose to meet his – had become something far more powerful. He had fallen in love with Bethany.

ii.

Bethany could feel the waves of pent up anger coming off Beulah as they left the book club gathering and made their way along the path through the orchard. Their walk to the A-Frame was marked by a stony silence. Bethany was relieved that Lisa-Marie would be over at the Camp until at least 11:00. She knew Beulah well enough to know that her anger was not going to stay unspoken for long.

Beulah slammed the door behind her and confronted Bethany before she had even reached the kitchen. Her feet astride and her arms crossed, Beulah angrily demanded, "What the hell is going on with you?"

Bethany kept walking, "Nothing is going on with me, Beulah. There's no need to shout. I'm not deaf, you know. You can stop with the drama queen act, OK?"

"First you take a little secret trip to town. Jesus jumped up Christ . . . as if that wasn't enough of a shock . . . and you tell me about it like you do it every goddamn day. And now . . . well, now . . . would it be too much to ask for some type of fucking warning before you get all confessional . . . telling your life story at the bloody book club. Are you cracking up or something?"

"I'm not a child, Beulah. I can go to town if I want and I don't have to clear with you first what I want to say at the book club."

Bethany turned her back on Beulah's confrontational stance and made to leave the room. "If I was you, Bethany, I would think twice about just walking out while I'm talking"

Bethany stopped suddenly and whirled around to face Beulah. "What are you going to do? Hit me?"

Beulah sat down on the sofa. She slowly crossed one leg over the other at the ankle and stared ahead of her for an agonizing moment while Bethany's words hung in the air between them. "You know damn well I'm not going to hit you, Bethany. Not my style at all." When she went on her voice was quietly cutting, with a deep bitterness below the surface of her words, "Don't forget what shape you were in when you came here, when I took you in. Don't forget who stands between you and the world. And don't forget who puts up with your little, I-guess-I'll-just-be-a-lesbian game.

Bethany matched Beulah's stare and tried not to flinch, "What's that supposed to mean? What are you trying to say?"

"Oh, I think you know exactly what I mean." Beulah paused to give her final, dagger-thrust remark a bit more power, "You can't handle being alone with a guy and you don't want to be alone. We both know that. So I guess I get you in my bed – my little, lesbian lover by default. Don't forget who puts up with that, Bethany."

Bethany glared at Beulah, then turned and walked into the bedroom to grab a quilt folded at the end of the bed. She returned to the living room and flung the quilt on the sofa. "It's my bed too, Beulah, and guess what? For tonight, I don't want you`in it," and having got the last word, she returned to the bedroom and slammed the door.

Beulah stared at the closed door that was still shaking in its frame. Her anger disappeared as easily as it had flared up. Well, she thought, surprise, surprise, surprise. Apparently, Bethany now went to town as if she had never resisted such an idea. She now spoke openly in public about painful events from her past. And now Bethany could actually go as far as to kick Beulah out of her own bed. With grudging admiration, Beulah curled up on the sofa under the quilt. Her last thought before falling asleep was that she couldn't ever remember wanting Bethany as much as she did in that moment when Bethany flung the quilt on the sofa and waltzed into the bedroom.

iii.

Dan came up the three steps to the porch of the guest cabin and opened the sliding glass door. He was hit with a blast of heat. Shit, he had forgotten to leave everything open earlier, as Izzy and Lisa-Marie were constantly reminding him to do. He went in and opened the door wide, pulling the screen shut behind him. That was the other thing Izzy kept reminding him to do – keep the screens shut to avoid being eaten alive all night. Placing the flashlight he had just borrowed on the counter with the three other borrowed ones, he grabbed for the bag of one-bite brownies Beulah had delivered earlier in the day.

Dan went back out to the porch and sat down in the old rocker. Wisps of cloud were scudding slowly across the waning moon. The stars lit up the sky in a marvellous array of light. Dan was caught in the grip of a confusion of emotions that clamoured for his attention. He allowed himself to scan back over his memories of recent events. Without examining any one event in too much detail, he was trying to get a hint of when his world might have stopped ticking along the way it was supposed to.

The trip to town with Bethany was a good place to start. He thought it went well. Of course it hadn't end in a hotel room. Still, he viewed the trip as definite progress. He was sure he could feel her on the verge of tipping toward him. Earlier this week when they were in the boat, he had casually brushed her leg with his hand as he reached for the fishing rod. She was startled and seemed to be filled with emotion. Timing was everything in these matters and he was confident they would be making love together very soon. He had even chosen the perfect cove where they could pull the boat up on a soft sandy beach and have the overhanging trees for privacy.

His thoughts wandered back to the trip to town. Maybe he was missing something. He had taken as much pleasure in the trip as she had. Seeing her hanging back at first, so timid when they got out on the sidewalk in Dearborn, then watching her get into the fun of things. He wasn't able to take his eyes off of her. When she was sitting in the Jeep beside him, on the way back to the lake, she looked at him with those damn eyes of hers shining and told him how glad she was he had asked her to go. His heart had turned over.

Today in the boat, for no reason that Dan could really explain, he had found himself telling Bethany about a girl he had fallen in love with the summer before he entered the seminary. How he thought she was his soul-mate. He had been very naïve then. He made up his mind not to go to the seminary at all, to choose a completely different path for his life. When he bared his heart to this girl, telling her he had decided against the priesthood, that he wanted to marry her, she had smiled in a sad way. She told him she liked him but that he shouldn't change any life plans on her account. It took years to get over that one sentence – *don't change your life plans on my account.*

Even so many years later this story still had the power to twist his gut. After the words were out Dan had been surprised at himself. He wasn't a stranger to letting pseudo-personal details drop in order to find his way under a woman's defences; he was actually pretty adept at it, but this was different. This was his story, his life and it was real.

Bethany had looked at him with compassion. She said that she had spent some years when she was younger just drifting in and out of relationships and though she was sure it hurt to be rejected like that, at least he had the memory of loving with all his heart.

To regain the upper hand, Dan had followed up with his one tried and true question. "Do you love Beulah?"

Dan found that this question, properly timed, had an uncanny way of tipping the scales in his favour. The fact that he didn't just assume a woman loved her partner seemed to plunge the woman into second guessing about what she actually did feel. Once she had vocalized her doubts to Dan and had gained his sympathetic ear, it was an easy downhill slope to the bed.

Bethany's answer had hit him with a jolt of emotion he wasn't expecting. She looked at him for a long time and he was completely captivated by the light dancing in her eyes. Then she answered. "In the beginning I loved only that Beulah looked after me. She made the world a safe place for me." Bethany's eyes began to fill with tears that she brushed away unselfconsciously, "I didn't think I could really love anyone. I felt all empty inside, like I didn't have the emotions that other people seemed to have. But I could be true and loyal and I was determined to be those things." She looked over at Dan as the boat bobbed in the slow and lazy afternoon waves, "Lately, though, I think something has changed. I feel different somehow."

With that she stopped talking and reached for the oars. She had to mean different because of him, right? What else could she mean? Then tonight, listening to Bethany hint at the extent to which she had been hurt and witnessing the courage it had to have taken for her to tell that part of her story, Dan was the one to tip irretrievably over the edge. He reached for another brownie only to realize the bag was empty. He felt his heart thumping in panic. Since his ordination to the priesthood he could hardly count the number of sexual affairs he had enjoyed, but he knew from what he was feeling now that this one was not like the others. He was emotionally involved and that was bad – a total disaster, in fact.

CHAPTER THIRTY-TWO

i.

Lisa-Marie came through the door of the A-Frame and leaned forward to pet Gertrude and Alice who had padded out to greet her. She turned and saw the lump of Beulah on the sofa. As she moved across the darkened room toward the stairs, the covers jerked down slightly to reveal eyes narrowed to a squint. Lisa-Marie chuckled at the sight of Beulah and said, "Trouble in paradise, hey?"

Beulah glared out at her for a moment before replying, "I don't suppose your love life is going much better." This remark was followed by a loud snort as Beulah pulled the blanket over her head and turned to face the back of the sofa.

Sitting in the center of her bed, the water from the stream tumbling quietly in the background, Lisa-Marie heard a wolf howl up in the hills. She thought about Beulah's words and all and all, she had to agree. Not even twenty minutes ago she had stood at the bend of the trail with Justin, her heart pounding, willing him to make a move, to do something, anything. All he had to do was give her even the tiniest hint that she could move closer to him, move into the quiet that surrounded him. But once again, as on so many other nights, it hadn't happened. She flopped across the bed and grabbed her journal from under the pillow.

ii.

Dear Emma:

I'm with Justin almost every single day. I know there isn't anyone else – he isn't with any of the girls at the Camp. Whenever I'm there he only pays attention to me – he sits with me, he walks me home – we swim together almost every day. I watch him all the time – I'd know if there was another girl. Well, except Izzy, but I can't think about that. Justin has a stupid guy thing of staring at her because she is so freaking perfect. It can't be anything else!

I know he wants me. But what can I do if he won't make a move? I'm lying here on my bed and I feel like screaming and crying like a two-year old. I'm running out of time, pretty soon he's going to leave and I'll never see him again.

What if he is interested – you know – like that – but he thinks I'm too young? Maybe he thinks I've never been with a guy before? He might think that. You know how nice Justin is – he never looks at me the way that creep Jesse does – like he can tell how many guys I've ever been with and exactly what I did with each one of them and what I might do again with him. As if – Maddy's nuts for doing who knows what with him.

Maybe Justin doesn't want to take advantage of me. How can I make him see I'm not a kid? I can't just go up to him and say – guess what, Justin – I'm not a virgin. He'd think I was a total slut. You know how it is, Emma. Only guys can ever brag about how many girls they've had.

iii.

Lisa-Marie snapped her journal shut in frustration. She thought about what had happened earlier that day with Jesse. He had walked up behind her when she was perched on a stool, working at the paper cutter, carefully trimming soap labels. He had pressed his crotch against her lower back. Breathing down her neck he had said, "How about you and I go find somewhere a little more private." The last part of his invitation was accompanied by a grinding of his hips.

Lisa-Marie had elbowed him as hard as she could in the ribs and slid off the stool to turn on him, "Listen you asshole, if any part of your body ever gets that close to me again, I'll remove it." She emphasized her last few words by slamming the huge paper cutter down as hard as she could.

Jesse had smirked and walked away, getting the last word as usual, "Your loss . . . if you change your mind you know where to find me."

A guy like Jesse could be as in your face about sex as he wanted and no one thought there was anything wrong with him. He was being a normal guy – a creep – but a normal guy.

Lisa-Marie had looked, as she always did, to see what Maddy's reaction would be to Jesse's behaviour. Maddy had only shaken her head at him and gestured for Lisa-Marie to come over to the workbench where she was assembling stationery boxes. When Lisa-Marie had plopped down onto a stool with a groan of disgust, Maddy had said, "Don't let him bug you, Leez, he's only acting like that because he thinks he can get to Justin by pushing himself on you like some crazy, out-of-control, stud boy."

Lisa-Marie perked up, "Do you think Justin is jealous?"

"I think Justin wants to look out for you . . . like a friend," Maddy emphasized the word *friend,* and gave Lisa-Marie a stern look. But then she grinned and pushed Lisa-Marie with her shoulder, "The way you handled Jesse – pretty impressive for a little-girl." She ruffled Lisa-Marie's hair, "That part about the paper cutter and his body parts – I thought I'd pee myself." Maddy began to laugh so hard she almost fell off her stool.

i v .

Resting back on the old blanket over the rough-cut boards of the boat shed floor, Maddy gasped as she stretched and arched her back in a graceful curve. She reached over to poke Jesse. He was lying beside her, a smile playing around the corners of his mouth.

Maddy sighed, "Wow, Jesse, that was –," she paused, "– hmmm . . . what is the word I'm looking for?"

Jesse shrugged, "Good?"

Maddy hooted, "Ya, right . . . good. That would be the understatement of the year." The summer storm lashed rain against the side of the boat shed windows as Maddy edged closer to Jesse, "You seemed to know what I wanted before I did."

Jesse laughed a deep satisfied sound. "Well, that is the trick, isn't it?" They both rested for a moment breathing deeply. "Leave your iPod with me . . . I've got that new album you wanted."

Maddy nodded as she raised herself up on one elbow and looked at him in the dim light that sifted in the window from the small bulb outside the door. "Great, thanks –," she paused for a moment before saying, "– Jesse, can you do something for me?"

He shook his head and grinned. "Well, you'll have to give me a minute here . . . I'm good but not that good."

Maddy poked him again, "Seriously, Jess . . . could you lay off the come-ons with Lisa-Marie?"

Jesse thoughtfully scanned Maddy's face, "Are you jealous, Maddy?"

"Come on, you know that isn't it. We've got a good thing going here –," she met his eyes for a moment, blushing slightly, "– a really good thing. But we aren't exclusive, we both agreed to that from the start."

Jesse nodded, "Ya, right . . . we both agreed."

"She's just a kid, Jess. You're only doing it to get at Justin and you're wasting your time."

"How do you know I'm not doing it to get at you, Maddy?" Before she could answer, a creaking sound from outside the boat shed door made her jump halfway up and grab for her shirt. Jesse laughed. "It's nothing Maddy, just the rain and wind, relax."

She lay back beside him and whooshed out her breath, "God, since that night when Roland was skulking around I've been as jumpy as a cat down here."

Jesse snorted, "Don't worry about Roland. Haven't you ever heard the expression that lightning doesn't strike twice in the same spot? That prissy old fart isn't coming out here in this weather."

Maddy began to turn the sleeve of her T-shirt the right way around. Jesse reached out and stroked his hand along her naked side. He pulled her closer. "If things are so good, what's your hurry?"

CHAPTER THIRTY-THREE

i

"Did you miss me last night, Beth?" Beulah smiled across the bakery counter at Bethany.

Bethany narrowed her eyes slightly and shook her head. "I don't like it when you bully me Beulah and anyway, what you said about me isn't even true,"

Leaning on the counter with her eyes obviously resting on the front opening of Bethany's shirt, Beulah responded, "Hmmm . . . well, how is that, Bethy?"

Bethany folded her arms tightly over her chest, before she said, "I can be alone with a guy. I'm alone with Liam all the time and in case you haven't noticed, I'm out on the lake alone with Dan almost every afternoon. What you said about me not being able to be alone with a guy – it isn't even true."

Beulah laughed and reached her hand across the counter to trace her fingers over the curve of Bethany's cheek, down her neck and throat and very slowly across the top of her breast. "Well, here's the thing about that . . . Liam and Dan, Bethy? They're hardly men at all, are they?"

Seeing the look on Bethany's face, Beulah raised her hands as if in surrender, "Fine, I'm wrong, you're right. They are men and you have no trouble being alone with them." Beulah reached behind Bethany's head, pulled her close across the counter and kissed her full on the lips. "You can be alone with anyone you want Beth, as long as you are alone with me where it counts."

Beulah whispered the last words against Bethany's neck. The buzzer on the bread mixer went off and Beulah pushed herself away from the counter, "Duty calls Beth, let's get moving."

ii.

Before heading to bed, Dan had decided that he would not fish anymore with Bethany. When he wanted to fish all he had to do was go down and hop in the boat Izzy had said was his to use. It had been sitting down at the beach all this time – ready for him. It would be good to get out on the lake earlier in the day when the fish were bound to be biting better. He was stupid to have spent so much time bowing to Bethany's schedule.

He took his morning coffee to the table where his papers and piles of books sat. Dan told himself it was high time to begin working on his writing project. After an hour or so he decided that he was still tired. He thought that maybe he should go back to bed for a while. Taking the boat out was bound to be a lot of work. He could wait until tomorrow or maybe even the day after tomorrow. What was the rush? The fish weren't going anywhere.

iii.

Izzy poured herself a cup of coffee and followed Cook out to the empty dining room. They took a table overlooking the lake and sipped companionably for a moment or two.

"I love the afternoons here," Cook sighed, "It's the only quiet time of the whole day." All she got from Izzy was a silent nod. Cook eyed her knowingly and said, "You're not a happy camper these days, Isabella. What's up?"

Izzy smiled despite her gloomy state of mind. Only when people really wanted to get her attention did they ever resort to calling her Isabella. "Roland is driving me insane with his constant nitpicking. If he gives me one more of his suggestions –," Izzy frowned and shook her head, "– his idea of so-called best practices, I'll scream. He's seems to be complaining about something all the time. He doesn't understand a thing about how I work and he's so full of himself and his bloody PhD he can't seem to talk about anything else." Izzy gripped her coffee mug tightly in her hands and stared past Cook to the white caps out on the lake. "Now he's come up with a plan to change the counselling evaluations to every six weeks. He thinks that will impress the Board. I've been doing three month evaluations for years." Izzy stared down into her coffee, "Exactly what I need . . . more bloody paperwork. I'm sick of all his crap."

Cook sipped her coffee and studied Izzy carefully. "He's only been here a few months. It'll take him time to settle in. He wants to make his mark like everyone else, I suppose." Cook paused for a moment, before asking, "It isn't like you to get so worked up by the fact that someone has a PhD or that you might end up with some extra paperwork – what gives?" Izzy shrugged and continued to stare past Cook.

"Don't take this the wrong way or anything, Izzy, but you know what I think? You need a guy." Holding up her hand at Izzy's look of exasperation, Cook went on, "I don't mean that the way it sounds . . . like you need to get laid and then Roland's stuff won't bug you. Maybe that's true too –," she grinned, "– but that wasn't what I meant. I mean you're alone too much. Alone with the work you do and with that big place of yours . . . way too alone with your own thoughts." Watching Izzy's face carefully, Cook asked, "When's the last time you let someone get close to you?"

The memory of leaning into Liam in the workshop snapped into Izzy's mind. She could almost feel the touch of his hand on her shoulder and how she had felt resting into his warmth. She thought about sitting beside Liam at the beach, shaking with fear and the weight of her confession. Now it was Izzy's turn to shake her head. Those times didn't count – it was Liam for God's sake.

Cook tipped up her coffee cup while looking at the big clock on the dining room wall, "It's time for me to get moving. I know it can't be easy for you to get used to being without Caleb. He was one in a million, that guy. But being alone too much . . . for too long . . . it's not so good, Izzy. Makes you frown all the time. It'll give you crow's feet."

i v .

"If you think you might have a shot at something you really, really want, do you think you should go for it Liam . . . even though it might be taking a big chance?" Lisa-Marie was sitting on the cabin floor with Pearl who was sprawled out getting a belly rub and looking up at her with adoration. "I mean, who knows, life is strange, right? You can't win the lottery if you don't buy a ticket." Lisa-Marie took a drink from her Coke, "You'll never know if you don't try, right?"

"Are you having a sixth sense about the Lotto numbers or something?" Liam smiled as he took his freshly brewed tea over toward the rocker, "If so, spill the beans, kiddo. I could use a million bucks, for sure." Liam had come to enjoy Lisa-Marie's visits. She never overstayed her welcome, just breezed in, played with Pearl, drank a Coke, chatted to him about what was going on over at the Camp and then she was gone. Lisa-Marie had a real gift for making a story come alive and her sarcastic sense of humour added colour to things. He got a kick out of the way she would laugh and shrug her shoulders as if to say, *well, you see what I mean, right?*

"Ya, I wish," she replied, "But seriously, Liam, if you think you have a shot at something should you go for it, even if it might not work out?"

Liam sat quietly for a minute, "What kind of a shot are we talking about here, kiddo?"

Lisa-Marie kept her eyes on Pearl and spoke quietly, "Well, like a shot with another person." Her hands worked rhythmically back and forth over the dog's coat.

"Are we talking about Justin?"

Lisa-Marie gave Liam a sharp look, "What? Are you crazy or something? I'm talking about Roland for shit's sake, or maybe Dan."

Liam laughed before saying, "I can really see you and Roland together," then he paused for a moment and a frown settled on his face. "Stay away from Dan, though, OK?"

"Of course I mean Justin, who else?"

Liam didn't want to give Lisa-Marie advice. He believed most people roll out the advice-giving wagon without thinking about what they're doing. It's arrogant to imagine you can ever know what someone else should do. He had no idea if Lisa-Marie should take her shot with Justin. His twisting gut told him it was a mistake. Justin probably wasn't interested in Lisa-Marie as anything more than a summer friend. Even if he did want more from her, it didn't change the fact that he would be going away and out of Lisa-Maria's life very shortly. On the other hand, Liam's gut was always twisting and he didn't know for sure what other people felt or wanted.

"It's a funny thing about taking your shot, kiddo. Sometimes even when you miss the basket you still win the game. Know what I mean?"

Lisa-Marie raised her eyes to the ceiling and said, "Oh my God," stringing out each syllable as she jumped up from the floor and went to the sink to rinse out her Coke can.

After the porch door snapped shut behind Lisa-Marie, Liam sat rocking in his chair. His face was drawn in a deep frown because he couldn't stop worrying about her. This worrying had crept up on him, but he knew it had started even before Lisa-Marie told him about trying to kill herself. The fact that she had confided in him – possibly the only other person at Crater Lake who knew exactly what she meant – was odd and it had to be more than coincidence. They had been on each other's radar in a strange, connected way from the very start. He wanted to protect her and more often than not the only way he could think of doing that was to grab her and wrap her up in a heavy flannel shirt. The way she was constantly putting her body on display made Liam cringe. He was fairly certain Lisa-Marie could parade naked through Justin's bedroom and Justin still wouldn't fall in love with her the way a sixteen-year-old girl wanted to be loved. Liam sighed heavily; he didn't want her to get hurt but he really couldn't see how events might unfold in any other way.

V.

The next afternoon, as Liam passed the guest cabin on his way to the workshop, he stopped in his tracks at the sight of Dan seated at the table in front of the window surrounded by his books and papers. Dan looked up and Liam called out, "No fishing today?" Dan waved his hand to indicate the stack of papers and looked morose.

By the end of the week, when Bethany went out the back door of the A-Frame toward the boat, she spotted Dan coming down the path. As fishing time had approached that day, Dan rose from his untouched pile of papers and books. He shook his head in surrender and told himself there really was no use in fighting any of this. He gathered up his fishing stuff and headed over to the A-Frame.

CHAPTER THIRTY-FOUR

i.

Izzy frowned at the open file in front of her. She had a 3:00 o'clock appointment with Jesse. As she reviewed her notes for the last few sessions she had to face the fact that they were not making a hell of a lot of progress – more like no progress at all. She hadn't found a way past his easy smiles and glib, snap-back responses. He continued to work the counselling sessions like a pro; he didn't reveal anything and was adept at turning the conversation to his advantage at every turn. Now his six-week evaluation was due and she certainly wasn't looking forward to writing a report that could be summed up in two words – no progress.

Coming through the door to Izzy's office, Jesse immediately suggested they go for a walk. He had managed to grab a cinnamon bun while cutting through the kitchen and was crunching away at it. Izzy followed Jesse out the door. As she watched his single-minded chewing she wondered if she should ban eating from all her sessions.

They had been walking for ten minutes and Izzy was about to confront Jesse on his constant diversions. She tripped on an exposed root in the trail and lost her footing for a moment. Jesse's hand was there immediately on her arm to steady her and as she turned to thank him, he quickly moved around in front of her to grab her other arm. Effortlessly he backed her up against the trunk of a tree on the edge of the path. Izzy was shocked at the sudden turn of events and before she could react, he moved in against her and kissed her while his hand roved up her leg under her skirt.

The memory of Roland's words of caution rang in her ears. *Walking those trails alone with clients leaves you vulnerable Izzy. I'm not sure it's a good idea.* She had brushed off his comment as she had the habit of doing with most of what Roland said. Now she could definitely see his point.

She began to struggle in earnest. She used all her strength to push against Jesse's chest, jerking her face away from his and trying to stamp on his foot. For a split second she thought he wasn't going to stop. But Jesse broke away and backed up quickly with his hands in the air, saying, "OK, OK – already. No problem. I'm not going to force you, I'm not that desperate." Shaking his head he turned and walked back toward the Camp, leaving her leaning against the tree struggling to catch her breath.

i i .

About an hour later, Jesse sat in the small meeting room off Roland's office on one side of a table with Izzy and Roland on the other. Roland stood up suddenly and slammed the file in his hand down onto the table. "You can wipe that smirk off your face right now, Mr. McAlister. I'm not sure about how things work where you come from, but around here we take sexual assault very seriously," he stressed each word and stood with his arms folded over his chest glaring at Jesse.

"Hey, hold it right there," Jesse countered, his hands going up in a sign of denial, "I don't know what she told you," he stopped to glare at Izzy. "I did not assault her. Maybe I got the wrong idea, but when she told me to stop, I stopped. If she's said anything else, well that's just bullshit." He was staring with real anger at Izzy and glaring at Roland in turn.

"Oh come now, Mr. McAlister. Are you seriously going to sit there and insinuate that Ms. Montgomery gave you signals that could imply anything of a sexual nature? Stop wasting your time and ours."

"Well, maybe she didn't really give me any signals," Jesse emphasized the word, *me*. "How was I to know she was only putting out for golden boy?" He delivered this last indictment with a gloating look in Izzy's direction.

Roland walked around the table to stand in front of Jesse, "Who exactly are you referring to, Mr. McAlister?"

Jesse smirked and replied, "Oh everyone's golden boy, Justin. Your sweet and innocent Ms. Montgomery is pretty hot for him."

Roland pointed to the door. With mounting anger in his voice he said, "Get out, right now. Go back to your cabin and do not leave it until you receive further instructions from me." Jesse darted an angry glare at Izzy before he slammed out the door.

Roland returned to his chair and picked up the file to leaf through its contents, shaking his head and saying quietly, "That kid really takes the cake. His hormones must be on overdrive. What does he think this place is – his own private harem or something? Is there no limit to what some of these kids will say to cover their own irresponsible behaviour?" He ended his series of rhetorical questions and looked up at Izzy. "Well, I don't know Izzy. It's your call. None of his evaluations have anything really stellar to say about him. Should we terminate his contract?"

Izzy rose from her chair to walk over to the window and stare out at the grey water of the lake. After a moment she turned back to Roland and said, "Read his file, Roland . . . not the stuff since he came to Micah Camp . . . the stuff from before. He needs this program."

She now knew this with certainty because she had spent the last hour doing exactly what she was suggested Roland should do. Izzy prided herself on her practice of not reading the thick files that accompanied most of the residents to Micah Camp. She liked to get to know each client in her own way – without having to see the person through the numerous lenses provided by every social worker, foster-care giver, teacher or health care provider that the client had ever met.

Moving across the room to the closed door she stopped with her hand on the knob and turned back to face Roland, "I've been letting him run roughshod over our sessions, I know that. At first I wanted to take things slowly, get to know Jesse and let him get to know me. I didn't want to challenge him too quickly before building up some trust between us. I suspected he had some serious past trauma issues. He's obviously found a way to cope with that and he's a bright kid. I didn't want to rock his boat too much until he trusted me. I see now I'm the one who has missed the boat here. I need to take another shot at this before we decide what to do."

"Izzy, am I correct in assuming you've only . . . just now . . . read his entire file?" Roland asked this question in a strained voice, pitched slightly above his normal range. Izzy nodded wordlessly. "Well, if you had read the entire file before ever seeing him, you wouldn't have needed to guess about the seriousness of his past trauma issues. You do recall my suggestion that you reconsider your approach to the issue of client files?"

Roland seemed to have enough sense to not even pretend he expected an answer to his last question. "Was there anything in his file to indicate a predilection for sexual violence?" Izzy shook her head. "OK then. I'll give him a stern talk with reference to being on probation and all that entails. Do a full evaluation after each session and send it along to me."

Coming around the desk, Roland handed Izzy the file and she saw a look of disdain pass over his face. She wondered if his scorn was for Jesse's behaviour or hers or both. Then she told herself she had enough to handle without worrying about what Roland might think. As she went out the door, he called after her, "Izzy, don't forget to fill out the yellow incident report in triplicate."

Izzy walked back to her office, went in and locked the door. Sitting in one of the comfortable chairs with a peaceful view of the lake she covered her face with her hands and sobbed. Her tears were quickly spent and she grabbed for a Kleenex from the box placed conveniently for clients, blew her nose and took a deep breath. Going to her desk she mindlessly filled out the incident report, placing one copy in Jesse's file, one in her own files and one in a sealed envelope for submission to the Board.

Years ago, she and Caleb had been doing some renovations in the cabin. They had taken a heavy oak door off its hinges and had left it unfastened within the door jamb. Izzy was standing near the door, calling out to Caleb who was in another room. Suddenly, out of nowhere the door had tipped over and slammed into the side of her head. It had been so unexpected. She hadn't even had a chance to react.

Jesse's accusations about Justin reminded her of that moment of stunned disbelief. But this blow was followed by an awful realization. She was partially responsible for what had happened with Jesse. Izzy was overwhelmed by how far she had strayed from her ethical and professional responsibilities. She realized that being hit with the discordance between who she believed herself to be and her actual behavior was a good life lesson. She would benefit both personally and professionally from having this lesson brought home to her with such brutal clarity. But for now, her discomfort was slipping close to a level she wasn't sure she could handle.

iii.

Izzy had paced every room of the cabin four times over and she still felt like a caged animal. She was so jumpy she didn't know what to do with herself. She couldn't settle down to anything and she stood in the center of the living room holding her hair up on her head, feeling like her body was burning up. It was stuffy and hot in the cabin and it didn't seem to matter how many windows she opened. She wanted to rush down to the beach, throw her clothes in a heap on the sand and dive into the cold water. But she knew she wouldn't do that by herself.

She looked out the library window for what seemed like the hundredth time. Liam was still in the workshop, the light spilling from the window clearly visible on the gravel drive. She couldn't bring herself to go out and ask him to keep her company, maybe go for a swim again. She had started for the door a number of times, only to stop with the handle half turned and walk away to pace the entire cabin once more.

Izzy came down from the library and spotted the wind-up radio they kept on the shelf for emergencies. She grabbed the radio and a full bottle of wine. She called Dante and together they headed out to the cliff deck. She wound up the radio, set it on the railing so it faced south and adjusted the antenna. A quick spin of the dial picked up a distant music station. Izzy settled on the swing, one foot tucked under her and the other tapping out the rhythm of the music. She began to make her way steadily through the bottle of wine.

When Liam came out of the workshop he heard the faint strains of music from the cliff and out of curiosity followed the sound. As he came up to the deck he saw Izzy's foot keeping the beat and heard the opening notes of *Save the Last Dance for Me*. He called out hello, amazed that this song was playing. He stepped into the open area of the deck in front of the swing and reached out his hand for Izzy's. "You remember this one, don't you?" Izzy smiled up at him and rose in one fluid motion to come into Liam's arms.

iv.

Caleb had not been a dancer. But he had been a big fan of the Saturday night dances at the Legion in Dearborn. He would haul all of them along with him.

Beulah and Caleb would hold up the bar, talking to everyone in sight and playing darts. Bethany and Izzy danced practically every fast song together and for all the slow songs they dragged in Liam. No matter who was playing at the Legion, even if the patrons had to resort to the jukebox, *Save the Last Dance for Me* was always the final song of the evening.

Liam and Izzy were the perfect dance partners. They were the right height for each other and when their two dark heads bent together – he with his straight hair and she with her curls – they were a striking couple and more than one person would stop and stare. The staring was fine, because in those days Izzy and Caleb belonged so exclusively to each other that everyone knew Liam could dance the last dance with Izzy every night of the week and she would still be going home with Caleb.

V.

The music was fast enough to require some spins between the slow parts and as the last chorus wound down Liam brought Izzy out of a turn. He felt her come totally into his arms and right up against him, closer than he had ever held her before. Her free hand stretched to rest under his hair, against his neck. They danced that close for a couple of moments and then Izzy's lips were on his in a kiss that was far from what he might have expected their first kiss would be – tentative and explorative. Instead, Izzy's kiss was hot and demanding and it seemed to make a statement – *we both know what our bodies want; like this dance, we know the steps by heart.* Liam's arm was tightening around Izzy's waist and his body was responding in a wave of tension, when the song ended. The radio announcer said there would be a break for a message from the sponsor before the *Classic Rock* evening show resumed. Izzy suddenly pulled away from Liam, turning quickly to grab the radio and shut it off.

She sat down on the swing clutching the radio in her lap, "I'm so sorry, Liam, I'm really sorry . . . it's been a long day and I had some trouble at work earlier with a client. I'm tired." She waved her hand toward the empty wine bottle sitting on the deck, "And clearly I'm drinking too much."

She stood up and turned to call Dante over to her. At that moment the lone wolf howl began in the hills. Izzy stood still for a second, as if waiting for something. Then she rounded on Liam, "I'm sorry, I'm just . . . sorry. I don't know what else to say to you. And I can't fucking stand that bloody wolf much longer." She turned and walked quickly toward the main cabin.

Liam leaned against the railing staring out over the lake. Izzy had passion and strong ideas and because Liam had been around her and Caleb for years he had witnessed some sparks flying. Izzy's ultimate expression of frustration to Caleb had always been, *I can't fucking stand this,* with the emphasis on the f-word.

As Liam walked back to his cabin the feeling of Izzy in his arms and that kiss clung to him. He told himself, I agree with you Izzy, I can't fucking stand this either."

vi.

Izzy leaned with her back against the closed door of the cabin, her breath ragged and her heart thumping in her chest. What the hell is wrong with me? As if I don't already have enough problems.

In all the years she had known Liam she had never once thought of him with any kind of sexual desire. It would have been like stabbing Caleb in the back with his own knife. Liam was Caleb's best friend; he was like a brother to both of them. Liam was family. Pressed up against him just now – with the sensuous feeling of his long hair falling over her hands, the feel of his arm around her waist and the sound of his groan as he pulled her closer – it was all she could do to pull back. She had sat down on the swing chair so suddenly because she had literally felt weak in the knees with longing. She looked down at Dante and said, "This is really going beyond the beyond, boy." He stared back at her, his liquid eyes filled with dog-agreement while his tail thudded softly on the wood flooring.

CHAPTER THIRTY-FIVE

i.

The next morning Izzy carried a mug of coffee and a plate of Cook's oatmeal cookies to the table in the deserted dining-room where Jesse sat. She handed him the coffee and placed the plate in front of him. With his file open in her hand she sat down in the chair across from him.

Jesse took a gulp of the coffee and smirked across at Izzy before he loudly crunched into one of the cookies. "How do I rate this star treatment? Are you reconsidering your hasty rejection of me yesterday, Ms. Montgomery? Or maybe your job is on the line? Do you need me to take back what I said about you and golden boy?" Jesse looked like he was enjoying himself as he picked up another cookie.

"Cut the crap, Jesse," Izzy said, giving him a sharp look and then returning her gaze to his file. Finally, she looked up and locked eyes with him, "I really mean it. Cut the crap and get serious about what you have to lose here. I've been letting you waste my time and more importantly your own. That stops right now."

Jesse rocked the chair back on two legs and stared at Izzy for a moment. He shrugged and smiled at her. "I've played head games with counsellors a lot more hard-nosed than you are and come out on top. Don't feel bad."

Izzy shook her head impatiently. She glanced down at the file for another moment and then began to speak, "Let's see what we have here, OK? Broken arm at age six . . . a playground injury apparently; five stitches over your right eye when you were seven, says here you hit your head on a coffee table; concussion, age eight . . . seems like you fell down the stairs; nine-years old, broken rib . . . fell off your bike; another concussion age eleven . . . oh, another fall down the stairs. Either you were a pretty clumsy kid or something else was going on here."

She had his full attention now. "Got to be a bit too much for your mom to handle, hey? Says here you beat your own dad up. Hmmm . . . your mother called social services and told them she and your dad couldn't look after you anymore . . . you were too violent and it says here, noncompliant." Izzy drummed her fingers against the open file on the table, a thoughtful look on her face. "I just wonder, Jesse, what makes a kid so noncompliant?"

Jesse's eyes had narrowed to scowling slits but Izzy had seen the expressions racing across his face as she spoke – vulnerability, fear, pain and anger. She hadn't been wrong in her first assessment – the young man sitting across from her was suffering. Izzy closed the file slowly and left it lying on the table between them. "You're a smart kid, Jesse, and a good manipulator. You know how to work the system and I admit it – you played me, for sure. I get it . . . that's how you've survived; but I'm telling you for the last time – get serious about our sessions and start dealing with some of this crap in your life before you end up getting kicked out of this program." Izzy pointed to the closed file and added, "Then you can spend the rest of your life with this stuff dogging you like a bad dream you can't shake." She stood up, grabbed the file and started to turn away.

Jesse was still rocking the chair on its back legs and staring out at the lake. She had got through to him alright but she wasn't sure it would get her where they needed to be. Confronting a client with his past was risky – what she had done with Jesse could backfire on her. But her gut told her that she needed to take the risk. She was out of options.

She was several paces away from the table before she heard his voice. "Wait. My real dad is dead . . . my mom wasn't living with my real dad. I beat the shit out of my step-father as soon as I could take him on and I'd have done worse to him if they'd have left me there." Jesse paused and his fists clenched on the table as he brought the chair down hard on all four legs. "She knew it . . . my mother . . . that's why she had them take me away. She chose him. She always chose him."

Izzy watched the emotions play across Jesse's face and then she walked back to the table and spoke quietly, "I guess we have someplace to get started then, don't we? Roland feels you are a risk and that I should meet with you in public places only. Can I tell him that's not necessary?"

Jesse met her stare as he drew in a ragged breath, "Like I told you the other day, Ms. Montgomery, I don't have to force myself on anyone."

i i .

Later that afternoon Izzy was methodically and mindlessly weeding through the three vegetable beds in front of the greenhouse when Justin came into view on the garden path. Izzy stood up and pulled off her gardening gloves. She rubbed the stiffness in her lower back as she watched Justin approach. He was in front of her now and the emotion racing across his face was obvious.

"I heard about Jesse. Roland called a group meeting and told all of us what happened. He says Jesse's on probation, whatever the hell that means. Jesse was right there the whole frigging time – probation, my ass. I'd like to punch that stupid smirk right off his face. He should have got kicked out of the program for pulling something like that with you," Justin was holding his fists clenched as he spoke and his eyes were filled with anger.

"It's based on my recommendation to Roland that Jesse's on probation. Look, we have to talk, OK?" Izzy looked down at the half done weeding, "I need a break from this anyway. Let's get something cold to drink. It's way too hot out here for weeding."

Izzy suggested they take the tall glasses of iced tea out to the shaded deck overlooking the fish pond. In the afternoon heat, under these circumstances, it seemed the most soothing place she could think of – in the shade of the tall trees with the gentle sound of water flowing down into the pool where fish swam lazily among the water plants. Seated in a comfortable deck chair with Justin across from her, Izzy pondered the nearby statue of Lao Tzu.

She had always loved the story of Lao Tzu. Disguised as a blind beggar, he attempted to escape the court and the moral decay of his time. He meant to take up the life of a hermit. As he tried to make good his escape through the city gates, he was recognized by a sentry who begged Lao Tzu to stay and share his wisdom – to become the sentry's teacher. Izzy thought that she would beg just like that sentry – she could use Lao Tzu's wisdom about now.

Izzy looked over at Justin as he stared silently down at the glass in his hand. She could sense that he knew what was coming. Whatever she said now was going to hurt him. It shouldn't have been like this. She should never have let things get so out of hand.

"Justin, I owe you an apology."

He looked up at her in surprise. "You don't have anything to apologize to me for, Izzy." Justin frowned before going on, "I've been acting like a fool all summer . . . that's all on me. I heard the talk . . . what Jesse's been saying about you and me. He had no right. You never encouraged me in anyway. I've known all along there is no chance of you and me –," his voice trailed off.

Seeing how miserable and humiliating this was for him, Izzy felt pinioned by her own guilt. "No Justin, I do owe you an apology. I saw what was happening. I knew that the way you felt about me was going beyond what is appropriate for anyone to feel about a counsellor or employer. I didn't try to talk to you about what I saw. I let it go and that was wrong. It was my responsibility to bring out into the open what you were feeling so we could both deal with it. I didn't do my job and that was unfair to you. I acted against my ethical and professional responsibilities. I let things go on because it felt good for my ego and I had no right to do that to you."

Justin didn't even look up. She could see his eyes following the koi around the pool. "Look at me for a minute, Justin, please." He looked over at her and the pain in his eyes made her want to reach out and put her hand on his arm – she wanted to comfort him. But she couldn't touch him – not now. Izzy took a deep breath and said, "A counselling relationship has a special kind of intimacy. That can't be avoided if anything of lasting change is going to come from it. I was there beside you when you faced up to a lot of really difficult memories. Feeling close because of that is normal and sometimes close feelings do cross the line to become something else. You didn't do anything wrong. I don't regret a moment of the closeness that helped you get better and I hope you don't either. This other thing that has happened is my fault, not yours."

Justin raked his hand through his hair and sat back in his chair. As the sun pushed through the clouds to dapple and shadow the reflected leaves on the pond, a ray of light caught the summer gold of his hair swinging past the side of his jaw. Izzy stared at the play of light on his face. She felt her heart turn over and she wanted to cry – felt her eyes actually filling with tears. She would have given a lot, at that moment, to be in another time with another man who had basked in a similar glow of sunlight.

Justin glanced at Izzy in time to see her eyes brimming with tears as she lowered her head and stared down at her hands folded in her lap. He spoke quietly, "I always knew it was impossible. Maybe it would have been better if you had talked to me weeks ago but I don't know. I don't think I could have stopped feeling what I feel for you. It probably would have meant I couldn't work here and then I wouldn't have had even the little I did have – that sounds pretty lame and pathetic right?" Justin stared over at Izzy for a moment; the misery on his face was quickly replaced by resignation. He picked up his iced tea glass and drained it. "I better get to work, right? I'll finish off that weeding for you."

Oh my God, Izzy thought, he doesn't understand what I'm trying to tell him. He has no way of knowing that if I had done my job and talked to him about how he was feeling months ago – he would have been able to put it all in perspective. He would have understood that what was happening to him was normal and he would have been more kind to himself. He still could have worked here and none of the pain he's feeling now would have been necessary. Because he doesn't understand, he's willing to let me off the hook.

Izzy knew she had to let it go – Justin's wound was too fresh. Someday he might understand – figure out exactly how unprofessional she had been. When that day came he might even hate her and she knew he had every right to do so.

"Sounds good, Justin. The going away party is tonight. Are you still OK with that?"

Justin smiled, though Izzy could see it was a strained smile. "Wouldn't miss it." He was walking away down the path when he turned suddenly and said, "Thanks Izzy, for everything, OK. I really mean that." Then he was gone and his words had such a ring of goodbye it was as if some part of him was already gone.

i i i .

A party was the last thing Izzy wanted to be getting ready for, but everyone was expecting a going away gathering for Justin. A week ago, Lisa-Marie had stopped by Izzy's office to ask if she could show some of her photos at the party. Roland had said she could borrow the digital projector from the Camp. At the time, Izzy had been happy to agree but now she dreaded what Lisa-Marie's photographs might reveal. All she needed was to see herself projected life-size smiling at Justin with God knows what kind of a look on her face. Or worst yet, for Justin to have been caught with his emotions bared for all of them to see.

Izzy stared at Lao Tzu with tears running down her face. She'd messed things up royally. Roland had every right to report her to the Board for the way she had screwed up Jesse's case. What she had done to Justin was horrible – and for what? So she could have her forty-five-year-old ego stroked by a vulnerable kid who wasn't even twenty. And to top everything off, she had no idea how she would get through a whole evening not being able to look Liam in the face. After the way she had acted with him the night before, she couldn't imagine what he must think of her.

i v .

Dear Emma:

I do want to know why I did the things I did – but it's so hard to think about all of it. Why did I act like such a total slut? I just ended up making my life worse than it already was – hard to believe, but true. Why did I do something so stupid like try to kill myself? Auntie Beth thinks I should find out why – but I just want to forget. Is that so bad, Emma?

I just wanted someone to be nice to me – everything happened because no one had been nice to me in so long and I got all mixed up. With all the guys, I thought doing what they wanted would mean they would be nice to me. But none of them were.

Things are so different now, Emma. People here see me. Justin likes me – I know he does and tonight I will take my shot. I'm pretty nervous but everything is different now. It has to work out, Emma. It just has to. I'm glad to be alive because I'm sure Justin cares about me and when I'm with him tonight it's going to make all the other stuff disappear.

CHAPTER THIRTY-SIX

i.

Much to Izzy's relief, Justin's going away party was finally winding down. Earlier in the afternoon she had scrambled around trying to find an appropriate going away gift. Caleb's gold watch was obviously the wrong choice and her stomach rolled over at the thought that she could ever have considered giving that watch to Justin. Izzy saw Liam raise his eyebrows slightly when Justin opened Izzy's gift to reveal a leather-covered journal with silver accents; the kind of journal she favoured for her own use – the kind of journal Liam always gave her for a gift.

The evening was even more difficult than Izzy had anticipated it would be. She could tell that acting as if everything was fine was hard on Justin. Every time she avoided talking to Liam she could see the hurt in his eyes. Whenever Roland spoke to her she was sure he was patronizing her with his inside knowledge of her professional blunders. And Lisa-Marie's photo show was the last straw. There were all kinds of great shots of the Camp, the lake, the main cabin and garden and even the nearby town of Dearborn. There were pictures of all of them, carefully chosen to be complimentary and to emphasize Justin's connection to each of them. And there were lots and lots of pictures of Justin – working in the garden, playing the guitar at the Camp, diving in the lake, lounging in a chair on the kitchen deck, dressed up as Robin Hood for the garden gala.

When the show ended, the lights were turned on and everyone clapped. Lisa-Marie beamed with pride. But it was the way she looked over at Justin that broke through Izzy's denial. She finally saw what she should have seen from the very beginning – Lisa-Marie was head over heels in love with Justin.

Beulah and Bethany had already left and Dan went home soon after them, having borrowed Izzy's last flashlight. Liam was also on his way out. Izzy avoided saying goodbye to him by gathering up the dirty cake plates and glasses. She came down from the kitchen a few moments later to see Lisa-Marie in the entrance standing close to Justin. She was talking quickly to him and gesturing toward the beach, a half-bottle of wine tucked under her arm.

Izzy approached the two young people with the hope that Justin would make some attempt to say goodbye to her. She wanted him to show her that things were OK, though she squirmed inside at the thought of wanting something like that from him – she knew he didn't owe her anything.

Justin looked at her with thinly-veiled anguish mixed with anger. She understood the anguish but she wasn't expecting him to be angry at her so soon. She had hoped that stage might take a while to set in.

He flung an arm around Lisa-Marie and spoke to Izzy before she had a chance to say anything. "Well, thanks for the party. It was great. Lisa-Marie and I are heading down to the beach for a moonlight dip." Turning quickly and practically dragging Lisa-Marie off her feet, he walked out. Izzy was left alone, staring blankly at the closed door.

ii.

Liam walked along the dark path to his cabin. He banged his door open and then slammed it shut. He stomped across the wooden floor and up the stairs to the loft. He was consumed with a smouldering anger. Pearl, who had watched his progress as he walked right past her without even patting her head, whined softly at the bottom of the stairs. Liam leaned over the railing and addressed the dog, "Who the hell does she think she is, anyway? She can't kiss me like that one night and then act as though I don't exist, the next. Oh sorry, Liam, sorry, I had a bad day, I'm drinking too much." Pearl's ears perked up at Liam's voice – high-pitched and mocking. "She can blame it on the booze all she wants, Pearl. I know what that kiss meant and so does she." Liam watched

Pearl cock her head to one side and stare up at him. "Go to your bed, Pearl. Go lie down."

Liam opened the small window. The loft was stifling hot. He threw the quilt down to the end of the bed and quickly stripped off his clothes. He slid naked under the sheet. Feeling wide-awake he stared at the ceiling. It was going to be a long night.

iii.

Lisa-Marie slid over close to Justin and held up the wine bottle. She rested her free hand on his thigh, "Want some of this before I finish it off, Justin?"

Justin shook his head. He looked down at her hand on his leg and gently picked it up and put it down on the log in the small space Lisa-Marie had left between them. He watched her chug back most of what was left in the bottle before she threw it end over end, out towards the lake.

"Ughh, it really isn't my drink of choice, I must admit." She stood up and moved in front of Justin, leaning forward to rest her hands on his chest. "Come on Justin," she whispered, bending close to his face with her hair swinging towards him. He caught the smell of wine on her breath and something else – something clean and fresh like lemons. He saw her moisten her lips slowly and then she leaned in to kiss him.

He quickly grabbed her forearms and moved her easily and smoothly back to a sitting position on the log beside him, "Knock it off Leez, OK, please. You know things aren't like that between you and me." There was a moment of silence when Justin hoped that what he was sure was about to happen might not. And then, of course, it did and he knew it was going to be as bad as this type of thing always was.

Lisa-Marie jumped up and moved angrily down the beach, stooping to grab some rocks to throw out toward the lake. "It's Izzy, isn't it? I've seen the way you slobber over her day after fucking day. She's never going to let you touch her, Justin. You get that, right?"

Justin snapped his head up. Lisa-Marie's words felt like fingernails digging into the wound his afternoon talk with Izzy had inflicted. "What's going on with you and me has nothing to do with Izzy. You're just an immature kid if you think that. She was my counsellor; we talked about a lot of heavy stuff. That's all there was to it."

Lisa-Marie walked over to stand in front of him. He could see by the look on her face that she was sorry she had ever mentioned Izzy's name. She reached for his hand and brought it up under her tight top to rest on her breast. Her skin was warm. He could feel her nipple harden under his palm as she pressed it tight against her. She shivered visibly and her voice trembled, "Why not me, Justin? I know there isn't anyone else. I've been with you practically every day this summer – why not me?"

Justin ground his teeth and sucked in his breath. He felt edgy and tight like a coil about to spring out of control. He quickly disentangled his hand from her shirt and grabbed her by the shoulders, shaking her slightly. "Leez, try to listen to me, OK. I'm going away in a couple of days. It's not like I'll ever see you again. I've had a great time this summer. You're a cute kid and it's been fun hanging out. But you and I are not going to do this when we both know it can't mean what you want it to."

Lisa-Marie pulled away and plopped down onto the log beside him. She looked at him with a sexy pout. "It really doesn't have to be such a big deal. I just thought we could have a bit of fun."

"Fun . . . ya, right. Look, Leez, I've been around a lot of screwed up kids over the last few years. A lot of girls and guys, too, who say it doesn't have to mean anything. But it always means something and not a very nice something when you realize it meant more to you than it did to the other person."

Lisa-Marie stiffened, her hands clenched tightly and Justin saw something that looked like hate flicker over her face. "I'm not one of your fucked-up group home kids, Justin. There isn't anything wrong with me."

His patience was fast reaching the breaking point. He was regretting the way he had walked away from Izzy without a backward glance. Having everything end the way it had today left a hollow feeling in the pit of his stomach. He felt guilty for coming down to the beach with Lisa-Marie in the first place. He had set the stage for this whole screwed-up mess.

He got up abruptly and threw the nearby bucket of water over the flames. "Do you think I'm stupid, Leez? I've seen how you've looked at me the whole summer and your slide show tonight was pretty obvious. I know you want us to be more than friends and now you're going to sit there and try to tell me I could screw you here on the beach and it would all be for fun. What do you take me for, anyway? You can lie to me if you want, but don't lie to yourself."

"Fuck off Justin. I'm going swimming." Lisa-Marie got up and with her back to him, she slithered out of her shorts and pulled her tight shirt over her head so she was standing outlined in the moonlight in nothing but her thong underwear. She walked slowly into the water.

Justin had no idea what to do. He was angry and frustrated but desire was starting to edge all of that out. Lisa-Marie's little attention getting stunt – pulling her clothes off like that – was bringing him close to the limit of his endurance for one night. He wanted nothing more than to bury his aching ego in her warm and obviously available body. He wasn't going to do it though, no matter how crazy he felt; but she was giving his self-control a workout.

He didn't want to leave her out there in the water all by herself, probably feeling like a complete idiot – probably feeling just like he did when he walked away from Izzy tonight. He called out across the shallow water to where she was standing, "Hey Leez, don't be like this. How about you come on out of the water and I'll walk you home? Look, I'm turning around; I can't see anything . . . come out and get dressed."

Before he turned he saw her toss her hair out of her eyes as she looked back at him over her naked shoulder. Then as he turned away, he heard her voice and it contained every ounce of sarcasm, hate and frustration he suspected she had been holding in for a while. "Go on back to the Camp Justin and jerk off to your little fantasy of Izzy. I'm sure you've had a lot of practice doing that."

The crudeness of that remark was the last straw. He glanced back out at Lisa-Marie, up to her waist now in the dark water of the lake. "Have it your way then, Leez," he called out. Before he walked away, he put the extra flashlight he always carried on the log near her pile of clothes.

CHAPTER THIRTY-SEVEN

i.

Lisa-Marie dove under the water and swam out into the blackness of the lake. Finally, out of breath, she rolled over to float lazily on her back, the slight chop of the waves bobbing her up and down. She caught the glow of Justin's flashlight through a break in the trees. He must be almost at the A-Frame, she thought.

"Fuck him," she said softly to the stars over her head. "Who needs him anyway?" But tears were running down her face and emptying into the lake. She felt hot with humiliation. All her daydreams and fantasies were destroyed. She had reached for the gold ring and she had missed. Justin had walked away from her for good. Everything had quickly become like the wet ash that was hissing in the fire pit on the shore. He didn't want her.

Lisa-Marie began to shiver. She knew what to do – start swimming out further into the blackness and keep swimming until she couldn't swim anymore. Then the emptiness she felt would disappear. There would be no more Justin walking away from her forever; no more Izzy looking perfect all the time; no more Justin wanting Izzy and not her. It would all disappear.

There was something so familiar about what she felt – the irresistible urge to be done with everything, to stop fighting and to stop trying; it was almost comforting to be in such a recognizable space. Her body relaxed and she turned to face the distant shore. She began to move her arms and feet slowly through the water, there was no rush; she had all night. Her mind was drifting along, reaching out to the darkness all around her when out of nowhere she could almost feel the sensation of Liam's hand on her back. She could hear him saying, *try to think every day about what it's like to be alive.* She shook her head and tried to ignore his voice but it was like a stuck record – it wouldn't go away.

She suddenly swung herself around in the water and pushed strongly toward the shore. The slight chop dragged at her naked body and she was surprised she hadn't felt the force of the waves before. And the water was freezing cold. She hadn't noticed that either. She focused on the small pile of her clothes by the fire pit. She couldn't just leave her clothes there like that. Those were her favorite shorts. Eventually her desperate toes scrambled against the lake bottom. She stumbled out of the water and along the beach to flop onto the log by the dead fire. Holding her arms tight around herself she shook, sobbed and vomited wine and Justin's going away cake all over the sand.

She took a couple of wrenching breaths and got up to pull on her damp clothes. She walked over to the edge of the lake to kneel and scoop up some water in her hands. She rinsed her mouth and turned to grab the flashlight that was sitting on the log. She began to walk along the beach towards the south stairs. All she could think of was getting to Liam. Izzy had ruined everything for her with Justin but Izzy wasn't the only one who could make a guy want her. Lisa-Marie knew how to do that, too.

i i .

Still wide awake, Liam heard someone on the path. Pearl would have set up a chorus of barking if it were a stranger. He suspected that whoever was coming from the direction of Izzy's, flashlight beaming off the trees and reflecting back at him through the loft's upper window, was no stranger. The thumping of Pearl's tail against the floorboards downstairs confirmed his suspicion.

He sat up in the bed as the door creaked open and closed quietly. He heard gentle padding coming across the floor. Lisa-Marie's voice was low as she whispered, "Good dog." Overwhelming disappointment pushed away any questions about why Lisa-Marie would be in his cabin at this time of the night. Even though he was supremely pissed off at Izzy, he still had wanted it to be her.

Lisa-Marie came into view at the top of the stairs moments later. Liam could see she had been in the lake and her wet top clung like a second skin, outlining her breasts clearly. She stepped off the stairs and stood by the side of his bed. The whole scene was so bizarre that Liam felt as robbed of the ability to speak as she apparently was.

She stared at him with a look that seemed, even in the dim light, empty and lost. She pulled her wet top over her head and dropped it carelessly on the narrow band of floor. She stripped off her shorts and underwear in one smooth movement, never taking her eyes from Liam's face.

Liam couldn't think any more than he could speak. The first thing that registered was the powerful physical reaction he was having to the nearness of Lisa-Marie's naked body. And in that moment he knew that his so-called concern about her skimpy clothing had carried the seed of something else. This slamming realization, combined with his anger at Izzy and lust for her, gripped him like a vise. He let his eyes stare at Lisa-Marie's naked breasts and then wander down her body. It was all the permission she was looking for.

She was all over him in an instant. She pressed her naked body on top of him and attacked his mouth in a fierce kiss. Her skin was ice cold against the heat of his body. Everything was happening way too fast. Liam felt like he had disappeared, if he was ever present to Lisa-Marie in the first place. He couldn't keep up with her and he just wanted her to stop. "Oh shit, this is all wrong," he said as he disentangled their bodies and pushed Lisa-Marie gently but firmly across the bed toward the wall of the loft. "Slow down for God's sake." His voice was shaking.

Lisa-Marie began to tremble, then to shiver violently. She whispered, "Don't you like it, don't you want me like this? Don't you want me either? Please say you want me, Liam. I know you do." In her desperation she tried to reach for him, touch him and prove to both of them that his hardness meant he wanted her. Liam pushed her hands away and looked into her eyes. He knew exactly how close she was to falling into something dark and awful. She curled up into a fetal position, hugging her arms over her naked breasts and shrinking back against the wall like he had smacked her.

He had seen her and Justin heading down to the beach together as he walked back to his cabin. It didn't take a rocket scientist to figure out what had happened. It was obvious now that taking her shot hadn't worked out for Lisa-Marie. Liam wondered what had been going through her mind before she decided to come here, like this, to him. The way she was shaking now, begging him to want her, clutching to her belief that he did, was about as pitiful a thing as Liam had ever seen.

Jesus Christ, what a mess – what was he going to do? Rejecting her and telling her she would be glad at some later date wasn't going to work. The way he had looked at her, he had all but invited her to get into his bed a few short moments ago. How was he going to tell her he had changed his mind? No matter how he said that, she'd think it was because she wasn't good enough. He couldn't see her getting over that type of rejection twice in one night. He couldn't let her walk away feeling as though no one wanted the only thing she thought she had that was worth giving.

He spoke very slowly, "If you want to do this . . . are you sure you want to do this?" She nodded silently, her eyes as large as saucers in her pale face. "OK, kiddo, OK. Do it with me then." Very slowly he pulled her across the bed toward him and held her gently against his chest until she stopped shaking. Then he made love to Lisa-Marie, the young girl turned far too quickly into a woman.

i i i .

"Is that what it's supposed to be like, Liam?" Lisa-Marie asked this question in a shaky voice as she lay breathless and curled up beside Liam's body. She thought she knew what sex was about. Now she realized she didn't know anything at all. Before tonight she had no idea that sex could be slow and gentle and sort of sweet, or that it could culminate in what had seemed like endless waves of pulsing, warm pleasure. Oh my God, she thought, if it's like this for guys every time, no wonder all they think about is sex.

She was stunned to discover that it was possible to feel something other than discomfort and to learn she wouldn't always be being totally grossed out by how guys could act. She blushed with embarrassment when she recalled that she had clung to Liam and moaned right out loud. All of a sudden she really did feel like a stupid kid and she retreated to her personal comfort zone – humour tinged with sarcasm. "Well, I've never had sex in a bed before. I guess it makes a difference."

"Ya, kiddo, it is all about the bed for sure. A guy doesn't have to try too hard when he has that going for him." She could see Liam smiling in the dark of the loft. He had stretched to rest his arms behind his neck and he seemed to be waiting for something.

"What's supposed to happen now? I mean when you have sex in a bed?"

Liam chuckled softly, "Well generally, in my experience, the girl wants to talk and the guy dozes off." Then in a more serious tone he asked, "But you tell me. Why did you come here tonight?"

In that moment it was as if a page turned. Lisa-Marie was suddenly uncomfortable with lying next to Liam's naked body. She edged up on an elbow and moved over towards the wall of the loft, pulling a corner of the quilt from the end of the bed with her. Without looking at Liam she replied, "For this, I guess . . . but I didn't think it would be like this." She blushed again, glad of the dark and her next words came out in a rush, "I made a total fool of myself with Justin down on the beach and he'll never even want to be friends with me again. I went into the water, Liam and I felt so cold inside and scared, like the other time scared. I wanted to start swimming out deeper and deeper and keep going until I couldn't swim anymore. I can't believe it now – that I was really thinking of doing something that crazy."

Lisa-Marie was quiet for a moment, shaking her head in disbelief, then she went on, "For some reason, when I was out in the water, I thought about what you told me – remember what it feels like to be alive – and all I could think of was coming to you. I knew you wouldn't send me away." She swallowed sharply on the lump rising up in her throat and dug her fingernails into the flesh of her palms; she didn't want Liam to see her cry. "I didn't expect it to be like this. I've been with other guys before, Liam. I know you probably think I'm just a kid, but I'm not." Lisa-Marie sat up, clutching the blanket tightly, "I know I shouldn't have come here like this –," her voice started to shake, "– it's all my fault. I'm sorry. Everything is so unfair. Things shouldn't be like this." With her free hand she gestured at herself and Liam, "Why couldn't it be Justin who made me feel like that?"

The silence stretched out and Lisa-Marie was relieved that Liam had pulled the sheet up to his chest. She hugged the quilt against herself and tried not to burst into tears. Doing that would certainly be the absolute humiliation.

Finally, Liam reached over and gently turned her face towards him. "Listen to me now, kiddo. This is important –," he paused to wait for her to raise her eyes to his, "– you are just a kid and that doesn't change because you've been with a few guys. I don't get off the blame hook here. Understand?" Lisa-Marie nodded silently. "It isn't your fault – none of it – not what happened tonight with me or Justin – and not any of the other stuff you blame yourself for. Whatever happened to you – you didn't deserve it – it wasn't your fault – remember that."

Lisa-Marie nodded again, the tears she was holding back shone bright in her eyes. She quickly slithered past Liam to sit on the side of the bed where she could retrieve her clothes. Liam got up as well, pulling on his jeans and grabbing his shirt from the corner post of the bed. She could tell he was being careful in the tight space of the loft not to brush up against her. Everything had changed; nothing would ever be the same between them. She was into her wet clothes and already starting down the stairs before he had his pants buttoned.

"I've got to get back to the A-Frame. If Auntie Beth is awake she'll be worried about me and I sure don't want to face the wrath of Beulah by upsetting Auntie Beth."

Liam came down the stairs behind her. He grabbed a red flannel shirt from the back of the kitchen chair and handed it to her. She shrugged her arms into it. She had one hand on the door to leave when Liam said, "Lisa-Marie, don't tell –," his voice trailed off. He let the unsaid name hang there between them.

He didn't need to say Izzy's name. Lisa-Marie knew exactly how Liam felt about Izzy. First Izzy ruined everything with Justin and now Liam, too. The whole summer, it always seemed to be Izzy.

Lisa-Marie paused for a split second to let it all sink in. Letting her hand drop from the door knob she turned to face Liam. She spoke in a voice that made Pearl raise her head and begin to whine. "Izzy, right, Liam, please don't tell Izzy. You like her, right? Oh God, of course, everyone's half in love with her. I know that. I'm probably half in love with her myself. I get that." Lisa-Marie tugged the flannel shirt close to her body and paced the small room, "I get that. OK, already. I really do fucking get it," she strung each of the last words out in an exasperated drawl.

"She's beautiful, fairytale queen beautiful, right Liam? I know she would never lay a hand on Justin or let him touch her, but she lets him look at her the way he does, like he's handing her his heart on a silver platter. She just lets it happen, Liam, and she doesn't stop it. What kind of a person her age does that?" Liam shrugged helplessly. "And now you too? Fuck." The last word came out in a tone of resignation and disgust. She understood now that Liam's desire hadn't been for her at all. She'd merely been a substitute, a fill-in; and if Justin had gone along with her plans down on the beach the reality would have been the same.

Liam sat at the table and looked down at his hands. "Izzy wouldn't approve of what happened here tonight."

"Because she wants you for herself, right? Does she have to have every single guy slobbering after her?"

Liam shook his head, "I don't know about that, kiddo. But if she finds out about this I'm certain she'll ask me to leave here."

"Stop talking crap, Liam. What are you trying to say? You're talking like this was a rape or something. I'm old enough to know the difference between yes and no." Lisa-Marie blushed but forced the next words out, "When you gave me the choice, I said yes."

"All semantics, kiddo. In Izzy's world, sixteen-year-old girls don't consent to having sex with older men. I'm the adult here – it was up to me to act like one."

Lisa-Marie nodded her understanding but she spit out her next words, "Whatever . . . it's none of her fucking business if you ask me, but fine. She'll never hear it from me, Liam. I don't want to screw things up for you." She drew in her breath sharply and though her voice was starting to hitch in a way she hated, she went on, "You have been nicer to me than any other grown-up has ever been. Whenever you took the time to listen to me – it really mattered, Liam. I mean that. Izzy can't fuck that up like she's wrecked everything else for me."

Lisa-Marie turned toward the door and as she drew herself up to her full height and squared her shoulders, she made a decision. "I'll be leaving here soon anyway. I've decided to board in Victoria for school – so you don't need to worry about me being around here to say anything." She walked out into the dark without another word and started up the path to the road. She would go along that route and down the other trail to the A-Frame rather than cut past Izzy's. She truly did not want to cause Liam any problems.

Lisa-Marie stopped suddenly at the top of the trail to the A-Frame. The night sky was filled with stars and she could hear the distant sound of an owl hooting, low and mournful. She felt like something about her was different. Her heart was broken because Justin would never want her but that wasn't it. It was the other guys. The hold they had on her had disappeared. She would never again call herself a slut. The sex with Liam, the way she had felt, what he had said to her afterwards – it had wiped everything clean. She knew she was just a kid – none of what had happened with the other guys defined her. She had said yes to all of it; but the yes she said to Liam was the only one she had ever meant. She shrugged and shook her head in wonder – how could something so fucked-up, have turned out so right?

iv.

From the vantage point of the rocking chair on the back porch of the A-Frame, Beulah saw the bounce of light against the trees – someone was coming down the trail. She knocked the ash off the dark cigarillo she was smoking and raised it to her lips to inhale deeply. As Lisa-Marie came into view at the bottom of the trail and walked slowly up the stairs to the back porch, Beulah took in her appearance with a quick glance – dishevelled hair, flushed cheeks and Liam's red-flannel shirt flung over an obviously damp and clinging top. Liam's shirt ruled out Dan; thank the powers that be for that one. The thought of her drinking buddy Dan, entertaining Lisa-Marie in his dark cabin was as ridiculous as it was disturbing.

"You're coming the wrong direction from having a little skinny dip over at Izzy's beach –," Beulah held her hand up as Lisa-Marie opened her mouth to speak, "– don't bother with any lies. Justin stopped here well over two hours ago saying he left you at the beach and you weren't in any shape to be alone. He was worried. You can just thank your lucky stars, missy, that Bethany was asleep and didn't hear him. She would have been frantic." Beulah leaned forward and ground the cigarillo into the old tin lid on the railing, "I took the dogs over to the beach to look for you. You drowning your sorry self in the lake would be a big pain in my ass. Fortunately for you –," Beulah paused to stare hard at Lisa-Marie, "– or maybe not, but we'll get to that, I spotted you, heading up the south stairs."

Beulah replayed in her own mind the surprise and momentary relief she had felt when she caught sight of Lisa-Marie and her flashlight disappearing along the trail past the south stair. By the time Beulah got across the beach and up the stairs, Lisa-Marie was at least five minutes ahead of her. Beulah had experienced an uncharacteristic moment or two of indecision when she passed the dark guest-cabin and then stood down the slope from Liam's equally dark cabin. It was clear to her that Lisa-Marie had to have entered one of the two places. There was nowhere else to go, and bush-whacking through the dark trees with no destination in mind was too nuts even for a crazy kid like Lisa-Marie.

Busting in on Dan or Liam like some kind of avenging, outraged parent was something Beulah couldn't bring herself to do. It was hard for her to imagine what would have made her feel more ridiculous – staring into the face of the man who was alone or the one who wasn't. She had walked away deciding she would deal with the whole mess whenever Lisa-Marie chose to drag her sorry little butt back to the A-Frame.

"Well, Missy," Beulah said slowly, "Someone has certainly been in your pants tonight and it wasn't Justin, so how about explaining to me just exactly what went on over at Liam's."

Lisa-Marie sat down on the edge of the porch and drew her knees up toward her chin. She stared off in the direction of the stream that provided a constant backdrop of sound. It was almost hypnotic at times, appearing as if by magic only when you listened for it. She chose her words carefully, "OK . . . I made a complete fool of myself tonight. There, are you happy? I threw myself at Justin and he made it very clear he wasn't interested. Then I ran off to Liam's and tried the same thing with him and made an even bigger fool of myself. He gave me some health tea to calm me down and it tasted like stewed frigging hay or something."

Lisa-Marie heard Beulah's snort of suppressed laughter and she knew she was on the right track. Making fun of Liam would distract Beulah. She had to throw her off the scent because if Auntie Beth found out she would get mad at Liam and maybe tell Izzy. For that matter, Beulah herself might tell Izzy in order to get rid of Liam. Beulah had never tried to hide her dislike for him. Lisa-Marie had no idea what could have made Beulah hate Liam so much but giving her this kind of ammunition against him couldn't be good.

Beulah frowned and said, "The cabin was pretty dark for tea drinking when I looked."

"Well, it took him a while to get me to put my clothes back on and he had to convince me to go downstairs with him."

"So, nothing happened?" It was clear from Beulah's tone that this is what she wanted to believe. All of a sudden, Lisa-Marie understood that Beulah didn't want Liam to have done this thing. Although she seemed to hate him, she didn't want to believe he'd had sex with Bethany's sixteen-year-old niece.

Lisa-Marie wanted to protect Liam. No matter what he had said about it not being her fault, she felt bad for having put him in such a crappy position. She knew what she had to do – make this story as convincing as if she were up for an Oscar nomination.

"No . . . nothing happened like you're thinking. I could tell he wanted me though. Well, look at me –," she pointed down to her wet top, "– but he wouldn't give in. You know how you always say Liam wouldn't say shit if his mouth was full. It was like that. He went on and on and on . . . I'm just a child . . . . I'm Bethany's niece . . . Izzy wouldn't approve . . . I have my whole life in front of me . . . it's time for me to move on . . . someday I'll realize this was all for the best. He fed me a bunch of patronizing crap, as if I wasn't humiliated enough for one night. I sure didn't need him lecturing me."

Beulah laughed again, "For all his gutless ramblings he did you a big favour kid, whether you realize it right now or not. Come on think about it," Beulah rose and turned toward the screen door. "You don't want to have sex with that old guy." Lisa-Marie saw Beulah's eyes wander over her breasts, clearly outlined through the wet top. "It would be a damn waste is what it would be," she added. "Coming in or what?"

Lisa-Marie's heart was pounding and her palms were sticky with sweat as she stepped through the door and felt Beulah thump her on the back, "Cheer-up. Things will look better in the morning, they always do."

V.

Liam sat at the table staring out at the dark lake for a long time after Lisa-Marie left the cabin, for so long that the thin shades of morning grey were starting to light upon the water before he rose to set the kettle on the stove. He believed Lisa-Marie. She wouldn't tell Izzy or Bethany but she would tell someone. She wouldn't be able to help it. That's the way kids are. He felt like a man waiting for the guillotine blade to fall; he couldn't see how there was any way on this earth that Izzy wasn't going to find out. Things like this never stayed hidden.

He thought about what Izzy would think – how her worldview didn't allow for what he had done tonight with Lisa-Marie. She would interpret his behaviour as morally reprehensible. Liam's worldview was not quite so black and white. Life was complicated – it was impossible to judge any action as always wrong or always right for that matter. He had known, up in the loft, that when

Lisa-Marie said yes she meant yes. He hadn't chased after her and he hadn't coerced her. At the same time, he knew those things weren't enough to make what had happened OK.

He wasn't surprised when she said she'd been with other guys before – she didn't come to him acting like it was the first time. She hadn't needed to tell him she'd never felt the way he made her feel. He figured that out for himself. Liam had a pretty good idea of what her previous sexual experience must have been like. She was a kid who needed someone to want her and of course, guys had taken advantage of that. He knew how cruel young people could be to one another – the guys used her and the girls convinced her she had asked for it. So naturally she looked at him and said it was all her fault.

What happened tonight was wrong and he knew it. Lisa-Marie needed someone to show her that she was worth more than her body – no matter what she thought she wanted. It was wrong because Liam was in love with Izzy and he had wanted Izzy to be walking up the stairs to his loft and stripping off her clothes; and in the end he hadn't been able to hide that from Lisa-Marie. His gut gnawed with pain as he rose to the sound of the whistling kettle and began to make his morning tea. Maybe, after all, it was wrong for the obvious reasons Izzy would say it was wrong. Maybe the distinctions he was trying to make were just ways to rationalize his own behaviour – all semantics really.

CHAPTER THIRTY-EIGHT

i.

Sitting on her futon in the A-Frame quiet with sleep, Lisa-Marie stroked her fingers over the album of photos that Justin would never see. It had turned out better than she could have imagined. She had chosen twenty of her favourite shots and had them printed at the local drugstore where she also purchased thick, white photo mats with dark inner edgings. She and Liam had finished the midnight-blue album cover last week. She traced her fingers over the gold-embossed leaf design on the cover. She had placed a sheet of cream-coloured, gossamer-thin paper over each page to protect the photo. She brushed her hand across the bits and pieces of garden plants that were captured in the weave of the paper.

There were only three photos of people in the album. One was a black and white of Justin. His T-shirt was off and tucked through the back loop of his jeans. He had been leaning under the water tap soaking his head right before she snapped the picture. She had caught him in the moment when he threw his head back, the water drops streaming behind him and through his hair. The light sifted through the wisteria fronds at the edge of the garden causing the water to sparkle. Lisa-Marie thought it was the best photo she had ever taken.

Another photo was of Justin and Liam. This one was in colour, to emphasize the differences between the two of them – the light and the dark. They were digging out one of the compost bins. Liam had stood to swipe his hand across his brow and he was leaning slightly on his shovel; he must have been saying something to Justin. The strong, lean lines of Liam's body were outlined in profile, his dark hair hanging back over his shoulder. Justin was in mid throw of the compost from his shovel to the wheelbarrow and he was looking toward Liam. The smile on his face seemed to transcend the confines of the photo.

Lisa-Marie had not even taken the third photo. The night of the garden gala one of the harpists had offered to snap a picture of Lisa-Marie and Justin. They were standing together on the garden path with the white lights twinkling over them. Justin's arm was draped over her shoulder and he was smiling in his relaxed and easy way. She had pulled in close to him, her body pressed against the green of his Robin Hood tunic. Every time she looked at this photo she felt her stomach flip over; anyone would think Justin was her boyfriend.

Lisa-Marie put the album down on the bed and pulled her journal from under her pillow. Fighting back the tears, she opened the book to a blank page.

ii.

Dear Emma:

This is what it feels like to have your heart broken. Justin will never be my boyfriend now. He probably hates me for the way I acted tonight and the things I said to him. He will never see the photo album I made for him. I should have listened to Maddy – but it's too late now. I should have listened to Justin when he tried to talk me out of acting like such a fool. If I had listened then we would still be friends. Now we are nothing.

Truth – right, Emma. I could have killed myself tonight. What I did out in the water was very stupid and I could have drowned if I hadn't remembered what Liam told me. And because Liam has always been so nice to me – because he has always treated me like a real person, letting me drive his truck and listening to me – because he gave me this beautiful journal – guess what I did? Threw my clothes off in front of him and practically forced him to screw me. He says it isn't my fault – that nothing that ever happened to me was my fault. And for some crazy reason I believe it about the other guys. It wasn't my fault – at least not the way I thought it was – like I was this little slut who couldn't get enough of being treated like that. Liam is right about all the other guys but I still think what happened with him is my fault.

Justin didn't want me because of Izzy. I know that. And Liam didn't really want me either – not the way things worked out. He wanted Izzy just like Justin did. They both wanted Izzy and no one wanted me. It's not fair – if Izzy could have Liam then why did she want to hang onto Justin, too?

i i i .

Turning from the huge vat of paper mash and waving a gloved hand at the kids in the workshop, Josie said, "Break time guys. See you back here in fifteen minutes then we're all going to pitch in and get that soap order ready for shipping."

Lisa-Marie rose from the workbench where she had been folding and packaging sets of note cards. Maddy pulled off her black apron and gloves and was walked away from the soap vats. She met Lisa-Marie at the shop door. "Hey, Leez, where have you been for the last couple of days? You missed Josie blasting Jesse big time for leaning over the soap vat without a hairnet on. It was too funny." Maddy stopped her stream of chatter to look at Lisa-Marie's downcast face, "Hey, what's up?"

Lisa-Marie grabbed Maddy's arm and said, "I've got to talk to you," and started to pull her out of the doorway and toward the covered walkway.

"OK, OK – it must be important if you want to pass up coffee and Cook's chocolate chip cookies. You know it's chocolate chip cookie day, right?" Maddy followed along to a deserted spot on the covered walkway. She watched Lisa-Marie look carefully in both directions to make sure no one was around before she leaned against the railing. Maddy imitated Lisa-Marie's darting glances from side to side. "Who or what are we watching out for?" she whispered.

Lisa-Marie let out a long breath and looked from Maddy's face to the lake and then back to Maddy before she spilled out the words, "I made a complete fool of myself with Justin the other night. I threw myself at him and everything is screwed up and he hates me and I won't even get to say goodbye to him now." Lisa-Marie dropped her head down onto her folded arms on the railing.

Maddy sighed and shrugged, "I won't say I told you so because that would be just plain mean."

"I can take that he rejected me but I can't stand what he must think of me now. I'm sure he must hate me."

"Oh come on Leez, he won't hate you. He's used to stuff like this. Go and talk to him. He's a sweet guy. I bet he feels worse than you do about the whole thing."

Lisa-Marie shrugged miserably. She looked over at Maddy for a moment. She thought about how she had never had a friend, not a real friend you could tell awful stuff to, not since elementary school when she didn't really have anything awful to tell. All the really bad stuff she had gone through in high school, she went through alone. All of a sudden Lisa-Marie wanted to be like other kids who had friends to talk to. Straightening up from the railing, she leaned closer to Maddy and whispered, "Things are worse than what happened with Justin." Looking around to make sure no one was walking towards them, she added, "I did something else and it's really bad."

Maddy's eyes lit up and she grinned mischievously before asking, "You did something really bad? Quick tell me?"

"Maddy, stop fooling around, I mean it. If I tell you, you've got to promise not to tell anyone else."

Maddy stepped back from Lisa-Marie and looked serious for a moment, "I do promise Leez, you can trust me, you know that." She crossed her fingers over her heart and acted out sealing her lips, locking them with an imaginary key and throwing it over her shoulder.

"I went over to Liam's place after Justin dumped me down on the beach. I went up to his bedroom and took off all my clothes right in front of him and I was such a pathetic mess, he must have felt sorry for me. He didn't kick me out and we did it."

Maddy's eyes widened dramatically and her mouth formed a perfect O until she whooshed her breath out and said, "Wow, Liam? You had sex with Liam? Was it any good?" The question was accompanied by an avid look of curiosity.

Lisa-Marie grabbed Maddy's shoulders and shook her. "Oh my God – don't you get it? He's like forty-something and good friends with my aunt. My aunt's partner Beulah already hates him for some crazy reason. If she finds out, I don't know what she'll do and if Izzy finds out she'll think he raped me or something. It's all just one huge mess." Lisa-Marie hung her head and thought she might start crying in front of Maddy – she felt that bad.

"Leez," Maddy stared hard at Lisa-Marie and grabbed her arm so Lisa-Marie couldn't turn away, "It happened like you're saying, right? It was your idea? He didn't force you, right?"

Maddy looked so serious that Lisa-Marie's eyes did fill with tears as she muttered, "Ya, like I said – I pushed myself on him. He gave me every chance to change my mind. I'm pretty sure he wanted me to change my mind."

Maddy relaxed and said, "Well, OK, I can see you feel bummed about it. But I don't see what his age or his friends and enemies have to do with my question. Was it any good?" Maddy repeated herself, poking Lisa-Marie in the ribs.

Lisa-Marie didn't say anything for a moment and then she mumbled, "Well ya, it was good – the first time it's ever been good and that makes it all the more humiliating. I'll never be able to look him in the face after the way I acted."

"Oh my God –," Maddy whispered, "– you're blushing aren't you? Oh . . . my . . . God. You had an orgasm, right?"

Lisa-Marie held her hands up to her burning cheeks and pushed Maddy with her shoulder, "Stop it. Will you be serious for just one freaking minute?"

"OK, OK," Maddy made a valiant effort to wipe the smile off her face and tone down the jokes, "Look, why would all these people find out? Are you going to tell them?"

Lisa-Marie was shaking her head violently, "No, no, no – of course not."

"Do you think he will?"

Lisa-Marie lowered her head again and said, "No. I think he feels really bad about it. He won't tell anyone."

Maddy shook her head, "Oh pooh, pooh, to his bad feelings. He got to have sex with a hot, little sixteen-year-old. He should be kissing the ground in freaking gratitude and you got to have an orgasm. If you ask me, it sounds like a pretty good outcome all the way around."

Maddy started to tickle her and finally Lisa-Marie smiled a bit and then giggled and then looked serious again, "Maddy, I feel bad about the whole thing. Liam's a good person and he's been really nice to me and I don't want anything bad to happen to him because of me."

Maddy arched her eyebrows and said, "Ya, I can see how he was really nice to you," and she silently mouthed the word, orgasm. Seeing Lisa-Marie just shrug and look away, Maddy dropped the attitude and squeezed Lisa-Marie's arm for a second, "Look Leez, stuff like this happens. He won't be the first guy you hook up with and think afterwards it wasn't such a great idea. Look on the bright side. At least it didn't suck and there's nothing to be embarrassed about that, believe me. You'll find out it's way more humiliating when it doesn't work out but forget that. Tell me everything and don't spare any of the juicy details. What did he do to make it good?"

"Oh my God, you are crazy," Lisa-Marie pushed Maddy away, "I'm not saying another word about it, not a word, period. I'm embarrassed half to death it even happened let alone telling you the details."

Maddy laughed, "OK, OK . . . keep your secrets little girl. Do you want me to tell you what Jesse does to make me have an orgasm every time?"

Lisa-Marie pulled a disgusted face and clapped her hands over her ears, "Oh, gross, stop. I'm not listening, I'm not listening." She backed away down the walkway, then dropped her hands to say, "We better get moving before Josie comes looking for us. Thanks Maddy. Just don't tell anyone, OK?"

Maddy spoke quietly, her impish grin held in check, "I don't want to see anyone get hurt, Leez. I've seen more than enough hurt." She followed Lisa-Marie toward the workshop doors silently mouthing the word, orgasm, every time Lisa-Marie glanced at her. By the time they got back to the workbench and the piles of soap that needed wrapping, they were both laughing so hard Lisa-Marie had a stitch in her side and Maddy was gasping for breath.

iv.

At noon, Lisa-Marie came out of the Camp workshop, where the labelling, wrapping and preparing of two hundred bars of soap for shipment was finished. She headed for the path to the A-Frame. Glancing over to the beach area she saw Justin. He was sitting alone on his favorite picnic table. Lisa-Marie's footsteps faltered and she stopped. She knew Justin would be leaving Micah Camp for good the next day. More than anything she didn't want him to leave with thoughts of that night on the beach as the only thing he had to remember her by.

She walked slowly toward the table, thinking that Justin seemed reluctant to shift his eyes from the view. But when he spotted her he spoke up right away, "Leez, I'm glad it's you."

She began to talk quickly, "Justin, I just wanted you to know before you go and we never see each again . . . I'm so sorry about what I said and did the other night."

Justin stared at her and said, "I've been watching out for you the last few days and wanting to say the same thing. I never meant to hurt you, Leez. But I did and I'm sorry for that."

Lisa-Marie climbed up to sit on the table top next to Justin, "I am a stupid immature kid, like you said. I know that now. I wish I would have listened to you and not made such a fool of myself." She sighed in a sad, small way.

Justin shook his head quickly, "Hey, don't say stuff like that, OK? It isn't wrong to want something." Lisa-Marie knew his words weren't only about her. Justin looked back over the lake and his voice was low and thoughtful, "I didn't think it was going to be so hard to leave here."

"I'm going away too, Justin, to high school in Victoria. Do you think we'll ever see each other again . . . or be friends?" Lisa-Marie asked the last part of the question so quietly she wasn't sure he could even hear her.

Pushing her gently with his shoulder, Justin smiled before he said, "We never stopped being friends, Leez. As for seeing each other again, who knows? We're both going to the big city, right? Civilization –," he nudged her again, "– we can update each other on Facebook."

After a moment he straightened his shoulders and moved to jump down from the tabletop. Lisa-Marie followed. As they turned toward each other for a moment she began to stammer, "Well, I . . . . good luck . . . and –," Justin moved toward her and wrapped his arms around her in a tight bear hug. She clung to him, her heart pounding wildly. The hug was over quickly. He walked away down the path and her footsteps turned toward the A-Frame.

V.

As Lisa-Marie entered the cabin she could see that Beulah had already finished her lunch and was onto her coffee. The invoices for the day's bread order were spread out in front of her on the table. Aunt Bethany smiled and brought a pot of leftover chili to the table. Beulah looked up over her dark-rimmed reading glasses and nodded at Lisa-Marie with a half-smile. Beulah had been acting in a way that could only be considered as kind and somewhat conspiratorial since the back-porch of the A-Frame had become a confessional for Lisa-Marie's humiliation. Lisa-Marie moved across the room to sit down in her place at the table. She marvelled at how, in two short months, this had come to be her place.

Bethany settled in the chair across from Lisa-Marie and watched her as she began to eat the chili. "Everything is set up with the family Izzy knows in Victoria. I talked with the woman on the phone. Her name's Marlene and she seems really nice. The family has a great big house. You'll have your own room and Izzy says they live close to a good high school. The worker who is filling in for Mrs. Clayburn left a message saying we can go ahead with our plans while we wait for the legal stuff to happen." She paused with a satisfied smile, "Marlene asked if you could be there a couple of days before school starts so she can show you around. And of course you're going to want to go shopping for some new school things. It's all working out, Lisa."

Lisa-Marie started to nod her acceptance when she felt a lump in her throat. She put her spoon down, pushed the chili to one side and tried to swallow. The lump got worse and to Lisa-Marie's horror tears began to spill down her cheeks. Trying to catch her breath and stop only made it worse. There was nothing she could do; she was sobbing, no gentle little hitching sounds, but huge racking sobs.

Startled, Beulah looked up from the invoices and jumped back and off her chair as if she had been scalded. "Hey Lisa, what the hell, what the hell's the matter?" She looked helplessly to Bethany and mouthed wordlessly to her to do something for God's sake.

Bethany waved Beulah away and moved around the table to pull up a chair beside Lisa-Marie. She began to rub her back slowly, up and down, "It's OK, sweetie, it's OK," she repeated those two words over and over. Lisa-Marie's head fell forward on her arms and she sobbed as if she would never stop. Beulah gathered her things hastily from the end of the table and with a concerned look at both Bethany and Lisa-Marie, she went out the back door to stand on the porch.

Lisa-Marie sobbed with a sadness she couldn't hold in for one more second. The hug with Justin could never begin to fill the hopeless, aching need she had for him; but she knew it was all she was ever going to have. She sobbed because she would probably never see Grannie again or the place and things that had meant home to her. She sobbed because deep down, despite her tough girl attitude, she had believed every shitty thing her classmates had said about her for three long years. She let them define who she was and because of that, she had almost lost her life – a life she now knew had hardly begun.

And just as Liam had said, the worst part was learning too late that it was never really about her at all.

She sobbed with regret, because even though Maddy's jokes and twinkling eyes made her feel better, she knew the easy comfort she had enjoyed with Liam over the past two months was gone forever. She wanted to go back to the way things had been when Liam was the coolest, nicest adult she had ever met; but she knew she couldn't do that.

And she sobbed with relief because she knew she had been saved. She would never let another guy treat her the way those guys back home had treated her. She would never again have to put up with how the girls had made her feel. She was never going back to any of that. Auntie Beth and Beulah had rescued her and she knew that now everything was going to be different. Nothing had worked out the way she had wanted it to and yet she had been saved, just like all the fairytale princesses she had ever read about.

CHAPTER THIRTY-NINE

i.

Izzy sat on the kitchen deck with her morning coffee held tightly between her hands. A heavy bank of mist rose in a cloud off the lake's calm surface revealing the quiet campground on the opposite shore. The smell of fall was light yet persistent this early in September. Despite the clear-blue sky above the banked clouds, there was no escaping the fact that summer was drawing to an end. Izzy usually basked in the excitement of September – a time for fresh starts. This year she struggled to get out of bed each morning.

The garden was bursting with produce and with Bethany's help, they were putting up pints of green beans every day, freezing bags of broccoli and cauliflower, canning tomatoes and making pickles and salsa. Liam had picked all the apples only hours before a large, black bear took down a huge branch from one of the oldest trees. Izzy had sliced and frozen bags of the crisp, red apple chunks. She had planted dozens of bulbs and a long row of garlic. Beulah returned daily from her bread deliveries with ice cream pails full of blackberries that Izzy and Bethany, with Dan looking on and making a vague pretence of helping, were turning into jam.

The low-keyed summer schedule at the Camp had given way to academic programming. Izzy's regular fall counselling groups had to be organized. She would also be teaching two internet courses this semester and they required hours of planning and arranging.

Izzy knew what depression looked like. In examining her own life, she had never used the term. She thought of the way Winston Churchill had described his recurrent episodes of melancholia as *the black dog*. She certainly had a touch of *the black dog* these days but as long as she kept moving, she hoped to stay out in front of it.

She also knew what could happen when a person's coping mechanisms and denials were laid bare. It was a time ripe for change but it was also a time of vulnerability. No one wanted to get stuck in the spot where denial was gone before something else came along to take its place. And that's where Izzy knew she was now.

She had allowed herself a degree of latitude with Justin that was inexcusable and she had turned a willfully blind eye to the consequences. That behaviour would haunt her for some time to come. She couldn't hide from how much she'd hurt him. His outright refusal even to say goodbye to her, and the fact that he probably ended up banging Lisa-Marie on the night of his going away party, showed the level of his pain and anger. She hated herself for thinking of the two of them like that – so crudely. And she hated that even the awareness of her culpability didn't stop her from feeling jealous about the way Justin had turned to Lisa-Marie that night.

At least her sessions with Jesse were progressing quickly now. Still, Izzy had to live with the fact that her nonprofessional behaviour and inability to work with him effectively meant that two months of his precious time at the Camp had been wasted – more inexcusable behaviour on her part. And the fact that Roland never mentioned anything related to the mess with Jesse just emphasized to her that he was keeping her fall from the pedestal in mind. She suspected she was being unfair to Roland and she knew her current state of mind was veering toward the paranoid.

To add to these burdens of conscience, Lisa-Marie had suddenly left for Victoria. She'd disappeared, as if she had never been at Crater Lake at all. There were no goodbyes and that really caught Izzy off guard. On the afternoon Beulah took Lisa-Marie to the bus, Izzy sought Liam out in the workshop to ask him if he knew Lisa-Marie was leaving that day.

Liam only shrugged and said, "No, I didn't know it was today. I knew it would be soon, but I didn't know it was today." He quickly glanced away from Izzy with a guarded look on his face and fumbled with the paperwork spread on the desk in front of him. Izzy pushed for more information even though she could tell Liam was uncomfortable.

"But you two spent time together, I thought she was friendly with you. Don't you think it's odd that you didn't even know when she was going?" Liam just shrugged his shoulders. She realized with mounting frustration she wasn't going to get anything more out of him.

Naturally, Izzy's thoughts now turned to Liam. Except for questioning him about Lisa-Marie's departure, she had been doing everything she could to avoid him without being obvious about it. The kiss on the cliff deck and her feelings of desperate desire had sent her emotional equilibrium into a tailspin. She couldn't lie to herself anymore. Seemingly out of nowhere, her feelings for Liam had radically changed and she didn't know if this shift was simply physical desire or something more. She knew he noticed how she was trying to stay away from him. Lately, though, she was starting to wonder which one of them was doing the avoiding because it really shouldn't have been so easy for her to steer clear of Liam.

Izzy's thoughts looped around and around from Justin to Lisa-Marie, from her work to Liam, from her loneliness to her guilt. Finally her wandering thoughts brought her to Caleb. She dragged herself through alternating cycles of loss, guilt, love and anger. For almost two years, she had forced herself not to feel. Her current situation had blown the top right off her emotions and she felt like one large exposed nerve.

Izzy shook her head with mounting anxiety. She had to keep moving through this or she would drown in it. The mist had fully lifted and the sky was blue and cloudless. She called to Dante, "Want to try to walk off some of this angst, boy?" She ran her hands over his shining fur and rubbed the spot behind his ear that he loved. He stared back at her with his loyal and accepting eyes and Izzy knew that at least for one more day, she would keep moving.

i i .

Beulah came out of the post office juggling a parcel for Izzy and trying to sort the mail as she walked toward the truck. The day was warm for the second week of September but already there was a fall smell in the air that told her to keep a sweater nearby. She noticed a small envelope of camp stationery with

Lisa-Maria's name and a Victoria address in the upper left hand corner. She was surprised the letter was addressed to Liam and not to Bethany.

Beulah got into the truck and dropped everything on the passenger seat except the thin envelope of oatmeal-coloured paper. She tapped the envelope slowly against the steering wheel and tried to imagine why Lisa-Marie would write a letter to Liam even before she bothered to write to her aunt. There could be a million reasons why a kid like Lisa-Marie would do one thing or another. None of those reasons was likely to make much sense to Beulah but somehow her gut was telling her this letter addressed to Liam didn't fit. This wasn't how things should be.

She thought back to the night Lisa-Marie had been at Liam's cabin and how she'd been told that nothing had happened between the two of them. Maybe she had wanted too much to believe Lisa-Marie. After a few moments of thought, Beulah took the envelope, tucked it into Izzy's pile of mail and headed toward Crater Lake. Maybe someone else should see this letter, she thought. Maybe someone else would also feel that there was something not quite right about Lisa-Marie writing to Liam. What would happen after that was in the hands of fate and not really Beulah's problem at all.

iii.

Izzy was sitting impatiently at the repair shop waiting for the Jeep's rear tire to be fixed. She planned to drive to Victoria first thing the following morning for a Conference at the university. The last thing she wanted to do was come into Dearborn today and waste time getting a tire repaired. However, when she came out of the cabin for her morning's walk with Dante, she noticed the tire was definitely losing air. She didn't want to end up pulled over somewhere on a deserted piece of the Island Highway having to change her own tire.

To pass the time, Izzy reached into her bag and pulled out yesterday's mail. She had grabbed the stack off the side table in the cabin entryway with an opportunity like this in mind. She went through a couple of bills and then noticed the back of a Camp stationery envelope. She immediately assumed that Justin was writing to say how he had settled in at UBC. She didn't even bother to turn the envelope over. She tore it open from the back and removed the single sheet of paper from within. She saw immediately that the short letter was addressed to Liam and that Lisa-Maria's looping handwritten name was clearly legible at the end. Izzy flipped the envelope over to discover that it was indeed from Lisa-Marie and addressed to Liam.

For God's sake, Beulah, does it take that much effort to put people's mail in the right pile? She started to refold the letter and put it back in the envelope. But the loopy handwriting, still visible, stopped her. A single, three-letter word jumped out at her and because this word seemed so odd and out of all context, she smoothed the letter out again. She knew full-well what she was about to do was wrong, but she did it anyway.

i v .

Liam looked up from the open workshop door when he heard Izzy coming around the hairpin curve at the bottom of the roadway. The gravel scrunching under the Jeep's tires was unusually loud. He was surprised because Izzy usually took the steep slope and the curve very slowly. Her Jeep came into view seconds later. Liam heard the door slam and saw Izzy coming around the corner towards him with a piece of paper clutched in her hand and a look on her face that said – if I could kill you right now I would.

With weary resignation, Liam accepted that the inevitable had happened. Izzy knew. The waiting was over and the sharp blade of the guillotine was rushing full speed toward Liam's exposed neck. All he could do was bow his head and wait for the impact.

Without breaking stride Izzy slammed both her hands against Liam's chest sending him stumbling backwards through the door. "You fucking bastard," she said, slamming him again so he hardly caught himself with his back to the workbench. "You had sex with that sixteen-year-old kid. You fucking bastard."

Liam saw betrayal written all over Izzy's face. He had expected outrage, for her to judge him harshly, to hate him for being the sort of man who would do such a thing, but he hadn't expected to see betrayal in her eyes. That surprised him. Maybe she would grab something like the mattock leaning against the wall, easily within her reach, and go after him. Liam knew that betrayal was a killing emotion.

She threw the piece of paper on the wooden floor between them and began to back away towards the door, her eyes locked on his, "You had better be out of my cabin and off my property before I get back from Victoria, Liam, or I swear to God, I'll call the police and have you removed."

Liam leaned against the workbench staring down at the piece of paper. He doubted his knees could have held him up if he moved away. The emphasis Izzy had placed on the words, my cabin and my property was still ringing in his ears. He bent over slowly and retrieved the thin sheet of paper, turning to smooth it out against the counter in front of him.

Dear Liam:

I'll keep this short and sweet – ha-ha. I just wanted you to know that I am doing really great. And I'm sorry I didn't say goodbye or thank you for the hair thing – it's beautiful and I use it all the time. The family here is super nice and I have my own room and I love the new school. I'm in drama and I'm going to try out for a part in the next play and I'm on the school paper taking photos. I'm still using Dan's camera. He wanted to just give it to me but Beulah wouldn't let him so he said to bring it back at Christmas. I've already made a whole bunch of friends. It's hard to believe – but I'm sort of cool down here.

Don't worry about the sex, Liam. It's not a huge deal, no matter what some people might think. I miss Crater Lake and I miss Justin and I even miss the paper and soap. Give Pearl a belly rub from me. Bye. Lisa-Marie.

Liam recalled the blue, leather hair-piece with its delicate pattern of yellow flowers worked along the edges. He had left it in the mailbox at the top of the trail as a going away gift for Lisa-Marie. When she hadn't shown up for their last Thursday trip to town he knew he wouldn't see her again before she left. She was going to avoid him and that was probably better for both of them.

She really was a kid; a kid who was in grade eleven and trying out for a school play and working on a school newspaper. She might say she was fine and he sure as hell hoped that was true. Liam felt emptiness in his gut that no amount of Pepto-Bismol was going to cure. All of his regret was mixed with a useless sort of inevitability. Izzy's look of betrayal told him she had been far closer to falling in love with him than he had imagined and that only made everything seem so much more hopeless. He looked up to see Beulah across the open area of the gravel drive, watching him.

She had come from dropping off a black forest cake at Dan's cabin. She had rounded the corner in time to hear every word Izzy screamed at Liam and to see him stoop to retrieve the letter from the floor of the workshop. Beulah had watched Liam read the letter and had seen a look of complete and total defeat settle over him. As she headed up the gravel drive in her truck she replayed, over and over in her mind, the way Liam seemed to give into the defeat; that's what really got to her.

V.

Beulah lay in the bed beside Bethany who had once again confirmed to Beulah that their chemistry together was right. "You awake still, Bethy," she asked.

"Yes, barely."

Staring up at the ceiling Beulah said, "I'm going to tell you some things that will probably be a shock – are you going to be able to handle that?"

Bethany moved up on an elbow to stare at Beulah. "I'm just as much of an adult as you are, Beulah. I can handle knowing stuff."

Beulah nodded a silent OK and then said, "Lisa-Marie slept with Liam the night of Justin's going away party. She had some kind of fight with Justin down on the beach. He left her there but he stopped here and told me she was down there. He was worried about her. I took the dogs and went to look for her. But she had already gone to Liam's. I waited up for her and asked her what the hell she thought she was doing – she said nothing had happened with Liam. But Lisa-Marie sent Liam a letter and she must have said something in the letter about that night. I picked the letter up from the mail yesterday and because I thought it was strange for her to be writing to Liam, I put the letter in Izzy's pile. I guess I hoped she would open it and see what it said. Well – she did and she told Liam to get out of her cabin before she gets back from Victoria or she'll get the police after him."

Bethany was so stunned by Beulah's speech she couldn't take it all in. To stall for time she seized on one part and asked, "You put the letter in Izzy's pile on purpose?"

"Ya," Beulah said quietly, "Ya, I did." As if responding to the why that Bethany had left unsaid, Beulah rolled over and looked at her for a moment. She seemed to be trying to make her mind up about something. Finally she said, "I want to tell you what happened between Liam and me the day Caleb died."

When Beulah finished, she lay quiet in the bed, her wiry arms folded behind her head for several minutes before saying, "I'm the one who betrayed Caleb, all this time, not Liam."

Bethany sighed to herself, thinking, well, of course you did, you old fool, but she stayed close to Beulah nevertheless.

"I just hope there is no afterlife where dead people sit around and watch what the people they left behind are doing, because I don't want to imagine what Caleb would be thinking of me right now." The bedroom was silent for a time and finally Bethany heard Beulah say, "Caleb asked us to watch out for Izzy. I've tried to do that but what she's doing now is wrong. It's wrong to tell Liam to leave like that."

Bethany felt like punching Beulah right in the ribcage. Beulah had been suggesting Izzy do that very thing for most of the last two years. "So we won't let her do it, Beulah." Bethany wasn't able to think about how her close friend, Liam had slept with her niece, so she lay quietly and thought about Caleb instead. Until tonight she never knew how much Beulah must have loved him or how hard it all must have been for Liam, especially with Beulah blaming him every time she looked at him. The whole thing just broke her heart. The way she had felt when Caleb died was nothing to what Beulah and Liam must have been going through all this time.

"Do you want to talk about Lisa-Marie?"

Bethany shook her head quickly, "Not now, Beulah, not yet."

She heard Beulah mumble, "OK, but don't blame Liam for what happened. Like I said, I saw her when she came back from his place. She came onto him and it was just the one time. Sure he should have sent her little ass packing but the guy's only human, right?" Beulah then rolled over and went to sleep.

Bethany lay awake in the bed for some time with Beulah's words ringing in her ears. Yes, Liam was only human, she knew that; but as the tears washed down her face she realized he had always seemed so much more than human to her. Caleb had been everyone's hero. He was bigger than life, but Liam had been her knight in shining armor.

CHAPTER FORTY

i.

The next morning Liam forced himself to walk over to the A-Frame with the eggs. Bethany greeted him quietly and handed him a coffee. He took the cup gratefully; he was glad she hadn't kicked him right out the door. "I don't know what to say to you, Beth. I don't know how to find the words to explain. Or even if there are any words."

"I was pretty shocked when Beulah told me." Liam read the disappointment and confusion on Bethany's face. She was quiet for a moment before asking, "Is it right what Beulah said, that Lisa-Marie was a willing party? I need to know that . . . from you."

Liam nodded sadly, while a range of conflicting emotions raced over his face. "Yes . . . she came to me . . . I didn't go after her. But that sure as hell doesn't make what I did OK."

Bethany placed her hand over Liam's, "No . . . it doesn't . . . but it's better than the alternative, for sure." Bethany's stared down at the table for a moment before she said, "I understand what happened between you and Lisa-Marie is nothing like what happened to me. I want you to know that."

Liam nodded gratefully. He had been terrified that Bethany would interpret his behaviour in light of her own experiences and he didn't think he would have been able to face that, not after the way Izzy had looked at him. "Lisa-Marie told me about trying to kill herself and how bad things were for her back home." Liam looked down at Bethany's hand on his as he continued,

"She trusted me. She was so messed up when Justin didn't want her . . . things just got out of control. I'm sorry, Beth. I never meant to hurt her or you or anyone else."

"I'm glad she trusted you, Liam. I knew things hadn't worked out with Justin but she wouldn't talk about it. I heard her crying in her room a couple of times. And I knew there was something wrong when she wouldn't go to town with you that last Thursday or say goodbye to everyone. But Liam, she wasn't acting like a kid who had been taken advantage of; I would have recognized that. She was OK when she left here – sad but excited about school. You made a mistake, Liam, no doubt about that, but you have to let it go now . . . just let it go."

"Even if I could, we both know Izzy never will." Liam looked completely lost.

Bethany rose and walked around the table to put an arm around Liam's shoulder, "That wouldn't be a good thing for her Liam, so we won't let her make that mistake." Gently patting Liam's arm, Bethany said, "You stay put, promise me. Don't even think about moving out of that cabin," she waited until Liam had nodded. "Izzy has her own stuff to work out but she knows in her heart that telling you to leave is wrong. She'll come around . . . give her a bit of time."

i i .

Four days later, Izzy was waiting for Beulah outside the coffee shop, her bags stacked on the sidewalk beside her. The Jeep had started to make a disconcerting thumping noise outside of Dearborn and Izzy had decided not to take a chance by driving out on the gravel road to Crater Lake. After smashing her fists on the steering wheel and vowing to replace the goddamn, unreliable wreck of a thing as soon as she could, she left the vehicle at the garage. She grabbed a coffee and waited for Beulah to show up.

After Beulah turned the truck off the highway and onto the gravel road, she kept her eyes straight ahead of her and told Izzy, "He isn't gone. Liam is still at the cabin."

Izzy looked across at Beulah with disbelief written all over her face, "You have got to be kidding me." Beulah just shook her head. The rest of the drive passed in silence as Izzy stared wordlessly out the passenger window.

As Beulah pulled up at the top of the road, Izzy said, "Let me out here, Beulah. I'll walk down. You can drop the bag off later."

Izzy had the door open and was partway out of the truck when Beulah spoke, seriously and quickly, "One of the last things Caleb said before he died was that Liam should never leave here. I mean he said exactly those words, Izzy. You can't kick Liam out when you know Caleb wanted him to stay here."

Izzy slammed the truck door. Looking back through the open window she said, "Caleb wasn't always right, no matter what you or Liam think. And in case you hadn't noticed, Beulah, Caleb is no longer with us."

iii.

Liam heard Izzy coming along the darkened path before he saw the flashlight's tracing pattern along the tree line and Pearl's steadily thumping tail confirmed that it was indeed no stranger approaching. The door was flung open; Izzy didn't even bother to knock. She stomped inside with her yellow raincoat streaming water all over the floorboards. Liam watched her from the rocking chair he had pulled up in front of the woodstove. Izzy flung the raincoat over the back of the kitchen chair and shook the water from her eyes and hair, much as Pearl might have done in her position. The effect of her wildly cascading locks and gleaming dark eyes caused Liam's heart to thud painfully.

"What the hell, Liam. Do you want me to call the police? Why are you still here? It's been four days since I told you to leave. What part of get out of my cabin and get off of my fucking property don't you understand? Why are you still here?" Izzy's voice had risen to a volume that caused Pearl to back slowly on her haunches toward the bathroom, a low pitched whine in her throat.

Liam looked down at his hands and spoke very slowly, "I'm not leaving. I don't have anywhere else to go. And we both know you're not going to have the police drag me out of my home, even if it is your cabin on your property." Liam added the last words while meeting Izzy's eyes in a direct challenge. She slumped down on a chair by the table and raked her fingers through her wet curls. She looked over at Liam with such a cold stare that he flinched.

"This is the thing that bothers me the most, Liam. How can you know what I'll do? How in hell are you so damn certain I won't see your sorry ass out on the street after what you've done?" Izzy emphasized each word by pounding her hand on the tabletop. Pearl had now backed right into the bathroom and she was whining softly but incessantly.

"It's because of Caleb that I know you're not serious about kicking me out of here . . . because of what Caleb was to both of us . . . because of what we've both lost."

Liam didn't take his eyes from the amber glow of the fire as Izzy violently pushed her chair back and leaned menacingly over the table toward him, her voice raised to a shout, "So, I guess you think you know me the way Caleb knew me. You are so sure of yourself, aren't you, Liam. I simply can't fucking stand this."

She began to pace the small room, her arms hugging her body inside the oversized sweater she was wearing, "Caleb was always so sure of me, wasn't he, so damn sure. If he was here right now I would throw his trust and belief right in his face." She stopped in the middle of the small room, "Look at me, Liam . . . just look at me, for once. Caleb looked at me all the time and he never really saw me. You just never even look."

Izzy placed herself squarely in Liam's line of sight and waited for him to raise his eyes. "Do you know what I was doing when Caleb died, right before you called me?" Without pausing for an answer, Izzy went on in a rush of words, "I was in a bar in a fancy hotel in Montreal with another man's hand on my ass. And I was seriously thinking about telling him my room number. Do you think Caleb would have suspected that, Liam, do you?" Izzy slumped back into her chair, her whole body trembling. "Maybe you should think twice before you imagine you know what I might do."

Liam saw through Izzy's anger to the guilt and sorrow that lay underneath. Suddenly everything was very clear. His whole world pivoted and his feelings of impending doom disappeared. He was sure Izzy would forgive him. He loved her and she loved him. He would find a way to make her understand.

He rose slowly from the rocker and crossed the room to put the kettle on the stove. With his back to Izzy he carefully prepared the tea things. He walked across the small space, from the stove to the kitchen table and moved Izzy's dripping raincoat from the chair, wiping up the floor and the chair seat with the towel from over the sink. With slow, easy movements he brought the tea pot and cups to the table and sat down across from Izzy. Neither of them spoke as they waited for the tea to steep. Liam poured Izzy's tea and then his own. He saw her take a sip, then wrap her cold hands around the steaming mug and raise her eyes to his.

"I went to see Lisa-Marie in Victoria after the Conference. According to her she's fine and I should mind my own business and get off your case." Repeating Lisa-Marie's words, in an imitation of her voice, Izzy told Liam, "It wasn't like it was the first time I'd ever had sex, OK? He didn't force me – it was my idea if you have to know the details. It happened just that once and believe me, he regretted it – satisfied?" Izzy shook her head and narrowed her eyes as if she were thinking, what a load of crap. Then she stared out the darkened window and went on, "She was also at pains to tell me I don't know everything, even though it seems like I think I do." Izzy paused to sip her tea, "So apparently, having sex with a man who is certainly old enough to be her father is no big deal for her. She is doing just fine."

Not expecting Liam to make any reply, Izzy shook her head and changed the subject, "She gave me a photo album." A painful look crossed Izzy's face as she described it, "It was obviously meant to be a gift for Justin. She told me I might as well have it. It's beautiful, Liam. She must have spent hours doing it and the pictures are good. She has a real gift for photography. So, why didn't she give it to him?"

Liam sipped his tea. Then he asked, "Izzy, did Caleb ever tell you what my life was like before I came here?"

Izzy shook her head, "Oh Liam, you knew Caleb better than that. He was a tomb when it came to people's confidences. I often wondered if he was really that able to keep quiet or if he actually didn't remember the details of what people told him."

"I wanted to tell Caleb about my past. It was after that whole horrible mess with Bill and Lila and I felt like maybe anyone of us could be gone tomorrow. I decided to tell him one day when just the two of us went up to do the power system maintenance. You know how it was with Caleb, the system never needed much maintenance but it was his excuse for a damn fine hike to a place with a view to take your breath away. I can still hear him saying that. We were sitting together at the top. Caleb had just taken a drink from his flask and I told him I wanted him to know what my life was like before I came to Crater Lake. He looked at me for a moment and said that whatever my life was like before didn't matter to him. All that mattered was who I was now and that I was here," Liam paused a moment to sip at the bitterness of his tea.

"I insisted though. It took me a good while to build up my courage to tell him and I wasn't going to let him brush it all off that easily. Caleb sighed. You remember that sigh Caleb had, right Izzy?" Liam looked at her and Izzy nodded.

"I remember exactly what he said . . . people always seem to think that if others knew all this dark stuff about them, they wouldn't want to be around them anymore. But whatever it is – it doesn't matter. I know you man, I know who you are and what you are. So tell me if you think it will make you feel better but I promise you it won't change a thing."

Izzy looked up startled, because as Liam related Caleb's words it was like Caleb was sitting at the table between them. It was so exactly how he sounded when he talked, every inflection, every pause; it was so exactly what Caleb would say.

"I told him and he was quiet and thoughtful before saying . . . You're like a brother to me, Liam. Don't ever leave – OK."

Liam rose to put a log in the stove and bank up the flames. Turning back to Izzy he said, "Do you remember the old Einstein poster in the shop – *I want to know God's thoughts: The rest are just details.* That was Caleb. He saw into the center of a person and everything else was just details. Caleb saw you, Izzy. What he saw in you is who you are. It isn't all of you –," Liam held up his hands to forestall the protest he could see written all over Izzy's face, "– but it is who you are."

Liam continued to look at Izzy, "I'm not sure of you like that. I don't see you the way he did. But I am sure of one thing – you won't force me to leave here – not because of what happened with Lisa-Marie. I'm sure you will believe I never planned for that to happen. I didn't want her like that. It was a mistake. I never wanted to hurt her or you, Izzy."

Liam paused for a moment and when he continued to speak there was pain etched into every word, "She told me she had tried to kill herself before she came here. Her life was that bad. A sixteen-year-old kid was hurting so bad she tried to take her own life." Liam saw a momentary look of shock and then understanding move across Izzy's face. "She was so crazy about Justin and he rejected her. She came to me and there was this look in her eyes, Izzy . . . I don't know if you've ever seen someone with that look . . . probably you have. It's a look of being more than halfway over the line to nowhere."

Izzy stared at Liam's bowed head for a moment and she knew that whoever or whatever Liam had been before he came to Crater Lake, he had seen that look in his own eyes, and not just once or twice.

Liam refilled his tea cup from the kettle of water now warming on the woodstove. He sat down in the rocker and Izzy heard the slow creaking noise of the chair as it rocked back and forth. She stayed at the table, lost in her own thoughts. Lisa-Marie's suicide attempt explained a lot. Norma's cryptic note made perfect sense now. For all Izzy's brilliant ability to work with young people, she had not picked up on the extent of Lisa-Marie's vulnerability. Justin had been in the way. By focusing on him, she had missed seeing Lisa-Marie. After the way she had acted, how could she possibly be sitting in self-righteous judgment of Liam?

The gravity of what she had to feel guilty about hit home when Izzy experienced a flood of relief on hearing that Justin had rejected Lisa-Marie. It was a terrible thing to have to admit but she was glad the night of his going away party had not ended the way she thought it had. She now understood how much she had wanted Justin's exclusive admiration, even though she never had the slightest intention of giving him anything in return. She knew she had failed everyone.

Izzy came to a decision. Liam was right. Because of Caleb and a lot of other things she was only beginning to name, she wasn't going to make him leave. She had no right to do that. She couldn't change anything that had happened. She couldn't go back and do the things she should have done, but there was something she could do. Something she needed and wanted to do. Getting up slowly she walked to the sofa and sitting right across from Liam's rocker she said, "Turn this way, Liam, toward me."

Liam looked puzzled, but he lifted the rocker and turned so Izzy was right across from him. She could easily reach out her hands and place them on his knees. She waited until his eyes met hers. "Tell me, OK Liam. Tell me what happened to you before you came here."

Izzy knew it was a powerful experience to be accepted no matter what. When Caleb said it didn't matter who you had been or what you had done he meant it; and you knew he meant it. That type of acceptance could transform a person. But it was also important to be able to tell your painful stories and know that someone else really heard you – stepped onto the path of darkness and walked alongside of you. It mattered that another person wanted to know who you had been and what had happened to you. This wanting to know and the ability to hear was Izzy's gift – what she could do and Caleb couldn't. He hadn't been able to walk on the path of darkness with anyone because he simply had no point of reference.

As the rain lashed the outside of the small cabin and the wind swept down from the mountains and over the lake, Izzy sat quietly in front of Liam and bent all of her being into his words. She walked with the boy who had been desperately afraid to leave the reserve and go away to school. She stood beside the man who was drowning in the gulf his leaving had created, who was disappearing in the emptiness he felt inside and all around him. She stayed with Liam, through the drinking, the fire, the aftermath, the suicide attempts, the wanting to die more than anything else, wanting to have the pain end once and for all. When Liam finally said, "I still believe I could have saved her, I'll always believe that," Izzy nodded and tears filled her large, brown eyes.

She placed her hands gently on his knees and Liam felt their warmth right through his worn jeans. He felt the gift that Izzy had to offer flow through her hands and as he met her eyes, he was shocked to see the tears. Out of nowhere, the conviction he had always felt, from the moment he heard the baby had died, wavered slightly. He had always been so sure he could have saved the baby. Now, under Izzy's steady gaze, he wondered. For the first time he started to second guess himself and that rattled him. In fact it made him feel really pissed off.

"Why didn't you ever come and talk to me before, Liam?" Izzy had seen the look of pain on Liam's face turn to anger.

He shook his head, a short violent movement and spit his words out, "I thought it would break me . . . that if I told you it would tear me apart." His voice was beginning to shake with the anguish of holding his anger in check. "With Caleb it was like I had to tell him. I owed him that much. I owed him the right to reject me. I guess I knew on some level he wouldn't." Liam paused for a moment to grasp the arms of the rocking chair in a viselike grip, his next words coming out in a strangled gasp, "Telling you means something else."

Izzy watched Liam's face, her hands now folded neatly in her lap. She wouldn't need to say anything more. She was sure Liam understood that he hadn't talked to her because he knew she might question his long-held belief and he couldn't face that. His thinly concealed anger made that obvious. He had always known that if forced to challenge him, Izzy would ask, *how do you know you could have saved the baby, Liam? How can you know that for sure?*

"I know I could have saved her, I need to hang onto that. I need to feel that guilt everyday if I'm going to live with this, to make up for it somehow. A child died because of me . . . an innocent baby. You get that, right? I fucked up and a baby died. For the love of God, you hear me, right Izzy? A baby died."

Liam rose from his chair quickly, sending the rocker tilting back wildly. He couldn't remember ever feeling so violently anger in his whole life. Like the huge metal chains they used to haul the logs out of the bush, the tension was coiled in him and pulled tight to the snapping point. As he moved toward the door he had no idea where he intended to go. He just knew he had to get out of the cabin and as far away from Izzy as he could before the chain snapped and destroyed them both.

"Don't go, Liam."

Even though he was desperate to get away, Izzy's voice held him from across the room. He knew she was asking more of him than her words conveyed.

"Don't try to tell me I couldn't have saved her, don't try to do that." Liam moved back across the small room and collapsed into the kitchen chair. He began to shake, his voice broke and he repeated over and over, "I know I could have saved her." Huge racking sobs rose up from his gut and he choked as they tumbled out of his mouth. It sounded to his own ears as if he were howling like a dog in the final throws of a painful death. Finally, Liam raised his eyes to look at Izzy. He felt as though a twisting demon had risen from inside his gut and moved out of him on the air currents created by his howling.

"It wouldn't have mattered if I was sober or not, if I was awake or not. I couldn't have gotten up those stairs in time. Her door was closed, the fire started in her room, it was filled with smoke in seconds and the flames destroyed the whole top floor in no time. I couldn't have saved her. It was just some kind of fluke that I survived myself. I should have died in that fire, too." Liam bowed his head and stared at his hands. "And I couldn't save Caleb, no matter what Beulah thinks. I couldn't have done a damn thing. No one could have."

Izzy rose from the sofa and reached for her raincoat, "I know, Liam. I know. Even if we could go back, we couldn't change anything." She rubbed his back gently then shrugged into her coat before quietly slipping out the door. Pearl rose from her resting place in front of the fire and padded over to lay her warm head in Liam's lap. With her body leaning into his leg, she kept her large liquid eyes on his face.

CHAPTER FORTY-ONE

i.

Bethany tore open two buns and spread them with raspberry jam. She moved efficiently around the A-Frame's kitchen, filling the thermos of coffee and preparing for the time out fishing with Dan. Today would probably be the last day she and Dan would take the row boat out around the point to fish. The season was winding down; even the Indian summer would soon be coming to an end.

Bethany rehearsed in her mind some of the things she wanted to tell Dan. The days they spent in the boat together meant a lot to her. She had been touched by the way he listened to her and shared things about himself. She wanted him to know how important it was for her to be able to be alone with him, to trust him and feel OK. She wanted to thank him.

Thinking about what she wanted to tell him brought to mind the things she wouldn't say to him or anyone else. She wouldn't tell him that she found him physically attractive or that she could imagine being with him. It was possible for her to be alone with a guy and feel sexual attraction. And though it was possible, she still chose Beulah. She wasn't a lesbian or anything else by default. This was the life she wanted and now, for the first time, she knew she was free to choose.

Beulah came in from the bakery shed to see Bethany placing the food and thermos into the green-canvas pack she always took out on the boat. "You're not planning to fish today are you?" Beulah asked this with a slight tone of concern in her voice, looking across the A-Frame and out the main windows towards the lake.

"The weather report says it won't get really rough until early evening," Bethany replied as she headed past Beulah to the back door. "We'll have Gertrude and Alice. Best early warning system of all, right?" She paused to look back at Beulah for a moment and then turned and walked over to press her body into Beulah's angular frame, "Don't worry, everything is fine, really. I'm fine."

She smiled and went out the door and Beulah stood for a moment watching Bethany disappear around the back toward the stairs to the beach and the dock. She shook her head thinking, I don't know what the hell your being fine has to do with the weather. The weather could change quite quickly at this time of year. But Bethany had been fishing on the lake for years and she did have the dogs and Dan would be with her. Beulah grabbed her keys and headed out for the trip into town.

i i .

The small boat moved through the water, slightly within the invisible line required to keep the dogs in check. Soon Bethany and Dan would be within sight of the A-Frame. The dogs knew by heart the route the boat took over the course of the afternoon and they were already rushing ahead toward the bend of the point. It had been an uneventful fishing trip. Despite repeated changes of tackle neither Bethany nor Dan had gotten more than a couple of tentative nibbles all afternoon. Bethany let her mind wander as she rowed the boat. She didn't need to rush speaking to Dan – he wasn't going anywhere. Fishing season was over but she would still see him. He would continue to drop by for coffee and meals. He and Beulah had decided that with baseball done for the year they would take up watching hockey games. Dan had already spoken about coming over some afternoon when Beulah was gone so he and Bethany could clean out their tackle boxes together and look at some fishing gear catalogues.

Bethany was jolted out of her thoughts by the sudden shifting of the wind and a heavier chop on the water that was making the boat hard to steer. The clouds were gathering darkly in the sky and she could see stronger white caps marching down the lake toward them. She looked over at Dan to tell him that they needed to move quickly around the point and that maybe he should take over the rowing.

Dan chose that moment to lean forward across the boat and put his hand on Bethany's thigh. He took his other hand and holding her lightly by the back of the head, he pulled the upper half of her body towards him. He kissed her deeply and as his hand stroked her cheek he moved his lips from hers to say, "Bethany, I can't take it anymore, I need you so badly." He kissed her again, longer this time, pulling away for a moment to whisper, "Beulah won't know a thing, I promise you. She's away every afternoon. We can be together every day." Bethany's continued silence was fuel for Dan's fire, "Say yes, Beth, please say yes. I know you want me as much as I want you."

Bethany was silent because she didn't feel Dan's kisses or hear his whispered pleas. The moment his hand touched her thigh she froze and disappeared. The sensation was instant and completely familiar, though she hadn't felt that way in a long time. She was no longer sitting in the boat with Dan. She was far away on the shore watching the dark, churning water and large white caps as they bore down on the small boat. She saw a woman with her long, blonde hair blowing about in the wind, being kissed by a man who was oblivious to the danger about to slam into both of them.

The dogs were far from oblivious and it was the sound of their barking, like a lifeline that brought Bethany back with an amazing thud right into the boat and right into the moment. With a burst of strength and a tremendous push she sent Dan sprawling backwards over the bench he was perched on. She watched in fascination as he flailed for a moment on the edge of the boat's now dangerously heaving prow, lost his balance and went tumbling over into the dark water.

Hardly believing what she had done, Bethany scrambled to turn the boat around to get an oar in position for Dan to grasp onto. She was thinking she might manage to bring him around to the back of the boat where he could hang on; then she could row them both to shore. But she knew even that was going to be a tricky with the waves picking up the way they were. It was at this moment that she noticed the dogs charging into the water and swimming towards them.

Dan grabbed one edge of the boat as a large wave lifted it from the other side. At the same time Bethany was leaning towards Dan. His weight, the force of the wave and Bethany's movement in the wildly tipping boat sent her right over the edge into the water as well. As she struggled up to the surface for air the wind grabbed the empty boat and lifted it up and over. The last thing Bethany saw out of the corner of her eye, as she struggled to orient herself toward the shore, was Dan's black tackle box, right before it slammed into the side of her head.

iii.

Beulah jumped off the ATV at the bottom of the trail wondering what the hell was going on with the dogs. The moment she had turned the corner she could hear them barking wildly. As she came out in front of the A-Frame she saw the dogs enter the water. Beyond them she spotted the overturned boat being rocked wildly by the waves. She began to run.

Liam was working in the greenhouse when he heard the dogs. He knew something was wrong. Izzy saw Dante tear off towards the north stairs and across the beach like he was running for his life. As the barking of all four dogs reached a frenzied pitch, she stood up hastily on the kitchen deck, scattering the papers she'd been marking. She moved quickly to the deck railing. She saw Liam running along the beach and heard him screaming. "Izzy, call 9-1-1, quickly. The boat's tipped over and I can't see Bethany or Dan in the water."

Liam was close enough now to see Beulah tearing down the stairs from the A-Frame and running at full speed along the beach, kicking her shoes off as she went. She was into the water in one fluid movement and she appeared a moment later swimming strongly toward the overturned boat. It was then that Liam saw Dan's head and his arms thrashing wildly in the water. He was moving steadily toward the shore past the A-Frame.

Liam watched Gertrude and Alice turn in the waves and swim toward Beulah. He saw Beulah pull Bethany from the lead dog, wrap her arm firmly around Bethany's neck in a rescue hold and swim for the shore, the dogs flanking her on either side.

Izzy arrived on the beach carrying a load of blankets. She saw Dan seated on a log further down the shore, coughing and gasping but obviously breathing. She hurried over to where Liam was standing. Together they ran to the water's edge to help Beulah pull Bethany's very still body further up the beach. Beulah immediately dropped to the sand on one side of Bethany with Liam on the other.

Seeing the panic in Beulah's eyes, Liam called her name in a calm voice, "Beulah, remember, ABC – airway, breathing, circulation. Clear the airway Beulah, she's not breathing."

Beulah nodded and quickly tilted Bethany's head back to open the airway. She knelt close to listen while Liam counted down from five. "There's nothing, Liam, nothing," Beulah's voice was rising.

Liam was checking for a pulse in Bethany's wrist and neck and getting nothing. "Mouth to mouth, Beulah, hurry up now." He continued to watch for any movement but there was nothing. "I'll start CPR." Liam's voice was as calm as if he had said, "I'll put the kettle on." He waited until Beulah had completed two full breaths and then he began chest compressions, counting slowly to fifteen. He dropped to his haunches beside Bethany and motioned Beulah to do the rescue breathing again.

Izzy knelt helplessly in the sand at Bethany's feet. She watched the three people she had lived so closely with for so many years. It was like she was seeing all of them trapped within a Gothic painting, a dark and bleak hopelessness pervading the entire canvas. Time froze as Izzy focused only on Beulah's two rescue breaths and Liam's whispering count of the fifteen compressions before he sat back on his heels and motioned to Beulah once again. All of this was repeated over and over in four rounds per minute before they took turns checking for any sign of life then started yet again.

The pace was almost hypnotic. Pearl and Dante were lying on the sand whining and Gertrude and Alice, spent from their heroic swim, raised their heads every few minutes to keen softly. Izzy could see the look of panic returning to Beulah's face. Bethany was lying with her blonde hair spread out across her face and into the sand like a fairytale mermaid washed up on the shore. She looked so cold and lifeless. The only thing marring her pale face was the gash on her forehead.

In a brief glance sideways, Liam's eyes met Izzy's and he knew that she thought it had been too long. He shook his head violently at her. He thought wildly, no, no, it can't be too late. I will not let it be too late.

Beulah faltered while Liam worked his ceaseless rhythm and she moved her hands to grasp Bethany's cold face. Liam looked at her and said very quietly, "Beulah, I can take over the breathing, too, if you want, but listen to me –," his words reached over to include Izzy, "– we are not stopping until the chopper gets here; we are not stopping no matter how long it takes."

Liam's tone of voice and the energy emanating from him were powerful, like a force Izzy had never felt before. He was totally in charge of what was happening, rock solid in the face of whatever was coming. Beulah bent back to Bethany's face, tilting her head and breathing for her.

Izzy watched as agonizing moment after moment unfolded and all she wanted to do was scream, *stop Liam, please stop, she's gone. There's nothing more we can do.* She felt sure that the magic that had once surrounded them was fully spent and gone. It was too horrible to see Bethany lying there like the corpse she surely must be by now. Izzy felt she couldn't stand it one more moment and in seeing Liam's courage she realized her own weakness.

Liam glanced at Izzy and once again read her thoughts. He looked across Bethany's body to Beulah as she waited for him to count and he directed his words to her, an offering and a promise all at once. "We're not giving up on her; do you hear me, Beulah, we're not going to let her die. We're not giving up on each other anymore."

These words snapped Izzy out of the paralysis of her hopelessness. She pulled herself over to where Bethany's feet lay in the sand and she grasped their coldness in her warm hands. With all her heart and soul and being she willed the magic back, willed her life energy and force to flow through to Bethany. Moments later Izzy felt the foot she held twitch ever so slightly and Bethany gasped suddenly and choked. Liam quickly rolled her to her side and she brought up what seemed like half the lake. Beulah started to sob – deep, racking, gasping sobs. Izzy rushed for the blankets to cover Bethany while her own tears ran in a steady track down her face. The whirling sound of the air ambulance was barely audible above the wind.

Looking toward Izzy, Liam repeated, "We don't give up on each other anymore, Izzy, none of us," and she nodded silently.

CHAPTER FORTY-TWO

i.

The dark crept up on Izzy as she sat at her writing desk transfixed by white caps breaking on the grey surface of the lake. Twenty-four hours had passed since she had looked up from the kitchen deck to see Dante dashing madly down toward the end of the beach. She could close her eyes and see Gertrude and Alice swimming out toward the overturned boat. As she stretched her arms over her head, Izzy had to admit she was still in shock.

She was certain she would never forget the moment when Bethany's foot moved and she watched her return to life. Beulah had spent the night at the hospital with Bethany and she would be there tonight as well. She had phoned to say Bethany was doing well and they would both be home tomorrow.

Izzy had been left to deal with Dan who had stood alone on the beach shivering and forlorn. Liam had quickly disappeared down the trail towards his cabin as the sound of the air ambulance carrying Beulah and Bethany faded away. Izzy hadn't seen him since. Maybe he was as wrapped up in his own shock as she was in hers.

She thought about how she had taken Dan back to the main cabin yesterday, cold and clearly shaken up. She made sure he got changed into warm clothes and settled him in front of a blazing fire. Then she wrapped his hands around a big mug containing the last of Caleb's whiskey. It hadn't surprised Izzy that she was the one to hear Dan's confession. She had no absolution to offer him. That was not her brand of healing. She did what she had always done – suspended judgement and heard his story.

Dan admitted, before he passed out in front of the fire, that he'd had a number of affairs with married women over the years. But he claimed what he felt for Bethany was different. Dan told Izzy that he had been sure Bethany wanted him and that he was totally shocked when she pushed him away. He looked stunned when he told Izzy that he was in love with Bethany.

Izzy thought of all the stories she had held in her hands and how hearing a personal story was like holding a piece of someone's soul. She tried with everything in her not to violate the trust people placed in her and she would hold to that, even for Dan, even for a story that disturbed her all the more because she understood Dan's blindness.

That entire summer she had failed to notice what should have been obvious about her own behaviour and that of others. She had failed to be where she should have been. She got tired and lonely and self-focused and she hadn't seen what was right in front of her. Dan certainly hadn't cornered the market on blindness.

She drove him to the bus in Dearborn that morning and the trip was silent. What was there to say? She didn't know if his experience with Bethany would change anything about him. Probably he didn't know either. Maybe he would eventually understand that his selfish actions and rash assumptions had almost led to a tragic accident. Then again, maybe he would go on being blind to the impact his behaviour had on others. Izzy had no idea what the next chapter of Dan's story would be.

ii.

When the grey afternoon light gave way to the dark of evening, Izzy called Dante to her. "Come on boy . . . let's see if we can squeeze in one more fire out on the cliff deck this year." The dog followed her willingly out into the cold night. The breeze was moving across the lake and the clouds were scudding along the sky, providing an occasional glimpse of the half moon. Izzy built a fire in the small stove. Rocking back on her heels she watched the kindling catch and she thought of all the times over the summer when Justin had laid out the fire for her. His affection and caring had been clear in all of his actions.

She caught her breath for a moment as she recalled how good she had felt whenever he looked at her.

When she was sure the fire was going, she added a bigger log from the last few that were stacked against the deck railing. She sat down on the swing chair facing the lake. Sparks danced up the chimney and Izzy shivered as she hugged Caleb's green-flannel shirt tighter around her body. All of a sudden, she felt overwhelmingly alone. She couldn't remember a time at Crater Lake that she had felt so lonesome. She saw Dante raise his ears even before she noticed a circle of light bouncing off the trees along the path that led to Liam's place. Liam approached the deck silently. He hunkered down in front of the stove for a moment to add another log and then sat down beside Izzy. His black hair was loose against the collar of his faded jean-jacket.

When Izzy felt she couldn't take the silence between them any longer she spoke, "I thought I knew myself pretty well, Liam. I thought I knew a lot about other people too. I've known you for so long. But yesterday on the beach . . . watching you . . . it was like I was seeing you . . . really seeing you . . . for the first time. I looked at you and somehow I could tell you knew exactly what I was thinking."

He nodded, "Yes, it was as if I heard your voice inside my head." He remembered the look on Izzy's face as she had held onto Bethany's feet – her concentration and focus – and he knew that they had come as close to being part of a miracle as was likely ever to happen to any of them again.

Izzy was looking down, twisting the gold band on her left hand, "I thought I knew how the world works. But as Lisa-Marie says, it seems I don't know everything. I sure didn't see Dan very clearly. Bethany pushed him out of the boat because he kissed her. Can you believe that, Liam? He made a pass at her and she pushed him out of the boat." Izzy shook her head, realizing how significant that action must have been for Bethany. For all of Dan's misguided behaviour, he was a stepping-stone in the next stage of Bethany's healing journey.

Izzy glanced quickly over at Liam for a moment before she said, "I have a share in the blame, Liam – for what happened between you and Lisa-Marie. I know that."

Liam leaned forward and rested his elbows on his knees and steepled his fingers lightly against his chin. With his straight, black hair swinging forward he said, "How you've come to that conclusion, Izzy, will take a bit of explaining."

"I could see I was hurting you and driving you right to the edge by ignoring you the way I did at Justin's going away party. I couldn't stop myself. But that isn't the worst of what I did, Liam." Izzy took a deep breath, "I knew from the book club night . . . remember . . . *No Great Mischief* . . . I knew Lisa-Marie liked Justin. I saw even way back then that she noticed the way Justin was looking at me and that I was enjoying it. But I fooled myself into believing I didn't know anything. Lisa-Marie didn't trust me from that very first night and it wasn't her fault. It was my fault . . . because of Justin. If she could have been able to trust me, I could have helped her. It's just that Justin was between us," Izzy stopped talking and caught her breath. She needed to go on but she wasn't sure she could. She needed to trust Liam.

"He got to me more than any of the others. He had come through so much crap and it hadn't touched the center of who he was. He came out clean, unscathed. Every time I looked at him he was walking in sunlight." Izzy leaned forward to catch Liam's eye and her next words came out in a rush, "God, Liam, he could have been Caleb at nineteen, with his golden hair and that carefree smile. I'm forty-five years old –," Izzy sat back and shook her head in disgust, "– I was lonely and I was feeling old and it was like I had been frozen inside since Caleb died. I liked the way Justin made me feel. I knew every day that I should talk to him . . . put a stop to the whole thing. But I couldn't bring myself to do it."

Izzy pulled herself deeper into the soft folds of the worn flannel, "I know I would never have crossed any other lines with Justin but I still did enough damage. Lisa-Marie saw right through me. And she wasn't the only one. Jesse saw what was going on, too, and that was part of what happened with him. When I finally spoke to Justin, I ended up hurting him way more than was necessary."

Izzy sat up straight on the bench beside Liam and took a deep breath. "Lisa-Marie didn't trust me and she wouldn't come to me. But she trusted you, Liam. So she went to you and she ended up in your bed." Her voice shook slightly but she forced herself to go on, "At least you really saw her, Liam."

Liam reached out and took Izzy's hand, holding it palm up in his own. He traced her life-line as he spoke. "I wish with all my heart things hadn't turned out the way they did." He stared out over the lake and hoped that would be enough, that Izzy wouldn't ask him to say anything else about Lisa-Marie – ever. Liam meant what he said; he did wish it hadn't happened. But he also knew that if he were in the same situation again, with Lisa-Marie standing before him with the look she'd had in her eyes that night, he might end up making the same mistake.

Izzy and Liam sat together in silence watching the fire burn down. "You have a real gift, Izzy. I've always known that. The way you helped me the other night means a lot to me. I don't really know what you did. It doesn't seem like you did anything at all but something happened and I thank you for that." Liam looked up to the surrounding hills across the lake and then he repeated the words he had spoken on the beach, "We don't give up on each other anymore, OK?"

Izzy nodded and reached into the pocket of her shirt with her free hand. She pulled out Caleb's gold watch and handed it to Liam. "I should have given this to you from the start . . . for luck, Liam."

Liam took the watch from her, "For luck," he repeated and tightened his grip on her hand. "The other night, Izzy, you said I don't look at you." He paused and when she met his eyes he went on, "You're wrong about that. I've been looking at you for quite a while and I do see you." He reached out to touch her cheek, "Caleb's been gone a long time. I think you should fall in love with me because I am sure as hell in love with you."

Caressing the side of her face he leaned toward her and kissed her gently. She dropped her head against his chest and slid close to him, his arm tight around her and their hands still joined. After what seemed a long time Izzy spoke, "So, what happens now, Liam?"

He was looking at their joined hands as well when he replied, "Well, I don't know, but I'm not going anywhere."

Izzy laughed softly, "Ya, I get that." She disentangled herself from Liam's arms and rose from the swing chair. Before she stepped off the deck she turned back and with her hand extended to him, she asked, "Coming?"

As he rose to join her, she heard the lone wolf begin to howl. As Izzy and Liam walked toward the cabin together, an answering howl sounded from across the hills. Then a chorus of wolf calls began echoing over and over around the lake.

ACKNOWLEDGMENTS

Many heartfelt thanks to family and friends who have stayed in my corner, rooting for me through the years it has taken to bring this novel to completion. To my husband, Bruce – thank you for helping me live out my dreams. To my son, Doug – I am grateful that you encouraged me to bring this novel into the world. To my daughter, Kristen – thanks for always saying – you can do it, Mom. To my dear friend, Louise Butcher – words can't adequately express my gratitude for your ceaseless and invaluable assistance. I am also indebted to the wonderfully generous people who were willing to wade through earlier drafts and give feedback – you know who you are.

ABOUT THE AUTHOR

FRANCIS GUENETTE has spent most of her life on the west coast of British Columbia. She lives with her husband and dog and finds inspiration for writing in the beauty and drama of their lakeshore cabin and garden. She has a Master of Arts degree in Counselling Psychology and has worked as an educator, trauma counsellor and researcher. This is her first novel. Please visit disappearinginplainsight.com or subscribe to Francis' public Facebook page to learn more.

Jacket Image: Bruce Witzel

Lightning Source UK Ltd.
Milton Keynes UK
UKOW041323180313

207818UK00002B/433/P